Brainchew 2:
Out of Their Heads

WOL-VRIEY

Burning Bulb
PUBLISHING

Brainchew 2:
Out of Their Heads

WOL-VRIEY

Burning Bulb
PUBLISHING

Brainchew 2: Out of Their Heads
By **Wol-vriey**

Burning Bulb Publishing
P.O. Box 4721
Bridgeport, WV 26330-4721
United States of America
www.BurningBulbPublishing.com

Cover artwork by Anton Rosovsky.
Author Photo: Lolade Akinsowon © 2014.

First Edition.

Paperback Edition ISBN: 978-0997773064

Printed in the United States of America

CHAPTER 1

Carmela, Tiff

It was just past 10 p.m. when the silver Honda Accord pulled up to the reception building of the Sunflower Motel.

The Honda stopped. Carmela Cole, who was driving, flicked on the interior light. Then the car's four occupants, all women in their mid-to-late twenties, spent a while looking at each other.

"Well, here we are," Carmela said, turning in the driver's seat to regard Lisa and Monique, the pair seated in the back. Carmela's voice was subdued. A nervous young woman at the best of times, she felt particularly so tonight. "Look, I'm not saying we shouldn't go ahead with the plan, but . . . we can still turn around and drive off right now, if you know what I mean."

For support Carmela looked across at the passenger seat, at the final person in the car: Tiffany 'Tiff' Hooper. Tiff was responsible for them all being here in this sleepy little east Massachusetts town of Raynham tonight. "What'cha say, Tiff? It's not too late yet. Can we just forget about this and all go home before any harm's done?"

Carmela shuddered at the coldness on Tiff's face. *No, she's not about turning around and going home,* she decided.

"No, Carmela. Stop being a chicken about this. I want my fair turnaround. I want . . . no, I *need* to pay back that scumbag in his own coin. He took a lot from me, and I'm going to take even more away from him."

Tiff fell silent, looking like she'd break into tears. Then she turned away from the others and focused her attention ahead, on the motel reception building, through the glass of which they could see a dark-haired man regarding their car with some interest.

Sighing loudly, Carmela again faced the two seated in back. Now they'd arrived here, she wished she could rewind time. She'd been the one who'd told her older sister Lisa about 'it,' and as such, felt responsible for their actions even before they'd done anything.

She looked pleadingly at Lisa. "Sis . . . ?"

As expected, Lisa shook her head emphatically, the coolest of smiles on her lips. "Oh no. You heard the woman. Let's do this"— she pointed through the windshield at the curious man in the lobby— "before he calls the cops on suspicion of us wanting to stick him up."

Carmela turned to Monique for support. Monique didn't like the plan either. Monique shrugged back, then gestured forward with her chin at the silent woman in the seat ahead of hers. "Like she said— you heard the woman. Let's just get this over with."

Carmela accepted that she was defeated: Tiff wanted revenge, Lisa intended dishing out that revenge, and Monique had absolutely no say in the matter—Monique would do whatever Lisa told her to; she'd even eat dog poop off the sidewalk if Lisa ordered her to.

"Alright, girls," she grudgingly agreed, "get your damn backsides out of the damn car. If it's revenge you want, it's revenge you're gonna get. Let's go check in."

"About goddam time," Tiff spat from the front seat, then opened her door. Monique and Lisa followed suit and got out.

When the doors opened, a cold wind blew in over Carmela, freezing despite this being late spring, with summer well on the way. Then she realized that the chilliness she felt wasn't external, it was rather the coalescing of her worries about tonight's business. A lot could very well go wrong with their plan, and if it did . . .

Lisa leaned in through the front passenger window and hissed, "Hey, little sister, get your bony ass out of the damn vehicle!"

Carmela shrugged, nodded back at Lisa, then opened her door. She put a philosophical hat on things. *Yeah, well, stuff may go wrong tonight. But it's too late now to stop this insane river that's already rushing madly towards its crazy sea.*

She got out of the Honda. For a moment her mind filled with their surroundings. The reception building was a two-floor affair, whose lower windows afforded the man at the desk a wide view of the parking lot. To the left of this building was the front block, a long white extension with a split in its middle, and with four cars parked in front of it. Beyond that (and curving around the parking lot and behind Carmela and her companions) were trees. The trees, which on their right continued along the driveway, walled off the motel from the outside world. (Except for the lot and walkway lights, and the fact that outside the front block, a fat man was just alighting from a green Toyota SUV in company of a woman who looked like a hooker, Carmela would have considered the Sunflower Motel a really creepy place.)

Overhead, the night sky was dark—with neither an auspicious nor a foreboding tinge to it—just dark, with the moon playing hide-and-seek with thick clouds.

Alright, Carmela thought, *it had better not rain tonight. That'll simply further complicate an already messy state of affairs. Or maybe it'll wash us clean of our sins?*

Then she caught sight of Lisa gesturing impatiently to her from the steps of the reception building, and realized she'd gotten tangled up in her thoughts. She hurried after the others into the lobby of the Sunflower Motel.

***

On entering the motel lobby, Carmela noticed the male receptionist's eyes almost imperceptibly widen. Suddenly, she wasn't even sure why Lisa had suggested that they check into a motel tonight. Surely, considering what they'd come to Raynham to do, complete anonymity would be best? But Lisa had insisted. And once Lisa got insistent, that was essentially that.

She managed a cool smile as the man's eyes swept over them, like he was wondering whether to call the cops or proposition them for sex.

Dressed in a gray shirt over faded denim pants, the receptionist was tall and slim and ruggedly attractive; dark eyed, and with similarly dark shoulder-length hair. He also had a neat moustache and beard. Carmela guessed he had to be at least forty. In addition, he had lines on his face that spoke of heavy drinking.

At the moment, though, his eyes were clear and focused on them. (Strangely, like he almost recognized her from somewhere, his gaze seemed to linger longer on Carmela than on the others. She found that flattering. Usually, once 'gorgeous older sister' was in the social mix, she rarely got this kind of checking out.)

Finally, clearly unsure what to make of them, the receptionist resigned himself to a bemused smile.

Carmela thought she understood what he was thinking. It wasn't so much that they looked 'evil' or 'criminal' or anything immediately 'suspicious' like that. It was more that the summing together of the four of them on this particular night had a 'wrongness' to it that even a skunk would smell afar off. They were four quite attractive (okay, except for Tiff, Carmela allowed), well-dressed young women, but . . . they were surely giving off an odd aura at the moment.

But that's how the silver ball falls tonight, she thought as they reached the desk. *Hopefully God's roulette wheel will keep spinning in our favor until we roll out of this town again.*

"Good evening, ladies," the man addressed them. "My name's Ambrose. Welcome both to the Sunflower Motel and to our quiet little town of Raynham."

He had an honest open smile and Carmela felt herself warming to him. And also, contrary to her expectations, his breath didn't reek of liquor like she'd expected it to.

"Now, what kinda room would you ladies like for the night?" Ambrose enquired.

"Do you have a single large enough for the four of us?" Lisa asked. "If not, we'll take two smaller ones next to each other. If they've a connecting door, that'll be great. We're driving south to Rhode Island to meet up with friends, but we set out rather late."

The other three nodded. Carmela understood that Lisa was establishing their alibi: that they'd spent the night here and departed south in the morning. Only they wouldn't be spending the entire night here. (They'd already stolen a Mercedes cargo van, which was currently parked farther down the road). And once they were through checking in . . .

"In that case, one of our front block rooms would be best suited to you," Ambrose replied. "They're more expensive than the others, but you'll find they've more than enough space for you four girls to get a good night's sleep." He gestured to a photo on the wall. "Here's one of 'em. As you can see, each room has a—"

"We'll take it," Tiff interrupted the sales pitch in a flat monotone. "How much for the night?"

Ambrose stared at her oddly for a moment. Carmela understood that look: It wasn't what Tiff had said, that had been innocuous enough. But . . . there had been a strange, strange note in Tiff's voice, something that wasn't good. Ambrose, not knowing what they'd come to Raynham to do, clearly couldn't put his finger on what had felt so odd about Tiff's response.

To Carmela, who did know, Tiff simply sounded psychotic.

Not good, not good, not good.

Lisa clearly shared her worries, because she immediately flashed Ambrose her winningest, most seductive smile and said, "Yeah, like she said, we'll take the room. How much is it?"

Ambrose ran a hand through his long hair, gave Tiff another odd look, then told Lisa the room's price. He got out the registration cards; she got out cash from her purse.

Carmela hoped Ambrose would chalk Tiff's oddness down to PMS or something. She also prayed that Tiff wouldn't up and do something crazy that would prove a definite red flag to Ambrose. The last thing they wanted here tonight was police involvement because the desk clerk got the impression one of his guests was nuts.

She had a good idea of how Ambrose must view them:

Tiff Hooper was short, blonde, and plump. Not really pretty anymore. (Carmela still found it amazing how much weight a depressed person could put on in such a short time.)

Carmela Cole was tall and slim, with her black hair cropped short. Like a seal on her nervous disposition, she'd bitten her fingernails down to the quick.

Monique Bangles was a busty redhead, with an icy beauty to her.

Lisa Cole was the best looking of the four of them, a gorgeous blonde with a great figure and fiery blue eyes. (Carmela was supremely envious of Lisa's good looks and all the male attention she got.)

Carmela and Lisa both wore T-shirts over baggy pants and gym shoes. Tiff was dressed in a leather jacket over a denim skirt and pumps. Monique, as if she was going to a party, wore a long blue dress and black knee-high boots.

What Ambrose couldn't know? Monique was a violent ex-con on parole, and Lisa was her parole officer. And he definitely couldn't even start guessing the most important fact of all about them: That Tiff, Carmela's BFF, had two-and-a-half months ago been abducted and held captive in a basement somewhere here in Raynham. And it was as a result of that incarceration that the four of them were here now to dish out some badass payback.

At the moment, Monique was looking away from the reception desk. She was staring out of the glass lobby door, her green eyes fixed at the end of the motel driveway. She had a longing look on her face, like she'd rather be anywhere else but here tonight. Carmela couldn't help but sympathize with her: Monique was already in trouble with the state law enforcement. A screw-up tonight would likely triple her trouble, send her away to a stone motel for a long, long time.

"Here's your key, ladies," Ambrose said. "You're in Room 9. If you need anything, just call me and I'll be right over to fix it for you."

He glanced at Tiff again. She regarded him with her deadpan stare that seemed to scream: *WHAT THE FUCK DO YOU WANT WITH ME, ASSHOLE!!!? EH, WHAT!!!!???*

"Thank you," Lisa said, distracting Ambrose again with her dazzling smile. "We shouldn't have any trouble settling in. We need to leave town real early though, to meet up with our appointment. Can we just leave the key in the room?"

"Sure, that's perfectly fine. I'll pick it up later in the day."

Carmela had heaved a sigh of envy-tinged relief on seeing Ambrose's look of bemusement switch back to the usual wowed look men gave her older sister. However, when his gaze again rested briefly on her, she once more got that same vibe—that he liked *her* in particular for some reason. Liked her even more than he did Lisa.

Behind her, Tiff, accompanied by a stony-faced Monique, was already pushing open the lobby door and stepping out into the night.

She considered walking after them, but instead waited for her sister, who was still working on charming Ambrose.

"So, thanks again," Lisa said, in what Carmela clearly heard as fake gaiety, but which Ambrose clearly misunderstood as genuine. Then she turned and they both left the lobby.

Carmela looked back once as they descended the lobby steps. Ambrose wasn't looking their way. Instead, the receptionist seemed to be filing away their card, his expression frozen somewhere between a grin and a grimace. *Oh, yep, big sister's charm works its evil magic again.*

Then she forgot all about the man. They were here for serious business tonight and there was no backing out now.

***

At Room 9, the four of them exited their car, offloaded their suitcase, and let themselves in.

Just like Ambrose had promised, the room was exceedingly luxurious. In Carmela's opinion, it compared favorably to the presidential suites of some hotels she'd seen on TV. It had seemingly acres of space and everything one could possibly desire for a night's comfort—living room section, kitchen section, huge TV, even huger wardrobes, and an empress-sized bed.

"Wow, just look at this place," Monique enthused. "Hell yeah, baby, I can just imagine bringing a trick in here and fucking his brains out." She flung herself down on the extra-wide bed.

"Don't you even dream about it, sugar," Lisa warned her in a half-serious voice. "The judge don't ever wanna see your face in court again."

"Party-pooper parole prude," Monique quipped then lay back and concentrated on staring at the ceiling fan.

Even Tiff grinned at that, though it was a glum sort of grin. Lisa didn't crack a smile, but she didn't look angry either. Carmela knew why: her sister wasn't any sort of prude; she liked sex and men and made no bones about it. Carmela often thought that if Lisa wasn't in law enforcement, she'd have been a huge success as a call girl. A kind of modern-era Xaviera Hollander. Lisa had that 'something extra' that men couldn't get enough of, while Carmela looked like a soccer mom (okay, a pretty one) before she'd even had kids.

She and Lisa lived together. Carmela had long ago gotten used to waking up to the sight of half-naked hunks passed out in their living room.

Lisa and Tiff dumped the large suitcase on the bed beside Monique.

While they opened it up, Carmela crossed to the bathroom to relieve herself. The bathroom duplicated the luxury of the front room. It was opulent to a fault, so much so that Carmela easily imagined she was someplace else at the moment.

Oh yes, she thought as her nether waters tinkled down into the ceramic bowl, *Monique's right—this would be a great place to bring a guy for a sexy weekend.*

Here, in the calm announcing the storm, Carmela was once again struck by an intense feeling of apprehension. *I really don't want to do this. But none of us have any real choice in the matter now, do we? Not me or Lisa, not Monique, and definitely not Tiff. At the moment Tiff barely seems to be holding herself together. If we don't do this tonight, Tiff will most likely wind up in a padded cell.*

Carmela mentally reviewed the look Tiff had given the receptionist. The look had been zebra-striped with hatred and revulsion, only Tiff's rage and loathing were turned inward on herself, so she looked blank.

The problem was, her unvoiced anger was eating her up.

Oh yes, currently Tiff was barely resident inside her own head. And since she'd doggedly refused to get psychiatric help for her frayed emotions and psychic pain, or even to report her abduction to the police (which would also have resulted in her getting psychiatric help), there was nothing anyone could do to help her.

Except—by her own request—this.

***

Carmela was a nurse at Boston's Brigham and Women's Hospital. Tiff worked with a computer supply firm up in the city's North End district.

Carmela clearly remembered the night when Tiff had wept bitterly on her shoulder, her loud sobs finally resolving into one repeated phrase: "I want to get even with that son-of-a-bitch! I want to get even with that son-of-a-bitch! I want to get even with that son-of-a-bitch!"

The next evening, Carmela had mentioned this to Lisa. And Lisa, the ice-cool personality that she was, had smoothly replied, "Sure, but how're we gonna find his ass to pay him back?"

They'd been at home in Roslindale that evening. Lisa had been painting her toenails black at the time, while Carmela flipped through a nursing journal.

Lisa had paused her pedicure to stare at her sister. She'd shaken her head, her silky blond hair flowing across her bare shoulders, above the towel wrapped around her breasts. "Look," she'd continued, "finding that rapist jerk might be possible if Tiff would just report everything to the police; then I could get the info from friends on the force. But the little fool won't, will she?"

"Hey, don't call her that," Carmela immediately objected. "Tiff isn't a fool. You've no idea what she's been through."

"Anyone who won't report being kidnapped and sexually abused due to some Victorian sense of reverse-morality *is* a fool."

"Don't you call her that!" Carmela objected again. Then she calmed. "Look, she's not ashamed that she's been sexually assaulted. She doesn't blame herself for what happened to her. It's not *that*. She just has a mental block about talking to anyone about it. Even a shrink."

Lisa smeared three long strokes of black along her left big toenail before looking up and replying. "Okay, so I'm being hard on her. I know she's your best friend and all, but . . . girl, it's been more than two months since then and even if the guy came like a horse each time he fucked her, his DNA can't be anywhere on her now, and no one's gonna be able to prove anything."

"Sis, you just said that if Tiff reported it to the police even now, you might be able to get some info."

Lisa regarded her toes for a moment, splayed out as they were between wads of cotton wool. "Yes, we might, by backtracking. It's a long, convoluted process though, and I won't guarantee that we'd find him . . . but at least we'd have the dedicated forces of Massachusetts law enforcement looking for the creep." She sighed. "C'mon, sis, don't think I don't sympathize with Tiff. I do—what happened to her is absolutely horrible and disgusting. I'd love to help her pay that guy back too. It's just that there's so little to go on in this case. I mean, come on—Tiff doesn't even know where she was held captive."

Carmela nodded sagely to that. Much as she hated to admit it, Lisa was right. That was the oddest part of the case: by her own admission, Tiff didn't know where she'd been held captive, just that it was in a basement. But it could have been in anyone's basement, and just about anywhere in the eastern part of the state.

"So, you're saying there's absolutely nothing you can do to help her?"

Lisa decided her toenails looked fab enough. She capped the bottle of nail paint and set it neatly aside, then stretched her legs out to let her nails dry, putting both feet up on the coffee table. "Not unless we somehow find the guy who put her in her current state." She shrugged helplessly and reached for her iPad. "And for that to happen, little sis, we'd really need a frigging miracle."

Lisa's phone rang then. Carmela watched her pick it up, then in half-amusement watched her beautiful face squeeze up in anger. "What? . . . Bobby, are you serious? You just saw Monique picking up a trick? . . . Oh, baby, she'd better not be. Shit, if that tranny slut is

9

back hustling ass again, I'll have her back behind bars before she's even through wiping the guy's poop off her dick!"

Bobby was Lisa's current steady, a hunky cop Carmela wished she'd met before her sister had. Monique, she didn't know; just another parolee who now had to endure her sister's zero-tolerance temper. The woman was apparently a just-out-of-jail transgender prostitute. Somehow, maybe it was sexual karma at work (God showing her what her own life might have been if she'd veered from the straight-and-narrow?), Lisa got more than her fair share of parolee hookers to work with.

Lisa's phone anger shortly gave way to gushing expressions of love and statements of lustful intent to Bobby.

Carmela more-or-less surfed over her sister's phone replies from then on. Her mind switched to considering Lisa's last statement to her. She agreed: finding the man who'd abducted Tiff would take a miracle. And those kinds of miracles were generally hard to come by.

So she'd resigned herself to watching Tiff slowly fall apart, her mental dissolution working steadily inwards from her already well-frayed seams, till one day she'd wake up screaming and scratching her skin bloody, and the paramedics would cart her off to a comfy padded cell.

Carmela could only hope that Tiff wouldn't be so far gone when she finally cracked up that she'd decide to blow her brains out or slit her wrists rather than throw a psychotic scream party.

***

But it hadn't worked out like that at all. A week ago, Lisa's 'miracle' *had* occurred. Tiff had herself found the man who'd held her captive.

He was here in Raynham.

How she'd found him? That part was sheer coincidence: Tiff, driving Carmela's car, had been motoring up from her mother's place in Somerset. She'd stopped at a filling station named the Red Eagle to buy gas, then afterwards decided to get herself a Pepsi from the station's convenience store.

About to push the store door open, Tiff had instead frozen in shock. Her mouth had dropped open and she'd almost wet herself from pure surprise.

The man behind the counter, the big muscular one currently bagging an old woman's purchases for her . . . it was her abductor. She'd recognize that face anywhere—small piggish nose, thick lips, and the long jaw. The cropped brown hair and mutton chop sideburns like he'd just fallen out of a movie about the Confederate Army. A wisp of brown mustache and small ears.

And that air of evil about him . . . those pale, pale eyes like the Devil himself had leeched away all their color as a sign of the man's devoted service to Hell.

He was grinning at the old woman, and Tiff wondered that the old girl wasn't terrified and running screaming out of there.

Quickly, before the huge storekeeper noticed her, Tiff ducked out of sight.

Oh, God. Suddenly she felt utterly sick. Only an effort of will kept her from puking up her entire lunch there and then. She felt like she was stuck inside a time machine and being rewound back to start over and over again, with no escape; her life on permanent sexual assault replay.

Her fears beat on her like hammers: *If he sees me, if he takes me away again to his basement and the handcuffs and knives and . . .*

Finally she managed to get a hold of herself. The old woman was just coming out of the store. She stared oddly at Tiff, wondering why she was loitering outside and not going in.

Tiff gave her the most reassuring smile she could, which apparently creeped her out even more, so that she practically ran across the filling station to where her even older husband waited in their white Chevrolet Camaro.

Her actions helped bring Tiff down to earth again. *The old girl thinks I'm a psycho. How's that for damn irony?*

After the couple drove off, Tiff stole several peeks inside the store. With no other customers to attend to, the man was now relaxed in his chair with a copy of Sports Illustrated, and she could study his face.

Yes, it is him. She had no doubts; after what she'd been through in his hands, his face was burned on her soul as indelibly as a brand on a cow's backside.

Tiff found that the longer she stared at the man's despicable features, the less fear of him she felt, and concurrently, the greater became her desire for violent and bloody revenge on him, as if fear and anger were two sides of the same coin, and given the right catalyst, you could convert from one to the other of them simply by flipping your mind over.

Finally, she turned away from looking at him and walked hastily back to her car, got in and drove off. A mile further down the road, she parked. After her accelerated breathing had normalized, she got out her phone and called her bestie Carmela, the only person she'd so far been able to tell the horrors she'd experienced.

"Hey, girl," she said once Carmela picked up, "I've found the son-of-a-bitch?"

"You've what? Who?"

"The son-of-a-bitch who abducted me and kept me in his basement and—"

She was interrupted by Carmela's loud gasp of disbelief. "*You have? Tiff, where the hell are you?*"

"I'm down in Raynham."

"Tiff, are you certain it's *him?*"

"I'm so positive, I could be a calculus symbol."

"Okay. What do you want to do now? Hey, do you have that gun on you? Don't you dare shoot him."

"No I don't. Lucky for him or else he'd be dead by now."

"Okay, okay. Now, just calm down and drive back home to Boston. I'll call Lisa and tell her and . . . we'll work out what to do about the asshole."

"Hey, I am calm. We're gonna get even with him, right?"

"More even than you can imagine, Tiff. Just come on home *now*. And drive *slowly*. Don't you dare speed and bash up my car."

Tiff had hung up and put the car in motion again. Though she did drive slowly as requested, she couldn't calm down. She couldn't get to Boston fast enough to begin to plot her revenge.

***

Carmela sighed loudly. Her reminiscences over, she wiped, flushed, and went back outside to join the others.

In the front room, assault preparations were well in progress. Tiff was already changed into Lisa's prescribed garb for them tonight ("Just make sure everything's black."). She had on a black spandex gym suit, black sneakers, a black leather jacket, and a black baseball cap.

Lisa was just zipping up her black leather trousers. Carmela grinned. *Yeah, trust my sister; everything just has to be sexy enough to die for.*

Watching her sister and Monique pull on their own nightshade clothes, Carmela couldn't fault the disguises: they looked like the ultimate set of party animals, or a female dance troupe about to run riot in the nearest nightclub. Of course, it helped that this was Saturday night, when even a little town like this had to have some fun going on.

Monique's 'disguise' was a black catsuit that hugged her buttocks provocatively, and thick boots. Her breasts stood out so proudly, they could have been advertisements for patriotism. Carmela winced. *Er . . . girlfriend, don't you get it? We're supposed to be diverting male attention away from ourselves, not attracting their eyes to devour our figures?*

Lisa paused in pulling on her spiky black jacket. "Hey, stop comparing your tits with hers and get changed too."

Carmela nodded, walked over to the almost empty suitcase, and took out her own clothes—a black T-shirt and pants. (Like Lisa, she was keeping the shoes she already had on.) That left just a small purse and two tasers in the suitcase.

While she dressed, Lisa went over the fine details of their plan again:

"Okay, guys, now remember: Monique and I are the ones going to make the snatch. Tiff and Carmela, you two stay out of sight in the van. Don't come out until we signal you to." She looked pointedly at Tiff. "That particularly means *you*. Don't show your face; we don't want him recognizing you."

Carmela said, "We do need to buy some gas into the van. The fuel gauge is reading very low."

Lisa shook her head firmly. "Not there. We don't want to leave any bank card details floating around in the pumps. Our alibi for tonight is that after checking in here, we four were all so ragged out that we fell asleep almost immediately. If we buy gas when we're supposedly asleep . . ." She stared hard at Carmela. "D'you get it now?"

Carmela nodded. She'd not forgotten. She was making conversation just to make conversation.

She couldn't fault Lisa's preparations for tonight's work. The four of them had gone over the plan with a microscope. And then Lisa (simply because she had to have the last say in everything in life), had gone over it again on her own till she was satisfied.

13

Lisa (along with Tiff) had actually driven down here to Raynham this past Tuesday, both to case the Red Eagle filling station and to confirm that Josh Penham (the scumbag they were after) actually did work here and hadn't just been filling in for someone else that day.

With her boyfriend Bobby's help, Lisa had also pulled up Josh's criminal record: Joshua Ronald Penham, Male Caucasian, 32 years old. Height 1.85 meters.

No real dirt on him though—just some domestic disturbance problems with a couple of girlfriends.

But that too had been good confirmation: Tiff remembered that her abductor had had a girlfriend. She'd never seen the woman's face though. For some reason, Josh's girlfriend hadn't ever descended into the basement to watch her being abused. Tiff would just hear her voice filter down the basement steps from time to time; to which Josh wouldn't reply. Or hadn't the unseen woman known of the horrors being committed right under her feet? That likelihood—that Josh's girlfriend was innocently dating a serial killer—seemed almost impossible to Tiff.

As an additional bonus, Josh's criminal record came along with his mug shot, which was all the confirmation Tiff had needed. "Oh fuck yes, that is the son-of-a-bitch!" Seeing that sadistic face, Carmela had shuddered too.

Lisa had also pointed out most of the precautions they needed to take; the important stuff that would prevent the police from suspecting and finding them afterwards.

The idea of stealing the van for instance. The van—a black Mercedes cargo vehicle with a sliding side door—was currently parked further along Carver Street, in tree-shrouded darkness four houses from the motel. They'd stolen the van from outside of a Mansfield factory on their drive down from Boston. (It had taken Monique and Lisa literally ages to get the old van to start—something to do with bypassing its security systems—while Tiff and Carmela watched for the police. All the time Monique and Lisa were trying to start the van, Carmela had been chewing her fingernails and almost peeing her pants. It had seemed like at any moment a cop cruiser would pull up and cart them all off to jail.)

Carmela reconsidered: No, they'd not 'stolen' the vehicle; they'd just 'borrowed' it for a few hours. Once done using it, they would drive it back up to Mansfield and park it back where they'd taken it from. And hopefully no one would be any the wiser—Lisa had said she doubted anyone would turn up at the factory before Monday.

Lisa had been the one who'd driven the van behind their car all the way down to Raynham. Carmela knew her sister had nerves of steel. (Carmela, who would never dare attempt such a feat, put Lisa's fearlessness down to her having developed such misplaced confidence in herself due to her attractiveness to the male half of the human species that she couldn't actually foresee anything evil happening to her.)

But yes, the idea of stealing the van is pure genius, Carmela thought. *If my Honda Accord is parked outside our room all night, we're clearly still inside it, right? And once we return the van afterwards, no one will ever suspect us.*

Lisa picked both tasers out of the suitcase. She handed one to Monique, then tucked the other away in a pocket of her metal-studded jacket. "Alright, girls," she said, "anyone wanna pee, you'd better go now. Next stop, Kick-ass-ville." She picked her gun up off the bed, and stashed it in her jacket also.

After arranging a black 'I Love MA' baseball cap on her head, Lisa went into the bathroom to pee. The others sat to wait for her.

Carmela took the interlude to regard her companions one last time before they set out:

Tiff was perched on the edge of the bed nearest to the front door. She sat stiff, her overweight body a mass of barely suppressed tension. Her eyes were cold as ice. Her lips were ledges of carved pink stone set in the frosty cliffside of her face.

Then, for the briefest of moments, a smile flickered over Tiff's lips. That smile gave Carmela the shivers. It was an intensely sadistic smile—in it Carmela read delighted anticipation and assurance that soon, very soon, she'd have her hands on *him*. Then, just as abruptly as it had appeared, the smile switched off again, and Tiff was back to being the 'aggrieved victim' version of herself. For the thousandth time Carmela's heart went out to her: *Oh my God, I've no idea what she must be experiencing at the moment. I really hope she gets her closure tonight.*

She looked from Tiff to Monique. The redhead sat almost opposite Tiff, on one of the room's two plush couches. She was positioned sideways on the couch, her legs over its edge and her chin propped on her arms which were folded over its backrest. In contrast to Tiff's straitlaced pose of tension, Monique looked relaxed. She was humming softly to herself.

Monique had their other gun. That detail worried Carmela a little. Other than that this woman was a transsexual and a prostitute, she knew nothing about her. And her sister hadn't yet told her what Monique had gone to jail for anyway. Carmela doubted it was just for providing sexual satisfaction for Boston's menfolk. The way Lisa had put it: "She's coming along 'cos I both need someone else who can handle a gun competently, and someone who'll do whatever I tell them to."

(Monique had to be really crooked though. She'd been responsible for buying the tasers from her 'friends,' who Carmela assumed were underworld contacts. The electroshock weapons were both second-hand purchases. As Lisa had explained it, she'd gone this route so they wouldn't have to worry about being tracked down by the tasers' 'confetti' tags—the folks they'd been stolen from lived way out west in Idaho. Sure it was all illegal as hell, but desperate needs inspired desperate deeds.)

Of course, what this all meant was that though Monique might not show it, she was certain to harbor resentment against Lisa for strong-arming her into another criminal act.

Carmela flashed Monique a reassuring smile. *Sorry, girl, you're in this like the rest of us.* Monique nodded back, her lime-hued eyes subdued, and kept humming her song.

Carmela had argued against involving any outsiders at all, but Lisa had smirked and overruled her. ("I need *reliable* backup, and you, darling sister, are scared of your own shadow. In a messy situation you'll be completely useless. Monique won't.")

Okay, Carmela could agree with that. But next, Lisa had also overruled her on something she considered of vital importance: the need for them all to wear gloves tonight.

Carmela winced. Ah, but Lisa was just so full of herself! Carmela had suggested that they all wore gloves for this operation, so as to leave no fingerprints. Lisa had airily vetoed her suggestion, arguing that seeing as the van was being both stolen from and returned out of town, there was no need to take a precaution that wasn't actually a precaution. Carmela thought Lisa was just pissed off that *she'd* not thought of the gloves idea, and viewed adopting her younger sister's suggestion as a breaking of her authority over their group.

Carmela *had* defiantly brought a pair of surgical gloves along anyway, just for herself. (They were hidden in her pants pocket.) But she'd already decided she wouldn't wear them. She didn't want the drama of confronting Lisa.

Tiff pointed towards the bathroom door, then asked, "Why the hell is she taking so long in there?" Her question rang with impatience.

"Maybe she's wanking," Monique replied with a smile. "Masturbation's a great way for alpha-females under pressure to relieve stress."

"We need to get a move on," Tiff insisted, checking the time on her phone. "It's almost eleven now. Josh closes shop at eleven-thirty."

Thankfully, at that moment flushing sounds came from behind the bathroom door, and Carmela, who'd also been wondering why her sister was taking so long urinating, relaxed.

While waiting for Lisa to reemerge, she also considered herself, here in this motel room. *Hell yeah, I look ready to boogie the night away.*

Her gaze fell on the single untouched object left in their suitcase—her little purse containing a hypo and two drug vials.

On picking up the purse, for a brief moment Carmela felt disconnected from herself. For that surreal instant she looked down on herself from above (like she were God in Heaven) and honestly contemplated this insanity she'd involved herself in.

Poop! How in the world did I talk myself into this? Sure, I fucking love Tiff like a sister, but . . .

But then, just like it had over their past week of planning, the feeling of worry and caution dispersed and she was once again left with the cold calm certainty that nothing could go amiss. Tonight, 'wrong' just couldn't happen. They'd planned for every eventuality. They'd left nothing to chance. They'd thought of all possible unforeseens. After work, they'd brainstormed for hours, for days, figuring out all the angles.

Lisa stepped out of the bathroom, the most beautiful party animal of the four of them. "Alright, guys, let's go," she said. "And one last thing—turn off all your cellphones, all of you. We don't put them on again except in an emergency." Licking her lips, she looked at each of them in turn. "I for one, don't need Bobby Finch calling me and the cellphone tower recording that I'm currently in Raynham. He thinks I'm home with the runs."

Everyone turned off their phones.

Next, like night shadows fading before the dawn, they left the room.

The critical detail here was sneaking out of the motel without being seen by anyone. Carmela agreed that this either made or broke their alibi. She now appreciated their good fortune in being given Room 9, right at the end of the front block. Room 10 was unoccupied, and beyond it, across the driveway leading to the rear blocks, stood a dark shelter of trees to hide them, these woods (like she'd previously noted) extending forward to meet those bordering the road. To the left of their room, beyond the vehicles parked in front of the other rooms, vague slots of white light spilled from the reception building onto the front lot. The lobby, however, lacked any windows facing towards the front block.

All they had to do was check that the front walkway was clear of people and then, one by one, hurry past Room 10 and out across the gravel drive, into the tree cover.

Lisa went first. She was delayed by the need to make absolutely certain that no one from the rear blocks could see them cross the drive. Once she'd confirmed this, she signaled to the others to come across.

Shortly afterwards, they were all hidden among the trees.

"Okay," Lisa said, "let's go get our man."

"About damn time," Tiff spat into the damp night air.

They set off for the road and the stolen van, with Carmela bearing her little purse behind the others.

As they padded through the trees, their shoes crunching the soft grass, Carmela once again struggled with the feeling that they were about getting into a world of trouble.

No, she reassured herself. *Stop worrying. Nothing will go wrong tonight.*

Her worries didn't cease, but seeing as she knew she was anxiety-prone anyway, after a while she simply ignored them.

CHAPTER 2

Josh

The Red Eagle gas station was located on the corner of Broadway and Britton Street.

Josh Penham was just about closing up the Red Eagle's convenience store for the night when he heard a loud commotion outside among the gas pumps.

Aw shit, not tonight! Josh thought. He was supposed to meet his girlfriend Ida Green at the Liquid Solace bar in twenty minutes and she'd be beyond mad if he was late again.

Unable to see clearly from behind the counter what was happening out in the filling station, Josh crossed to the storefront door and peered out through the glass.

What the . . . ? Two women in black clothes were having a brawl over by Pump No. 4.

Josh watched them for a couple of seconds. Damn, it was a real catfight—hair pulling and lots of screaming. Then they fell to the floor and began rolling around everywhere, while still flinging punches at each other and seemingly trying to pluck one another's hair out by the roots. The combatants' black van was parked by the pump, with the gas nozzle stuck in their fuel tank. The van looked like there was no one else in it.

Aw shucks! Josh thought, scratching his mustache. *These two broads ain't gonna kill themselves out there now, are they?*

He considered just leaving them to it, but the gas nozzle in the van's tank worried him. If one of them crazy women lit a match . . .

Josh also had several problems with calling the cops to the scene.

Firstly, if he called the boys in blue to come break up the fight, he wasn't going to make it to the Liquid Solace in time, and Ida would . . . his head almost hurt at the memory of how strident Ida's voice got when she screamed at him. Angry, Ida was a human air-raid siren, so goddam irritating you'd consider suicide rather than listening to her.

And also, Josh reasoned, *if I call the cops and these women have stopped fightin' and driven off before they get here, what then? I'll be accused of making a false report, and I already got a police record and I don't need any additional trouble.*

Okay, he knew that if he insisted he was telling the truth and the police pulled the gas station CCTV footage, they'd see that he wasn't lying. But who wanted all that damn hassle just because two hookers had had too much to drink on a Saturday night?

Outside, the battle was raging as violently as ever. Both women were back up on their feet again. One of them had the other by her ears and was banging her head against the pump like she wanted to shatter her skull.

Shit! Wincing, Josh decided to go break up the fight himself. He was a big, big man; there was no way two drunken chicks could be any match for him. He'd stick them in their goddam vehicle and send them on their merry way. And thankfully, they didn't appear to be armed. If they insisted on fighting regardless of his intervention, one or two smacks to the head would knock the booze out of them.

He pushed open the store door and stepped outside. As he did so, his cellphone rang up on the counter. He winced again. That would be Ida, wondering where he was while also slowly revving up her eardrum-piercing engines. He considered answering the phone, then decided against it. Best to break up this escalating altercation first. He'd simply stuff his ears with cotton wool before calling Ida back.

"Hey, ladies," Josh said as he reached them, "for fuck's sake, stop your goddam brawling!"

The only response to his request was for one of the fighting women—a blonde—to howl at the other, "I'm gonna disembowel you, you boyfriend-snatching skank!" then slam her head hard against the side of their van.

Dammit! Josh thought. *These girls sure do mean business. I gotta put a stop to this!*

He leaned forward, grabbed each woman by a shoulder, and pulled them away from the van. Then, while they still spat and clawed at each other, he forced himself in between them.

Finally, he had them separated from one another. The blond was behind him; the other woman, a lovely redhead, in front. The redhead was breathing heavily. Josh peeked quickly behind him to ensure that the blonde was alright. He felt somewhat relieved—despite all the rolling about and hair-pulling, neither woman seemed to have more than a few scratches on her.

"Okay, girls," he said in a tough voice, "that's enough fightin'." He stepped back from between them, peered hard at them both in turn, then gestured to the fuel nozzle they'd left stuck in the van's gas tank. "Now fill up and leave."

"Sure we'll leave," the redhead said with an odd smile that Josh couldn't place. "But you're coming with us."

He looked to the blonde. "Please, just fill up your damn tank and drive off. It's too late at night to be fightin' over some guy who's likely right now bangin' someone else."

"She's right," the blonde agreed with a cryptic smile. "You're coming with us, man."

Josh imagined both women were joking. *What is this? First they wanna kill each other, and now they want a threesome?* Then he remembered Ida, and winced. *Holy hell, am I gonna get a damn earful tonight.*

He hardened his face again and stared meaningfully at both women. The blonde in particular was making him uneasy. She looked out-of-place having a fight at a filling station. Sure, all women lost it on occasion—his girlfriend Ida was a great example of that—but this blonde suddenly seemed to have shed her anger completely, like she'd been playacting all along. He looked across to the redhead. She too seemed to have forgotten all about her gripe with the blonde. *Now, just what the hell's goin' on here?* Josh pondered. He wasn't overly worried though. At six-foot-one in height, and muscular like he was, no way were two chicks gonna take him down.

"C'mon, hurry it up," he said gruffly. "It's time you two went home. I gotta date and you're making me late."

However, neither woman stepped towards the gas nozzle. Instead, the redhead slipped something out of her jacket pocket.

Josh couldn't see clearly what it was that she'd pulled out. In the shadows overlapping her body, he thought it was a cigarette pack.

"Hey—no smoking here!" he cautioned quickly. "What the hell is wrong with you two women! Are you suicidal?"

Next he saw that the blonde too was pulling something from her jacket. This time there were no shadows; he got a good look at the stubby black object—a gun that wasn't exactly a handgun—with a blue electric arc sparking between the two metal protrusions on its front end.

Understanding came to Josh too late to save him. Next thing he knew, the prongs from the blonde's taser had hit him and he was shuddering in a muscle-anaesthetizing current of electricity, 50,000 volts almost making him piss and poop himself, and he'd lost control over his body and crumpled to the filling station floor.

And then, while Josh Penham stared dazed at the base of Gas Pump 4, his world turned into a haze of mingled impressions—what he saw, felt, and heard forming a blurred multimedia experience:

"Okay, yeah, we've gotten the bastard."

"Yeah, get the others."

This was followed by a banging on the side of the black van, the sound of its side door sliding open, and the sound of several more feet walking around his prone body, along with two additional female voices.

Josh was too weak to think, close to unconscious even. However, despite his flesh seeming dead, words, feelings, and impressions continued to filter in through his dulled senses, confusing more than enlightening him as to what was going on.

"Okay, guys, let's get him inside."

Many hands proceeded to lift him off the ground. "Damn, this man is heavy."

"Just don't drop him!"

A sensation followed of being carried and of being swung through the air, and then came a hard landing on a metal floor.

Josh desperately hoped that someone would drive into the Red Eagle to fill up. But they had to arrive *now*, right *now* before it was too late.

"Alright, he's in. Fucking fold his legs in too, Monique, and let's go."

He was folded in and the side door slid shut. Someone taped over his mouth with duct tape. Next, his wrists and ankles were also taped together. Resistance was impossible, his muscles felt paralyzed.

Through bleary eyes, Josh made out a young woman crouched beside him and staring down at him—another blond. This one was large, almost fat. He was sure he recognized her from somewhere, somewhen. Wasn't she the girl he'd . . . ?

Remembering was too much trouble. The large blonde spat in his face and smirked at him.

There was the sound of people getting into the front seats, concurrent with the shift of weight as the vehicle became noticeably heavier forward. Then a chorused slamming of doors.

"Alright, lady kidnappers, let's get the hell out of here before someone comes."

A worried, nervous voice: "Sis, are you damn certain the cameras haven't recorded us?"

The first blonde's confident reply: "Carmela, I've told you it's a blind spot. That camera at the end of the building is supposed to capture everything that happens here, but someone messed up their calculations."

"Are you *sure?*" the plump blonde asked as the van drove out of the filling station.

"Yes, Tiff, for goddam fuck's sake I'm sure; don't turn into Carmela on me. Hey, little sister, have you doped him yet? He's *big*. If he gets his strength back, he'll be worse than a bull in a china shop."

"I'm just about to." The speaker was the other girl who'd been hiding inside the van, a thin and angular young woman with a moody expression on her face like she'd had prunes and cod liver oil for dinner. Like the others, she was dressed wholly in black. Like the plump blonde, she was crouched beside his prone form. Oddly, she looked scared, or at best incredibly anxious. She was holding up a hypodermic syringe, and depressing the plunger just a little so a pale blue fluid squirted from a really fat needle.

Aw shit, these crazy women really mean business. Josh felt the van slow, then turn right, then speed up again, his body rolling sideways to compensate for each change in direction. They seemed headed down through the middle of town now. That ruled out any chance of Ida seeing the van and noting its number.

Josh was aware of a sense of high excitement in the air among his four abductors, along with nervousness, and . . . anger?

He next felt a pin-prick in his left arm and the intrusion of liquid into his body. His about-to-recede paralysis took a firm hold of him again, and it took all his strength to stay awake and keep his eyes open.

But what the goddam fuck? The girl with the injections was sticking another needle into him. He felt strange now. He was still as knocked out as before, but suddenly he could feel and hear and see everything clearly. He just couldn't help himself for shit.

Then she was looking down at him again, a mix of worry and excitement scribbled across her face.

"Alright, he's ready," she told the one driving. "He's completely helpless now."

"Ha ha! Next stop, the damn graveyard."

"Ha ha! Oh, I am so looking forward to this."

"Hey, Lisa, slow down the fucking van! I know you're impatient to start, but . . . do you want the cops to pull us over?"

"Calm down, will you? There's no goddam police in sight and besides, this entire center-of-town strip looks like Main Street in a damn ghost town anyhow. What's the population of Raynham? Fifty people?"

"Just drive *slowly*. The turnoff to the cemetery should be coming up right about now."

A surge of fear rushed through Josh. *We're headed for the cemetery? Oh no!* Okay, so he'd done some bad, even crazy things in his life, including a shitload of illegal stuff, and there were all those women too, when he couldn't control his temper . . . but . . . surely they weren't going to bury him alive, were they? *C'mon, you crazy women*, he thought desperately, trying to scream through his gag with limp lips, *let me fucking go! Let me go!*

"Okay, here's the Pleasant Street turning," the driver said. "Next stop, the Pleasant Street Cemetery."

Josh rolled against the side of the van as it made a lurching left turn then balanced again. Clearly, the other woman's speed warning to the blonde driver wasn't being heeded.

"Alright, everyone, this is our destination up ahead. Time I kill the lights."

They slowed to make another left turn. Josh did his best to fight down his rising terror of being buried alive.

CHAPTER 3

Tiff

During the short drive off the road and into the Pleasant Street Cemetery, Tiffany Hooper was there with the others in body, but not actually present in mind. At the moment, her three companions were merely extensions of the night, at once as real and unreal as the hanging darkness outside the van and the gibbous moon glowing overhead. Similarly, the cemetery trees they rolled beneath were perceived by Tiff more as pillars of darkness than even shadows.

Seated beside Carmela on the floor of the cargo van, Tiff's attention was focused primarily on their captive. Like a vulture waiting for him to die so she could devour his entrails, she regarded the bound and drugged man with a fixed stare.

Yes, I've got you now, you evil man! Ha ha! Did you really think you'd get away with hurting me?

She controlled her urge to spit on him again. She regretted doing so the first time—that was coming down to his level. With the lights off, she couldn't see his face, but she hoped his eyes were as terrified and uncomprehending as hers had been during the week he'd held her captive.

Looking at his darkened face, she felt her mind swell. Then, in her head, a huge bubble of blood burst, and she was suddenly back in that her horrible yesterday, watching a severed hand floating atop a pile of severed limbs, and Josh's ugly face grinning at her across the room . . . while he held up a dead woman's lower jaw without the rest of her face—just shattered teeth jutting from a curved expanse of raw bone and bleeding meat with an attached left ear.

She shuddered, for the moment still trapped in his basement, doubting even that she'd escaped. (Had she? Or was this revenge quest of hers all wishful thinking? A product of her subconscious? Just a

25

dream she was having on the night before he butchered her like he had so many others before her?) Escape from there had seemed impossible to her, something one only dreamed of, like she was a victim in a slasher movie, doomed to death by the scriptwriter with whatever logic filmmakers applied when determining their movie's sequence of kills. Chained there in this bastard's basement, she'd not been the heroine, that was for certain. Her escape had been a fluke, possibly even an oversight by God, whom she'd been certain disliked her and was punishing her, even if she didn't know what she'd done to offend Him. (Even now her feelings/thoughts towards deity were ambiguous—had He saved her because He liked her, or simply because she'd not yet suffered enough in this world? Because even the most violent of deaths was an exit, and if God had merely saved her for more suffering, the rest of her life—her entire future—must surely be very bleak indeed.)

The van turned and slowed, then turned again. Tiff was aware that they'd now rolled off the graveyard's internal routes and were motoring beneath a thick clump of trees.

The impressions arrived and faded like ghosts. They weren't worth focusing on; better to watch their captive's helpless bulk tremble below her. Besides, she knew where they were headed. *She'd* suggested this place to Lisa: her maternal Aunt Matilda was buried here.

The black van slowed to a halt like a corpse arriving at its final resting place.

Tiff inhaled deeply, filling her lungs with the smell of the night, with that of the van and its mingled female scents . . . and with *his* smell, the smell of her most hated one. It was an intoxicating inrush of air, one full of brutal promise. For a moment, Josh swirled about as atoms in her brain. She smirked. He smelt cleaner than she remembered, but she figured one couldn't continually reek of gore and expect to hold down a steady job. Or keep a steady girlfriend, for that matter.

At this point her mind backtracked a little:

The *girlfriend*—Josh's girlfriend. From the offset of their plan Tiff had been concerned about Josh's lady love being at the gas station when they snatched him.

Lisa had told her not to worry about it, and Lisa had been proven right. (Carmela would of course disagree, but Lisa was generally right about most things.)

But . . . peeking from a window as their van pulled out of the gas station, Tiff had glimpsed two people—a man and a woman, she'd thought—walking down the road (Broadway) toward them. Her view had been momentary though; she hadn't been certain. And besides, none of the others had noticed the approaching pair.

She'd said nothing. She'd seen no point in alerting and possibly alarming the others, particularly Carmela, who was already a bundle of nerves. (Highly strung at the best of times, tonight Carmela reminded Tiff of a wobbling jellyfish.) She'd figured that even if it had been Josh's girlfriend coming to look for him, and she and her male companion *had* noticed the van, they wouldn't have bothered with checking out its number—they hadn't yet reached the gas station, and so had no idea that Josh wasn't there.

But of course, once the woman couldn't find her beau . . .

Lisa's voice cut through her reverie. "Okay, everyone, we've arrived."

The van stopped for good and Lisa flicked on some sort of cop-light that she'd brought along—it gave off a dim red glow, just bright enough to see by. Tiff didn't know if it was infra-red or whatever. She just knew it made them all look extra-creepy, like demons in one of Hell's caves.

Yes, we all look like spirits of vengeance.

Her anticipation ramped up a little. Her fugue state dispersed so she was once again all there with the others.

"Say, why're we doing this in a graveyard again?" Monique asked. "I mean, it's dark and cold and creepy here and we're certain to get bugs all over our hair and dirt under our nails."

Lisa gave the answer Tiff would have. "I already told you why. We're . . ."

Monique had only been drafted in at the last moment, after all the planning was done—and Tiff still didn't know why Lisa had insisted that she come along. If anything, Monique was a total prima-donna—constantly on about her makeup getting messed up, and her hair falling out of alignment, and her lips losing their gloss, and she seemed to have little in her pretty red airhead except herself and how good she needed to look at all times. (There was also something competitive about her that was off-putting in a vague way. To Tiff's mind, Monique seemed to be trying too hard to show everyone how feminine she was, like it was important to her to let every other woman around know that she was just as much of (if not even more of) a woman as they were. She seemed unable to just relax and be female; like she was on gender watch 24/7.)

Tiff grimaced. Oh, Monique did look good, that was undeniable. *Even before I started eating to fight the pain of being kidnapped, I never looked that cute, and now, with all the pizza and candy and chocolate I've been consuming . . . I'm a frigging blimp!*

She was suddenly filled with an intense burning rage directed at the paralyzed man lying in front of her, this jerk who'd taken her life away from her. If she had a shotgun now, she'd . . .

In the front seat, Lisa was telling Monique, ". . . Really secluded place. No one'll see . . ."

"But a damn graveyard? C'mon, Lisa, what is this? Some Goth chick-flick we're making?"

Lisa's face turned hard in the red light. She looked really scary. "STFU, Monique, just do it like I said we do it."

Monique flinched like she'd been whipped, but she fell in line. "Yeah, sure, boss. Whatever you frigging say."

"And don't sass me. You're my bitch, I got you on a leash."

Monique just nodded glumly.

Carmela said, "Guys, let's get on with this, huh?"

"Yeah," Tiff agreed. "I'm dying to get started on this dickhead."

Lisa laughed and turned around in the front seat. "Now that's what I want to hear. Alright, open the side door and let's get him out. . . . Shit, Carmela, do it quietly, will you?"

"Sorry."

"Yeah, whatever. Just don't bring the goddam cemetery men running over 'cos they think they're having a zombie revival."

"Bitches versus Zombies. Now wouldn't that make a great movie?" Monique said acidly.

Lisa didn't answer her.

***

They got Josh out of the van and positioned him at the spot Tiff and Lisa had previously agreed on.

This was on a single, solitary grave deep under the web of tangled leaf cover. The grave was shut off within a wide rectangle of metal pickets. Even considering its out-of-the-way placement, the secluded burial place might still have been viewed as normal enough, except that its concrete top was clearly *bolted* down over the interment vault.

All that was written on the tombstone (also bolted in place) was the name 'Brian Chu.'

Now this is really strange, Tiff thought as they stripped Josh Penham naked and laid him out face-up and spread-eagled on the tomb's concrete slab. *It's almost like they are expecting a zombie resurrection here. Bolting down the top of a grave like they're trying to keep something locked inside it?*

But she didn't concern herself too long with those thoughts. Now that they had Josh naked and spread out, she had other things on her mind. Seeing him arranged like that greatly excited her. She wondered what her abductor was feeling; he had to be terrified. She really hoped he was. She knew he was both fully awake and fully aware of all that was happening around him. Carmela had told her that one of the drugs she'd injected Josh with was a synthetic variant of curare, meaning he would hear and feel everything they did to him, yet would remain totally paralyzed until an antidote was administered.

She was impatient to start. She looked around at the others. Carmela was kneeling beside Josh, checking his pulse. Over by the van, Lisa and Monique were whispering together.

Tiff decided that if she'd already waited this long for her revenge, a few minutes longer made little difference. Still, it had to be almost midnight now. She had no way of checking though: she wasn't wearing a watch, and just like Lisa had told them to, they'd all switched off their cellphones.

She looked back at the van again. To her relief, Lisa, baseball bat in hand, was now walking towards her; a violent angel of the night. She peered past Lisa. Did the vehicle's dashboard have a working timepiece that she could check, or didn't it? She hadn't noticed, and finally realized the illogic of her mental query anyway: the van's clock would likely only work when its engine was running. *Duh?* she chided herself.

She put her curiosity aside for the time being. Just before Lisa reached her, Tiff scanned their current location with satisfaction. This was genius planning. The tree foliage was so dense here that even the van was completely hidden from view. And it was great (fortuitous? preordained?) how the overhanging and overlapping branches had all formed a sort of natural cave over the grave to hide them. Driving off the cemetery's fixed routes, however, did mean that the vehicle might have left tire tracks on the lawn. But they were so far off the normally used roadways in this place that it was unlikely anyone would notice said tracks, so that was a minor worry. For all purposes and intents, they weren't even here at the moment, but rather, back at the motel asleep. All they needed to do now was keep the noise down. Which might prove difficult.

Then Lisa reached her, and it was time to begin.

"Alright, girl, are you ready?" Lisa asked, wrapping a friendly arm around Tiff's shoulders. She pointed the baseball bat down at Josh. "I daresay *he's* ready."

"I've been ready for months," Tiff replied. Without hesitation, she took the baseball bat from Lisa and stepped towards the prone man.

She couldn't wait to get started. She removed her jacket, folded it up, then knelt on it on Josh's left. Lisa and the others stood opposite her.

For a long moment, she held the baseball bat raised overhead. "You deserve this beating, you pig," she hissed at Josh, then began hitting him with the bat.

She didn't pay attention to where the bat landed, so long as it wasn't on his head. Lisa had explained as much: "If you hit him in the head, you'll knock him out, and then he won't be able to feel the beating anymore till we wake him up again."

Fair enough, no blows to the face then. But still, Tiff whacked him as hard as she could, each dull thud of the baseball bat against his motionless flesh a step towards mentally escaping from him for good.

"Take that, you kidnapping jerk . . . and that . . . and this too, asshole!"

A harsh whisper penetrated her anger: "Hey, Tiff! Lower your goddam voice, wilya! You wanna wake up the neighbors?"

"Yeah, Tiff, remember the police station's just around the corner."

"Oh, yeah, alright."

She did lower her voice, but she kept hitting Josh. She hit him left, right, and center, striking his legs, arms, and torso in no particular order, letting her rage direct her. And she hit him HARD. Thrice it sounded to her like she heard bones shattering beneath her bludgeoning. These crunching noises merely spurred her on to greater heights of violence.

Oops. In the crimson darkness (the red light glowing like the tip of a lit cigarette) she noticed that she'd damaged Josh's face with her blows. So much for good intentions. His nose looked broken, and she could see the dark spill of blood across his frozen mouth and matting his mutton chop sideburns. Aw well, he was still conscious, that was what mattered. His eyes were dark pits and she imagined them as lakes filled with tears, brimming with the salty water of his repentance for what he'd done to her.

Fuck him—he deserves this! She hit him some more, a whole lot more. And a whole lot harder. Her arms and knees were aching now (her kneeling position being less than conducive to swinging a bat), but damn, this was such enjoyable release! She felt really excited, turned on. She was shocked to realize she was sexually aroused. She hadn't had any sex since her abduction and this bastard was responsible for her celibacy, and now she had him exactly how she wanted him and he was going to pay and pay and pay.

"Stupid goddam rapist son-of-a-bitch!"

The blows fell harder and harder on Josh and she got wetter and wetter, until suddenly, she realized she was approaching orgasm. And then her climax was blindingly close, it would hit her at any moment.

She hit him again and again. "I hate you!" she gasped down at him between clenched teeth. "Oh god, how I fucking hate you!"

And then she was coming hard, and her months of horror and fear and dread and the obscene memory of all he'd done to her were gushing out of her in torrents, and being replaced by the sense of she exorcising herself of this demon in human form; and she kept smacking the baseball bat into his prone body until the sweet empowering sensation ebbed. It was only when she felt the others pulling her up that she realized that she'd collapsed forward on him.

Soft friendly hands laid her on her side by the grave.

Tiff felt intense satisfaction. *Oh, I have reclaimed me*, she gushed inside with a deep flow of peace in her soul. *I've gotten myself back again.*

(What Tiff had utterly hoped and prayed for for the past two months had been the chance to take out her anger and rage on her abuser. She'd wanted him one-on-one and helpless so she could do to him whatever she pleased. She'd been certain that if she could just have the bastard all to herself for an hour and beat the crap out of him, she'd be healed, all her 'crazy' consigned to the vaults of the past. And—that's what true friends were for—Carmela, Lisa, and Monique

31

[who she now liked a whole lot better] had helped her achieve her desire, and she was immensely grateful to them.)

For a while all four women were silent, the emotion in the air seemingly rendering it too thick for speech.

Then Carmela sat cross-legged beside Tiff, lifted Tiff's head into her lap, and held her hand. "Hey, bestie, you okay now?"

"Yeah."

"I mean, as in, *really* okay?"

"Yeah. Fuck, I think so."

"Good. All this was worth it then. I was worried that after we got him, you'd still feel as shitty as before."

"Nah, I'm fine now. I feel euphoric that I've gotten my own back on the pig." She grinned in the dark at the naked man who now looked more like a bleeding sack of meat than anything else (and did his left arm look broken?). "My first order of business once we're back home is to lose all this stupid weight I've gained and find me a new boyfriend."

"Matt's still fawning after you."

"Matt beats his women. Tammi told me so."

"For real?"

"For real. Tammi said he broke two of her sister's ribs during an argument. Linda was gonna press charges but they finally settled out of court." Tiff felt serene like this, her head cradled in her best friend's lap.

"Matt's family is super-rich," Carmela said. "They won't miss the dough. Chick feed."

"That's the problem though, isn't it? Now Matt'll feel like he has the right to treat any woman he wants like dirt. Count me out of dating him. I'm just not cut out to be anyone's punching bag."

"View it as an investment: he beats you up, you sue him."

"Or we bring him here and do him like we're doing Josh now?"

"Ha ha! Next thing you'll be thinking of setting up a 'female revenge' club."

On that statement Josh Penham gave a mighty wheeze that made all four young women look worriedly at him. But no, the drugs hadn't worn off; he still lay immobilized. His chest was visibly heaving though.

Damn, Tiff thought, *his face really is bloody.* The guilty baseball bat lay beside Josh, its business end mottled with dark glistening stains. She stretched out a hand, and with weakened fingers, retrieved her folded-up jacket from beside the bat so it wouldn't get stained too.

As if their victim's behavior was topping up her anxiety tanks, Carmela gestured violently at her sister. Lisa and Monique had stepped out over the pickets and walked away from the grave. The pair stood whispering to each other beside a tree.

"Hey, Lisa," Carmela called, waving an arm at her. "Hey, Lisa, what's next on the agenda?"

Carmela's question, asked with her usual tinge of distaste at having to defer to Lisa's opinion in just about everything, made Tiff once again reflect on the sort-of-strained relationship between the Cole siblings:

They weren't exactly estranged—they lived together—but . . . Carmela disliked her older sister. It wasn't obvious, but it was there. Hate possibly, but buried beneath so many years' accumulation of sisterly goodwill that Carmela herself no longer recognized it as hatred.

And Lisa, who seemed well aware of Carmela's dislike of her, didn't appear to care much about it. As far as Tiff could tell, Lisa simply assumed it was because Carmela considered her too slutty, and because she bossed Carmela about.

There was a five-year age difference between the sisters, and Lisa had been looking after Carmela since their parents' tragic deaths eleven years ago. Back when Tiff and Carmela were both teens, Carmela had griped endlessly to Tiff about how Lisa was more strict with her than any of their other friends' parents were with them. Numerous were the times she'd pondered aloud in Tiff's hearing: "You know, maybe I should just run away from home?"

Often too, Tiff would notice Lisa giving Carmela a look that said: *Hey, I know you dislike me, little sis, even though you hide it well. But for the life of me, why?*

And then, Lisa's querying look would be gone and the pair were once again loving siblings.

Tiff was suddenly aware of the oddest of sensations—it felt like the ground was throbbing. No, it wasn't throbbing—it was just a quiver, like the kind of nervous twitching one felt beneath an animal's skin if one placed one's hand on it, but much magnified.

And then it was gone again.

"Did you feel that?" she asked Carmela.

Carmela stroked her hand in the darkness. "Feel what?" she asked languidly. "Did I just fondle your breast by accident?"

"No, no, no—I'm serious. It felt like there was a little earthquake." She peered up at her friend as if to convince her.

Carmela shook her head. "No, I didn't. It's likely just the afterglow of your evil orgasm. Ha ha ha! Man, I had no idea you were a sadist. You should have heard yourself moaning while you whacked him with that bat."

"Shush!" Tiff whispered. "Keep your damn voice down." She was suddenly embarrassed. "You knew I came? You could tell?" She stole a quick glance over at the others. "Could they tell too? How'd you know?"

"We *all* knew. You sounded like a bad porno actress. You were going 'whack-moan-whack-moan-whack-moan' like the baseball bat was in your pussy."

Though quite mortified now, Tiff said nothing further on the matter. She grinned up at Carmela, but was really only half-interested in their conversation. She was certain she'd earlier felt something moving the ground. Even now, if she lay still and relaxed herself and concentrated . . . There! She'd just felt it again, like something—some mechanical engine—was throbbing underground. But what kind of engine would someone bury in a graveyard? And why? It seemed impossible, so she decided it was. Even if she was picking up vibrations, they were most likely being conveyed through the soil from a short distance away. She couldn't, however, hear any factory noise nearby.

"Listen," she told Carmela finally, wanting to confirm her experience by sharing it, "just quieten down and *feel* the earth. What I'm talking about feels almost like an underground machine at work."

Carmela stroked Tiff's hair. Then she relaxed her body, till her buttocks seemed to merge with the graveside soil and its carpet of overgrown grass. "Yes, I do hear something rumbling down below," she said after a while, "but I think it's just gas filling up my colon. Don't blame me if I fart."

Tiff rolled her eyes at the leaves overhead. Outside of their secret space, through a break in the leafy canopy, she made out the moon in its quarter of the heavens, shedding an unwelcome light on the graveyard.

It's particularly brilliant tonight, she thought, *as if to illuminate our unholy doings.*

She looked down. Lisa and Monique were both standing over Josh again.

"Hey, Lisa," Monique said, "I gotta go pee. I'll be right back."

"Yeah, sure. But hurry up."

The redhead turned to leave the picketed enclosure, only for Lisa to pull her back.

"Hey, Monique, I've got a better idea. Piss all over Josh."

"Aw, c'mon, Lisa."

"Do it, Monique. Get your dick out and give our boy a golden shower."

Tiff froze stiff on the tomb-side grass. *Dick? She's got a dick? How in the world didn't I figure that out?*

She watched Monique unzip her catsuit. Even in the semi-dark, she could clearly make out the woman's freed penis.

"And now, Josh baby," Lisa said, giggling. "I'd like you to meet the lovely Miss Bangles. She's gonna wash all that nasty blood off of your hurting body. Now isn't that really considerate of her?"

Tremors of anticipation moved Tiff's flesh. Oh, she just had to see this. If the ground vibrated now, she didn't notice it. Her mouth felt dry. She leaned up on her elbow to watch the transsexual drenching.

Monique began pissing all over Josh. She had a lot of urine to get rid off. For some reason she concentrated on his face and head. When Josh snorted like Monique had pissed into his nose, Tiff realized that she'd not killed him. For a while he'd been so motionless that she'd imagined she'd bludgeoned him to death.

To death.

As Tiff looked at Josh Penham lying there on the grave, she saw him more as an abstraction than a person. Try as she might to see her abductor as a fellow human deserving of pity, Tiff could only view him as the soulless embodiment of pure evil. It didn't matter that she believed she'd gotten her own back on him now and was already well on her road to recovery, she just couldn't empathize with him at all. And she was (at least she'd been until he'd taken her captive) at heart a very empathetic person, one deeply touched by the suffering of others. It didn't help matters any that the red glow around them all made Josh's face seem demonic. And the way he lay there—like a doll, like an object to be abused and violated, all of him weak and helpless—dehumanized him even further in her mind. The man was primarily a concept now, except for his strong and mighty penis (even flaccid and shrunken as it was now, she still saw it as erect and violent in her memory and it horrified her), that EVIL product of misguided testosterone responsible for filling him with the confidence to terrify and harm her.

To death. Monique was done urinating now. The smell of piss hung thick around them as the yellow liquid dribbled off Josh's body, making Carmela shift out of its way.

"Damn, that's sleazy," Monique said in clear disgust.

"Stop pretending. It isn't like you haven't pissed on a trick before."

"Yes, I have, but he was paying me to."

"Hey, Tiff?"

"Yes, Lisa?"

"How do you feel now? Ready to go?"

"Please give me five minutes more. My arms and knees ache."

"Alright, you got it. But not a second longer, we need to get a move on back to the motel."

Tiff again tried to make out the suffering man's face. All she saw were a mass of shadows, a shade darker where she'd broken his nose. She hoped that inside his mind he was crying, weeping and repenting of his sins. She hoped he was sorry he'd ever abducted her, and sorry he'd abducted all those other girls too . . . all those poor young women whose families were certain to be weeping bucketloads for them now.

Then Tiff remembered something else and looked up at Carmela. "Did *you* know? I mean, know that Monique is . . . ?"

Carmela was silent for a moment, so quiet that Tiff could hear her breathing over the rustle of the night. Finally she giggled and said, "Yes, I admit I did. I didn't think it'd come to this though. Quite a surprise, isn't it?"

Tiff laughed. "Oh, I'm surprised alright." She waved a hand across the redness, at their captive. "Not as surprised as he is now, I'm sure."

"One wonderful thing about having a penis is that you can direct the stream of pee wherever you want it to go. Not like us—you don't squat and it dribbles away down your thighs."

Tiff was amused. "I can pee standing up. You need to spread your legs wide though and . . . okay, you gotta squat a little bit too . . . just a teensy bit."

To death. I thought I'd beaten him to death. Tiff's thoughts split off from the sounds around her and folded in on themselves. The whisper of the wind through their cavern of leaves, the rustle of those same leaves against each other as if applauding Josh Penham being delivered his just deserts (or as if the trees were making love), the soft crunch of damp grass as Lisa silently paced, and the beating of Tiff's own heart, all those sounds became secondary things, background muzak over which the credits of a bloody movie would shortly scroll.

To death. Oh yes, they were going to *kill* Josh Penham. They'd all agreed on it; even Monique had. Josh's capital offence wasn't just the abduction and rape. No, this man was bigger than mundane misogynous misbehavior like that.

Once more Tiff's mind did a 'time machine' flip back into the past:

The day after she arrived in Josh's nightmare basement, he'd uncovered a bloody tub of chopped-up meat and told her it was his basement's previous 'tenant.'

(At the time, Tiff had been chained nude to the basement wall, her wrists and ankles all chafed sore from trying to escape her shackles. Her captor was a partly-shadowed horror in front of her, a hulking mass of muscle wearing blood-spotted jeans. He stood over six feet tall, his face half-hidden by a surgical mask. The surgical mask had been a constant during her week of captivity. Tiff had never been sure if he wore it to terrify her further, or to hide his identity.)

Like one hypnotized, Tiff had stared at the gory mess of bloody disconnected flesh, recognizing, amongst other things, some sliced up coils of intestine like plumbing pipe, dark trapezoidal chunks of liver, lighter colored cubes of lung connected to more plumbing-fitting windpipe, bits of scalp with long blonde hair, a cracked rib, and a hand with cracked and dirty fingernails.

Tiff had instantly begun puking, spewing what remained of yesterday's lunch.

"Yeah," Josh had explained to her, while stepping backward so her vomit didn't spray on his pants, and while stroking his mutton chop sideburns with his huge fingers, "Traci here just got tired of livin'. Of livin' down here, I mean. I fed her and fucked her—what else does a woman want from a man? But no, she wasn't satisfied with . . . with the effort I put into keeping her. And what can a nice man do with an ungrateful bitch like that, huh?" He'd scowled. "So I just sent her up to Heaven, to rest with the good Lord above. There's supposed to be a better place up there, ain't there? Dammit, girl, I sure as hell don't know; I never paid attention in Sunday school."

Tiff had just gaped at him in horror and wet herself.

"So, just you be a good li'l girl now and don't you ever grow tired of living down here with me, and nothin' bad's ever gonna happen to you," Josh had assured her.

Then he'd singled-handedly carried the massive plastic tub of destroyed female flesh up the basement stairs and left Tiff alone in the semi-darkness to meditate on the horrors that awaited her.

And, oh yes, those horrors had come. Josh had proven himself a first class psychopath. Tiff's body bore the scars that proved his proficiency in torture and evil. She still woke up terrified, breathless as a fish on land, from what he'd done to her.

(For reasons of his own understanding, that was the single time in the entire duration of her captivity that he'd spoken to her—thenceforth all communication had been via coughs and guttural grunts from behind his surgical mask.)

So, yes, they were going to kill Mr. Penham tonight. And that was that. It had been a simple decision to reach. This wasn't so much murder as refuse disposal, making the world a safer place by clearing out a toxic waste of male skin.

Tiff toyed with the idea of beating Josh up again before they killed him, but she knew they were running out of time.

"Okay, Tiffany Hooper, your five minutes are up," Lisa announced suddenly.

"Yeah, alright." Tiff sat up.

Lisa was perched with her behind against the 'Brian Chu' tombstone, her feet beside Josh's head. "Well, girls, now we kill him," she intoned like an evil Mother Superior. "He's outlived his usefulness to planet Earth."

"Who's gonna do it?" Carmela asked. Tiff could hear the nervousness back in her voice now, and she fully understood why. Oh, it was easy enough to think of killing someone, but when it came to time to actually do it . . . Oddly, now that she thought about it, all through their planning sessions, they'd never decided on who would be the executioner tonight. The general consensus had seemed to be that the choice would make itself, that the moment would pick its own volunteer.

But it had to be done. If Josh Penham had hated women before, that hatred was surely nothing compared to what he must be feeling now that they'd completely humiliated him.

"Well, who wants to kill him?" Lisa asked. "Any takers?"

There was silence all around the four of them. Even their breathing sounded subdued.

Tiff knew what the problem was: none of the four of them (okay, she wasn't sure about Monique though) had ever killed anyone before. Tiff didn't think she herself had the guts to do so now. Killing a person—particularly one as helpless as their captive—seemed akin to voluntarily damning oneself. Tiff wasn't religious (the last six times she'd been in church were for her friends' weddings), but she did have a highly developed sense of right and wrong. She viewed justice as a set of scales that one tried not to overbalance. The good one did in life must be more than the bad. A good person did more good than evil; that was it. One should never do *serious* evil unless one had sufficient credit of good already stored up. Enough to, if not completely neutralize the bad, at least counterbalance it somewhat.

And now, Tiff realized that even though she hated Josh Penham, even though she was scared of what he'd do if left alive . . . she no longer felt like killing him. She couldn't imagine herself actually putting a knife to his throat. She had a sudden horrible vision—likely helped by the red glow about them—of his blood spilling over her hands and never washing off again, no matter how hard she scrubbed and scoured them, until she died. Oh no!

She said nothing. Neither did Monique. The transsexual woman had taken Lisa's place, leaning on the other side of Brian Chu's tombstone. She had her face turned skyward, as if watching the stars through the leaf cover. Lisa had moved to sit by Josh's feet on the grave slab.

"Who's gonna kill him?" Lisa insisted. Behind her, their van seemed a giant insect peeking through the trees.

"Maybe we should just let him go?" Carmela whispered back. She sounded scared now. "C'mon, we don't need to kill him. He isn't gonna tell anyone what we did to him."

"Shut the fuck up, you little wimp. Just listen to yourself: let him go so he can butcher some other girls? Of course he won't tell the cops what we just did—he'll simply take it out on the next woman he abducts. That is, before hacking her into bits."

Lisa leaned forward and clutched her knees. "Hey, Tiff, do you want to do it? Rid the world of the scumbag?"

Tiff cringed. Lisa was making it sound like an honor. "Nope, I don't have the balls for that."

Lisa laughed. "Well if it takes balls . . . Hey, Monique, you come and slit his throat!"

Monique looked down at them. "Forget it. I already pissed on him, I don't want his blood on me."

"Monique, I told you—I own you, you punk bitch. Get your trans ass over here right now and slit this asshole's neck."

"Go suck a dick. I ain't killing anybody."

"Who the hell are you talking to?"

"I'm talking to you, you goddam bully." Then she calmed. "Look, Lisa, for fuck's sake, just slit the guy's throat yourself already? I sure as hell ain't doin' it, and I can tell you your kid sister won't either. And neither will Miss Victim over there, so . . ."

It was being referred to as 'Miss Victim' that pushed Tiff over the edge of reason. Hating Monique with all her heart for referring to her that way, she leapt to her feet. "*I'm not* a frigging victim," she growled. "Give me that goddam knife!"

"Finally, someone with balls," Lisa said sarcastically. "I was beginning to think we'd be all night doing this. Alright . . . Hey— what's that rumbling?"

"What rumbling?" Monique asked.

"The ground just felt like it was shaking," Lisa explained. She waited a few seconds then added, "It's stopped now though. But it was odd . . . I felt—"

"Tiff was saying the same earlier," Carmela said. "I thought she was just imagining it."

"Hey—here it is again! Shit, now it's stopped again. What is going on here?"

"It's probably the vibrations from a huge underground water main," Monique said. "Likely flood drainage. When we were working out our route on the map, I noticed that there's a large pond just in back of here."

"Well it's really creepy," Lisa said, "almost like there's a mining engine drilling underground." Giggling, she leapt to her feet and made claws of her hands. Then, arms stretched in front of her, she began a slow, wavering walk forward. "Or like there's zombies digging themselves out of the earth."

"Stop trying to fucking scare us!" Carmela yelped.

Lisa pantomimed some more zombie steps. Monique laughed softly.

As far as Tiff was concerned they'd gotten well off track now. *Shit, have you all forgotten what we came here for?* "Give me the knife," she repeated loudly. "Let's get this piece of trash disposed of."

Lisa stopped joking and walked close to her. They stood together, their lips at kissing distance. "Are you sure you can?" Lisa asked quietly, an honest concern in her voice that Tiff had rarely ever associated with her.

"Why ask?" she replied bitterly. "You've been goading someone to do it for the past five minutes."

Lisa leaned close to her ear and whispered, so the others wouldn't hear, "Not true. I'll kill him myself—all the talk was just to scare him shitless first. None of us can possibly imagine how terrified the bastard must be now—hearing us four casually discussing his death the way a shopper would point to a cut of meat and say, 'I want that one, chop it up for me,' then suddenly change her mind and say instead, 'Oh no, sorry, I think I prefer that leg of lamb over there.'" She touched Tiff lightly on the cheek. "You don't have to do this, girl. Honest. It'll be a weight of guilt on you for a long time." Her expression saddened. "Me, I'm used to guilt. It's been an acquaintance of mine forever."

"Guilt?" Tiff smirked. "Not for this piece of shit, it won't." She glanced down at Josh, a long pale lump lying on a grave; its current location a prophecy of its morbid end. She sighed. "Lisa, give me the knife. I'm serious that I'll do it."

Lisa handed Tiff the knife. "Okay, now remember, a single deep cut into the jugular vein is all it'll take. Just keep a steady hand and slice as far as you can into the side of his neck. Watch out for the blood or it'll get all over you."

Tiff nodded. Even in this red dark, she could make out the worry on Lisa's face. She shrugged off Lisa's concerns and took the three steps that would bring her to her destiny.

She knelt over Josh and felt his face with her hands. He was a sculpture in the dim red light, a soft bleeding rock with human features. She was struck with the sudden strong desire to see him clearly. She wanted to see if he was crying.

"Anyone got a penlight?" she asked. "I wanna see the look on his face."

"Too dangerous. Try to imagine it."

Frustrated in her desire, Tiff did try to imagine it. She pressed the blade of the knife against Josh's throat, and with her other hand felt his eyes. Yes, there were tears in the bastard's eyes. A wind of euphoria blew through her and for a moment, she wasn't herself anymore, she was Nemesis, the goddess of vengeance, digging the knife deep into his neck . . . DEEP. She felt his blood wet her fingers, and at the same time felt tears spill from his eyes and wet the fingers of her other hand.

It was wonderful. Perfect.

She sliced and sliced and sliced. And beneath her, Josh Penham died.

Finally, Tiff was aware of Lisa and Monique pulling her off Josh.

"Shit," Carmela was whispering, somewhere far away. "I thought you said you were *over* him! You've almost cut his head off."

Tiff wasn't sure how she felt, but she was certain of one thing now: Josh Penham definitely wouldn't be haunting her nightmares anymore. Except if he had special access to them from Hell.

And then, suddenly, the ground began vibrating beneath their feet again.

"I felt that," Carmela said.

"Me too," Monique said. "What the hell?"

Tiff didn't say anything. She felt suddenly nauseated, the previously compelling sweet smell of her victim's blood now making her stomach turn. She shrugged off the arms restraining her, staggered to the edge of the grave, and puked over the pickets. Through her feet she felt the earth continue its strange movement.

The other three had meanwhile forgotten her trouble. They'd seemingly even forgotten the dead man beside them.

Monique was pointing down at the bolted-down grave. "Something's very wrong here. What the hell did these idiots do? Dig a grave over a generator?"

The underground throbbing had now settled to a more subtle tremoring. Tiff kept throwing up.

Carmela asked in a nervous voice, "Or was this 'Brian Chu' guy a terrorist, and someone buried a time bomb with him?"

"Tell you what," Lisa said. "How about if the four of us vulnerable young females stop speculating and just get the hell out of here?" She pointed over at their parked van.

Carmela nodded. "Yes, I second that. Let's just *go*."

Tiff looked up from her puking and said, "I *third* that suggestion. If there's going to be an explosion here, we definitely don't want to be caught in it . . . or associated with it if someone calls the police." Another wave of nausea hit her and she gulped in fresh air to steady herself. Carmela pulled her aside again to wash her hands, then handed her the dead man's shirt to wipe them dry.

"Okay, I'm fine," Tiff said finally. She accepted her jacket from Carmela and slipped back into it. Its warm fabric around her body seemed to damp a threatened chill in her soul.

Lisa picked up the red-light and they all turned towards the van.

"Hey, guys?" Monique called as they set off towards it.

As one, they turned back to stare at her. "What is it?" Lisa asked drolly. "You into necrophilia now? You wanna fuck his dead ass?"

Monique pointed down at Josh's corpse. "What about that note we were gonna pin on him?"

Lisa shrugged. "It won't work anymore. Tiff almost sliced his head off his neck. No one's gonna believe this is a suicide."

"Yeah," Carmela added. "And . . . all those bruises from the beating she gave him make him look like the victim of a gang assault. He can't have done that to himself either."

Monique mused on that. "I feel we should write something on the corpse anyway, just to throw the cops off. Something like 'Die Rapist Pig!' Something like that."

Lisa's response was patience itself. "Hey, redhead, get your donut butthole over here and into the van right now. What part of 'the goddamn motherfucking ground is shaking like it's gonna explode under us' do you find hard to understand?"

To a loud rustle of displaced leaves and branches, Tiff was already scrambling into the van beside Carmela. She was relieved when a few moments later, Monique climbed in the front beside Lisa.

Lisa started up the vehicle. For a moment, the revving engine sounded unnaturally loud in the darkness. It seemed impossible that someone wouldn't come running from the cemetery caretaker's buildings.

But no one emerged to see them.

"I'm sure those vibrations were just from a water main," Monique protested adamantly as Lisa backed the van out of the clump of trees. "I already told you guys about the pond behind the graveyard. I remember its name now—Johnsons. We really should wait and write something on the body, and . . ."

She kept on talking to herself. To herself, because no one paid her the slightest attention. The others kept silent as Lisa drove through the cemetery to the main road. They were pleased at a mission accomplished, but also a bit worried.

As the black Mercedes van left the Pleasant Street Cemetery, Tiff finally fulfilled her earlier wish to see what time it was by the dashboard clock. 00:00. Perfectly on the stoke of midnight.

Well, that's taken care of, she thought with satisfaction. *Now we just need to get back to the motel and sneak back into our room to establish our alibi.* She rolled her eyes heavenward in a heartfelt plea: *And, God, please—I don't want any dream replays of me killing Josh Penham tonight.*

CHAPTER 4

Ambrose

"Oh wow, Nancy, that feels so good!" Ambrose Duggan gasped. Next, he sagged against the Sunflower's reception desk.

Nancy Pine, on her knees behind the desk, grinned around her mouthful of his penis and sucked harder. She grabbed a handful of his testicles and squeezed them gently, then slid her mouth almost completely off Ambrose's erection and sucked on just the head of it.

Ambrose groaned and ran his fingers through her honey-toned hair. He was trying to hold off the inevitable climax for as long as he could, but it was a losing battle. Damn, she did it so good! So good indeed that his initial worry of them being discovered by one of the motel's guests had long ago fluttered off to the rear of his mind. All that was left now was the pleasure, as he leaned against the desk with his jeans down around his ankles and Nancy fellating him.

Then he felt her tickling his anus with a fingernail, and the sensation in his groin overloaded.

"Oh my God!" He grabbed her ears and spurted into her mouth.

Feeling Ambrose start ejaculating, Nancy grabbed firm hold of his buttocks and forced her mouth all the way down on his penis, until its tip was buried deep in her throat and his pubic hair was brushing against her lips. Going completely weak-kneed from the sensation, Ambrose just managed to hold himself upright through the duration of his orgasm. "Oh God, oh God, oh God!"

Nancy waited till he'd stopped trembling before drawing her lips off his member. Then she sucked hard on the penis head to empty it completely, swallowed twice, and wiped her lips dry with the back of her hand.

Ambrose stood there with his pants on the floor, trying to recover himself.

Nancy got up and regarded him with a pleased, impish smile on her face.

Nancy Pine was twenty-five years old and short, but pretty with it. She had curly brown hair and brown eyes. As with many women under 5'3" in height, her small figure bordered on plump, with her bosom and hips really pushing out her clothes. She looked like she'd get fat after a child or two.

"So, how was it?" she asked Ambrose coyly. "Good?"

"You have no frigging idea," Ambrose replied with a weak smile. "I never would have imagined . . ."

She giggled with that endearing manner she had. "I told you I'll be good for you, Ambrose," she said. "Way better than Crystal is." She stepped close and hugged him.

Ambrose smiled over her head and ran his fingers through her curls. She only reached to his chest and there was something oddly comforting about hugging her, an almost paternal feeling she stirred in him. Which wasn't what *she* wanted. But he was so much older than her—sixteen years older to be exact—and he wasn't certain if he could give her what she wanted. That was the thing about dating younger women—you had no idea if they had 'daddy issues' they were resolving through you or not. (A warped concept it was: If a woman loved her father, she might want you because you reminded her of him. Similarly, if a woman hated her father, she might also want you because you reminded her of him; only in this latter case, she'd now expect from you all the love he'd denied her.) Ambrose shrugged. Best it was to simply love the woman who loved you without bothering about why she loved you.

Nancy Pine, however, clearly didn't care about the difference in their ages. Even if he'd been blind, Ambrose could've seen that much. As they separated now and she pulled her diminutive form up onto the stool beside his, the desire for him in her eyes was obvious. And it wasn't just sex—she'd told him in no uncertain terms that she loved him. As in *really* loved him. "Ambrose," she'd told him, gasping the words out after a long, long kiss that seemed to use up all the air in both their lungs, "I fucking love you; and I don't ever plan on stoppin'."

Surely, a woman couldn't be more direct than that.

They'd been going steady for the past week.

(Ambrose was Nancy's landlord. Nancy, a florist's assistant, lived two houses away from the Sunflower Motel, sharing house with her older brother Owlsy, a big chap who worked for Ambrose's uncle Ed McKinney on his pig farm. Owlsy was a nice enough sort; he never said much and minded his own business. Nancy, more effervescent than bicarbonate of soda, was his exact opposite—the life of the nonexistent party. Now that they were dating, Ambrose wondered how he'd ever be able to keep up with her.)

Suddenly remembering that a guest might walk into the lobby, Ambrose bent down and pulled up his jeans. As he zipped them up and buckled his belt, he watched Nancy. She smiled innocently back at him. She had a winning smile, so choir-girl innocent that Ambrose wondered if she'd really been the one who'd just almost sucked his balls out of their sack.

"Wow, Nancy," he said admiringly. "You sure are one hot chick!"

She preened herself, running fingers through her hair. "And there's more of me to come. I haven't even gotten started with you yet, baby." She leaned forward at him, her left arm braced on the reception desk. "Okay, darling, how 'bout a drink? I need something to chase the come down."

Ambrose laughed. He knew she was toying with him. "Stop tryin' to tempt an old alcoholic back to the bottle."

She laughed back. "C'mon, Ambrose, you might be an alcoholic, but you sure as hell ain't old." Then her expression grew serious. "But what's it like? I mean, not drinkin' anymore?"

His eyes clouded before his reply. "Different . . . yeah, different, that's the best way I can put it. There's no haze anymore, no buffer zone against reality. Things hurt you and they hurt badly and there's nothing you can do about it except let them hurt you, you know? The world—the past—is always here with me, and it's hard and cold, and I see and feel everything, and"—he forced a sad smile—"sometimes, when Crystal comes over and she's drinkin', I'm almost tempted to have a drink too, but . . ."

"But what, baby?" At his mention of 'Crystal,' Nancy's face had creased up in anger.

(Ambrose understood her jealousy: Crystal Parr, Raynham's top prostitute, was his best friend, and Nancy, who thought he was still sleeping with Crystal, didn't like that one bit. Ambrose *wasn't* sleeping with Crystal anymore—which Crystal didn't like either. Thankfully

Crystal was at the moment out of town, on call girl duty down on a millionaire's ranch in Texas. Of course, the moment she got back to town and discovered he'd begun dating Nancy, there'd be a major emo meltdown. Ambrose would have hell to pay on both sides. *Damn, I might even have to start drinking again to cope.)*

He laughed at Nancy's question. "But . . . each time I'm tempted to drink again, I recall Chief Kravitz's promise . . . or threat."

***

Ambrose Charles Duggan, once Raynham's most famous lush, had stopped drinking himself to death because Tina Kravitz, Raynham's Chief of Police had thrown him into a solitary cell down at the Raynham Police Station and hadn't let him out for three weeks. Those three weeks had been more than long enough for the booze to exit his system permanently.

Initially, Ambrose had raved and howled and complained and . . . No one paid him any notice. All he got to drink for those three weeks of incarceration were water and coffee.

"Hey, what about my damn rights?" he'd asked the Chief the first time she'd come to see him in his cell. Like an old-time convict, he'd been chained around the ankle to keep him near his bed, so he didn't start banging on the bars of his cell.

"You don't have any."

"Tina, this is America, you can't just throw a guy in jail and deprive him of his liquor!" He frowned. "Look, I'm not even asking for my phone call to a lawyer. I just want a bottle of J.D."

The Chief, a massively corpulent woman, had grinned broadly at Ambrose. "Buddy, this is my damn town and my damn police station, and I can do whatever the hell I damn want in here." She'd pointed a thick finger at him. "And what I want is for you to stop drinking."

"That's too hard. Ask me to die for my country instead."

Chief Kravitz sighed loudly. "Ambrose, you're a *hero*. We need you sober."

"It's really hard, Tina. Each time the memories come, I feel like I'm breaking down all over again."

She went and sat next to him on his bunk and draped an arm over his shoulders. Her scent of musk and roses enveloped him. "Ambrose, you gotta get through this. That's the past—you have to leave it

48

behind you. You've already defeated the monster that killed your family. You've even defeated Brainchew *twice*." She sighed again, softly this time. "We *love* you, Ambrose, we don't need you drunk."

"Brainchew's dead for good, you don't need me. But me? *I* need the booze to help me forget."

"What if it wakes up again?"

"It can't. It won't. Not the way you've got it secured now."

"What if you're wrong? Then we'll need you, our hero, to defeat it again. You can't do that if you've drunk yourself to death."

He'd leaned away from her, a roughish smile on his face. "Hey, maybe being drunk helps me defeat it."

She'd given him a look of intense disgust. Tina Kravitz had a pretty face that was sort-of mismatched to her immense body. "Don't even think of pulling that crap excuse, Ambrose. You're gonna quit drinking and that's final."

He turned defiant. "And if I don't?"

She got up and faced him, fat hands on immense hips, her gaze equally defiant. "Don't you frigging dare me, Ambrose. I run this town, and I assure you that if you so much as even look longingly at another bottle of whiskey once I let you out of here, I'll have you back in here so fast you'll be dizzier than a baseball that's just taken a home run hit. And this time you'll be on bread and black coffee for three whole months."

Without waiting for his reply, she turned and walked out of his cell.

Ambrose had watched her go. He didn't doubt that she was serious—here he was now with a chain around his ankle after all.

But what happened to my rights? he wondered. *I got rights, ain't I?*

Two weeks later Ambrose was let out of the Raynham Police Station. He'd been sober ever since.

***

Opposite him, Nancy was still grinning coyly. "What'cha thinkin', Ambrose?"

He grinned back. "Lotsa stuff. Particularly how hard a jail bed is. Girl, you've no idea what it was like getting off the bottle. And staying off the damn bottle is even harder." His voice broke. "But I'm doing it, one damn day at a time."

The next moment Nancy had crossed the distance between them and was in his arms, sweet and soft against his chest again. "Oh, Ambrose, I understand. I really do. Let me into your heart, baby. Let me help you heal your hurt." She looked pleadingly up at him and there were tears in her eyes now. "C'mon, baby, don't shut me out."

He nodded back down at her and held her close. "Hell, Nancy, you've no idea what losing your entire family is like."

"But that was so long ago. Years ago. I'm here now. I'll be your family if you'll let me. I'll help you stop hurtin'."

Ambrose leaned forward and kissed her lemon-scented curls. He pondered her words. Yes, it was almost four years now since Brainchew (the name filled him with intense disgust) had killed his wife Nina and their young son Michael. It was about time he rested their ghosts in peace. And here, sobbing on his chest now, was a wonderful young woman who was clearly besotted with him.

Yeah, Ambrose Duggan thought, a smile spreading over his craggy face. It seemed time to take a chance on love again. Maybe—if Nancy was as real as she seemed—they might even get married and start a new family.

He raised her face to his and kissed her soft lips. "Yeah, Nancy, you're my family now."

She squealed with delight, hugged him tight, and then glanced at the clock on the lobby wall across from them and groaned. "Aw shit, it's past twelve . . . I gotta hurry home before Owlsy gets back."

"He ain't back from Rehoboth yet?" She'd told him her brother had driven south out of town to Foxmerle Farm pick up a load of young pigs.

"Nah, he called earlier to say he'd stopped at a bar to do some drinkin' with a couple of old friends. He should just be arriving back now." She kissed Ambrose on the cheek, separated from him, and looked around for her purse. "I'll call you once I'm home to let you know I ain't been abducted."

He laughed. That was a good joke. The house separating hers from the motel was currently empty and she'd often told him how creepy it felt walking past it.

"C'mon, I'll walk you over," he offered gallantly.

She shook her head. "No need for that, Sir Gala-hard"—she grabbed his crotch so he winced—"but if you hear anyone screamin', come running fast. I'll be your damsel in distress."

Ambrose laughed. He was glad when she let go of his crotch. He was about getting a follow-up erection and . . . seeing as she was leaving, that would have been very uncomfortable.

Nancy traipsed happily around the reception desk and leaned over it facing him, her plump breasts propped up on the lacquered surface. "See you later today?" she enquired hopefully. "It's Sunday."

"I'll call you in the morning. Michelle said she might be able to cover for me if her dad's arthritis is better. We could drive out of town for lunch." (Michelle was the motel cleaner.)

"Great!" Nancy blew him a wet kiss and dashed off. She paused in the lobby doorway to blow him another kiss and then was gone.

Ambrose watched her go—pint-sized packed of energy that she was—with deep admiration. Yeah, he certainly did like this girl. Enough to let it bloom into love. She had a certain earthiness to her, a homeliness that wasn't about her looks, but rather a domestic vibe she gave off, like she'd always be there waiting at home for him to soothe his troubled mind.

***

After Nancy vanished with her happy aura, Ambrose was left alone with his midnight thoughts, the sober reflection on everything that might have been, that once was, and now no longer was. Midnight might be the Witching Hour for some, but for Ambrose, it tended to be the Misery Hour, when, as if seeking him out at his most vulnerable, his blackest thoughts came calling. It was then that he replayed his life, including the series of tragedies—the deaths of his father and two siblings—which had made him sole owner of the Sunflower Motel.

For a moment, he was tempted to have a drink in honor of the departed. A single shot of good American whiskey.

He shook the urge off. He had no desire to drown his sorrows in alcohol again. That way lay, if not madness, at the very least death by liver cirrhosis.

Stroking his beard and mustache as if to calm himself, he looked across the lobby, out through the glass front door. He could see clear down the motel driveway to Carver Street, where the streetlights illuminated a pack of strays frolicking around a bitch in heat. The horny dogs danced out of sight. Ambrose's gaze swept right to the border of trees—old gnarled oaks and others—then back inside. It was a calm night. Nancy should have gotten home safe by now.

And then—unusual for him at this hour—Ambrose suddenly felt happy, optimistic even. He had a sudden vision of himself and Nancy and a baby . . . of Nancy in the kitchen upstairs pulling bread from the oven . . . of the two of them bathing the kid while laughing happily.

It was a sweet image, and it cheered Ambrose up immensely for a while, but . . .

The 'but' was Crystal Parr, who was certain to be utterly livid once Ambrose told her what he was up to.

Ambrose's happy feeling vanished again and he rolled his eyes heavenward. *Dammit, God, how come I got such a complicated life?*

On the surface his dilemma wasn't much of one. Choosing between an adamant prostitute who (by her own admission) had no intention of ever quitting the game, and a sweet, clean-cut young girl like Nancy Pine was really a no-brainer. Crystal wouldn't ever make anyone a wife. Nancy would.

But then, if I know that's the truth, why the hell do I feel so conflicted over it?

He knew the answer to that. He trusted Crystal; that was it. She was close to him in age and they'd gotten drunk together enough times and had sex enough times that . . . No, it wasn't just *that*; their connection went way deeper than just boozing and screwing. *We're friends, goddamit!* Yeah, that was it: they had no secrets from each other. Crystal told him everything she'd done or was gonna do, even though some of it turned his stomach.

And Nancy? Young and fresh and pretty Nancy, who seemed to want nothing more from life than to have his kids and live happily ever after with him? And the sixteen-year age difference? *Doesn't it matter?* He knew little about Nancy other than that she was madly in love with him. Was that enough? Wasn't love supposed to be enough?

Well, she sure can suck dick, he consoled himself. *That's a definite plus. But she also digs country music—all that Lady Antebellum stuff that I can't stand; Lord, give me AC/DC or Black Sabbath or Jane's Addiction any day . . . but then Nina was a Garth Brooks fan too . . .*

And then, by random association with his dead wife, Ambrose's thoughts leapt back to earlier in the evening, when those four young women had checked in.

Room 9, he'd given them. He hoped they were okay. (Yesterday, Mrs. Shamrock, who'd been staying in Room 22 in the middle block, had complained about a mouse that wasn't letting her get any sleep. Ambrose had had to move her into Room 23, then he'd spent half of the morning trapping the damn mouse. Walking over to fling the mewling rodent into the nearby bushes—he'd been unable to bring himself to kill it—he'd wondered how it had gotten into her room in the first place. Or had Mrs. Shamrock unknowingly packed it amongst her things when she'd left home? Weird and unlikely as that was, it had been known to happen. Like with the Van Dale twins, who, unknown to their parents, had brought their pet alligator along on holiday. And then they'd somehow forgotten it here. [Or maybe they'd just grown tired of it?] Michelle had fled screaming when she'd found the gator in the bathtub afterwards. The thing had been huge. And two 8-year-old girls had put it in a suitcase and shipped it up from Alabama?)

Those four young women in Room 9? There'd been one of them he'd particularly liked. What was her name again?

About to open the laptop on the desk to check, he remembered: Carmela . . . Carmela Cole. Yeah, that was she. The tall and skinny one with the short black hair. Early twenties, maybe twenty-four max. She wasn't overly pretty, but she had nice blue eyes, and, underneath that slightly crooked nose of hers, a fleshy mouth you just wanted to kiss. Yeah, she'd caught his attention immediately she'd walked in with her friends. In a way she resembled his late wife Nina; the way she wore her black hair short, and those nice lips and . . .

And then, in another mental switch, Ambrose's thoughts leapt from Nina to the monster that had killed her:

Damn Brainchew! Ambrose swallowed his hurt. At least the evil creature wasn't about harming anyone again. He'd seen to that.

Brainchew was asleep, locked in a metal casket which was in turn locked inside a reinforced concrete tomb with the lid bolted down on it. There was no way it was gonna get out of there. No way any blood was getting down there to revive it either.

The good people of Raynham town could at last sleep easy.

Besides, lightning never struck twice in the same place. Or (Ambrose uneasily adding the monster's previous resurrection as its second coming), it never struck *thrice* at the same spot, did it? Nowhere could be that damn unlucky. (Just to ensure that Brainchew remained out of sight, it had been left in the same secluded corner of the Pleasant Street Cemetery as previously.)

Ambrose forgot Brainchew. The damn monster wasn't leaving its grave any time soon, not with all the security precautions the town had taken to imprison it.

But why hasn't Nancy yet called me to say she's gotten home? Has Brainchew gotten out and gotten her?

He laughed at his own joke. Brainchew? No. Like he'd assured Chief of Police Tina Kravitz, that monster's brain-munching days were over.

He considered phoning Nancy to check that she was okay, then relaxed. She'd probably just forgotten to call. Or, more likely, her brother Owlsy was home now and he was drunk and hungry and growling at her for dinner at past midnight. Owlsy looked to be a handful to manage once drunk.

Ambrose grinned. *I didn't heard her screaming, so she has to be okay.*

He looked out through the glass lobby door again, then ran his fingers through his dark hair. Didn't look like anyone else would be dropping by tonight. But then, one never knew. Sometimes folk got stranded on the highway and turned up here at the damnest of hours.

Ambrose got up from behind the reception desk and went to lock the lobby door. It was late, and he was tired, and he was off to bed. Anyone who wanted him could buzz him awake again.

CHAPTER 5

The Monster

Ambrose couldn't have been more wrong if he'd been christened with a 'Dunce' hat on. Lightning *was* currently striking thrice in the same place.

Over in that deep corner of the Pleasant Street Cemetery where 'Brian Chu' was buried, an explosion was occurring underground.

The single, and most costly mistake everyone had made while containing Brainchew—and which they'd keep making—wasn't really anyone's fault. It stemmed from a lack of knowledge of how powerful the monster's sense of smell was.

No one realized that they should shut it away in an *airtight* container.

Brainchew didn't really hear too good, and its eyesight was so-so, but it smelt better than a shark locating blood in water. Its sense of smell was so acute, it could practically 'see' the object that had emitted the odor. Even in its dormant petrified state the slightest scent of blood instantly set its senses ticking over, shifting it into 'standby' mode (like someone switching on a TV before picking up the remote).

And now four women had just left a dead man on its grave.

Brainchew had become alert the moment Tiff Hooper broke Josh Penham's nose. The smell of blood had seeped down through the seams of its concrete tomb and into the metal casket that held it. It had smelt and instantly understood—there were five people above it: four women and a man with a wounded head.

Food!

The word flared in its tiny mind. With the promise of nourishment just overhead, it thawed out and began fighting against its confinement.

The metal casket, however, at first proved very difficult to escape from.

Brainchew's battle to be free of the casket was the shaking of the ground that Tiff, Monique, Lisa, and Carmela had noticed.

***

Brainchew's most recent spate of killings (which had occurred the previous year) had been hushed up. The Raynham town administrator, board of selectmen, and chief of police had all conspired to keep the deaths out of the news, so as not to give the town a bad reputation.

All the deaths had occurred in or around the Sunflower Motel, and all on the same night, so it had been relatively easy for the town authorities to keep a lid on any news of Raynham's most infamous resident escaping to the rest of the world.

Indeed, they'd done such a stellar job, most of their own townsfolk had no idea that their 'pet monster' had once again gotten free.

The Raynham authorities had already agreed to 'sell' Brainchew to Massachusetts billionaire Ellis Drake, who'd offered them ten million dollars for it. So technically, Brainchew now belonged to Ellis Drake. (If, of course, something that insanely murderous could legally be considered anyone's property.)

There was just one little snag: Once removed from Raynham, Brainchew tended to 'magically' relocate back there again. No one knew why that was. Ellis Drake currently had people researching the phenomena in hopes of finding a solution to this dilemma. In the meantime, the people of Raynham town had kept their fingers crossed that Brainchew wouldn't get out again.

Their hopes were about to be violently dashed.

***

Brainchew finally 'ignited' itself. This was a last resort, but one that had always worked in the past.

It worked this time also.

'Igniting' involved converting the surface of its body into a gaseous state and setting the gas on fire, causing an explosion. Brainchew did this without thinking, not understanding how it was able to burn a part of itself, only knowing that the fire would free, and not hurt, it.

Such was the case now. There was little noise, the wall of heat it had created around itself not giving the metal casket sufficient time to protest its end.

Like water evaporating, the metal prison disintegrated around Brainchew. Shortly it was completely free. The controlled explosion also both burnt and shattered the walls of the concrete tomb, and blew out its top, the latter process flinging Josh Penham's body to one side with his hair on fire.

Brainchew pulled itself out of the hole in the ground.

It already knew the four women were gone. It had smelt them leaving. That was no problem—it had their scent and would hunt them down and feast on their delicious juicy brains, and drink their sweet liquids.

But first . . .

In a fit of ravenous hunger, it flung itself on Josh Penham's corpse, locked its mouth over the back of his head—not minding the taste of his charred hair—and bit in deep.

Its mouth was instantly filled with the sweet taste of the dead man's brain, a delicious reward for the labor of unearthing itself. It quickly ate the brain, crunching the braincase like it was a cracker, chewing and swallowing the resulting chunky mush to replace the energy it had used to free itself.

Finally, its hunger appeased for the moment, it turned its attention to slaking its thirst. The dead man's blood (which had spewed everywhere from his slit throat) had long since clotted, so Brainchew took the second alternative. It rolled the man over, and after a moment's contemplation of his naked corpse, sliced his lower abdomen open with one of its razor-sharp claws. Next, without hesitation, it ripped out the dead man's bladder. Quick as a flash, it raised the extracted organ to its mouth and drank the urine trickling from it.

The bladder thus emptied, Brainchew cast it aside and stood for a moment on its erstwhile tomb, taking stock of itself and the world it had reentered.

***

Had the four women who'd roused it from its sleep been watching, they would have imagined themselves caught in the grip of a nightmare.

Brainchew was UGLY, almost goblinesque in its grotesqueness. It resembled a short gray-skinned man who lacked genitals and had an ENORMOUS head. Yes, it was sexless, and its head was its most distinctive feature. Though of normal width, its head was over two feet high, and elevated the pigmy monster's height to well over six feet.

At the moment Brainchew looked skinny, as emaciated as a death camp survivor. The explosion to free itself had used up fully half of its body tissue. Its immense head was still the same size, but now its body resembled that of a human child of say, eight or nine years of age.

To restore its body to its previous state (and strength), it would need to eat a whole lot tonight. However, Brainchew didn't imagine that would be a problem. There was a huge amount of food nearby; and—it caught the sweet tantalizing odors of the four women who'd just departed from here—it smelt very appetizing too.

***

Brainchew stepped out from the tree cover and howled wordlessly at the oval moon. It stood there, its tiny red eyes focused on the white satellite, enjoying the soft glow on its face. For a moment, frozen in place, Brainchew seemed itself a part of the graveyard, its warty gray skin portraying it as a gargoyle of peculiar design amidst the ranks of tombstones.

It unfroze and looked out at the road that ran past the cemetery. A solitary red car was pulling away into the night.

The departing vehicle's speed created a sense of urgency in the monster. There were things to be done and done fast. It gave another silent howl, the action revealing its disarrayed mess of uneven and unequal teeth, teeth that could bite through bone without difficulty.

Finally Brainchew turned and stalked out of the graveyard. It smelt brains, lots of brains, fresh and juicy humans brains it was going to eat.

It headed towards North Main Street, where it could clearly smell the women in the departed car.

CHAPTER 6

Monique

As they made the right turn from Pleasant Street back onto North Main Street, Monique relaxed. The cemetery and its dead were behind them now, along with their own acts of violence. The quiet gloominess in the black van's interior vanished in quick degrees. The oppressive feeling like fingers tightening around her throat also disappeared.

At least *she* felt that way. She looked sideways; Lisa drove on, an almost-smile on her lips.

She glanced back at Tiff and Carmela who sat side by side on the floor in the rear, their backs against the vehicle's side, their legs pulled up close to their breasts. (By unspoken agreement, the van's interior lights had been left on; at the moment complete darkness seemed much too threatening to cope with.) In a gesture of comfort, Carmela had her arm around Tiff's shoulders and was holding her close. Tiff looked shell-shocked. Carmela just looked nervous. By now Monique understood that Lisa's kid sister was always worried about something or other. She was competent enough otherwise though.

She smiled reassuringly at Tiff, then looked forward again. The road ahead had the appearance of an asphalt-lined throat, just the single approaching car and that was it.

"So . . ." she prompted, to start a conversation in the van. No one took the bait however, so she added, "Are you guys all okay? We did good back there, right?"

"Yeah, I guess so," Carmela agreed from behind. "He won't be murdering any more women, that's for sure."

Beside her, Tiff smiled. The sad smile of someone who'd just heard that they'd both won a lottery and had terminal cancer. Monique understood that: Tiff wasn't sure if she should be happy or sad. She'd avenged herself, but was now confused over if she'd been right or wrong to take the law into her own hands.

Yeah, at the moment she's wondering if maybe she should just have called the cops instead.

Which thought made Monique glance over at her companion in the driver's seat: gorgeous fucking Lisa, with her long blonde hair and luscious lips and her perfect face and figure. Lisa now looked amused. Of all of them in the van, Lisa seemed unbothered, like killing a man was really no different from eating dinner. But then, to Monique, Lisa always seemed made of stone anyway. She saw what she wanted and went for it, whether it be a man, or some job advantage, or (like in this case) revenge. For certain, Lisa Cole was as emotional as the next woman, but she had a talent for, if not exactly controlling her feelings, being able to focus them where she wanted to achieve her desired end. Monique wondered how Bobby Finch coped with her.

But, she reasoned, *maybe Lisa's beauty and her ability in bed compensate for her horrible character? Maybe she fucks as good as she looks? Maybe Bobby simply can't see deeper than her perfect exterior and the erotic pleasure she gives him?*

Monique Bangles greatly disliked her parole officer. *Lisa is a horrible bitch and a bully and she's got me dangling on her puppet strings.* Silently, she cursed herself for her own bad decision making and her lack of self control, both of which had put her into this situation where she could be strong-armed into coming along on a vigilante mission. *And things could just get worse for me. If the cops ever find out what we've done and . . .*

On a sudden damning realization, a massive tremor of fear surged through her, leaving her yet angrier still. *Shit! None of the four of us bothered to wear gloves tonight. Fingerprints! Fingerprints! How on earth could we overlook something so basic? Shit! Damn Lisa!*

But her rage was a waste of emotion. Lisa had a firm grip on Monique's testicles, and Monique knew it. She didn't do what she was told and she was going back into the slammer, and for a very long time. And, having a penis despite her gorgeous female looks, she was going to a *male* prison, full of randy inmates who'd waste no time before getting to work on fucking her anus sore.

For a moment, she remembered how she'd urinated on that man back in the cemetery. She smiled coldly; that hadn't been bad. She had no sympathy for their victim—working as a trans-hooker had brought her into contact with too many creeps and weirdos. Twice she'd barely escaped with her life. She had a long scar down her left thigh where one loony trick had stabbed her.

No, they'd done the right thing in ridding the world of Josh Penham. Men like that had no right to be born. He should have been aborted. The problem was, there was no prenatal test for sociopathy.

She pushed red hair out of her face and winced. *And as for me, I really need to get my act together. At the moment, Lisa can do whatever she wants with me. About the only thing she's not suggested yet is that I join her and Bobby in a threesome. Not that I'm sure she hasn't thought about it, but she's likely scared of being overshadowed in bed.*

That, she knew, was a recurrent problem with women and threesomes. If one woman called another into her sexual bed, she got worried and upset when her man enjoyed that other woman. Female threesomes seemed to work best when they involved one woman and two men. Then the woman was the center of attention, and she felt in control of the situation.

And Lisa Cole *always* had to be in control of the situation.

The silence began to eat at Monique again. She turned and stared at the two women in the rear of the van. "Shit, guys, lighten up, wilya? It ain't like we've just attended a funeral."

Lisa laughed. "Haven't we just, Monique?"

"We're okay," Carmela said. "I'll just feel more okay once we're back in our motel room again. Then I'm gonna take a pill and sleep forever."

She hugged Tiff close and petted her like a baby. Tiff still wasn't talking, still looked frozen in her vigilante la-la-land. Monique smiled at her and tried to think of something to get her tongue moving.

And then the van stopped. Just like that. It lurched once like a drunk, then its engine died.

"Oh shit!" Lisa said before Monique had even turned back around to look at her. "We're outa gas." Utilizing the last of the vehicle's forward motion, she steered it to the roadside and parked. Several turns of the starter key produced only an annoyed protest from the van's engine. "I don't believe this!"

The night rushed in on Monique like it hated her, ready to fill her with fears and worries. "We're *what?*"

Lisa swiveled on her seat to stare at the others. "Guys, the tank's empty."

Tiff gazed dully up at Lisa. "You're just making a joke, right? Having some fun with us? Trying to scare us?"

Lisa said nothing; Carmela replied for her: "No, she's not. Remember how I said we were low on gas before we left the motel, but she said we couldn't buy any?" She glared at her older sister. "Now see the result?"

Lisa still didn't say anything.

"You know," Tiff added, while, like a snail exiting its shell, slowly detaching herself from Carmela's embrace, "this just gets better. First, the grave starts vibrating after we've done what we came here for, and now . . ."

"Let's just think of a solution," Lisa said in dangerously calm tones, her eyes locked on Carmela's. "Like it or not, we can't abandon the van here. We need to return it to Mansfield."

"Yes, yes," Tiff agreed, the current crisis seeming to pull her back to real life from wherever she'd been sheltering her mind. "So let's think of something fast."

Monique looked outside the van. The night was dark and quiet. Luckily for them too, they'd stopped a good distance from anyone's driveway, though the residences along this stretch of road were widely spaced anyway. Still, this wasn't a good place to be stranded at this late hour.

"Hey," Lisa said, "I recall seeing an empty can in the back of the van when we moved the cartons aside."

"Yeah, I noticed it too," Carmela said. "Hold on a sec while I find it." She moved past Tiff to the rear of the van and rummaged through the mess of piled Styrofoam pellets, crumpled strips of brown wrapping paper, and empty cartons there, till finally she came up holding a red plastic 5-gallon can.

She waved the can at Lisa. "So . . . ?"

"There's at least two filling stations just up the road," Lisa said. "I suggest that two of us walk up there and buy some gas, while the other two of us stay here with the van."

"Yeah, that makes sense," Carmela agreed. "So who goes and who stays?"

"I'll go," Monique said quickly. She wanted to be out of the vehicle before the Cole sisters began throwing accusatory bombs at each other. She'd witnessed one of their arguments during the planning sessions for this trip and it hadn't been pretty.

"Okay," Lisa said. "I'll come along with—"

"No, *I'll* go with her," Tiff said flatly. She half-stretched in the vehicle's cramped interior, like she was just waking up. "I need to get some fresh air in my head to blow out Josh's stink for good."

Lisa first looked like she was going to protest, but then didn't. "Okay, you guys go then, we'll wait for you. But two things . . ."

Tiff said, "Yeah?"

"First, hurry up. And second, don't go to the Red Eagle gas station we abducted Josh from."

"Hmm, it might be a good idea to peek around there and see if there's any cop activity," Monique said.

Lisa shook her head flatly. "No. If the police are there and they see you, it'll be too much of a coincidence for them: two out-of-town women with a gas can at"—she glanced at the dashboard clock—"twelve-fifteen in the morning? And that'll mean they'll make you bring them back here to cross-check your story." She looked hard at Monique, giving her that 'I'm the Boss' look that Monique hated so much. "Or is that too much for *you* to process, darling? Maybe I should just go myself along with Tiff?"

Monique shook her head, hating her but unable to do squat about it. "No, we'll be fine. Don't worry about it."

"And one last thing . . ."

Tiff groaned audibly. "Yeah, what is it? Lisa, d'you want us to buy gas or not? What's with all the schoolmarmery?"

Lisa smiled sweetly. "Nothing much. Just *please* remember—don't turn on your damn phones except it's an emergency."

"Shit," Monique said, "this is worse than being in kindergarten." She smiled nastily at Lisa, said, "Yes, teacher," then opened her door.

She dropped to the ground, shut the door behind her, then walked a distance ahead of the van and waited for Tiff to join her. Tiff had the empty can with her. They both looked back once and saw that Lisa had now turned off the van's interior lights, then headed up the road towards the gas station.

To those inside the vehicle it looked like the darkness had eaten them both.

***

"Lisa means well," Tiff said after a while of silent side-by-side walking.

"Yeah, I know," Monique agreed. "But she's so smug and self-assured, so full of herself, that I can't stand her. Having a big head is the major failing of beautiful women."

"How'd *you* manage to avoid getting one then?"

It took Monique a moment to appreciate the compliment. "Oh, me? I'm not really good-looking—it's all the plastic surgery I've had."

"Oh, but you look great. I've been unable to take my eyes off you all night. If I had your looks . . ."

"Hell, it's a whole lot of work maintaining them if you weren't born with them. I'd have been a lot happier to . . ." She'd been about saying 'to look like you,' but then realized that Tiff was currently overweight and didn't look too good, and most likely wouldn't appreciate the statement, so she said instead, "I really wish I'd been born a genetic woman, and not have to go through all this goddam transition into becoming one—hormone therapy and electrolysis and cosmetic surgery, and . . ."

"Do you plan on going the whole way? I mean . . ."

"Exchange my penis for a vag? Oh, most definitely. I don't want to live in the intergender wasteland for the rest of my life. Don't get me wrong—I'm not ashamed of who I am, not in the least . . . but I'd like to not just *feel* completely female but also *look* it. Simply put, I need my mental image of myself to match my physical person." She grinned. "So once I've enough money, I'm heading in to see the butchers and donating them my man sausage."

Tiff laughed softly. "Ugh, how can you be so blasé about that? There's something so instinctively horrifying about what you're going to give up that I shudder to even contemplate it, and I'm a *woman* feeling this way, not a man. On a primal level it's simply inconceivable that anyone would want to give up their penis."

Monique shrugged. "I know what you mean, but I assure you, darling, I won't miss it. I have to take pills to make it work now anyway, what with all the antiandrogens and female hormones I'm on. Besides, I already don't need the dick anyway. At the moment, I can come just from anal sex."

"You can?"

"Um hum. Prostate orgasms, they're fantastic. The prostate is like a transsexual clitoris, and, oh my God, having a hard cock rub over it

64

is like . . . Oh, baby, you don't know what it's like. It's like someone giving you head inside your ass."

"Wow! That good?"

"If done right, it's better."

They stopped talking for a moment as they passed a short flagstoned driveway that lead in to a white two-story house with two SUVs parked in front of it. On the screened-in porch, a man sat in a deck chair working at a laptop. He was drinking wine and concentrating on whatever he was doing and clearly didn't notice them crossing the foot of his driveway.

Once they were back amidst the shadows of the roadside trees, Monique asked, "So how do you feel now?" She herself felt better since they'd left the van and Lisa's domineering company. And Tiff was proving nice to be around. (Of course, the fact that Tiff found her attractive—though clearly in a platonic sense—was great too. Though she occasionally slept with women as business, Monique preferred men. Having sex with women made her feel male, which she hated. Being loved by hard muscles and a hard penis made her feel like a woman. And if the man was soft and tender while he was also hard and deep inside her body, she was in heaven.)

"Oh, I'm okay, I guess." Tiff sounded as non-committal as her reply.

Monique looked at her sharply, trying to gauge exactly how much of a mental meltdown killing Josh had triggered in her. In the half-darkness, it was impossible to tell.

Tiff caught the sidelong glance and said, "No, really, I'm cool. I don't regret it, if that's what you mean. I'm just so tired out all of a sudden."

That Monique could relate to. "It's because you had an orgasm while beating him. You know how coming tires one out. And it's late at night too, we both really should be in bed by now." She didn't doubt that it was Tiff's recent orgasm making her tired. *Damn, I feel like I used up energy just peeing on the guy!*

They stepped along the road between the streetlights with their empty gas can.

"We should be near the gas station now, right?" Tiff asked. "You know, maybe we should just have let Carmela and Lisa make this hike."

"Yeah." Monique thought of a topic to distract Tiff. Talking would also shorten their walk. She looked back for a second. The black van was out of sight now, hidden in the night behind them. She looked forward again. By her estimation of where the closest gas station was, they still had about a mile of walking to do. Suddenly she felt fagged too, her legs losing strength like the sidewalk was draining it from them. If only someone—some knight in a shining BMW—would pull up next to them right now and offer them a ride to the nearest Shell or Exxon. But she knew it was a wasted hope. A lift at half-past-midnight?

"I'd like to ask you something, but I don't know if you're up to talking about it," she told Tiff.

"Go ahead," Tiff replied.

"Are you sure it's okay? It's a bit personal."

"Yes."

"Okay, what I wanna know is—what was it like being held captive in that guy's basement? I mean, I can imagine the situation was bad— like how you see it done in films, but the reality must have been much, much worse. And also, how did you ever get away from him? I can't even imagine how you'd escape a guy like that—he was so goddam big and mean." A momentary erotic chill swept through Monique at her memory of how muscular the dead man had been.

"That's what you want to know?" Tiff asked. "Oh, you're right, it was utterly horrible. Even now, remembering how I got caught makes me scared to leave my house."

Monique stopped Tiff for a moment beneath a streetlight, and stared intently into her eyes. "How *did* you get caught?"

Tiff sighed. "It was so easy and so dumb, you'd never believe it. I was driving up from Somerset—my mom lives down there—and, deciding I had time on my hands to spare, and with a sudden intense desire to experience the rustic countryside, I made a long detour east through Lakeville . . . which proved my undoing." She winced with memory. "Shit . . . no, fuck. See, on Route 28, just before you get to Bridgewater, there's this roadside diner called the Roadside Reformatory, probably named for the nearby prison. I stopped there for lunch. The parking lot was at the back of the place. After eating, I walked back around there to drive off. I remember hearing heavy footsteps behind me and trying to turn, and then next, he'd grabbed me and placed a cloth over my mouth, and there was a weird smell

66

coming from it and I was out cold . . . and next thing, I woke up in his chamber of horrors."

Tiff pointed down the road, indicating that they start walking again.

"When I woke up," she continued as they resumed their trek, "I was stripped naked and chained facing a yellow wall. My pussy and ass were both sore and there was semen dripping down my leg, so I knew he'd had his way with me while I was unconscious."

"Did you scream for help?"

"First thing I did. I yelled my lungs out. I howled until they hurt. When no one came running to help me, I realized I was either far out in the woods somewhere, or down in someone's basement, where he could do whatever he wanted with me. That's when the real horror set in."

While Tiff spoke, her voice had grown smaller, shriveling into that of a terrified child. Monique felt like hugging her and comforting her. But there was something forbidding about Tiff now—her recollection of her suffering shielded her like a wall.

Tiff continued: "That really was what scared me the most: the fact that no one would be able to find me, that no one would know where I was; and that even if I vanished off the face of the earth, there would be no traces left; for the next thirty or so years people would still be speculating over what had happened to me. They'd do a 'Disappeared' special on TV, and armchair detectives everywhere would cogitate on me and finally decide that I'd eloped to South America and changed my name or something like that." (Monique watched her shudder.) "That was even more scary that his abuse of me, you know? The fact that I'd just vanish for good; that I'd be just another Missing Persons statistic."

Monique nodded. They were approaching an intersection, but it didn't look like it had a gas station, just an auto shop on their right and a block of stores on their left.

"And then . . . he'd come in from time to time and laugh at me. He always wore a surgical mask. And except on the second day, when he showed me a tub full of a chopped-up girl, he never said a word to me. He'd just force-feed me and—"

"Hey—backtrack a bit," Monique interrupted. "If he never said anything to you, and always wore a surgical mask, how'd you later recognize him?"

"He took the mask off twice. Once to spit out a massive gob of phlegm—he coughed a lot—and the other after he'd chloroformed me again, and thought I was out cold. But I wasn't, see? That's when I saw what he looked like. Believe me, those two glances were more than sufficient. After getting away, I saw his ugly face every night in my dreams. How wouldn't I recognize it?" Her tone was accusatory, angry that Monique dared question her credibility.

"Sorry," Monique said. "I was just curious, that's all; I didn't mean any offence. Look, it's really okay if you don't want to say any more about it. I really don't think I should be putting you through that again." It wasn't that she didn't want to know, but she'd suddenly realized it had to be a fresh ordeal making Tiff relive her horrors.

"Don't worry," Tiff said with a cold, flat laugh. "It's good therapy. I need to get it out of my system one final time. From tomorrow, I'm restarting my life."

Monique nodded. They were now crossing the intersection, where oddly, the road split into five instead of four. Five bare routes that seemingly led nowhere, like the points of a star penetrating the heart of the night. Maybe because of Tiff's revelations, Monique felt the darkness tangled messily about her like a duvet she needed to be free of on a hot summer night.

"That was how I got away too," Tiff said. "He'd chloroformed me that time because he wanted to screw me and he didn't want me flailing about and trying to stop him. But I wasn't out cold like he'd thought: I played possum—instead of inhaling in a panic when he'd slapped the rag over my face, I managed to hold my breath for a while so I didn't get the full dose he intended—and then I stopped fighting him and pretended I was unconscious. It worked: he unchained me from the wall and draped me over a table. Then, after he'd had his dirty way with me, he left the basement—I think he went upstairs to bath—and I slipped out of the house as quietly as I could.

"And then I ran and ran and ran and ran and ran. It was in the dead of night and I had no idea in what direction I was headed, but that didn't matter so long as I was moving forward and getting as far away from him as I could. Every time I felt my legs weakening like I was going to fall over, I'd remember the girl he'd chopped up to bits in that plastic tub, and I was determined that I wasn't ever going to end up like that—in a thousand pieces, with my breasts and eyes floating all over my blood and intestines. So I kept moving all night. But I was naked and it was early spring and . . . the cold and the exposure nearly killed me. But I kept going, until finally I found a road, and a driver almost hit me, and he rushed me up to Norwood and a hospital. By then I was half out of my mind, and couldn't even clearly remember who I was, talk less of all that I'd been through, and the doctors were pumping me full of antibiotics and other shit so I didn't die of pneumonia from the exposure."

She grinned at her companion as they stepped up onto the opposite sidewalk. It was a manic grin. "Believe me, that was a really bad month for me."

Monique nodded. She couldn't think of an appropriate comment to make that wouldn't sound trite. (What could she say? Oh, I'm so sorry to hear that? Best to keep her mouth shut and thank God that they'd paid Josh Penham back in his own violent coin.)

They walked on in silence for a while, their shoes making soft slaps against the concrete. Then Tiff said to Monique, "I've been wondering about you too."

"Uh? About what?"

"Well, I don't understand what sort of a hold Lisa has over you that makes you do whatever she says. And . . . what in the world did you do to go to prison in the first place?"

Monique suddenly felt embarrassed. "I shot two policemen," she admitted finally.

Tiff looked at her oddly. "Why on earth would you do a thing like that?"

Monique sighed and explained: "I didn't really mean to. See, I was in love with this great guy who was also a drug dealer and . . ."

***

On a warm July morning six years ago, Monique Bangles and James 'Ducky' Polan had been lying in bed having sex. Stiff penises deep in each other's mouths, they were slurping away happily, performing sixty-nine on each other, when they heard someone kick in the front door downstairs.

"Shit, baby, it's Stones' boys!" Ducky growled as they hastily separated.

This information instantly sent Monique (who'd been about ejaculating in Ducky's mouth) scrambling for her clothes, and (unwisely as it turned out) for a weapon of some kind.

Weapons were easy to come by in Ducky's house. In addition to being one of Boston's most disreputable drug dealers, he also sold guns (and heavier artillery—grenades and rocket launchers) to anyone who needed an unlicensed firearm.

Ducky only balked at selling weapons to terrorists. He was a patriotic American and wanted no truck with blowing up his own country. (Ducky couldn't stomach terrorists or communists, or the Chinese, or the North Koreans, or the Afghans, or the Pakistanis, or the Iranians, or ISIS, or the Syrians [or even the Libyans when Gaddafi was still in charge there]. In short, he couldn't stand anyone who threatened to destroy the American way of life with its spirit of free enterprise. Besides, lots of the terrorist-sponsoring countries also had stringent anti-drug legislation [damn, they're gonna decapitate a guy just for dealing coke?] and that just pissed Ducky off no end.)

For those whose anger didn't have militant-religious overtones, however, Ducky was the go-to guy for the illegal weapon of your choice.

(Afterwards, Monique cursed whichever demon had made her pick up that gun that Thursday morning. It must have been paranoia from all the drugs she and Ducky had been doing since the previous night.)

Ducky and Monique both thought it was Ronnie Stones' gang after him, because Ronnie owed Ducky a hundred grand that he didn't want to pay back. Word had gotten back to Ducky of Ronnie boasting in clubs about how he was 'going to bury that fag so far underground that even a mining team won't be able to unearth him.'

"Let the bastard come," Ducky had told his informers and Monique. "We'll see then who the real fag is. I'll shove my dick so far up his tail, they'll make him the goddam Gay Mardi Gras mascot."

And now it looked like 'the bastard' *had* come.

Ducky, who was tall and plump with brown hippie-length hair, was walking around the huge bedroom with cocaine ruling his brain, staring at the guns racked in his walk-in gun closet, and trying to work out whether he wanted to take on Ronnie Stones and his hoodlums with an Uzi or with his new Russian rocket launcher; or with just some old-fashioned Nazi stick grenades.

For her part, Monique had grabbed the first handgun her fingers touched, a Smith & Wesson 9mm semiautomatic that lay on the nightstand. She knew the weapon was loaded: Ducky had yesterday slipped out its magazine and put it back in. Once she had the gun, she quickly pulled on some panties and a T-shirt, then ducked between the bed and a wall and waited for the bedroom door to burst open.

When it didn't open quick enough, she looked around for a rubber band to tie her red hair down. When the door still didn't burst open, it was all she could do to not sit at the dresser and start applying her makeup—she was that nervous.

Ducky meanwhile, was strolling around the bedroom like some psycho kid from Marysville Pilchuck High on his way to slaughter his classmates. He was carrying an Uzi, had the Russian rocket launcher slung over his back, and had two pistols stuck in his waistband.

He looked back once at her, blew her a kiss, and gave her a thumbs up. Then, like he was following her lead, he put on a red sweatband to hold down his straggly hair. Total Rambo, except that he was dressed in just his boxer shorts.

Then he got out some cocaine and did a few lines.

Monique considered hurrying over to use some of the coke too, but a thread of common sense held her in her place of concealment. Something told her that doing coke at a time like this was a very bad idea indeed.

***

Monique had been dating Ducky for four months at that point. (Ducky hated the 'fag' tag that went with their romance though.) He was violent to her occasionally (brutality went with the territory of being a drug dealer, she'd philosophically decided after the first time he'd slapped her for sassing him), but he paid her bills (all of them, including her medicals), made love to her competently, and treated her like a lady.

Most important of all, him keeping her beat her working the street to pay her way. (For a transitioning transsexual good work was often hard to come by. If you were lucky, you were already employed when you started the change and couldn't get sacked because of the anti-discriminatory laws. Otherwise, you'd most likely find yourself continually overlooked by employers in favor of some less qualified cis-gender person. Monique thought employers weren't as much bothered by hiring transgender employees per se, as they were by the associated 'issues' such employees brought along with them—things like which pronouns to use to address them and which toilets they'd use, etc. It was easier to stick with the uncomplicated male/female human species divisions. At least gay/lesbian men and women still answered to the regular he/she and used the same bathrooms as their straight coworkers.)

***

Just when Monique thought she'd die of anticipation, the bedroom door shattered inward and all hell broke loose. Two shiny canisters flew into the room and it filled up with smoke and . . .

"Police, put your goddam hands up!"

"Fuck tha police!" Energized by cocaine, Ducky instead began shooting. Then the cops began shooting back, and there were bullets flying everywhere.

And Monique, panicking (and somewhere in her mind feeling like if she didn't shoot too, she'd be the first to die), began firing also.

The room was so full of smoke that she couldn't see anything except the muzzle flashes from Ducky's gun. So she kept shooting, just not in Ducky's general direction. And police bullets smashed over her head and ripped the walls beside her to shreds, and sprayed her with plaster and glass and wood shards. She was aware of dark figures stalking the large bedroom, and of a sudden sharp pain in her right thigh, which she ignored.

And while firing at random, the thought occurred to her that if Ducky suddenly got so crazy as to let off that rocket launcher of his in the limited space of his bedroom, Heaven and Hell were going to be welcoming a whole lot of new tenants in the next few minutes.

Her pistol clicked empty then. The room, however, was still as full of smoke and commotion as before. She flung the gun away, then flung herself hard to the floor and crawled into the bathroom and shut the door behind her. She lay in there on the bathroom floor, waiting for the cops to come in and kill her.

After a while the war-zone noise outside faded, and someone kicked in the bathroom door. It was a cop with a hard, cold face, dressed in SWAT body armor.

"Hey, his girlfriend's still alive! She's hurt though!"

It was only then that Monique realized a ricochet had drilled through her right thigh. The cops carried her downstairs and to an ambulance, where they summarily arrested her then took her to hospital.

***

"Wow," Tiff said, "that's some mess you got into."

Monique sighed. "You've no idea of the half of it. Ducky was stone cold dead of course; the police gunfire had done a major number on him. Two slugs had ripped off his face, and another had completely sliced his aorta in half. He had holes in him just about everywhere you looked. He was so shot-up that when they carried his body past me to the ambulance, I doubted he'd be resurrecting even in the afterlife."

"Wow, that's so sad," Tiff said with deep feeling.

"Yes, it was," Monique agreed, "'cos I really cared about him." Before continuing, she flung her hands outwards in an exasperated gesture. "And as for me? Oh, I was still very much alive. However, to my eternal regret, my totally random shooting had lodged two slugs in police parts—one in a guy's butt, the other in a guy's thigh. I was more-or-less cooked; well garnished Massachusetts goose barbeque. They read me my rights, handcuffed me, and took me away."

"Oops," Tiff said.

Monique nodded. "As expected, the DA didn't mess about none. He threw the entire book at me, including its dust jacket."

"Hell, I can imagine."

"Oh, there was more to it."

"More?"

"Yeah. See, the major problem wasn't even just my shooting those two guys."

"How do you mean?"

"Someone had tipped the BPD off that Ducky was supplying an ISIS sleeper cell with chemical weapons, which was what had brought them out to our place on Marlborough Street, and which turned out to be a complete waste of their time and resources. They were real pissed about that. The terrorist connection was of course total bullshit—Ducky hated those ISIS bastards. Thankfully, it was disproved in court. But still, even if we weren't terrorist shitheads like they'd initially believed, *I had* wounded those two cops during the raid. There was no side-stepping that. My lawyer, though, persuaded the jury that I'd thought it was a rival gang coming to kill us. Which was almost true—I had no idea where the cops were. I never actually saw anyone I was shooting at—there was too much smoke in the bedroom. I mean, half the North Korean army could have been in there for all I knew."

They trudged under another streetlight. Monique shivered, just like she had in court back then, with everywhere so silent you could've heard a feather drop, and all eyes on her, and the judge about to read out her sentence. "Anyhow, I got sent down the river. I got ten years for my involvement—resisting arrest, aggravated assault, discharging a firearm at cops doing their duty, injuring two cops doing their duty . . . then all the other stuff . . . drug dealing, prostitution . . . you name it."

"Wow!"

"Girl, I was damn lucky. My lawyer was great or else I might have gotten half a century behind bars. Anyway, I did four years of my sentence then was paroled for good behavior, on the understanding that if I stepped off the straight-and-narrow again they'd throw me back behind bars to complete the years I owed the state." She laughed without mirth. "And of course, like God is angry with me . . . I wind up with Lisa Cole as my parole officer. And you know what she's like. Okay, I do tend to violate the conditions of my parole a lot, and she gives me lots of leeway, but I get to pay for that with stuff like tonight's snuff job on Josh."

"She's had you do something like this before?"

Monique was amused at the surprised horror in Tiff's voice. She shook her head. "No, no. It's usually little stuff like running demeaning errands for her. View it this way—she generally uses me for her ego-tripping practice." *Where's the goddam filling station*, she was wondering. *How long do we have to walk tonight? And we can't even call back to the van to let the others know we're alright.*

"It's wrong to let her have so much control over you," Tiff said.

"Let it go. I'm fine."

"No, no—I'm grateful that Lisa is doing all this to help me out, but it's horrible that she's forced you to involve yourself."

"Thanks," Monique said. "I honestly appreciate your concern. I really do. But I was okay with helping you out. I've had my own painful encounters with jerks like that, some of which you'd not believe if I told you."

They lapsed into silence again, with Monique thinking, *Oh, there's more to it than I've told you, Tiff baby. Believe me, there's a whole lot more. Lisa's got such a grip on me, girl, she might as well have shoved a hook up my butt.*

* * *

Monique had served her jail sentence at the Massachusetts Correctional Institution in Norfolk. Her initial dread that she was doomed to life as a 24-hour-a-day sex slave proved unfounded. Yes, her anus did get more than its fair share of overuse while she was incarcerated, but . . . it wasn't totally bad. News of why she was being sentenced had preceded her to the prison, and on her arrival, Marko Velli, Ducky's mentor in the drug trade, immediately took her under his wing.

Marko Velli was a small, thickset middle-aged man with a face that seemed chiseled out of ice, and pale eyes that were even colder than that. He wore his hair in a black buzzcut. When Marko frowned, you felt he might shortly kill someone. And he frowned a lot.

No one in MCI-Norfolk messed with Marko. No one. They still hadn't forgotten how Stringy Newton, who'd called Marko a 'dumb punk Croat' and spat in his face in the dining hall, was found dead in the toilets two days later with his throat slit ear-to-ear and all his fingers cut off and shoved down his windpipe. All fingers pointed to it being Marko's work, but it was never proven.

Marko also had Hell Angels credentials. So no, Monique didn't get raped endlessly like she'd expected. She still got fucked a lot by Marko and his friends and anyone else Marko wanted to keep sweet . . . and anyone else she liked, but she survived. Marko made sure everyone used condoms with her though; he wasn't looking to get AIDS. He also saw to it that she got her hormone shots and other medication regularly. He had good connections both inside and outside the prison.

Of course, all that anal sex did have its side effects. For instance, Monique soon found it really easy to take a shit. It was harder to keep the poop inside her ass than let it out.

After a while, she got used to prison life. She was almost a queen in MCI-Norfolk, and when shemale porno superstar Kendra Yang—

aka KY—arrived there also to serve a five year sentence for major tax evasion (and other financial offences), Monique was even jealous that her exclusive notoriety and desirability were at an end.

But shortly after that, Monique's time in jail did end. Her parole board hearing came up, and she was so popular in MCI-Norfolk, there was no alternative but that she was getting out easy.

Marko Velli called her into his cell the day before she met with the parole board. She at first thought he was going to tell her to stiff them (she would have if he'd insisted), but he had something completely different on his mind.

"Once you're back on the outside again, Monique, there's some business you gotta take care of for me." A small muscular figure on the bed, he spoke as quietly as he always did.

"What business?" she asked. She'd not been expecting this at all.

He smiled coldly. "Ronnie Stones."

"What about him, Marko?"

"He's the one who set Ducky up to get killed. The punk lied about you and Ducky being terrorist stooges. Once you were both out of the picture, he took over Ducky's business." His smile turned even colder, chilling Monique like she'd just walked into a mortuary. "Which—since I was funding Ducky—means he took over my business. And now Ronnie's trying to move in on some of my other boys."

"Marko, you certain of this?" He'd been in her ass so many times, she wasn't scared to demand the truth from him.

He scowled back so she first thought he was angry with her. Then he smiled again, but warmer this time. "Girl, have I ever lied to you? Yeah, Ronnie set you two up. And now that you're getting out, I want you to take care of him. That son-of-a-bitch ain't due any kind of a natural death." He coughed. "I'd wait do it myself, but I ain't leaving here for at least another ten years, and I don't want him drinking or fucking himself to death before I get a chance at him. Besides there's a good chance that Ronnie might get me before I get him. I'm hearing bad stuff over the prison grapevine. The rumor is, he's planning to hit me in here."

He leaned forward and peered closely at Monique. "You got the balls for this, girl? You don't *have* to do it." He gestured around the cell. "That's why we're talking alone in here. If you don't think you can handle it, I'll wait till someone else I trust is getting out. And if I'm dead before then . . ."

"I'll put the bastard in his grave, Marko," Monique said quietly, anger and hatred filling her heart. "Just you leave it to me."

Marko nodded at her. "Good girl." Then his frown turned to a lecherous grin. "Now come over her and give me a blowjob. Oh, how I'm gonna miss you, baby."

She went over and took his penis in her mouth. While fellating Marko, she ran her mind over different violent scenarios for killing Ronnie Stones.

***

Three months later, Monique was a free woman again. Once through with her parole business with Lisa Cole (whom she disliked on first meeting), she got on with her life.

Marko Velli had made things easy for her. He'd gotten her a job working as a secretary with Johnny Horowitz, one of his many mob associates.

Monique spent the next few weeks reinserting herself into Boston's transsexual circles, meeting with Lisa Cole, and more quietly, working on her revenge mission.

She fast discovered that revenge was easier thought of than done. She and Marko had gone over endless payback scenarios in the months before her release, but none of them seemed really workable or satisfactory now.

Marko wanted a subtle execution—he wanted Ronnie killed without anyone suspecting his involvement in the man's death. It would be too hard to coordinate a gang war from inside his prison cell. He just wanted Ronnie Stones put underground so he could sleep with both eyes closed each night.

"The constant stress of thinking about that punk is making me hypertensive," he'd told Monique.

She'd been wondering how exactly she'd get in contact with Ronnie Stones. She couldn't exactly go knocking on his door, could she? Not when Ronnie's prison contacts were certain to have informed him that she'd been Marko's paramour for the past four years.

And, did she even want to get in touch with Ronnie? Planning his death from far away had seemed so easy, but now that she actually had to do it . . . There was no chance of getting near him with a gun—his bodyguards would simply blow her ass to shreds.

In the end, Ronnie came looking for *her*.

Late one Friday night, two months after her release from prison, a somewhat drunk Monique was standing outside her fourth floor Beacon Street apartment, rooting through her purse for her keys, when she heard the elevator opening.

She looked that way and saw a man get out of the elevator. He wore a brown hat, was wrapped in a coat despite the warm weather, and had sunglasses on despite the late hour. A black scarf hid the lower half of his face.

He began walking briskly towards her.

An instant chill went through Monique. It was a hit man coming to kill her!

Desperate now, she somehow found her keys and fumbled them into the lock. Before she'd gotten the door open, however, he was behind her and jamming something hard into her back.

"Open the door, bitch, and don't you dare make any damn noise, or you'll get it right outside here."

Monique complied. She opened the door and was first pushed inside, then rushed through her living room into her bedroom, where she was thrust face-down on her bed.

She waited for the bullets that never came, then turned around slowly. Then she heaved a sigh of relief. She instantly saw that she wasn't about being murdered. At least not yet.

The 'hitman' was Ronnie Stones. He'd removed his hat and glasses and scarf and thrown them over a chair.

Once he unbuttoned his coat, however, Monique gaped in *real* shock. Ronnie was naked beneath it, was wearing nothing except his shoes and socks. He stood there tall and skinny and buck naked for her appraisal.

Her eyes widened further still and she gasped. What had been sticking her in the back—what she'd mistaken for a gun—was his penis, which looked rock hard.

"Hi, babe!" Ronnie said, peeling off his coat so he was completely naked. "I heard you're back in town and just thought to drop by for old times' sake."

Monique couldn't take her eyes off his swollen penis. The cock was visibly jerking and throbbing, like *it* had ordered Ronnie to come visit her.

She played it cool, managing to filter her hatred and anger at him out of her voice. "Nice to see you too, baby." She pointed to his erection. "Is that a special gift for me?"

He sat down beside her on the bed. "Who else? I heard you were old Velli's bitch in prison and thought I'd come over and give you a taste of what a real man fucks like." He laughed. "I mean, you're unlikely to have any real idea of that now, are you? Seeing as you were screwing that limp-dicked faggot Ducky before you got sent away for terrorist activities. That hurt me no end, you know—how could you guys turn on your own country?"

Listening to him, Monique was so incensed that she could have bitten his penis off. Or shot him. Or both. Marko's friend Horowitz had provided her with an unregistered revolver. The gun was in her dresser drawer; all she needed to do was pull it out and blow this son-of-a-bitch away, shoot him in his balls for good measure. How dare he insult her lover Ducky?

But she didn't. If she shot him, she was going back to prison, and this time likely for good. She could claim rape, but that would be hard to prove. Or . . . she could claim assault and tip him out of her window, and say he fell out during a struggle. Her room was high up enough for the fall to kill him; but what if it didn't? Then she'd *really* be in the shit. (And of course, there was also his gang to consider; sure as sex was fun, they'd be after her ass for vengeance.)

So instead, she smiled at Ronnie, who was high on coke anyway.

"Come on, baby, let's party," she said with a sluttish wink. "I appreciate the gift you've brought me. Just gimme a moment to get undressed."

Once she had her clothes off, she pulled him down to her on the bed and took his penis in her mouth and licked it like a pro, while he gasped and groaned and called her 'honey pie.' And then they got to work on each other's bodies, feasting on the sensations of one another's flesh and sweating hard through the midnight hours.

Oh, Ronnie really fucked her that night. By morning her ass was sore as hell, so much so that she could barely walk.

But what was more important (and of vital importance to Monique's plans) was her discussion with Ronnie (somewhere between their second and fourth orgasms, if she'd counted correctly).

"Look," he'd said, "I want you for my own woman."

She'd hedged. "C'mon, Ronnie, you know I'm with Marko's crew now. Marko is scared that you're gunning for him. He'll blow my ass away if he hears I'm screwing you."

Ronnie had grinned. "He won't hear about it, Monique. I got this secret hideaway down in Roxbury . . ."

Monique had listened to him lay out what he had in mind for them. Now she understood: Ronnie Stones had been jealous of Ducky all along; he'd wanted her for his own. This revelation increased her rage at him, both for getting Ducky killed, and for getting her sent to jail to have her ass mercilessly stretched.

Of course, there was also the 'faggot' tag consideration, which she figured was the real reason Ronnie wanted the two of them to meet somewhere secret.

"Hey," she'd asked him, "How come all you *straight* guys want to fuck us trannys, but you never want to be seen with us in public?" She winced. "That sucks, you know. I mean that figuratively, of course."

He'd grinned back smugly. "I can imagine. Use your head, girl. What kind of street cred would I have if word got around that I'm sleeping with you? And speaking of sucking, girl"—he'd pointed at his penis—"get back to doing it."

Monique had controlled her anger and disgust with him. Ronnie wasn't anything like Ducky, with whom she'd had a give-and-take relationship. Ducky hadn't minded being either 'top' or 'bottom' when they'd had sex; both the male and female role were fine with him. Ronnie, on the other hand, just wanted blowjobs and her ass. He wasn't giving her anything back, not even emotionally. She just managed to come with him, but that was all.

They took to meeting once or twice a week at Ronnie's out-of-town place, a small cottage with an attached garage. Ronnie always arrived there alone, without his bodyguards; always without any clothes on under his coat, and always with a raging erection. Then they'd literally fuck for hours and he'd drive off again, after leaving Monique a couple of thousand in cash. Oh yes, and an aching butthole too. Damn, could Ronnie fuck!

He never suspected she was playing him. Or that his 'no homo' ego secretiveness (even his own bodyguards had no idea where he went those two days a week) was leading him to his death.

She poisoned him a month later. She didn't even know what the poison was. Horowitz supplied it to her in a plastic bottle labelled 'Azapine,' along with the simple instructions, "Put a teaspoonful in a glass of Ronnie's wine. Afterwards, wash the glass then pour more wine into it. That'll throw the cops off."

She looked at the bottle, with its colorless liquid content. "What's it do?"

"I dunno, but my supplier assures me it's damn effective. A sip or two of that and Ronnie'll be joining the choir in Homo Heaven."

She did like she was told. She and Ronnie were used to drinking between bouts of sex, so, using the excuse that she needed to fetch a fresh bottle of bubbly from the fridge, she poured them each a glass of champagne and spiked his.

Ronnie, all sweaty despite the open windows, shimmied down to sit under the fan at the foot of the bed. He finished his champagne in one long swallow then grinned.

"Hell, Monique, I get so damn thirsty nowadays. It's like I'm—"

Then, eyes bulging out of his face, he grabbed hold of his throat and keeled over, landing flat on his front on the floor, where he proceeded to roll spastically over the rug for two minutes flat, foaming at the mouth and pissing and shitting himself, while Monique just stared at him in horror, her fingers pressed to her lips.

Okay, so she'd looked forward to watching Ronnie Stones breathe his last, but this was just horrible to witness.

Ronnie rolled over onto his back and stared at her while twitching. Then blood began spurting from his nose and ears, and dribbling from his mouth. Then Ronnie began coughing up blood, foot-high spurts of liquid crimson that looped through the air towards Monique like they were accusing her of his murder. And he was still shitting and pissing himself like mad, like his guts and bladder had an argument with him.

Then finally, to her relief, he stopped moving.

She gaped around in complete disbelief. The bedroom was a total bloody mess. And there were clumps of excrement smeared everywhere too. In addition, the pee-reek in the room was worse than in a public toilet. *Shit! Shit! Shit!!*

After a while, she calmed down enough to call Horowitz.

"Yeah, what is it?" he asked when he finally picked up the phone. He sounded grumpy, like she'd interrupted him in the middle of something important.

"Ronnie's dead," she replied in a trembling voice.

"Yeah? Good. That was the plan. So, what's the problem?"

"That poison you gave me completely fucked him up. You need to see this place now. There's blood everywhere. I mean, fucking *everywhere*."

Horowitz was quiet for a few moments. In the background Monique heard a woman groan, "Oh, fuck! Johnny, please get off the damn phone and come back to bed and finish eating my pussy, will you? It really needs your tongue right now."

Then Horowitz said, "Alright, Monique, get your stuff and clear out of there. I'll send a cleanup crew over to the place. Just get out *now*. If those boys meet you there, they might decide to clean you up too."

He hung up. Monique did like he'd said. After several more guilty stares at Ronnie's messy corpse, she dressed and hurried out the front door and drove off as fast as she could.

Once she was back home, the full horror of what she'd done hit her and she almost puked her guts out. Then she took a massive dose of sleeping pills and went to bed.

This all happened on a Monday. Two days afterwards, she read in the papers that a fire had gutted Ronnie's Roxbury cottage.

(So officially, Ronnie Stones died in a fire. Forensics tests later turned up a strange substance [the rare tropical poison 'azapine'] in his charred remains, but the police were so delighted that Mr. Ronald Stones was dead that they honestly didn't care who'd poisoned him. They couldn't be bothered to spend the honest taxpayer's money investigating the demise of a drug-dealing scumbag, so they let the case go cold.)

Monique was off the murder hook, or thought she was. She'd however made just one little mistake:

That Friday, Lisa Cole visited Monique's workplace to see if she was still working there. Monique wasn't at work, and no one knew why, so Lisa drove over to Monique's apartment.

Horowitz was out at the time of Lisa's visit, but a secretary called ahead to alert Monique of her parole officer's impending arrival at her door. So when Lisa arrived, Monique was alert enough (after two cups of black coffee) to answer the front door and present a semblance of normalcy.

Lisa sat down in Monique's living room and studied her. Monique knew she looked more ragged than a shirt ten Doberman puppies had been playing hide-and-seek in.

"I feel like shit," she excused her appearance, cursing the sleeping pills she'd been gobbling each night since Ronnie's messy death so she didn't have nightmares about him. "Like I've picked up some bug."

Lisa smirked. "Girl, you look like you've been partying all night long. Hey, have you been hooking again? 'Cos if you have, you know what'll happen if I bust you."

Monique starred dully at her parole officer's lovely face in its oval blonde frame. "Me, darling? You've got the wrong ex-con." She hated the way Lisa always looked so smug, so cool, so feminine-perfect without ever seeming to work on it. She also couldn't shake the feeling that Lisa was condescending to her, that Lisa considered her a 'second-class woman' because she was a transsexual and still had her male equipment attached.

Lisa was looking around the living room with a suspicious eye. "Hmmm, this sudden illness of yours. Monique, are you doing drugs again? Or selling them?"

"C'mon, lady boss," she replied in conciliatory tones, "Gimme a break, huh? I've been puking worse than the Devil's hangover since I woke up and . . ."

"Monique, you're just a junior secretary in a grubby office. You can't afford a place like this on your measly income. So tell me—are you selling your ass again? Or maybe, muleing drugs for Ducky's successor?"

"I plead the goddam Fifth Amendment." Monique rubbed her bleary green eyes. "Even if I am dealing, what's it to you?"

Lisa grinned coldly. "Do you miss the macho men in prison that much? Being surrounded by all that muscular criminal beef? Is that it—law-abiding guys aren't sexy enough for you anymore? Oh, I can imagine how ex-convict sex just ain't the same after having your anus stretched to the limit every night for four years."

"Aw, you're just jealous of me."

"Jealous of you? Monique, what in the world gives you that impression?"

"You wish you had a dick too so you could be locked up in a male jail too."

"Alright, now you're really convincing me that you're using drugs again."

"Give me a goddam break."

"That's the second break you've asked me for in five minutes. What the hell do I look like to you—an auto spare parts dealer? Girl, sit your ass down in that wicker chair and tell me what the hell you've been up to that you haven't been in to work all week."

Monique instead gestured towards her kitchenette. "I was just about to make coffee. You want some?"

"Sure, cream and two sugars. Thanks."

"Alright, sit tight, and I'll be right back."

Then suddenly, Monique felt sick, sick, sick. Coffee was going to have to wait.

"Oops, excuse me!"

She dashed off to the bathroom and bent over the toilet bowl, just managing to hold off long enough to get the seat up. She hunched over there vomiting. After she was done, she didn't come out again for several minutes. Instead, she took the time to clean herself up, brushing her teeth so her mouth didn't smell, and applying some perfume. She brushed her hair too, then regarded herself in the mirror. At least she no longer looked like her own ghost. And as for that bitch Lisa Cole out there . . .

She made the damn coffee.

Carrying two steaming cups, feeling a resurgence of her confidence, Monique tramped back out into her living room. She walked around her sofa and put down the coffee cups and sat facing Lisa with a look of defiance on her face.

"Here we are, darling."

Then, realizing what Lisa was holding up (carefully, her index finger and thumb just gripping the bottle's cover), all Monique's confidence drained from her.

Lisa was holding the bottle of poison with which Monique had killed Ronnie Stones. Monique hadn't yet removed it from her handbag, which lay open on the coffee table.

She attempted to bluff her way out of her dilemma. "Hey, how dare you go through my purse?"

Lisa smiled at her. "I didn't 'go through' your purse, honey. It happened to be poking out. Azapine? What is it anyway?" Then she smirked. "And why do you have a copy of Wednesday's paper with Ronnie Stones' death in it?" She tapped the copy of the Boston Globe, which Monique had conveniently left both open and folded in half so Ronnie's grayscaled face was staring at the ceiling.

Monique felt a noose tightening around her neck. But then she realized that Lisa—perfect evil Lisa—was *smiling* at her.

(Unknown to Monique, Lisa was *very* familiar with her past history. Lisa's current boyfriend Bobby had been one of the SWAT team who'd taken she and Ducky down. In fact, Bobby Finch was the cop Monique had shot in the thigh. Bobby was fond of remarking to Lisa, "Oh, God sure likes me, honey. Two inches to the left and that tranny bitch would have blown my dick off!"

Bobby had also told Lisa that it was Ronnie Stones who'd sold out Ducky to them. [The BPD were still smarting over his fake ISIS info.] So Lisa knew just about everything there was to know about the case. And with the evidence so glaringly laid out in front of her, it was easy for her to put two and two together.)

"It wasn't me, and you can't prove anything," Monique blurted out desperately.

"It *was* you, and besides, I don't *need* to prove anything," Lisa countered simply, her smile still intact. "I don't even need to arrest your fat butt and return it to jail. All I need to do is pass the info along to Ronnie Stones' people that you had something to do with his death." She grinned at Monique. "Should I? Then you can go right ahead and prove your innocence to *them*."

Monique almost pissed herself from fright. "No, no! I'll do whatever you want me to, but please don't tell anyone."

"So it was you? Why? Revenge for your dead boyfriend?"

She nodded contritely. She wished she'd remembered to remove the newspaper from the coffee table when she'd heard that Lisa was coming over to see her. Now it was too late. *Shit! I'm in really big trouble here. It isn't just Ronnie's gang I have to worry about now! Shit! Once Horowitz hears I've been caught, he'll likely have me eliminated so the trail doesn't lead back to him!* (For a reckless moment she considered grabbing the bottle of azapine from Lisa and dashing into the bathroom, and locking herself in there to destroy the evidence: empty the poison into the toilet bowl, then pulverize the bottle. But that wouldn't prevent Lisa from telling

Ronnie's gang of her involvement. And if *they* got their hands on her, she'd be worse off than dead.)

Tears in her eyes, she hurried around the side of the coffee table and knelt down and clasped Lisa's legs. "Please, fucking please, don't tell anyone. I mean it—I'll do whatever you say. Anything at all."

Lisa frowned awhile, appearing to consider Monique's plea. Then she smiled smugly again. "Alright, girl, you got yourself a deal. I'll keep my lips completely zipped about this, and"—still holding the azapine bottle by its cover, she dropped it into her purse—"just in case you think of calling my bluff, I'll hold onto this too. It's certain to have your fingerprints on it."

Monique just nodded, too relieved to care.

"And now that you're my bitch," Lisa said, rising to her feet and stripping off her jacket and top, "come into the bedroom and lick me to orgasm. Bobby's been too busy for my pussy lately."

Monique followed her inside meekly. Lisa was already peeling off her pants, revealing her exquisite, curvaceous body.

Once she was fully nude, Lisa lay back on Monique's bed and spread her perfect legs wide, revealing her plush pubic paradise. "Alright, baby, now come over here and get to playing on my sex organ. Licking my clitoris and making me squirm is great fun . . . Bobby says so anyway."

Monique obediently walked over to Lisa's waiting vagina and dug her tongue into it. Lisa instantly began gasping and moaning. Less than a minute later she was coming.

It had been like that ever since. Lisa regularly had Monique perform cunnilingus on her. She said a proper fuck would be cheating on Bobby, and she didn't want that.

As far as Monique could tell, this aspect of Lisa's behavior to her didn't truly stem from sexual frustration. Lisa was just power-tripping on her.

But she had no choice. The alternative was death. And a slow and painful death at that.

And so it was that Monique got drafted into Lisa's plan to take out Josh Penham.

But of course, she wasn't about telling Tiff that. Tiff might start blackmailing her with the information too.

***

86

"I'm tired of walking," Tiff interjected into her thoughts. "My orgasm drained me more than I thought. Who'd ever have imagined such a thing—that I'd come so hard while beating someone up?" She lifted her empty red can and rapped it loudly with her knuckles. "And now my legs feel like they're about giving out under me."

"Yeah," Monique agreed glumly. "Over a mile's walk to get gas ain't my idea of fun either. And we still gotta walk back a—"

She shut up. A solitary approaching vehicle was bathing them in its headlights from behind.

"It's heading our way," Tiff confirmed with a look back, which showed her twin lights growing larger. "Quick, stick your thumb out! If I walk anymore tonight, I'll drop dead by the roadside."

"Yeah!"

They stuck their thumbs out, then waved. The vehicle—it was a green pickup truck—slowed, then rolled past them a short distance.

"Hey stop, wilya!"

The pickup truck stopped and reversed. As it halted beside them, Monique became aware of animal noises from the vehicle's open rear bed. She looked in the back. From what she could see, and from the sounds, it was ferrying a cargo of young pigs somewhere. The piglets were penned in wooden crates.

Monique was nearer the front of the truck than Tiff. She turned from regarding the piglets and bent in through the front passenger window.

"Hi, girls, where you two headed at this time of tonight?" the driver asked, leaning toward her. The pickup truck's interior lights were off and Monique couldn't really make out the man's face in the dark, but he sounded friendly enough. He was quite large, filling up most of the driver's area. He also smelt like he'd been drinking.

"Our van ran out of gas," she explained. "You might have passed it back there. We've been walking for half an hour to get to a gas station."

"There's one just up ahead. Hop in—I'll drive you there and back to your van. It's dangerous for you ladies to be walkin' around late at night like this. Brainchew might get ya."

"Thanks, that's really nice of you. Uh, Brainchew? What's that?"

He laughed. "Just a local joke we use to scare the kids when they're bad." He reached back between the front seats to unlock the rear door for Tiff. "Get in, get in."

Monique climbed in the front of the truck beside him. Tiff got in the back. After a moment, the pickup truck began moving again.

"I apologize for the smell from the back," the driver said cheerily. "Gotta deliver the little hogs to the boss at the farm tomorrow morning." He grinned, his teeth white in the dark. "By the way, my name's Owlsy Pine."

"We're Monique and Tiff," came the reply from behind.

"Pleased to meet both you ladies," Owlsy replied. Then he shut up and concentrated on his driving, which pleased Monique. He'd clearly had a lot to drink—the fumes from his mouth threatened to intoxicate her too—and him running his truck off the road and wrapping it around a tree was a distinct possibility she didn't like considering.

The smell of pigs seemed a part of the vehicle, almost like they were driving through a herd of the animals.

Soon, the lights of a gas station showed up ahead. They pulled into it and slowed.

In the station lights, Monique got her first proper look at the driver. A big muscular fellow he was, with short brown hair and mutton chop sideburns. She winced. Did everyone in this town have the same outdated haircut? But for his lack of a mustache, Owlsy could have been Josh Penham's twin. Instinctively, she felt the taser in her pocket, its plastic-metal solidity a promise of safety. She was relieved that this guy Owlsy was friendly. Big as he was, if he too had serial killer tendencies, he'd be a real handful to handle.

Then she grinned. Well, not with 50,000 volts in him, he wouldn't.

And . . . and . . . just what was that he'd said again, about the local bogeyman? Brainchew?

Monique's mind replayed what Owlsy had said. *A local joke*, the man had explained. But to Monique, the name sounded worryingly close to what had been written on the grave they'd killed Josh Penham over. *Brainchew? Brian Chu? What if it's more than a joke? What if there really was something buried down there that was trying to get out of its grave?*

She shrugged it off as a dumb supposition. Except on TV, the dead stayed dead. But if that was so, why'd she feel so uneasy all of a sudden?

The truck stopped by Pump No. 2.

"Alright, ladies," Owlsy said, "fill up your can, and I'll drive you safely back down the road. We wouldn't want Brainchew to get you both now, would we?"

Repressing a sudden shudder, Monique nodded and got out of the truck.

CHAPTER 7

Steve

Steve Birchfield hadn't noticed the two young women pass the foot of his driveway. His mind was far away, in a totally different place.

Steve—tall, slim, and in his late forties with thinning black hair—currently had his full attention focused on the screen of his laptop, where a young blonde woman was being whipped. The curvaceous blonde was chained to an X-shaped frame and being beaten by a muscular man wearing black leather pants and a black mask that completely hid his face. The woman wore a white embroidered eye mask. Her red lips split into gasps which each strike of the whip.

Her back, buttocks, and thighs were crisscrossed with thin red lines. As though it knew what the viewer desired most to see, the camera zoomed in on the woman's behind, framing the tormented expanse of her white flesh in 16:9 HD resolution. Stripped&Whipped.com, read the neat blue script at the bottom right of the monitor. Stripped & Whipped was the new BDSM website Steve had just discovered. Maybe the best ever, in his opinion,. The site had a constant turnover of beautiful women, and they all seemed to be enjoying themselves.

Steve currently had an erection like he couldn't believe. His manhood was so damn hard. He didn't touch it though. He might relieve himself later when he was back inside the house, but for the moment, he just wanted to watch.

On the screen now, the man had loosened the cuffs around his partner's wrists and was turning her around to face the camera. Once he'd reversed her position, he began whipping her front. The camera faithfully zoomed in on her small but shapely breasts. Steve gasped as parallel red stripes appeared on their pale white flesh, trapping her nipples between them. The camera held the shot, so he could see the beads of sweat dripping down her punished skin.

Damn! This was so goddam hot! Steve almost came in his pants there and then.

He paused the video. He leaned back in the deck chair and fanned himself with a hand. It felt so hot out here all of a sudden. He grabbed up his glass of red wine and took a long sip. Then he adjusted himself comfortably in his chair and regarded the night through the bug curtains. It was complete darkness out there beyond the vague dimness fostered by the house lights. Nothing moving at this hour.

"The streets are as dead as my sex life with Audrey," he regretted aloud. Then he reflexively looked back through the front door—he always left it open when he was outside like this so she couldn't sneak up on him unannounced. (Steve was an architect; Audrey was used to him bringing work home and doing it outside on hot nights.) Oh, Audrey was just so dull in bed nowadays. Nothing like the exquisite hot number he'd married fifteen years ago. Now, all she wanted to do at night was sleep, sleep, sleep. Audrey was always too tired after the day's work to make love, and whenever he persuaded her to, all she wanted to do was missionary position; even doggy-style required too much energy from her.

Steve was certain that if he listened hard enough now, he'd hear her snoring gently in her bedroom. *His* bedroom, *her* bedroom; it was annoying. They'd only started sleeping apart when their sex life fizzled out.

He felt sad about that. They still loved each other—he knew they did—but somehow their sex life had gone to the dogs. All the sizzle and sparkle of their bodies sweating over the sheets had faded. How? It had just happened, like a natural disaster creeping up on an unaware community.

Oh, how Steve wished he could get Audrey interested in the BDSM scene. Not that he wanted to whip her all red like the hot girls at Stripped&Whipped.com, but just to add a little spice to get their sex life up and running again. Audrey was still a damn pretty woman, with a great body and all, and he'd love to try out a little kinky stuff with her.

He stared longingly at his laptop again. The screen was still frozen on the shot of the blonde model's abused breasts. He winced—he still had his erection. *Maybe I'll go see if she isn't asleep yet. But . . .*

Oops, I forgot. One reason Steve always stayed up this late at night was his Stripped & Whipped chatmate, Wellcaned69. Like himself, Wellcaned was stuck in a sexually stale marriage, her love life empty because her husband was now more interested in work than in satisfying her. He was also too obtuse to pick up on the endless signals she'd given him that she'd like to spice up their sex life with some hot BDSM.

What a loser, Steve thought. Then he looked sadly up from the porch in the direction of Audrey's bedroom. *But then, aren't I a loser too? Not in sixty million years of sexual evolution is Audrey ever gonna agree to trying out anything even remotely kinky.*

Sighing, Steve minimized the video window and called up the Stripped & Whipped chat window instead.

A message from Wellcaned was already waiting beside her icon, a set of sexy feet in black high heeled sandals: *Hi, baby. I feel like being whipped hard tonight. Are you up to the job?*

His breath sticking in his throat, Steve quickly typed out a reply (his own screen name was Thick8, his icon a male crotch with a red codpiece): *Oh, baby, hell yes, you know I am.*

There was a pause of maybe thirty seconds, then the reply came in: *Oh, Thickie darling, so you finally came? Baby, can you handle me tonight? I mean, can you? I need a REAL man. A rock HARD man who knows how to use a whip as well as his dick. I need to be tied down hard and dominated, caned good 'cos I've been a really bad girl today. I need to be cuffed to the bed, and my soft butt smacked so hard I can't sit for hours.*

Steve felt delirious. *Oh yeah, girl, believe me, I'm the man for you. You don't know it like I do. I'll flog that tender ass of yours so hard, you'll be cumming stars.*

Wellcaned replied: *No, Thickie, I don't think you're up to it. I'm a hard bitch to tame. Doggy bones don't work with me. I need real meat!!!!*

Steve wrote: *Wow, honey, we really need to get together.* (Steve didn't really mean that. This was all harmless fun. Besides she lived way down in Florida. He'd made certain she was far away before striking up a chat. Steve had no intention of cheating on Audrey. Also, the Stripped & Whipped anonymity policy protected him—one couldn't post or receive personal pictures without written consent being given by both sides, and he wasn't about letting Wellcaned see him. What if she wanted more? What if she wanted to go beyond merely chatting online, wanted to delve into what they both fantasized about? No,

Steve wasn't ready to go that far. Things could get really complicated and ugly like that. Better to keep hoping against hope that Audrey would someday see the kinky light.)

Wellcaned replied: *You're most likely like my husband—all talk and no fuck. Damn stick-in-the-mud sleeps like a train engine. You can hear him snoring down the street. But, maybe you really are the right one for me, Thickie. If you are, we can meet up and really get things whipping. But let's see, macho man: are you really as HARD as you claim to be? Alright, tell me what you're gonna do to me tonight, honey. How are you gonna discipline my soft tender skin . . . how are you gonna make me suffer for my sins?*

Steve groaned aloud. *Oh, shit! Audrey, why can't you just get interested in this scene with me?* It hurt to have secrets he couldn't share with her. Steve had a momentary vision of the two of them enacting a classic D/s role play scenario—Audrey bound hand-and-foot in bed with silken cords, her buttocks crisscrossed by thin red lines, while he teased her clitoris with the whip handle.

The vision faded. It would never happen; Audrey was too set in her ways.

He remembered that Wellcaned awaited his reply. He began describing his fantasy: *First, you naughty li'l seafront slut, I'm gonna tie you down on your back on the bed. Then I'm gonna smack your face a few times so you know who's boss around here. Then I'm gonna put painful clamps on your soft nipples, and when you squeal from the pain, I'm going to gag you too. Then I'll take a flogger and start work on the inside of your thighs . . .*

Oh shit! came Wellcaned's reply. *Oh fuck, baby, you're making me come! Oh God, I'm coming!*

Feeling inspired, Steve resumed typing: *Next I'll turn you over on your side and grab hold of your bruised and reddened ass cheeks and I'll redden them some more with my belt. And then I'll get a birch switch and lash those tender buttocks all over until you start squirting from the pain . . .*

***

From a cover of roadside trees, Brainchew regarded the white house.

The monster had chosen to come here rather than head for the black van. The two women who had left the van (and had recently walked past this house) had influenced its decision: from here it would have gone after them too. But then the two women had gotten into another vehicle—one with many small animals in the back of it. That vehicle was now parked farther down the road, at an open space that smelt of mined substances.

Brainchew contained its feelings of frustration. A further decision on direction would come later. For the moment, it focused its attention on the white house facing it. There were the two people there: the man seated outside, and a woman upstairs in bed. It needed these two as food to restore its body. Even after eating the head contents of the man on its grave, its body was still too small, so shrunken that it could feel the weight of its enormous head on its neck.

Brainchew stealthily approached the white building, its anticipation rising with each step.

**

Steve Birchfield was happily chatting away with Wellcaned69 when he smelt something unpleasant. It was a really bad smell, one that grew steadily thicker with each passing second.

Finally, Steve was forced to stop typing. The stink was just . . . ugh! Like all the frogs and newts in Johnsons Pond (at the back of the house) had suddenly died and turned rancid.

Distracted, unable to continue chatting with the stink so intense around him, he left his newest reply incomplete, put his laptop down on the stool that held his wineglass, and got to his feet.

Steve opened the screen door and peeked out. *What the hell is that smell!?* The odor was simply atrocious. Now it smelt like someone had just unearthed a rotting corpse in a damp and moldy basement.

The stink grew yet thicker around him. And then he heard a sound on his right.

He turned and saw *it*—coming towards the house from between his and Audrey's parked SUVs. It looked big and small at the same time, which made no sense to him until he understood why it had that odd appearance—its HUGE head (*Damn, that has to be the largest head in existence!*) sat atop a kid's body, maybe a ten-year-old's.

Oh shit! It's Brainchew! It's real? Steve had always imagined Brainchew to be a mere myth.

Then the creature—this misshapen monster with the little body and large head—was ripping through the fiberglass screen mesh like it was wet newspaper, and Steve was staring at its sunken red eyes which seemed to hypnotize him into immobility, and he was uncertain if he should scream or flee, and then . . .

And then the monster had him. And despite its short stature, its huge head made it even taller than he was.

Steve's paresis broke as Brainchew's razor-sharp claws dug into his shoulder. He was going to yell for help, but the monster's hand was suddenly covering his mouth. It was incredibly strong; he couldn't shake it off. Its horrible stink of something recently buried was choking him.

And next thing, it spun him around so he was facing away from it and staring at his laptop, on which he saw that Wellcaned69 had just sent him a new message.

Steve's vision telescoped, magnifying the computer screen. He could clearly make out what she'd written: *Oh, whip me, whip me, Thickie! Give this hot bitch the sweet lashing she needs! Fuck, I'm gonna come again* . . .

That was all Steve's panicked and staring eyes took in. In shocked horror he realized that Brainchew was now wrapping its mouth around the back of his head. It was a horrible clammy feeling, like falling headfirst into goo. Oh, God! And the pain! Its teeth ripped open his scalp as they slid through his hair like they were combing it.

No! NOOO! Steve screamed in his mind, his voice blocked off by the monster's palm. He found it impossible to understand how he was dying like this. *I've got two guns in the house!* This was just inconceivable.

Then it ended. A sudden biting pain in his head made Steve flail and kick his laptop off the stool. Then *nothing.*

As Steve's laptop crashed to the porch floor, a fresh message was just coming in from Wellcaned69: *Oh, honey, I just came again. You're so gooood—oh fuck, I think I love you. We really should meet up for real!*

However, by this time Brainchew was already dragging Steve's brainless corpse into the house, leaving a thick trail of blood behind them.

***

Brainchew took its time with chewing the dead man's brain. The soft, delicious white meat seem to dissolve in its mouth, flavored with blood and made nice and crunchy by the chunk of braincase it had bitten off. As it ate, it felt its body rebuild itself; soon its head was noticeably less of a burden on its shoulders. Feeling thirst, it ripped open the man's neck and drank its fill of the sweet refreshing blood, thrilling in the red liquid's coppery tang.

Finally, it flung the man's corpse away and headed for the rear of the house, where it glimpsed a stairway to the upper floor. It had considered first ripping out the man's bladder and drinking his urine, but it was in too much of a hurry to eat another brain, and there was a fresh juicy female one right overhead.

Even though thinking wasn't its strong point, Brainchew understood its luck here: the open front door. Brainchew didn't understand locks. For the monster, opening locks was a hit-or-miss affair (as was everything else that required a process of logic and deduction). It preferred not to have to deal with them.

It reached the stairway and began climbing. Each step filled its nose with the scent of the woman upstairs. She was in bed but not asleep.

It grinned its horrible grin, made all the more horrible now by the coating of blood all over his mouth and chest.

A thrill of delight pulsed through Brainchew's evil heart. Oh, the juicy woman upstairs was in for a nasty shock.

CHAPTER 8

Tiff, mostly

As the gas station lights seeped into the pickup truck, abolishing its interior darkness, Tiff suddenly felt sick, like she'd been punched in the gut.

She looked once at Owlsy, who wasn't saying anything to her or even looking her way. The man was tapping on his steering wheel and whistling a country and western tune like she wasn't even in the vehicle.

Her ill-feeling intensified; Tiff knew she would puke really soon. In this truck even, if she didn't get out right now.

"Gotta go pee, man," she said quickly, then leapt out the door before he'd even finished replying a nonchalant "Yeah, sure, girl."

Once out of the confines of the pickup truck, she quickly whispered to Monique (who had the silver gas nozzle stuck in their red can), "I'm going to the restroom. Make an excuse to Owlsy and come join me. Hurry up, it's urgent!"

Then she was off and running to the toilet building.

She stood in there waiting, her heart in her mouth. She'd have thrown up, but it felt like she'd emptied her belly in the cemetery.

Monique joined her thirty seconds later. "Okay, I told him I needed to pee too. He agreed to wait, and I left the gas can in the van with him." She gestured at her jacket and catsuit. "With the way we're dressed, he likely thinks we're a pair of junkie hookers off to shoot up." Then she took proper note of the horrified look on Tiff's face. "Hey, girl, what's the matter with you? You having period pains or—"

Tiff could hardly find the words. "Monique, I think we fucked up."

"Huh? What are you talking about?"

"I think we killed the wrong man." It was a damning possibility. Tiff heard her voice echoing off the restroom walls and tiles like a thousand accusations against herself. And all the voices proclaimed her guilty as charged.

Monique's eyes instantly became as round as saucers. "What!?"

"Shush! Keep your voice down." Tiff could feel her heart pounding like it was trying to burst out of her chest. "Yes. I'm almost a hundred percent certain that Owlsy—the *nice guy* who's just offered us a lift—is the one who abducted me!"

Monique's countenance fell. "Aw shit. I agree they do look alike—with the same damn hairstyle and all, but that's just coincidence, right? It has to be. People look alike all the time. It doesn't mean that . . ." She saw that Tiff was shaking her head and asked, "How sure are you? What makes you so certain?"

Tiff let the words out in a flood of damning emotion. "His *voice*. Remember how I said he only ever spoke to me once? Well, it's the *same* voice—gruff, but not-too-low pitched—I'm sure of it. And I never really heard Josh talk, did I?"

"You didn't hear him from inside the van? How not?"

"I wasn't listening—I was too tense. And to make things worse, Carmela was close to freaking out from all that racket you and Lisa were making out there, and I was calming her down." Her eyes now bored into Monique's like drills. "Tell me, what did Josh's voice sound like?"

Monique made a face while she searched her memory. "It was all thin and reedy-like. Yeah, I remember that about it. It was thinnish."

Hearing that, Tiff felt like shit. "I'm right then. Josh was the wrong victim. Dammit, Monique, I just killed—murdered—an *innocent* man."

"*We* murdered an innocent man." It didn't help Tiff's feeling of absolute horror that Monique looked more upset than she did.

They stood in silence for half a minute, both dueling with their consciences, then Monique said. "We'd better call the sisters and tell 'em."

"Lisa and Carmela?" Tiff shook her head. "No, not yet. We need to confirm that Owlsy *is* our man. Lisa will be mad if we're wrong, and it'll mess up our alibi too."

"Confirm that he's our man?" Monique gaped at her. "And then what?"

"We're gonna kill him too," Tiff replied, her voice much calmer than she'd thought it would be. "Try to understand this: in addition to his other crimes, that son-of-a-bitch has just made me guilty of murder. I'm not leaving this town until he's dead too."

She watched Monique ponder her words. Monique stood worrying the ends of her red hair with her fingers, her brow furrowed, her gaze concentrated like it was focused somewhere outside the four walls of the restroom.

"Okay," Monique said finally. "I understand you. Oh, Lisa'll be mad when she hears this." She grimaced. "If you're right, that is." She wagged a 'be quiet' finger at Tiff's respondent look of anger. "No, no, no, I'm not buying this completely yet. An hour ago you thought Josh Penham was the right guy. Now, you think it's this guy Owlsy outside. Who's to say you'll not wake up after we do Owlsy and claim it's someone else?"

"I'm not making things up!" Tiff spat angrily. "I'm sure it's him."

"I'm not done talking yet," Monique retorted. "I'm not saying I completely doubt you, just that I wanna be extra-sure before we kill another person tonight." She smiled without mirth. "Reason along with me for a minute, huh? So, *you* recognize the guy out in the pickup truck as your abductor? How come *he* doesn't recognize *you*? Explain that?"

Tiff had already figured that out. "Because I'm sitting in the back, as in, I'm *behind* him? And the truck's interior lights are off, and *you've* been doing most of the talking for us? And I'm all fat now, nowhere near as hot as I was when he kidnapped me, so he's not even bothering to give me a second glance? All he sees is another overweight girl? Instead, he's been ogling you since you got in; planning on how to get the redhead into bed."

Monique laughed at that last comment, then her green eyes narrowed to cold focus again. "Okay, you said we'd confirm that Owlsy's our man. How do you plan on us doing that?"

Tiff exhaled loudly. The rotten smell coming from one of the toilet stalls exactly complimented how horrible she felt. *How could I be so frigging wrong? But Monique's right—am I wrong?*

She told Monique, "We'll seduce him and get him to take us home with him."

Monique nodded slowly, then looked perplexed. "You'll recognize his penis when you see it?"

"Don't make jokes. I'm talking about his house."

"How? You said you were only half conscious when you escaped."

Tiff nodded back. "Yes, yes, I was. But I do remember two details about the place."

"Oh? What are they?"

"First of all, the front door was a bright blue, with a—"

"Not proof enough," Monique interrupted while shaking her head. "Lots of houses have blue doors. Just like this is a suburbanish, rural kinda town; lots of big strapping guys here can easily be mistaken for your abductor."

Tiff ignored the slur on the reliability of her recollections. "C'mon, girl, hear me out, will you? The other thing I remember? On one corner of the front porch, a large chunk of stone had fallen out. I know that 'cos as I was leaving I almost tripped into the hole it left. Trust me, Monique, that hole is unmissable. And the extracted block of stone seemed to have been left there to act as a step. That's how I got down off the porch anyway. Once I see that I'll know it's the right house."

"Hmmm, so a house with a blue door and a damaged porch? And once we find it, what then?"

Tiff smirked. "Then we tase Owlsy, load him back into his own fucking truck, and drive back to the Pleasant Street Cemetery to finish the job." She saw Monique looking less than convinced and asked, "What's the problem now? And we need to hurry up before Owlsy thinks we're screwing in here."

"I'm just bothered. I don't think the Pleasant Street Cemetery's the best place to return to tonight. Don't you remember how the ground was shaking?"

Tiff had forgotten. "We'll find somewhere else then."

They checked themselves out in the restroom mirror. "Do we look hot enough to tempt him?" Tiff asked worriedly.

Monique laughed. "Are you kidding? You think a guy who's been drinking like Owlsy has is gonna turn down some free pussy?" She sniggered. "Few guys ever do." Then she understood that Tiff was really concerned about her own attractiveness and added gently, "C'mon, girl, you look mighty fine; Owlsy's gonna be all over you." Then she frowned. "Just remain incognito in the back seat and let me do all the seductive talking, in case he remembers your voice like you do his."

They made to leave the restroom. Monique looked meaningfully at Tiff then nodded over at the stalls.

"Girl, you wanna pee before we hit the road?"

Tiff shook her head. "No, I'll piss on the bastard's grave instead. I might even shit on it."

***

Outside, Owlsy was still waiting. *A real northern gentleman,* Tiff thought sourly, *when he ain't rapin' and killin' womenfolks.*

They climbed up into the pickup truck where their full can of gas waited. Like they were glad to see the two women again, Owlsy's rear load of piglets instantly started a round of squealing.

Once seated, Monique got to work. "Hey, Owlsy baby," she said in a voice dripping with bedroom innuendo, "my friend and I were just wondering if you'd mind putting us up for the night. It's so late and cold, and just like you said, it ain't safe for women to be out on the streets at this hour."

"W-well, I-I-I dunno," Owlsy stuttered. "This is kinda sudden . . ."

"C'mon, baby," Monique said, placing her hand on his right thigh. "What're you scared off, you hunk? Two li'l women? Surely, a big strong stud like you can handle the pair of us if we get a li'l rowdy?"

"Why, yeah, sure . . ." Owlsy seemed to be having problems coordinating his thoughts. After peeking forward between the seats, Tiff understood why:

It wasn't just all the booze he'd been drinking distracting him. Monique now had her hand on Owlsy's crotch and was kneading it fiercely.

That clearly was keeping things extra-realistic, Tiff agreed, though she thought she detected some real lust in the transsexual's voice too. As for herself, she felt sick, sick, sick to her stomach. If the house he took them to had a blue door and that broken-in porch . . . shit!

"So what'cha say, honey? Do we head to your place for a sleepover?"

Owlsy nodded. "Yeah, most definitely, yeah. But, please, please, please take your hand off my dick, woman, before I mess up my pants."

On that note, he put the pickup truck in gear and headed out of the gas station.

Tiff glumly watched the road stream past them, a black river hemmed in by upright shadows. She hoped for the life of her that she was wrong, and that this was the actual case of mistaken identity, not the first one with Josh Penham.

CHAPTER 9

Audrey

Audrey Birchfield froze for a moment with the vibrator hard against her clitoris.

What was that?

She'd heard a sharp noise from downstairs, as if her husband Steve had dropped his glass of wine again. No, it had been louder than that. It sounded more like Steve had dropped his laptop.

She listened for a moment longer, her head cocked sideways like a dog's, then decided there was no problem. Whatever the matter was, Steve must have fixed it or he'd be calling for her.

She returned her attentions to her pleasure.

Audrey Birchfield was a pretty forty-five, with soft hazel eyes, long dark hair, and a nice body. At the moment she lay in bed, propped up on soft fluffy pillows against the headboard. She was masturbating with a yellow vibrator while watching a video from the bondage website Stripped & Whipped. The scene was of a hairy, portly man and a voluptuous blonde woman. Both were completely naked. The man was masked, his female lover chained wrist and ankle to a wall. The man was beating her large buttocks with a paddle that left wide red marks.

"Oh, oh, oh!" Audrey gasped with each hit of the paddle on the woman's ass. It felt like she was the one being so tied and dominated.

***

Audrey Birchfield often wished she could tell her husband Steve of her intense desire to experiment with BDSM culture. Not *too* deeply— she had no interest in the more extreme forms of it, but . . . Audrey often fantasized of being tied to a wall or frame in a darkened room, while Steve—in black hood and leather getup—whipped her; not violently enough to draw blood, but hard enough so she'd really feel it. Even the merest thought of him doing a D/s scene with her set her ladyparts ablaze.

But, oh no, Audrey knew her husband much too well to even suggest such to him. Steve was so straight-laced, he could have been a preacher without any conversion needed.

Audrey still loved Steve deeply. Oh, there was no question about that in her mind. She truly did love him, and didn't desire a replacement. But, like a sailor on a ship sinking in the middle of the Pacific Ocean, she'd slowly watched her sex life capsize without a sensual lifeboat anywhere in sight.

Audrey ran a real-estate business. Yes, it was a demanding job, but it wasn't any more demanding that it used to be. Saying she was fagged out simply sounded better than confessing to Steve that she no longer felt the flames of passion for him.

She didn't even understand when or how it had started. She figured it happened to all couples after a while: they became too used to each other's bodies and the pleasures that separate flesh afforded, and even though when one made the effort to fuck, the enjoyment of the other was still the same, the desire to make that effort grew less and less. Mind and body both tired of what they knew and loved, and craved outside stimulation. Some couples fixed this impasse by having affairs; some did so by getting divorced, each partner ending their sexual boredom between a fresh lover's legs. A few of Audrey's friends had tried swinging with varying results.

Audrey (call her old-fashioned if you liked, she didn't mind) had never really been interested in anyone except Steve.

And then, out of the blue and just when her libido seemed to be completely dead, she'd become interested in the BDSM scene. Why? She couldn't tell. How did one explain one's own fetish? Could one even explain such a thing?

She had no idea why the thought of being tied up and caned and dominated turned her on. And she was utterly terrified to even let Steve suspect her interest. Oh, she'd tried: Thrice, after discovering the Stripped & Whipped website, she'd sneaked into Steve's computer when he wasn't home, opened up the S&W webpage, and left it minimized. Steve had a tendency to leave multiple windows open, even when the laptop was asleep, which made it easy for her. After loading the Stripped & Whipped page, she'd dragged it to the middle of the open tabs, then put the laptop back to sleep. Then she'd waited to see what her husband would say.

He'd never said a word. That surprised her. She'd imagined he'd have been raging about some 'damn internet malware that was downloading filth onto his PC,' but no, he'd not said a thing.

After the third failure, she'd quit and sought her pleasure alone. True, she'd have loved Steve to treat her the way the men in the S&W videos did their female partners—with nipple clamps and gagballs and butt plugs and dripping hot wax and those multitudes of whips and floggers—but watching it being done was the next best thing. And then she'd discovered the pleasures of the Stripped & Whipped chat window; and met her special S&W friend, Thick8, whose avatar was a male crotch cradled in a bulging red codpiece.

Audrey's own screen name was Wellcaned69.

***

Thick8. Now there was a man who understood her. (Audrey could only imagine what he looked like—tall and sexy with Tom Cruise's looks and Dwayne Johnson's physique. Their nightly chats were everything (short of physical contact) that she could expect from a lover. Oh, Steve, oh! Darling, if you could only look in my heart now and see what you're missing!

She reread Thick8's earlier posts on how he wanted to bruise her tender buttocks and clamp her soft breasts and . . . she almost began coming again.

You dirty sex bitch, he'd written, *I'm going to flog your ass raw. I'm going to write my name in red welts on your white ass cheeks. THICK8'S BITCH FOREVER! You belong to me, woman, and don't you dare forget it!*

Then, just as Audrey had been having her third orgasm, Thick8 had abruptly gone offline. Her two follow-up messages had failed to elicit any response. Bad weather conditions most likely.

***

Audrey flinched at a sudden noise, and looked nervously about. *If my husband comes in and catches me wanking to S&M porn, he'll blow his gaskets . . .*

Then, remembering that Steve never came upstairs once out on the porch designing buildings (even though she always left her bedroom door slightly ajar so she'd hear him on the stairs if he did), she relaxed.

Or tried to. About to settle once more into the delights of her body, Audrey found herself distracted by a sudden nasty smell in the air. She sniffed and almost gagged. It was utterly disgusting. *Like the earth is rotting somewhere,* was the best description she could give it. The smell was just abruptly there with her, as intense as the stink in a toilet after one had just defecated.

Oh, my dear Lord in heaven, what the hell is that atrocious reek? Yes, what in God's holy name was it? Had a dog died somewhere on their property?

But then, just as suddenly as it had appeared, the fetid smell vanished. Audrey heaved a sigh of relief. After a few sniffs to assure herself that the terrible odor wasn't going to return, she resumed her masturbation, plundering further delicious sensations from her body.

Thick8 was still offline, but the S&W video was still streaming live.

Onscreen, the woman—now wearing a hood that covered her eyes and ears—had her partner's penis in her mouth. She sucked lustily on the swollen organ, while he yanked on the chain attached to her nipple clamps, making her breasts bob up and down in a fast rhythm. The woman's cheeks were puckered in from her intense suction on his penis.

Audrey tingled at the sight, imagining it was herself sucking Thick8's erection.

Her mind slipped off her chat-lover and onto her real love, her husband. *Ah,* she thought wistfully, *if I could just get Steve to agree to . . . even a hard bent-over-the-knee spanking once in a while would be great.*

Oh yes! She felt herself bubbling up to a fresh orgasm. She dug the yellow vibrator into her sex and stroked herself. Slowly, slowly, sloooowwwly did it . . . And then finally, she was there again in her genital paradise, stranded on a sexual island around which swam sharks of pleasure she desired to have eat her. All the while she kept her eyes on the onscreen couple—the woman bent over, the man licking her anus, his tongue roving wetly up and down in the crack between her buttocks.

Audrey shuddered and tingled in ecstasy. Oh wow!

This orgasm was so mind-blowing that she initially missed the sudden return of the horrible smell from earlier (a smell that now seemed to be coming from within the house). And when she did notice the foul odor, she at first imagined that she was imagining it. *Are there olfactory hallucinations? Oh, I need to research them.* She froze tingling, the vibrator now pressed hard against her slick genital crack, her juices seeping from her body into the sheets, her clitoris aflame with erotic fire.

After a slight pause, she fed the vibrator back into her blossoming sex, one exquisite inch at a time, then slid it in and out. It was a wonderful orgasm, dark and sweet; at once pure and dirty and scary and comforting, like all great sex should be.

She was still climaxing, her body melting into her fantastic universe of herself, when her bedroom door burst open and the monster rushed in at her.

Recognition flashed through Audrey's mind. *It's Brainchew!* She knew the creature from its legend and was shocked that it was somehow now in her bedroom.

Oh, God, help me! Audrey thought in utter terror as she saw its horrible bloody mouth yawn open at her, revealing a disaster zone of jagged uneven teeth. *Noooo!* Her intense fear locked her voice in her throat, her tongue fluttering in her mouth like a bird hovering in a cage with an open door yet unable to free itself.

After a moment, she unfroze from her shock and gathered her breath to scream. By then Brainchew was already flying through the air at her.

Audrey got off a single short, sharp yelp, and then then it was on top of her on the bed and it had a hand over her mouth. Her follow up screams were all muffled to farty protests by its smelly palm, and she was fighting for her life with all of her might, while all the while knowing she was wasting her time.

***

Keeping a firm hand over her mouth, Brainchew dragged the struggling woman to the middle of the bed, beside the strange unfolded black rectangle that flickered with an image.

For the briefest of moments, Brainchew regarded the rectangle's display of two mating humans, wondering why they had no smell to them. Perplexed, it touched the picture with a claw. It concluded that they were real but unreal; imagination.

It returned its attention to feeding on its victim.

This woman had a nice meaty aroma to her, the musky smell of an aroused beast. She also reeked of the man downstairs, the odor of a long association. Her dark hair smelt of sweet flowers. Her dripping sex had a mingled scent of fresh fruit in its musk.

The woman's primary smell at the moment, however, was fear. Fear of itself. It thrilled at her terror, at her hazel eyes almost popping from her face as she squirmed on the bed. She was weak from her earlier pleasures, but still put up quite a fight. She was lying on her back and Brainchew needed to roll her over to get at her brain, something she was resisting with all her might.

(Brainchew had no idea why such a normally easy task as turning someone over had now become so difficult for it to accomplish; even the man downstairs had almost freed himself from its grasp. If the monster had been smarter, it would have understood that its troubles stemmed from its still shrunken, childlike body, with that body's corresponding lack of strength. Now, it merely growled its silent frustration and fought the woman on the bed.)

She was scratching its face and biting its hand that covered her mouth. To quieten her, it ripped a hand across her pale belly. Her blood flew out of the cuts, bright red against the pure white skin. Then she moved at just the wrong moment, and its claws went right through her skin and muscle and deep into her abdomen. Pulling its hand out merely widened the hole.

Her blood spilled everywhere: up over Brainchew, over the machine with the flickering picture, and all over the bed. (Ordinarily, Brainchew would have bemoaned this wastage of her precious body fluid, but now it was no longer thirsty—it had slaked its thirst on her husband—so it let the blood pour.) Soon the bed sheets looked like the top of a chopping block, and both previously lovely pillows looked like raw beef haunches.

The woman was weakening, but not fast enough. Brainchew was losing patience.

It realized she was no longer able to scream the terror in her eyes.

In a flurry of sudden motion, its claws moving like knives, it savaged the woman. First, it ripped her belly completely open and excavated her guts, dropping them in a messy heap onto her 'picture machine.' Then it flipped her over so that the machine (with its strange display of a thin and bald man whipping an obese woman) was now stuck inside the woman's empty belly.

As the pictures flickered inside her, with bright pulses of colored light showing through her skin, the woman jerked weakly in unbelief, twitching along with the screen's flickers as her blood short-circuited its functions. She wasn't completely dead yet, but with her guts draped over her bed, Brainchew knew she was in utter agony, her life all but over. It felt intense delight at having damaged her so badly.

With a wordless howl of triumph, Brainchew finally locked its teeth on the back of her head.

**

Audrey Birchfield's final thoughts as she felt Brainchew's mouth slobber over the back of her head and lock itself in position, were of how stupid she surely must look dying like this, with her laptop stuck inside her belly and showing an S&M scene. She could even hear the whip crack against the submissive's buttocks.

Oh, Steve! Darling, how did this ever happen to us? She had no doubt that downstairs her husband was dead too. Audrey regretted that they'd both expired as meaninglessly as their sex life had.

And then, just as Brainchew's teeth snapped through her skull, she had a moment of the most intense horror imaginable. She was standing at the edge of a pit filled with darkness and with horrible burning eyes staring up at her in anticipation.

And then she was dead, and amidst the munching sound of the monster eating her brain, the laptop buried in Audrey Birchfield's belly played its requiem of her sexual fantasies.

**

After eating the woman's brain, Brainchew fished out her bladder and drank its fill from it. Then it lay on her corpse and rested. While it rested, the three brains it had so far eaten became fully part of it, replacing the body tissue it had burnt to free itself on awakening.

It lay quiescent on the dead woman in her bloody bed. It lay motionless, both its eyes and its mouth closed, almost as if it was dead again. It was neither awake nor asleep, its senses both as alert and as dull as a newborn child's. It smelt the world around it, where everyone was and what they were doing. (At this hour most humans were sleeping; some were making love, some were fighting, some getting drunk.) But for these minutes as it regenerated, none of those mattered.

It even smelt its old enemy Ambrose over in the Sunflower Motel. *AMBROSE*, who twice now had stopped its rampaging and killed it.

But as with everything else, at this moment even its most hated archenemy was irrelevant.

Brainchew might have been utterly useless at reasoning out even kindergarten-level concepts, but there was one thing it knew for sure. Something it was absolutely certain of. Something very relevant to the fate of this slumbering little town of Raynham tonight:

Brainchew *knew* that once it was fully regenerated, it was going to be hungrier than ever. Hungrier than it had been in ages. And it was going to take a whole lot of brains to satisfy that hunger.

Brainchew *knew* it was going to bite open a whole pile of human heads tonight.

CHAPTER 10

Lisa & Carmela

Lisa checked her watch. "Where the hell have those two gotten to?"

"Oh, I dunno," Carmela replied her. "How long's it been since they left? Is it time for us to start worrying yet?"

(After Tiff and Monique had departed to buy gas, Carmela had moved to the van's front passenger seat beside her sister.)

Lisa did some calculations. "Twenty-five minutes." She regarded Carmela with a smile. "No, I guess it's not too long yet. It just seems that way 'cos it's so late at night."

"I'm feeling edgy, sis. Too much can go wrong, and we'll all be stuck behind bars for life."

Lisa grinned and reached over to place a hand on Carmela's arm. "Don't worry, we'll be fine. Once they come back with the gas, we'll park the van as before and that's it. No evidence and no witnesses means no jail sentences."

Carmela nodded. She really wanted to believe Lisa, but found it hard to. And . . . with some shock she realized that this was the closest she'd felt to her elder sister for a long time. For years in fact.

Lisa too felt this sudden surge of tenderness between them. At first it was an uncomfortable feeling, a strange difference from the usual unspoken tension, but then she relaxed into what was after all a pleasant change in their sibling relationship, even if it proved to be only a temporary respite in their simmering emotional conflict.

As others in their circle had long suspected and suggested, Lisa too understood that at a really deep level, Carmela disliked her.

Why? Lisa had no definite answer. Some of her friends said it was merely envy—Lisa had clearly gotten all of their mother's good looks, leaving Carmela to primarily inherit her nervous disposition.

But Lisa herself suspected something else might be the cause of Carmela's unvoiced vexation with her, something a lot darker than mere irritation over the unequal genetic distribution of beauty between them. And what she thought might be the cause was something she couldn't ever voice out to anyone; there was no point stirring up old waters.

Besides, Carmela had been just twelve at the time, still full of wonder and worry at getting breasts and periods, much too concerned about the ghastly new happenings in her own body ("Mom, help! Call an ambulance—I'm bleeding to death between the legs!") and her sudden overnight interest in the boys at her school to notice goings-on at home. At least, Lisa hoped she'd not noticed anything. And then the tragedy of their parents' death had occurred and they'd had only each other since then.

After their parents died, Lisa had put all her energies into looking after Carmela. She'd even put off her own dreams of postgraduate studies in Criminal Psychology and taken her present job, all so that she could give Carmela everything she'd missed out on due to their mother and stepfather's deaths.

Which should have been enough, she felt, to atone for ancient wrongs.

Lisa loved her younger sister with honest affection. She loved her deeply and intensely. Maybe in future, when she got married and had children, she might experience a dilution of her feelings towards Carmela, but for the moment, Carmela was all she had, and she was damned sure going to let the little bundle of nerves know she cared about her.

"Sis?"

Lisa smiled sweetly at her sister. "Yeah?"

"What're you thinking about?"

Beside her, Lisa sensed Carmela as an extension of herself. Less pretty, nervous to a fault (Lisa assumed *she'd* inherited all the 'spunky genes' as well), but nonetheless a part of her. Despite the wall between them, a wall that now felt as flimsy as toilet paper.

Unsure if now was the right time (or if she even dared) to rip through what remained of that flimsy emotional barrier, she sidestepped Carmela's question: "C'mon, girl, lets go look for those two."

"But you just said—"

"A walk will do us good anyway. They might have gotten lost or in trouble."

Carmela sounded unconvinced. "In trouble? How? They're just walking up the road."

Lisa laughed. In that statement she heard a fresh complement of worries for her sister to chew on. No wonder her fingernails never grew. For her own part, Lisa never pondered too much on negatives. She was an 'up' person. Whenever the situation looked dull and grim, she recharged her expectations with positivity, replaying through her mind all that she'd so far accomplished, and using that to illuminate her future. *If I've already done this much,* she told herself, *I'll get the rest done too. It might take a while, but I'll achieve it.* That was Lisa's attitude to life, to keep ploughing ahead even when it hurt. If her unshakeable self-confidence had its roots in how good-looking she was, she'd also added a rubber-ball-like personality. It didn't matter how hard life knocked her down, she was getting up again and coming back at it.

In a way, Carmela's deep-buried dislike of her had also helped toughen Lisa over the years. Looking after a younger sister who constantly gave off a queer vibe of ingratitude had served as practice for dealing with the jerks and bitches of the world.

Lisa felt good all of a sudden. "C'mon, let's just walk," she urged her sister. "It beats sitting here in the van, where we can't even play the radio 'cos we might attract attention."

"If we leave the van and someone comes . . ."

Lisa pushed open the driver's side door, then pointed past Lisa at the other one. "Get out of the van, kid. No one's gonna steal it. There's no gas in the tank, remember?"

"Alright." Carmela opened her door too and climbed down. (She hated Lisa calling her 'kid,' but the five-year age gap between them made the tag legitimate, so she couldn't complain.)

Lisa took her by the hand and pulled her along up the road. The moon was out again, this time accompanied by some stars. The air smelt nice and sweet.

Lisa was still on her 'up.' A positive thing had been accomplished tonight. An abductor and rapist had been killed. Dead innocent women had been avenged; future attacks on other innocents had been prevented. What was there not to be pleased about?

"You seem happy," Carmela said. "You're grinning like a guilty raccoon."

Lisa nodded. "Yes, I am happy. I'd like to be in bed and asleep now though." Then she winced. "Oh shoot! I still haven't yet figured out what to tell Bobby if he's been calling me."

"Just say you went to get laid."

"Be serious."

"Okay, I was only joking, but it really does surprise me how much you like sex. Sis, how come you don't ever get tired of it?"

Lisa clearly heard the envy in Carmela's question, though it was coated with saccharine sisterly sweetness. She ignored it like she always did. "Little sister of mine, there's no such thing as an excess of sexual enjoyment. You need to get your head out of your romance novels and start dating more regularly, instead of waiting around to get suddenly discovered like the New World and married."

"Hey, wait!"

Lisa stopped. She'd been expecting an angry retort, so the totally unexpected alarm in Carmela's whisper felt like walking into a wall. "What?"

"Look!" Carmela pointed inwards, up the driveway they were just passing.

Lisa looked that way, at a white two-story house with a couple of SUVs parked in front of it and a screened-in porch. "What?" she asked again, wondering if Carmela merely felt embarrassed by the sex chat she'd initiated and was trying to change the topic.

"Look upstairs, on that middle window. Is that blood?"

Lisa looked up, and for a moment felt extremely strange. She had a very eerie feeling. On the middle window which Carmela was indicating—a wide one with parted blue drapes—Lisa clearly made out an odd dark splotch that seemed to drip down the glass. Oh, that had to be blood.

"We're too far off to tell," she told her sister.

"Let's walk in then and see," Carmela suggested. "The guy might have murdered his wife."

"We can't," Lisa pointed out. "We can't risk getting involved in whatever's going on in there." She suddenly wanted nothing more than to be well away from this place. The eerie feeling she'd gotten on seeing that dark splatter on the glass hadn't yet left her. She had no intention of walking up this driveway here to encounter some madman with an axe. There were a couple of odd dark splatters on the screen netting too, which Carmela clearly hadn't yet noticed.

"We should do something," Carmela protested. "Like call for help. We could use *their* phones."

Lisa understood that it was the 'nurse' in her younger sister acting up, that programmed desire to help the sick and wounded. *Call for help? Use their phones? Girl, are you serious?*

"Oh no we're not, kid sister," she growled and grabbed Carmela's hand firmly. "You and me, we're getting ourselves well away from here right now. Let the townsfolk find out for themselves whatever's gone wrong in there when the day breaks."

"Lisa, she might still be alive!"

"From the size of that smear—assuming it is blood—I doubt that very much."

She tugged her sister up the road. Carmela went reluctantly, scuffing her soles, peeking back through the roadside trees, trying to keep the white house in view.

As they left the driveway behind them, Lisa's eerie feeling lessened. But not by much. She'd definitely sensed something about that house that didn't feel right. Something they didn't need as an additional complication tonight.

But then, being who she was, Lisa Cole forced her thoughts back onto the business at hand, which was finding their companions and getting themselves all back to the Sunflower Motel and into bed to establish their alibi.

She also began working on a good tale for her boyfriend.

CHAPTER 11

Monique & Tiff

The green pickup truck turned off Broadway and onto Carver Street. A moment later, they rolled past the Sunflower Motel where they were lodging.

Owlsy drove past the next building, a bungalow with all its lights off, then turned up into the driveway of the third house on the right. Monique heard Tiff's almost inaudible gasp as the truck's headlights illuminated the building's small front porch.

It had a blue door.

On seeing that, it was all Monique could do not to swivel in her seat and stare at Tiff. *Oh please, please let Tiff be wrong,* she prayed. *Okay, there is that other test of the porch—if it's damaged on its far side.*

The angle of their approach from the road, however (the house sat on a slight rise), made that impossible to tell without alighting.

"So, ladies," Owlsy said as he slowed the truck, "you're both welcome to my humble abode." He laughed in his beer-sodden way. "Might not look like much from the outside, but it sure is comfortable inside." A queer, almost wistful note now entered his voice. "All my previous lady guests have slept soundly anyway."

Again, Monique resisted the urge to turn around. She could just imagine the expression on Tiff's face now: worms of anticipation writhing over her features like they'd burst through her skin. She doubted she looked any different herself.

Owlsy parked and got out of the truck.

Tiff opened the right rear door to also alight, but once she saw Owlsy was out of hearing range, she leaned forward instead and quickly whispered to Monique, "Remember how we planned it at the gas station . . ."

Monique nodded, said, "I remember," then watched Tiff get out of the truck.

The plan was simple: Tiff would hurry up the porch steps ahead of Owlsy. Then, if this *was* the right house, she'd signal back to Monique who'd tase him.

And then . . .

Owlsy meanwhile, was checking on his load of piglets. His doing so gave Tiff ample opportunity to walk ahead of him to the house, an old stone two-story without a garage. The large yard was surrounded by trees. (As far as Monique could tell this late at night, this tree encirclement applied to every house on the street.) Several lights were on, both upstairs and downstairs (including the porch light), but she saw no movement behind any of the drapes.

Alright, here it goes.

She pushed her door open and leapt down. Her role in this involved getting behind Owlsy without him suspecting anything. And also, if they were doing this, they had to be quiet about it, knock him out real quick and drive off before whoever else was in the house came out to investigate. Tiff had insisted that her abductor had a girlfriend. It wouldn't do to have her see them and try to rescue him.

"Hey, you okay?" Owlsy called to her across the front of the truck. "Come on inside where it's nice and cosy."

"Oh, sure thing, baby," she replied airily. "You just lead the way; I'm right behind you. I can't wait to warm myself in your fire."

Leaving his load of piglets, most of which had now fallen asleep, he stepped towards the house. She followed him. She dragged her feet so that by the time he was halfway to the porch steps she was behind him. Her right hand was in her jacket pocket, gripping the taser. She hoped they wouldn't have to use it though. In her left jacket pocket she felt her gun lightly bump her hip. But that was only for the most extreme of emergencies.

And then she saw Tiff turn on the porch—her plump body perfectly framed by the blue door—and signal to her.

Aw shit, he's the real one?

With a groan of dismay, Monique jerked the taser from her pocket and let Owlsy have it.

***

Tiff saw it—the missing corner square—immediately she stepped up onto the porch. For a moment it felt like she was falling through the gap in the concrete floor.

Oh no—WE HAVE killed an innocent man!

Tears in her eyes, she turned and nodded and waved at Monique. The next moment, she watched Owlsy shudder and jerk like he'd stepped on a downed power line, then crumble forward like a sack of coal someone had knocked over.

He lay there jerking.

She hurried down the steps again.

"Alright, let's get him in his truck!" she whispered breathlessly to Monique. Then she couldn't control her anger at herself any longer and gave Owlsy several hard kicks to the head. "Ugh! I should fucking kill myself. How could I have been so goddam dumb? You goddam piece-of-shit woman-snatcher, you made us kill an innocent man!" Then she stopped kicking the prone Owlsy and stared instead at her companion. "Oh, Monique, how in the world could I have been so mistaken? I . . . we . . . I've made us . . ."

"Don't worry about it," Monique replied gently. "Everyone screws up sometimes." She pointed down at the incapacitated Owlsy. "And while we may not be able to raise the dead, we sure can kill more of the living as compensation."

"Alright, let's load him up and leave."

"No," Monique said, her green eyes regarding Owlsy's house with a deep look of cunning, "I've got a better idea."

"What? C'mon, Monique, we need to hurry. Lisa and Carmela—"

Monique shook her head. "No. Let's do this bastard here. In his own house—in his own basement."

Tiff didn't immediately reply. She too turned to stare at the house.

"It's poetic justice, not to mention wonderfully ironic, if we kill him here, at the scene of his crimes," Monique said.

Tiff turned back to her. "Lisa won't like any change of plans. You know she's already going to nuke out once she hears how I fingered the wrong guy."

Monique frowned. "Girl, don't you dare start turning into Carmela on me. Worrying's *her* job. Reason along with me now: this guy's been killing women for ages and hasn't been discovered, right?"

Tiff nodded; Monique went on: "Which means his basement's a perfect hiding place. Also, we're right next to the motel. We can even park our van here overnight and drive off from here in the morning, with no one the wiser to our visit. And also . . . I don't have a good feeling concerning us going back to that cemetery tonight."

"You're forgetting something," Tiff whispered harshly. "This douchebag doesn't live alone." She gestured to the house. "His girlfriend is likely in there right at this moment, watching us and getting ready to call the cops."

Monique was suddenly conscious that they were standing outside in a wide open space in the middle of the night, the moon shining bright and incriminatingly down on them, with an unconscious man at their feet. She gazed down at Owlsy to confirm the last. He was still out cold, put to sleep by one of Tiff's angry kicks.

She shook her head. "Nah, the girlfriend won't be calling the police. Like us, they're doing something illegal—murder. Imagine how pleased with her big shithead here's gonna be if she calls the cops and they discover his dungeon of doom."

Tiff nodded her agreement. "Okay, so what do we do now?"

Monique gestured over at the blue front door. "We search him for the house keys; they're likely on the ring with the car keys. Then we let ourselves in, carry him into the house and tie him up, then look for his Sleeping Beauty and tie her up too."

"What makes you think she's asleep?"

Monique flicked a bug off her arm. "She must be. She hasn't come to open the front door, has she? And we've been out here for at least five minutes. Who else is gonna be awake at this crappy hour except violent criminals like us?" She faked a yawn. "And once we've got them both secured, we'll drive the guy's truck back to get Lisa or . . . we can call from *their* phones."

"Lisa and Carmela's phones will be switched off."

"Shit, I forgot. Okay, so we'll drive back there. Come on, hurry, let's find the house keys."

***

Owlsy's keys were on the ground under him, spilled from his shirt pocket when he'd hit the floor. The girls carried/dragged him up the steps to the porch, cursing over how damn heavy he was. Then, while Tiff got her breath back, Monique unlocked the blue door, quietly opened it, and peeked in.

"Like we expected, there's no one awake," she told Tiff.

They picked Owlsy up again and carried him inside.

The living room was large, with sturdy old furniture and green carpeting. They dropped their human burden on the living room floor. Owlsy had blood all over his lips and nose. He gasped loudly, like he was having a nightmare, and his eyelids fluttered, but he didn't wake up.

"Okay, you stay here with him while I go fetch Sleeping Beauty," Monique instructed Tiff.

"Why are you changing the plan?" Tiff enquired worriedly. "Look, I don't like this anymore. You said we'd first tie him up and then go after his girlfriend. So why the sudden alteration?"

Monique tried to allay her fears. "I just realized that if we're both humping this son-of-a-bitch down the stairs to the basement, I can't shoot at the same time. And also . . ." she gestured around them, "I don't see anything to tie him up with in here, and searching the house'll take some time."

While smiling reassuringly at Tiff, she retrieved the taser from on top of Owlsy's body (where she'd placed it so they could carry him in) and popped out the spent cartridge. She got out a fresh cartridge from her pocket, reloaded the taser, and handed it to Tiff. "Just give him another dose if he starts coming around."

Tiff weighed the electroshock weapon in her hand. "I don't want to kill him."

Monique considered the look on Tiff's face as she said this— mingled disgust, desire for vengeance, and sadistic lust. She nodded. "No, not yet, we don't. He still has to pay the piper girl her dues, right?"

Tiff reply was a chilling smile.

Monique said, "Don't worry, another dose of energy won't kill him. He's a big strong stud."

She left Tiff there, staring at Owlsy the way an alligator does at a naked swimmer, and, gun in hand, walked through the house looking for the stairs.

She found them and climbed slowly.

The moment she stepped up onto the landing, something cold was pressed against the side of her head, shoved hard against her left ear.

She turned and saw it was the muzzle of a shotgun. *Oh, fuck!*

The young woman pressing the shotgun to her head, said, "Drop the gun, bitch, or I'll blow your brains out here and now."

Wincing, Monique did as she was told.

The woman stepped back a few paces. "Alright, now come closer so I can see you properly."

Monique obeyed and followed her along the hallway.

"Damn, now ain't you a sexy thing?" the woman said. "And a redhead too, for that matter."

Monique looked her captor over beneath the hallway light. The young woman was a short plumpish brunette wearing a pink nightgown. She reminded Monique of Tiff, but was much better-looking. (She also seemed to be about Tiff's age as well.) Then Monique corrected herself: It wasn't that this brunette—actually her hair was honey-colored, but too dark to be considered blonde—was prettier than Tiff. She just had an intense femininity to her bearing— an unspoken female confidence—which Tiff most definitely lacked. She bulged a little too (with an overly generous allocation of bosom and hips, and a thick waist), but she carried the extra weight with verve and swagger.

The other thing Monique quickly realized about this girl currently holding a shotgun on her was that she was dangerous. Very dangerous.

Monique said, "Look, I'm sorry I'm in your house. Owlsy invited me home for a drink or two. I didn't know he had a girlfriend."

The young woman laughed. "Girlfriend? *Girlfriend?* Hell no, I'm his sister Nancy." Then she frowned. "And if my brother invited you home for drinks, what the hell are you doing bringing a gun upstairs? Were you planning on shooting the competition?"

She laughed at Monique's lack of a reply. "Yeah, I didn't believe you either. Alright, girl, turn around. We're headed back downstairs together. And don't you try any stupid tricks. I'd hate to smear your brains all over the stairway walls. Even after cleaning the walls never seem the same again."

This remark was made with such flippancy that Monique shuddered. Then, realizing she was out of options, she turned back towards the stairway entrance.

A moment later, the shotgun's butt hit her in the back of the head and she collapsed unconscious.

***

Downstairs in the living room, Tiff was keeping an eagle-eye watch on Owlsy Pine as he lay unconscious on the green carpet. She'd moved a chair right next to him so she could see his eyes twitch. The moment the man opened his eyes, she was zapping him again.

She'd begun worrying about Monique though. The redhead had been gone for what, like ten minutes now?

Where the heck has she gotten to? Shit, do I have to go and start looking for her upstairs? Oh my God, Lisa must be raving mad by now! Through her decade-long friendship with Carmela, Tiff was well familiar with Lisa's temper when she imagined she'd been thwarted in some objective. Oh, this was going to be bad, bad, bad for the pair of them. *Even if I am righting a huge wrong here, Lisa is going to demand to know why we didn't ask her opinion first. Shit!*

Owlsy groaned then. She looked down and saw that he was just opening his eyes.

"Oh, damn, my head hurts," Owlsy moaned, moving his hands feebly and blinking at the ceiling. "What the hell did you two bitches do to me?"

Tiff prepared to tase him again. Then she'd go upstairs and see what Monique was up to. Hopefully, Monique wasn't screwing Owlsy's whore as pre-payback. Penises gave people strange ideas sometimes.

She raised the taser.

"Don't you dare do it."

It was a woman's voice, but not Monique's.

Tiff froze with her arm raised. "Oh, shit!" she said, turning and staring at the short woman in the pink nightdress now pointing a shotgun at her from the passageway entrance.

"Put the damn taser down," the short woman instructed. Once Tiff had done so, she tossed her a pair of open handcuffs. "Now just be a good girl and put these on yourself. No, no, don't you get up; just stay there in the chair. We're all gonna have us some fun and games tonight."

The short woman waved the shotgun at Tiff. Tiff had no choice but to comply. Handcuffing oneself was a tricky business, she shortly discovered. Being right-handed, she had no trouble with securing her left wrist in one of the metal circles, but cuffing her right wrist proved impossible to accomplish—the chain linking both handcuffs was too short. She looked up and saw that the woman with the shotgun was grinning, like the command to 'handcuff herself' was a practical joke she was playing on Tiff. Then, all at once, the woman stopped grinning and walked over and locked the second metal cuff in place on Tiff's right wrist.

And just like that, Tiff Hooper found herself completely trapped again. She couldn't believe it. She was utterly stumped; she had no idea what to think.

And then Owlsy said weakly, "Nancy, you remember this chick, don't you? Tiffany? The pretty one that got away?"

The woman with the shotgun laughed. "How can I ever forget? You were telling me you were in love with her. I guess Tiff's in love with you too, that's why she came back here. She's gotten all fat now though."

"You know me, I don't mind a little padding on my women. Besides, true love runs deeper than looks anyway."

Listening to their conversation from her chair, Tiff was horrified. *He recognized me from the get-go! He knew who I was!*

"Where's her redhead friend?" Owlsy enquired, slowly making attempts to get up. He made it up to sit on a couch.

"Oh, she's just havin' a li'l nap," Nancy replied.

Owlsy wheezed, then began working some feeling back into his hands. "You know they mistook me for Josh Penham? I think she and her friend even killed Josh."

Tiff saw Nancy was peering at her in surprise and horror. "You did *what?*"

She admitted it. "Y-y-you b-both look so alike . . . h-h-how?" The question just popped out of her mouth; she had to know. "How c-c-come you t-t-two look so alike?"

Owlsy laughed weakly. "We've got the same daddy, that's why."

"H-h-he's your b-b-brother?"

"Half-brother, more like," Owlsy corrected, getting to his feet. He wiped the blood off his face. "Not that anyone knows it though. His ma was married to someone else when my dad knocked her up, so she didn't tell no one who the real father was. I don't think even Josh knows he isn't—shit, you killed him?—I mean, *knew* he weren't Jebediah Penham's son."

"We only know 'cos our daddy told us just before he died," Nancy added. "And that was only 'cos I had a thing for Josh, and he didn't want his kids screwing one another."

"Yeah, pa was conscientious like that," Owlsy confirmed. "As for myself and Josh, everyone just kept commenting on how alike we looked, and then we became friends and we started wearing our hair the same way and all. And most townsfolks mistook us for each other until they got a better look." After stroking his brown buzzcut and mutton chop sideburns, he unbuttoned his shirt. "See—I got a tattoo on my left shoulder which Josh didn't have."

Owlsy was quite recovered by now, Tiff realized to her dismay. He strode back and forth across the living room, then bent and picked up the taser and stared at it in wonder. "Damn, I always see these things on TV and think they're a joke, but they pack a punch like Bobby Lashley just kicked my ass . . ."

He stopped speaking and instead stared wonderingly at Tiff.

His gaze made her uneasy. She felt like forcing her way backwards through the upholstery of her chair till it sealed over her and shielded her from his gaze. It wasn't like he was undressing her with his pale eyes—it felt more like those eyes were knives skinning her alive. Suddenly, in a distressing vision, she was in his brain, seeing herself as he saw her: ripped open, with her guts pulled out and exposed to the air while he sodomized her dying body.

Finally he smiled. "You know, until tonight I never saw the benefits of having Josh and me look so alike you couldn't tell the difference." He stepped near to Tiff, crouched, and put his face close to hers, so she could smell the booze on his breath. "Most times it was disadvantageous, see? Twice I got busted by the cops because Josh was dealing pot, and then another time when he'd gotten drunker than a skunk and smacked up his girlfriend Ida."

"Ida was likely askin' for it though," Nancy said. "She's got a mouth on her like a trumpet; loud like you wouldn't believe. And once she's riled up? Even sailors don't cuss that bad. You need to hear her to believe me."

Tiff nodded. It was all she could do, along with ponder on how what had seemed like such a great plan fifteen minutes ago had now turned so wrong. She stole a glance down at her chain-linked wrists. She saw no way they'd get out of this. According to Owlsy's sister (*sister, not girlfriend!*), Monique was out for the count, which most likely meant that she'd also been disarmed and handcuffed. So for the moment it was all up to herself. What could she do? Scream for help? Who'd hear her this late at night? Or rather, who'd hear her in time? True, Owlsy and Nancy were unlikely to shoot her if she yelled, but she'd certainly not get more than one scream off before they knocked her out, and then anyone who'd woken up would be unable to tell what direction the noise had come from.

Even if someone did come here to investigate, Nancy could simply pretend that she'd screamed herself awake from a bad nightmare.

Oh shit, am I so in trouble again! All I can do now is be strong and try to escape again. An opportunity is sure to come.

Owlsy still had his face close to hers. "What?" she asked him courageously. "Have I got mouth odor?"

In response, he grabbed her left breast roughly and fondled it, then leaned forward and kissed her. She squirmed her mouth away from his, but he followed her, like a leech crawling around her face. She felt she was going to vomit, and did everything she could to hold it back. She already knew he was crazy. If she puked in his mouth . . . he might break her nose in retaliation. And he was likely to have no compunctions about doing so; she'd already kicked him in the face tonight.

Finally, he pulled his stinking mouth off hers, straightened up again, and stepped back two paces. "Oh yeah, Nancy," he told his sister, "my girl here's just as sweet as I remembered. The extra weight ain't submerged her lovemaking talent, that's for sure."

Tiff spat at him.

Owlsy frowned back. "Hey, where'd you two bitches bury Josh?"

Tiff wasn't going to tell him that. Lisa would be furious. "We . . . er . . . we . . ."

"Oh look, she's *shy*," Nancy interrupted angrily. "You killed our brother and now you're too bashful to tell us where his corpse is?"

"I . . . I . . . I . . . don't . . ."

Then, in a character switch so rapid that Tiff was almost uncertain Nancy had just been angry at her, the woman grinned at her instead. Her honey-toned curls seemed to bounce on her head with pleasure; that was how wide her smile became. Her dark eyes gleamed nicely at Tiff, and she said, "Oh, we'll forget that little detail for the moment. See, Tiff, am I glad to see you. You certainly don't know it, but you came back to the family just in time. Owlsy's last girlfriend just died"—she looked fondly at her brother—"again." She shrugged. "His fault; he keeps picking up all these frail types who can't keep up with his hard lovin' style."

"Not like you, baby," Owlsy said, leering at Tiff. "You're a real *hog* of a woman—built for hard usage."

That 'hog' comment stung Tiff deeply. *This goddam douchebag ruined my entire existence—made me eat like a pig to dull the pain—and now he's mocking me with the same weight gain he caused me?* Her initial dread of the sibling pair was now replaced by an even more intense rage at their adding insult to her injury. *If I ever get out of this mess, oh God help me, what I'll do to these two . . .*

Nancy laughed. "Well, once again, welcome back home, Tiffany! C'mon, Owlsy, let's get both of our guests down to the basement motel and settled in."

God no—not the basement! Tiff thought in an attack of almost mind-curdling panic.

"No—!" She'd opened her mouth to scream, but Owlsy had already covered it with a huge smelly hand. And next, all Tiff could do was kick and flail her arms as he effortlessly lifted her out of her chair and bore her away through the house and downstairs.

***

From out of a sphere of padded darkness, Monique felt the shock of something wet splashing her face.

She opened her eyes just as more water hit her face. While blinking the water out of her eyes, and trying to focus through the echoes of the headache that had knocked her out, she slowly put the world around her together again.

Shit! she thought, on realizing she was chained ankles-and-wrists to a wall (her arms stretched above her head) in a room with no windows. *I'm in the goddam basement!*

A surge of desperation filled her, the impotent urge to flee screaming. Panic threatened to unhinge her mind. Her splitting headache reached up for her with its claws of annihilation, forcing her to shut her eyes again. She willed the pain away, then took proper stock of her surroundings.

Yes, she was in *the* basement, which was painted a ghastly yellow that instantly filled her with the urge to puke herself silly. She resisted the urge and continued her desperate appraisal of her captivity:

Tiff was chained on her left. She was topless, stripped half-naked down to the waist. (Monique herself was still fully clothed, though she doubted that would last long. And also, they were both barefoot now, their shoes clearly removed so their ankles could be cuffed.) Tiff looked dazed, like she'd either been slapped silly or drugged. Monique thought she smelt chloroform. Over and above the chemical smell, however, was the reek of raw meat, fresh and wet meat. Monique again felt sick.

Their two captors stood opposite them, in the middle of the room. Neither was currently looking their way. Nancy was whispering something to Owlsy, who'd just replaced the glass from which he'd thrown the water in her face on a metal table.

Monique shuddered when she saw what else lay on the table: an array of kitchen knives and cleavers, medical saws and scalpels and surgical retractors, and household tools like hammers and pliers. All were covered in blood and scraps of gore, as was the surface of the table they rested on. The table next to that one bore both a circular saw and a large chainsaw, both also blood-and-gore-coated.

Seeing those, Monique felt hope seeping from her. She doubted she'd ever be more scared in her life.

She was wrong about that. When Nancy stopped whispering to her older brother and stepped away from him (leaving a gap between their bodies), Monique saw what all the medical instruments and other tools had previously been used on:

On the floor behind Nancy and Owlsy were several plastic buckets. All were full of human body parts. In the nearest bucket, Monique clearly made out several severed fingers sticking out of a mess of long black hair that hung over the bucket's rim, and from which blood was overflowing onto the basement floor.

Monique's horror finally overloaded. She threw up.

Nancy heard her puking and turned around. "Oh, I see you've met my brother's last girlfriend Kayoko. She died just yesterday." Nancy reached down into the next bucket of body parts and pulled up something like a white purse, which, on seeing the small brown circle attached to it, Monique understood was a woman's severed breast.

"Lovely big tits my Japanese girl had," Owlsy said with a dreamy smile, taking the fatty lump of flesh from Nancy and lovingly caressing its blood-smeared surface. He leered at Monique. "Touching this almost makes me want to give her one last fuck."

"Dammit, Owlsy, you're always saying that," Nancy chided softly. "That's why I always advise you not to be in such a haste to wear these girls out. Then once they're dead and gone you start pining after them"

"Yeah, yeah," Owlsy agreed, his expression all sad as he pinched Kayoko's large nipple. "Damn, what a waste."

While speaking, his eyes never left Monique's face, not even when he dropped the severed breast back into the bucket it had come from. "But I got me some good replacements now. Right, Nancy?"

She laughed. "Oh yes you do."

"Fucking let us go!" Monique protested in a panic. "You'll never get away with this." Beside her, she was aware of Tiff's parallel horror, but Tiff still wasn't saying anything yet. (Maybe she was in shock at being re-abducted?) "Let us go, damn you!" She pulled and kicked against her chains, but her actions were wasted violence that merely chafed the sensitive skin of her ankles and wrists. And in the position she was, stretched out, with her hands raised well over her head, her arms had already begun aching.

Nancy grinned back at her. "Oh, but *we will* get away with it," she said gleefully. "We've been getting away with it for two whole years now. We only ever pick up out-of-towners like yourselves, or runaways." She giggled. "And . . . disposing of Owlsy's exes? That's the easiest thing in the world, as easy as eating pumpkin pie. See, my brother works at Mr. McKinney's pig farm. We just grind all the bodies up and feed 'em to the hogs there and no one's ever been any the wiser. Of course, seein' as old Mr. McKinney is our Chief of Police's daddy, no one's gonna come around investigating the place anyway."

"Oh fuck!" Monique thought, and promptly fainted.

She was revived by more water thrown in her face.

"We didn't come to Raynham alone," she sputtered as she came to. "Our friends will come looking for us."

"Yes, that's right," she heard Tiff mumble on her left. "Our friends will be searching for us."

Nancy shook her head, then wagged a finger at them both. "Maybe, but if so, they ain't gonna find you. No one can." She smiled smugly at their puzzled expressions. "Girls, you both left your phones turned off—they've no way of knowing where you are." Then her expression turned cunning. "I don't get that though. Why'd you switch off your phones? And don't bullshit us that your batteries are flat—we already checked and they aren't."

Monique stared at Tiff, who stared back at her in equal horror. Each could read the other's mind. *Oh shit! Lisa, you idiot!*

Then Nancy gave a little gasp of horror which made them all look at her.

"What's the matter?" Owlsy asked.

Nancy looked utterly horrified. "Shit! I promised Ambrose I'd call him the moment I got home to let him know I was safe. He must be worried stiff about me! Shit! Shit! Shit!"

And next thing, she turned and dashed off out of the blood-splattered basement. "Oh god, oh god, how'd I forget to call him?"

Owlsy looked after her bemused for a moment, then turned back to his captive audience. "Don't you two worry none about that," he said with a grin. "You know how you ladies act when you're in love. Personally though, I've no idea what she sees in the guy—Ambrose Duggan that is, he runs the Sunflower Motel next door. He used to be an alcoholic, but he's retired from drinkin' now, and he's all of twenty years older than she is." He sighed. "Oh, I dunno, I guess I'll never understand you ladies anyway—maybe Nancy's got daddy issues or something. But the girl, she's got such a thing for Ambrose like I ain't *never* seen before." He peered intensely at Tiff, who reflexively cringed back from him, though the wall behind her meant there was nowhere for her to go. "Damn, I wish I could have a woman love me that wholeheartedly. And Nancy ain't faking it either—she's so much in love with that Ambrose Duggan fellow that she'd convert to alcoholism herself if he ordered her to. I mean, I just don't get it: she cares more about him than she does about me, her own brother."

Listening to Owlsy's rant, Monique wondered: *How in the world did we miss the traces of madness in his voice on the drive up here? But that's the genius of the sociopath, isn't it? The fact that, except when under the spell of their mania, they seem normal people.*

"But let's get started," Owlsy said all of a sudden. "Little sister can join in the fun once she's done romancing her sugar daddy."

Grinning, he turned from them and advanced on his tables of tools and surgical implements. "Now, how'm I gonna welcome you both to your new home?" he pondered to himself. "Which'll be best: the pliers, or a scalpel, or a little skinnin' action?" He looked back over his shoulder. "For you, Tiffany, my runaway bride, I need something extra-special to welcome you home again. I mean, I already told you—*you know* how much I just hate ungrateful women in relationships. I gave you a good home here; I fed and unclothed you, gave you sex whenever I wanted it, and you didn't appreciate my love. You ran off and left me miserable and helpless . . ."

He began crying, blubbering his eyes out. Then he once more turned away from them and began muttering to himself, while picking items off the table and replacing them again and shaking his head in frustration. "Nah, not this one. Nah, this one ain't right either . . ."

Monique looked from the maniac in front of them, to the ranked buckets containing the remains of his most recent 'love affair,' to Tiff's terrified eyes.

"This is worse than being in an Eli Roth movie," she whispered to Tiff. "What the hell are we gonna do now?"

"Pray for a goddam miracle," Tiff whispered back in a completely hopeless voice (manacled hand and foot like they were, they clearly weren't going anywhere), "and hope God's not too busy answering prayers on the other side of the world at the moment to save us both."

"Tiff, how come he's so talkative now?" Monique whispered. "You said that last time he hardly said a word to you."

"I don't frigging know, okay!?" Tiff exploded. "Maybe it's because he's got two of us this time, or maybe it's because he's been drinking! Or, maybe, the jerk has a special liking for redheads and he's utterly delighted to meet *you!?*" (Though still whispering, she was gushing the words out like a tap, clearly close to a mental crack-up.) "How the hell should I know? What am I—his wife!? Just wait a few days, he'll get used to you too and quieten down again."

"Shush—he'll hear you!"

"I don't goddam care!"

"Well I do." Monique did. Owlsy overhearing them might mean even more pain and suffering, and from every appearance, they were already in for a hefty dose of both. Then she saw that their captor had turned from his tool table and was regarding them both coolly, Tiff in particular.

Oh hell, he heard us discussing him.

"Last time you were here I had real bad bronchitis," Owlsy informed Tiff. "Damn sore throat alone was so bad, I could hardly say a word for a week. It's also why I wore that damn mask so I didn't infect you too. And it's the reason too why Nancy never came down into the basement while you were here back then. The silly girl was so scared of catching what I had, she avoided me all week except when she was broke and needing money." He looked pained all of a sudden. "See, that's the sad thing about you women: Now, if it was *Ambrose* that had gotten sick like that, Nancy would have been all over him with honey drinks an' home remedies, fussing and nursing him back up onto his feet again. She'd even try to catch his bugs so they could be ill together, so she could feel closer to him. Shit!"

That said, Owlsy turned away again and resumed muttering to himself, while contemplating which blade would be best to cut them with.

The two women stared at themselves again, wordless this time. After a while Tiff began crying. The only reason Monique didn't cry also was because she knew it was a waste of emotion.

CHAPTER 12

Ambrose

Unable to sleep, Ambrose Duggan made his way downstairs. He wasn't sure why he'd left the comfort of his bed, had no idea why he was suddenly so insomniac. Nowadays, sleep came easy to him. He'd fall into bed at the end of a long hard day serving the motel's guests, and before he could even begin counting sheep, he was out.

But tonight? Tonight felt different in some ineffable way. It had a heavy and ominous atmosphere to it, the feeling of lots of strange and evil goings-on, but all happening just beyond the reach of his perception.

Like the Devil's having a party I ain't invited to, he thought as he stepped off the bottom stair and into the reception building's inner hallway.

The hall seemed even darker than he'd left it, but for some reason he couldn't find the light switch. Noting the oddity of this, but not finding it really significant, he decided to just walk through the hallway to the lobby. Opposite him, the lobby door was a soft lambent rectangle, its shape filled in by spillage from the parking lot lights.

Ambrose crossed to it. Standing there framed within the wall, he discovered to his horror that the front lobby door was open. He hurried over to it.

"Oh heck." The door casing was all buckled up like someone had rammed a car into it. And he'd been mistaken: the door itself hadn't been opened. It had been ripped off its hinges and thrown out into the parking lot, where it lay in separate parts of metal framework and shattered glass.

After standing on the reception building's front steps for a moment scratching his beard in confusion and staring out at the destroyed door, Ambrose turned and dashed back into the lobby for his shotgun. This was kept in the rear of the big reception desk.

But something was wrong. Right as he turned the side of the desk, a smell hit him like a punch to the gut—a smell so vile, it was all he could do not to keel over retching.

What the hell?

Ambrose knew that smell better than he knew his own name: Brain-frigging-chew! *Aw shucks! It's back again? But it can't be!*

He stepped into the space behind the reception desk and reached into its topmost shelf for the shotgun. The weapon wasn't there. Thinking he'd unknowingly pushed it farther in, he felt deeper into the enclosure, then peeked inside.

The shotgun wasn't in there anymore.

Pulling his head out again, Ambrose suddenly found himself in the grip of a terror like he'd never known before. Brainchew was practically invulnerable. Then he remembered (how had he forgotten?) the antidote to Brainchew.

The knife! The knife! Where'd I put the stone knife?

Yes, where was the ancient relic that had been found along with the monster?

Try hard as he might, however, Ambrose simply couldn't recall where he'd kept the damn knife. Yes, he'd hidden it away somewhere so the cops couldn't take it from him, but where? He found it simply unforgivable, that he couldn't remember where he'd kept something so valuable; it was like losing a billionaire's last will and testament written in favor of oneself.

Where the heck did I hide the blasted thing? Did I put it in with those old crates in the storeroom, or . . . she-it! Oh, please don't tell me I accidentally threw it out with the trash! No I didn't, I'm sure of that—I remember showing it to Crystal about three months ago, when we were debating over what the runes on it meant. But after that. . . . It's not in the bedroom, that's for sure . . . so where?

Brainchew's stink was everywhere now, its 'rotting earth' reek like earthworms burrowing through buried meat. The fetid odor even seemed to seep from the cubbyholes where the motel cards where kept. But of the monster stinking up the place, there was no trace.

Perplexed and worried, Ambrose looked across the lobby, out to the crashed door on the lot floor. Was that someone's scarf beside it? Then a gust of wind picked up the blue strip of fabric, flapped it like a wing, and carried it off into the darkness. As it blew away, Ambrose imagined he saw drops of red on it.

He turned from the door, still racking his brain as to where he'd kept the stone knife needed to defeat Brainchew now. Where the hell was it? While he pondered this, the creature's obscene stink thickened in the lobby. Its smell seemed to fall on him in waves. This sense of a dousing from above grew so intense that Ambrose imagined the monster was hanging overhead and tilted his face up to look for it.

There was nothing up there. The ceiling was as bare as his mind was concerning Brainchew's whereabouts.

Then, just as he was about lowering his eyes again, he sensed the rush of something big and gray and powerful passing in front of him.

He quickly looked down to see what it was, but it was gone, vanished out into the night. In addition to its trail of stink, however, it had left bloody footprints in its wake, large three-toed footprints that clearly weren't human.

Those were Brainchew's footprints.

And then, a desperate female scream came from outside: "Help, Ambrose! It's got me!"

That's Nancy yelling! Brainchew's got her!

Ambrose broke into motion. He dashed around the side of the reception desk and charged for the door. Then, just before exiting, he remembered he needed a weapon. He paused.

Outside and unseen, Nancy was screaming, "Oh God, no! NOOOO!"

Ambrose looked around, grabbed the first thing he noticed that had some weight to it—a carved Red Indian statuette—and ran out of the door.

Nancy's screams were coming from around the right edge of the building. Ambrose hurried around that way.

Brainchew and Nancy were on the lawn which separated the reception building from the front block. Brainchew had ripped the fish-shaped fountain out of the ground and was smashing Nancy's legs with it. Nancy lay naked and spread-eagled on the flooded grass, her entire body below her waist a bloody pulp. Her cries of agony were loud enough to wake the dead down in the Pleasant Street Cemetery.

All of a sudden, Nancy shrieked so loudly that Ambrose dropped the statuette he was holding and covered his ears instead.

As she screamed, she wept. Like missiles, her words penetrated Ambrose's auditory blockade of them. "I'm dying, darling! I'm dying!"

Brainchew was still busy pounding Nancy Pine to mush. It was up to her breasts now.

Ambrose felt paralyzed. Nancy was clearly beyond any help, but, combined with the monster's evil stink, her goddam yelling was driving him nuts. He could feel the noise fraying his sanity, feel himself going crazy—it felt like his nerves were peeling away from their connections in his brain and unravelling.

This had to stop. Ambrose unblocked his ears, picked up the Indian carving, and ran over to Brainchew's side.

There, after a brief look at Nancy's pleading face, he raised the statuette and slammed it down on her head. She still didn't shut up, so he struck her with it again. Then again and again and again, till her entire face was a flat mess like raw hamburger patty, a mess flanked by honey-colored curls.

Then, now that she was properly dead, Ambrose stared at his reddened hands in horror. *What the hell did I just do? What the hell did I just do that for? I'm supposed to kill the damn monster, not her! I love her!*

He walked forward through the mess of Nancy's body, her mangled flesh sticking to his feet. He stopped at the spot where the fountain had been uprooted and bent to wash his hands clean of Nancy's blood in the gushing water.

That was when he felt Brainchew's horrible rubbery lips wrap themselves around his head like warm putty. (In his sorrow and horror at murdering Nancy, he'd forgotten all about the monster.)

His eyes widened in terror: *NOOOOOOOOOO!!*

***

"NOOOOOOOOOO!"

Ambrose woke up mumbling his protests into his darkened bedroom. He lay there reentering the real world, beads of sweat on his forehead, scared to move.

Oh, thank heavens, it was just a nightmare.

But the nightmare had been a horribly vivid one. Especially the part about him not saving Nancy, but instead helping Brainchew kill her. Remembering that brought a sour taste to his mouth.

He reached over and flicked the reading lamp on. He checked the time. It was 01:05. *I've only been asleep for thirty minutes?*

Clad in just his pajama bottoms, he sat up in bed and took a few deep breaths, waiting for his pounding heart to calm. By the time it had done so, he realized he wasn't likely to get back to sleep again any time soon. Just like in the nightmare, the night now felt sinister to him, the darkness outside his bedroom window full of eerie foreboding. He knew it was merely the nightmare working on his subconscious, but he couldn't help feeling that way.

He got out of bed and walked over to the bedroom door to turn the room lights on. He had to confirm something. One aspect of his bad dream really worried him—the fact that he'd been unable to find the stone knife which would kill Brainchew. True, he'd hidden it from the police and pretended he'd lost it, but he knew where it was (something he'd later admitted to Chief of Police Tina Kravitz).

He crossed from the door to the wardrobe and pulled out a small attaché case from the recess at the top of the wardrobe. He carried the brown case across to his bed and sat and opened it up.

Like he'd known it would be (despite the dream claiming otherwise), the knife was still in there, wrapped in its accompanying leather scroll of indecipherable script.

Ambrose unwrapped the weapon, then held it up to the light and examined it. The knife was fashioned—both blade and grip—from a single piece of dark gray rock. It was however nothing like the crude stone blades of primitive cultures. This one displayed exquisite craftsmanship; from the sharp, double-edged blade that could cut paper as easily as it sliced through skin and muscle, to the strange runes etched into its surface, runes that covered it from the tip of its blade to the base of its handle.

Ambrose wrapped the stone knife up again and put it back in the brown attaché case. One thing he'd discovered while studying the knife was that the writing carved on it was a exact duplicate of that on the leather scroll. But as for what it all meant . . .

He put the case away again in its recess above the wardrobe, then yawned and stretched. He waited a moment afterward to determine if he yet felt sleepy again. He didn't, so he pulled on his pajama top and some slippers, opened his bedroom door, and headed downstairs to the lobby.

Ambrose didn't feel like either watching late night TV or reading a book, so he'd decided to do some work: review the coming week's reservations and balance the Sunflower's accounts. He'd originally planned to do it tomorrow—actually later today, now that it was past twelve—but since he'd promised Nancy he'd take her out of town for lunch, he figured he might as well do his bookkeeping now.

While descending the steps to the ground floor, his mind returned to his dream. Brainchew. Hmmm, he was glad he'd seen the last of the creature. Yes, it had killed his entire family and made him start drinking like a fish, but he bore the evil thing no further ill will, so long as it stayed buried in the Pleasant Street Cemetery.

So long as it stayed there.

Shit, Ambrose mused, *the damn demon doesn't even belong to this town anymore.* (Ambrose had always considered Brainchew a runaway from Hell. He couldn't, for the life of him, fathom where else something that evil could have originated.)

Like just about everyone else in Raynham, Ambrose had been delighted when billionaire Ellis Drake had offered to buy Brainchew from them. And they'd all been even more delighted when the town authorities had agreed to sell it to him. So, yes, Brainchew now belonged to Mr. Drake, who, in Ambrose's humble opinion, clearly had more money that sense, since he wanted to move the monster out to his house, a large mansion out west near Springfield.

But—and Ambrose winced at this thought—*Brainchew, of course, is doing its utter damnest to thwart leavin' us in peace here. She-it. Mr. Drake's already carted the damn demon away twice, only for him to find it magically out of his house by the next morning and back over here in our cemetery again.*

Ambrose scowled as he reached the bottom of the stairs. *Well, it's welcome to stay in its grave here till Mr. Drake works out how to take it away for good. I don't give a rat's turd so long as it doesn't show its ugly mug aboveground.*

On that thought, a deep chill ran through him. This sudden and inexplicable feeling of icy water dripping down his spine subtly reinforced the impression of tonight's weirdness that had accompanied his waking.

Then Ambrose's cellphone rang upstairs in the bedroom. Black Sabbath pumping out mini-decibels of *Paranoid.*

Ah, that'll be Nancy, he thought with a grin. *She's only just remembered she promised to call me.*

He returned upstairs to fetch the phone, which stopped ringing before he entered the bedroom, then started again.

It wasn't Nancy Pine calling. It was Crystal Parr.

Still grinning, Ambrose accepted the call. *I wonder why she's calling at this hour.*

"Hi, baby," Crystal said, sounding a little tipsy. "How's tonight going? I just called 'cos I thought you might be lonely."

"I'm fine," Ambrose replied while descending the stairs again. "Thanks for thinking of me. And you, what're you up to, girl?"

"Oh, I've been getting humped like a rabbit. Ambrose baby, these rich Texans sure as hell can fuck! It felt like they were drilling me for oil. And they come like oil wells too." She giggled. "At the moment, I'm doing stretching exercises."

"Stretching *what?* Crystal, you don't sound like you're in a gym."

She giggled, and he heard her slurp something before replying, "No, no, no, you silly man, nothing like that. I'm stretching my asshole."

"What?" Ambrose had just stepped down off the staircase. Feeling suddenly overwhelmed by this phone call that was topping up tonight's oddity, he sat down on the bottom step. Staring through the dimness at the door to the lobby, he thought, *Oh, dear Lord in heaven, why in the world did you give me a prostitute as my best friend?*

But of course he'd never say that aloud. Instead he asked, "Crystal, hon, why the hell are you stretching your anus at a quarter-past-one in the morning?" He didn't really want to know though.

"Oh, it's 'cos of Jimmy and his friend Cody."

She paused there. Ambrose didn't say anything. Crystal made several drinking slurps then continued over the line, "See, Jimmy and Cody both wanna fuck my ass at the same time." She giggled. "Personally I think they just wanna rub their cocks against each others' but don't wanna be thought gay. I keep getting this feeling that they're actually in love with each other, but . . ." She burped. "Anyhow, I told them to let me clean up first, then I came to the bathroom and I started fisting myself just to loosen up my ass a li'l bit so I don't tear back there, you know? And then I remembered you, and how you're likely to be so lonely now that I'm out of town, and so . . ."

"I'm not lonely. Nancy came over and we—" Ambrose shut up, instantly regretting that he'd introduced Nancy into their conversation. He just knew what Crystal was going to say now.

She didn't disappoint him. "Nancy Pine?" The concern for him in her voice was instantly replaced by a clear thread of anger. "Ambrose, how many times do I have to tell you that she's crazy?"

"She don't seem crazy to me," Ambrose replied, immediately on the defensive. "Crystal, how can you advise me on my relationships, when by your own admission you're about to be double-teamed in the same hole by two men?"

"That's different; that's business. I'm providing a sexual service. My relationship with Jimmy and Cody is with their dough and their dicks. Once they come, I'm gone, out of their lives till they want to come again."

She sounded so convincing over the phone that Ambrose almost laughed. Almost. He wished she'd just accept Nancy Pine for the nice young lady she was. And he hadn't yet even told her they were officially dating yet.

"Ouch!" Crystal yelped suddenly.

Ambrose was instantly worried about her. "What?"

"I just stabbed my fingernails into the wall of my rectum. That hurts."

"Oh." He felt foolish for worrying.

"O.K.," Crystal said, "that's more than enough widening of my butthole for the moment. Where's the goddam KY? Hey, Ambrose, hold on a sec while I finish off my banana daiquiri." Sultry slurping sounds were followed the sound of her smacking her lips. "Hey, Ambrose, you still on the line?"

"Go on." He looked glumly around the dark hallway, his eyes flicking from one piece of its sparse furniture to the next. For a dire moment, he imagined that one of the hall's distorted shadows was Brainchew. He scratched an itch in his crotch.

"See, hon," Crystal went on, "it's not that I'm against you finding a woman. Let me put it like this—I'm your best friend, right?"

"Yeah, you are."

"Alright then. Then you'll agree too that as your BFF I simply always want what's best for you, right?"

"Yes, yes. But you sound like my mom trying to veto my prom date 'cos she ain't hot enough."

"You're just hearing me wrong, that's all. I want you to marry a really good woman. You deserve someone nice in your life. Baby, I'd happily marry you myself if it wasn't for this job of mine. You do understand that, don't you?"

Ambrose nodded into the darkness. The cellphone felt uncomfortably warm and clammy in his grip.

"You still there?"

"Yeah, I'm admiring the shadows. They look sexy as hell tonight. Crystal, you know you could just quit hooking. We could run the motel together. You know how I'm always up to my neck in work here and could use some help."

"Ha ha ha! Ambrose darling, I'm a pussy businesswoman and proud of what I do. I fuck for a living and I don't intend to ever stop, so I can't marry you. But"—she rushed on—"I also don't want you making any silly romantic mistakes."

"Crystal, how exactly does sweet little Nancy Pine, the ultimate 'girl next door,' qualify as a 'silly romantic mistake?'"

"I don't trust her. Now don't get me wrong—I don't suspect she has a boyfriend hidden away somewhere and she's just after you for your money, or even that she'll cheat on you, but . . . she's just *wrong* in some funny way that I can't put a fingernail on. That kid's just somehow *off*. And besides, she's much too young for you anyway. Sooner or later she'll—" She broke off talking for a moment and Ambrose heard another voice seep over the phone, a gruff male one, indistinct but urgent. "Oh, they're calling for me from the bedroom, Ambrose. I gotta go fuck, wish my asshole luck. Dammit, where's my tube of lube?"

Ambrose was relieved. Her hanging up meant he didn't have to listen to her badmouth his young girlfriend anymore. "Alright, so have fun, and I'll—"

"Wait, don't hang up yet!" she gasped suddenly. "I almost forgot something!"

"Girl, go service your clients before they refuse to pay you. We can discuss me and Nancy when you get back home."

"No, no, no, it's not that. Last night I had this horrible dream about you. A real nightmare. Brainchew was in it."

On hearing her mention Brainchew, Ambrose felt the return of his previous dread and horror. Immediately, the previously benign hallway shadows all seemed alive and malevolent, like they were watching and stalking him. He tried to shrug his unease off. "Brainchew? C'mon, Crystal, it was just a dream."

"Yeah sure, but it was really vivid-like, ya know? Just listen—here's how it went: You were in a restaurant, and Nancy was there too, along with another girl with huge blue eyes and long black hair down to her feet, hair so long it covered her entire body. And then,"—in the background the gruff male voice called her again—"anyhow, Brainchew was dressed in a tuxedo and was sitting in the restaurant too and was ordering and eating endless plates of brains. And Nancy was the waitress serving brains to everyone, only her head was empty 'cos Brainchew had already eaten *hers*—I mean eaten her brain." She giggled. "Okay, I'll admit it sounds damn silly now that I'm telling it to you on the phone, but it was horribly vivid when I woke up. I ain't been scared out of my sleep like that in a long time. Ambrose, are you still listening to me?"

"Yes, yes, I am. Like you said, it's just a—"

"Alright, baby, I'm off to use my skills to pay my bills. Gotta run. Bye!"

She smacked him a kiss over the line. Then she yelled (not to Ambrose, but to the man calling her in the background), "I'm coming, Cody darling! I got my ass loose and juicy as my pussy for you guys! Oh, I was just talking to my accountant!" and hung up.

Cellphone in hand, Ambrose didn't move. His ass felt dead on its seat. It wasn't that he took Crystal's dream about Brainchew seriously, or that he put too much credence in dreams in general, but . . . *Both of us having gory nightmares about the monster?*

There was such a thing as too much of a coincidence.

Maybe, he thought grimly, *maybe I better take this coincidence seriously.*

He got up off the bottom step and ascended the stairs again. He'd decided to get the knife out of its case and keep it with him downstairs while he checked his books. There was no chance in hell of him falling asleep now.

As he entered his bedroom, his phone rang again.

A smile spread over his lips. This time it *was* Nancy.

"Hi, darling," she gushed breathlessly, "I'm so sorry I forgot to call you. Oh, I can be such an airhead sometimes."

"That's alright." After his vivid nightmare and Crystal's phone call, it was comforting to hear her voice. Finally someone *normal* to talk to. At least Nancy wasn't filling her ass with KY Jelly and having sex with anonymous (and possibly gay) Texans with too much money.

"Hey, I didn't wake you up, did I? It's been quite a while since I got home, and Owlsy was delayed, and I don't remember why I didn't call, and—" (Ambrose had noticed that grammatically, Nancy Pine was a bit of a chameleon, with her speech altering to match her company. [Occasionally, this also seemed to depend on how excited she was.] With her brother Owlsy, for instance, who mostly spoke the very loose informal (almost backwoods) lingo they'd inherited from their dead parents, she adopted the same. When at her florist job or with him or with friends, however, she spoke 'normally,' with little drawling or dropped consonants and vowels. Nancy's quirky, unpredictable way of talking was one of the many things Ambrose found so delightfully charming about her.)

"No, it's okay," he replied. "I was already awake. Had a bad dream."

"Yeah? I like dreams. What was it about?"

Ambrose wasn't about recounting it to her. Not that he'd been bashing her head in. Oh no. So instead he laughed and said, "Don't worry about it, sweetheart. It was just some stupid nonsense. There was most likely too much cheese in my last pizza."

She laughed too, in that tinkling way she had that filled him with so much joy, joy like Crystal too once used to give him. For a moment he felt sad that he'd sobered up and could no longer appreciate what Crystal could give him. But then, he reasoned, he needn't feel any guilt over it. Even if they were no longer 'friends with benefits,' they were still friends, and best friends at that, much closer than before now that sex no longer interfered with their communication of emotions.

But how to tell Crystal about he and Nancy? That was the sticky question.

He said, "So are we still on for tomorrow?"

"You mean later *today?*"

"I keep forgetting it's already Sunday."

"Have you cleared it with Michelle yet?"

"No, but I will. If her dad's still poorly, I'll ask Ida to mind the reception desk for me."

"Ida Green? Josh Penham's Ida? I don't think she'll be in the mood."

Did he just imagine it or was there something odd in Nancy's tone as she said that? "Why? I mean, how can you be sure of that?"

She sighed. "Oh, it's just a feeling I have. You know how her mum's Parkinson's gets really bad at times. And since it's Sunday, she'll want Ida to take her to church and maybe to visit her friends afterwards."

Nancy laughed, which oddly, again sounded forced to Ambrose. *What's the matter with her? Or am I just being overly suspicious now that Crystal's seeded ideas in my head? But suspicious of what?*

"And also," Nancy added, "she'll likely lose you lots of customers. You know how bad she swears all the time."

Now Ambrose laughed. "Yeah, now there you're right—it might not be the smartest of ideas to ask her. But don't worry, sweetheart, I'll find someone to man or woman the desk, and you and me, we'll drive out of town and have fun, just the two of us."

"Okay, baby, I gotta go to bed now. I feel like I'm out on my feet. I just served Owlsy his dinner and . . ."

Once again, Ambrose had the feeling that she was lying to him. And once again he put it down to Crystal's phone call.

"Love you, darling," Nancy said and blew him a kiss over the line.

"Love you too, sweetie-pie, kiss you soon," he replied and hung up.

Then he got down the case with the stone knife from over his wardrobe and opened it up again.

Once he had the weapon in hand, he felt an immediate return of his anxiety. It was utterly preposterous.

Alright, that does it, Ambrose decided. *I'm having an attack of nerves here. Me and Crystal's dreams don't mean shit. Brainchew ain't out of its grave, and hell no, Nancy Pine ain't hiding any dark secrets from me.*

Despite which thoughts, he still took the stone knife with him when he went down the steps for the third time that night.

CHAPTER 13

The Monster

At almost the exact second that Ambrose Duggan placed the stone knife on the top shelf in the rear of the reception desk, Brainchew 'woke up' again.

The creature, which for the past ten minutes had lain motionless, draped over the mess it had made of Audrey Birchfield, sat up in her blood-soaked bed. (The laptop stuck in Audrey's belly had long ago short-circuited and gone dead from all her body fluids that had dripped onto it.)

Brainchew stood up on the bed, its foot claws ripping deep holes across the mattress. Once upright, it examined itself, extending its bloody arms and flexing its muscles.

Yes, it felt 'right' now. Its body was once again the proper size; that of a short stocky man. Most important of all, its neck no longer felt the burden of the enormous head it supported.

However, the monster's restoration had come at a price. If Brainchew was stronger now, it was also much hungrier. Though essential, its rest of self-repair had used up a lot of its energy.

But . . . (and a thrill of evil joy surged through its tiny mind at this consideration) there was food—delicious hot human brains—nearby. It could smell them.

While one of its three-toed feet pressed Audrey's emptied head into a hole in her bed, Brainchew scanned the meaty scents of the night. The human smells came from near and far, from far and wide. Almost all of them came from within houses, were the odors of people behind walls and doors and in their beds, either asleep or mating.

For a frustrated moment, Brainchew's delight at the abundance of its potential feeding was dampened by its hatred of locks.

Then, through its gloom burst two scents it had already encountered: the two females from the vehicle parked down the road. The two women had passed the house while it had been regenerating. Currently they were about half a mile away; a short enough distance for it to cover.

Energized by bloodlust, Brainchew leapt down off the bed.

It grinned, blood and spittle dribbling from between its teeth and running down its elongated chin to splatter its muscular belly. Yes! And after eating those two women's brains, it would search out their two companions. It could smell those two also, they were in a house close to its enemy, Ambrose.

AMBROSE! For a moment, Brainchew's horror and dread of its arch-nemesis filled its soul. It howled soundlessly into the silent night, in its rage spewing chunks of gore through the air of the blood-spattered room, its mouth splitting wide to reveal the disarrayed rows of its shark-like teeth, those teeth like rows of random-sized claws and hooks set in alien flesh.

AMBROSE! AMBROSE!! KILL . . . KILL!!!

Utterly incensed and filled with hatred for Ambrose Duggan, Brainchew flailed about the bloody bedroom and slashed at objects at random. Then, to give full vent to its wrath, it dragged the dead woman's corpse off her bed and got to work savaging it further. It tore deep rips through her skin. It dug its claws into her muscles and organs and pulled them apart. It shredded her dead flesh into little chunks of mince and ribbon-like strips.

Then the monster froze in shock. Its anger dwindled into surprise. It saw . . . *itself?*

***

Brainchew stared entranced at its reflection in Audrey Birchfield's dresser mirror. It had been crouching over her defleshed body when it caught sight of its duplicated self. (Audrey's corpse was little more than bones now, its previous clothing of meat and skin scattered about the bedroom.)

Brainchew remained frozen in that crouched posture.

It was utterly confused. Was this another of its kind it was seeing? This 'other' also had the same HUGE head as itself, the same rough gray skin now coated over with blood, the same . . .

145

The creature in the glass seemed perplexed too, the gray flesh around its sunken red eyes creased by thought.

(Brainchew was used to seeing its reflection in glass windows, but those it easily understood to be 'false.' Those reflections were mostly unclear. They were vague and shadowy, like gods or spirits. [Brainchew considered window glass to be a type of hardened air.] It had also once seen its reflection in a pond surface. That had seemed almost as real as this one, until it had touched the surface of the water. Then the image had vanished. But this one . . .)

It touched the mirror, then scratched it. The glass was marred by its claw, but the 'other' remained unaltered, and . . . as it had touched the mirror, Brainchew had noticed the 'other' also drop the severed arm it held and reach forward to touch also. So maybe the 'other' had scratched the mirror, not itself.

It was aware of its two female targets getting farther away as it delayed, but it felt compelled to resolve this puzzle of this 'other' who looked exactly like itself. And even behaved like itself.

Was this 'other' trapped? Did it need its help?

The monster's tiny mind was trapped by the puzzle, tied in intricate knots by a simple trick of the light it couldn't comprehend.

All it could do was stare and stare and stare at its reflection.

So, while Lisa and Carmela Cole strode briskly up North Main Street, unaware that death had their scent in its nostrils, death's instrument stood entranced in its most recent victim's bedroom, for the moment unable to hunt them down, unable to free itself from the spell of a simple concept that was nonetheless well beyond its primitive understanding.

CHAPTER 14

Carmela & Lisa

The farther away they got from their van, the more worried Carmela became. She couldn't help herself. It wasn't just the fact that they were the only ones on a road in an unfamiliar town in the middle of the night. Something was definitely wrong; she felt it in her bones. Her memory of the bloody smear on that window they'd earlier passed didn't help calm her either.

"We've been walking for almost a mile now," she told her sister. "I didn't think the gas station was that far off."

"It has to be, we haven't reached it yet," Lisa replied with a grin. "But I know what you mean—even if we've not gotten there yet, our friends should have, and we should be meeting them on their way back."

"D-d-do you think the police got them?"

Lisa shook her head. "It's not against the law to buy gas. No, something else has happened to them." She pulled her pistol out of her pocket, held it up to the streetlight they were walking under, and inspected it. "I hope not, though. I really don't want to have to get rough with anyone else tonight. It'll mess up our schedule, and may possibly even ruin our alibi."

The calmness in her voice angered Carmela. She felt like screaming at her: *HOW THE HELL IS IT THAT YOU CAN'T SEE WE'VE GOT A FUCKING SITUATION HERE THAT NEEDS DEALING WITH, YOU NARCISSISTIC BITCH!*

She didn't scream. In addition to their current location not being a good one for loudly expressing one's emotions, screaming hardly ever worked with Lisa. She just screamed back; and being that they shared genes, both their voices were equally loud.

"Let's keep walking," Lisa said, putting her gun away again. They were at an intersection, with empty road in five directions now instead of two. "They may still be at the gas station."

Carmela didn't reply as they stepped off the curb into the road. Triggered by tonight's events, a familiar thread of resentment was replaying inside her. *This is all Lisa's goddam fault,* she fumed. *Even if, yes, I was the one who mentioned Tiff's desire for revenge to her, she should have poo-pooed it away and told me I was being childish. But no, she had to go all vigilante on me. And see what's happened now? Lisa always thinks she knows it all; she's got everything all worked out. So, big sister, how about explaining where Tiff and Monique are now, huh?*

This wasn't the first time Carmela had blamed Lisa for something turning rotten for them. In this case, though, while she knew she was just worried and overreacting, and was probably being unfair to her older sister, she couldn't help herself. She had too much resentment bottled up.

As Lisa had herself long suspected, her younger sibling's anger with her went back through the layered dust of many years to deep roots in the past.

In Carmela's opinion, her elder sister was responsible for a number of particularly bad occurrences in her life.

And the chain of Lisa's responsibility started with the first—and most disastrous—really bad thing that had happened to both of them:

***

Lisa and Carmela Cole had both grown up in the south Boston suburb of Roslindale, in a nice beige two-story house on Poplar Street.

Their birth father Jack Cole had died when Carmela was two, and she had no memories of him. Her stepfather, David O'Connor, whom her mother married when Carmela was six and Lisa eleven, was the father she knew and loved.

A construction foreman, David O'Connor was tall and dark and muscular and handsome. Carmela was completely smitten with him, and she loved it when people assumed she was his real daughter.

Lisa and Carmela's mother, Mary O'Connor, was a very pretty woman. A nurse by profession, she was slim and graceful and kind. She was a good mother who only wanted the best for her family, and Carmela's childhood was a happy one, even though by the time she was eight she'd already begun showing—by indications of a nervous disposition—signs that she resembled her mother in more ways than one.

Young Carmela's relationship with her adolescent sister, however, was less than pleasant. Although tall, blonde, and undeniably beautiful (in short, everything a younger sister desired to hero worship), Lisa was also as bossy as hell. She was always yelling and threatening a beating (that oddly never came) if Carmela played with any of her things.

'She Who Must Not Be Trifled With,' David O'Connor had already dubbed her after a particularly violent tantrum (which had included a two day hunger strike), over not being allowed to go to summer camp.

Lisa's fledgling attempt at anorexia hit its speed bump when her mother, the eternally-patient Mary, having had as much of her annoying sulking and whining as she could take, dragged Lisa downstairs by her blond locks, then, after slapping her senseless (Lisa was already so weak from not eating for two days that a single blow sufficed), duct-taped her to a dining room chair.

Once she had her taped down, Mary informed her 13-year-old daughter that she wouldn't un-tape her until she began eating again.

Secured like that, her body, legs, and one arm completely taped to the chair, Lisa looked encased in a silver cocoon. (A loop of tape around the wrist secured her 'free' right arm to the chair also, so she couldn't use it to release herself.)

"Dad, help!" Lisa pleaded from her cocoon.

David shook his handsome head. "Sorry, young lady, but I agree with your mother. You need to start eating again."

"I just want to go to summer camp. All my friends will be there."

Her mother smiled coldly at her. "And *you* won't be. And that isn't going to change, no matter what you do in protest. I'm like the US government—I don't negotiate with terrorists, and your mental bombardment is driving me crazy."

For her part, Carmela was amused. She'd never seen her mother this determined before, and watching the Almighty Elder Sister getting her long-delayed comeuppance was great. Carmela couldn't stop giggling. Lisa looked really funny, taped over everywhere with just one arm free.

And then, the tide turned. Lisa seemingly realized something. The belligerent look on her face turned to one of worry. "Mom, what about when I need to go? I mean, to the bathroom?"

Mary smiled back evilly. "Oh, you're not going anywhere for anything, darling. If nature calls you, do it in the chair."

"What?" The horrified expression on Lisa's face was so comical, Carmela began giggling even louder. "Mom, I can't poop and pee in my pants."

"You're going to have to. I've told you: you're not leaving that chair unless you call of this 'not eating' nonsense."

Lisa looked pleading at David. "Dad . . . *please.*"

He grinned back. "It's like your mom says: we both love you a lot and we don't want you looking like a fashion model. So . . ."

Tears filled Lisa's eyes. "Oh, I hate you both!" she screamed.

Lisa stopped screaming. She breathed in deeply, preparing to yell again. Then she gaped in disbelief when her stepfather placed a strip of duct tape over her mouth.

"Mmmph! Mmmph!"

"Sorry, kiddo," he said, "but you're not getting your way this time."

Her mother had since left the dining room. She returned now, bearing a camcorder which she arranged on a stool so it faced her bound daughter.

Smiling coldly, she explained what the camcorder was for: "We're making a home movie of you going to the bathroom in your pants. Then we'll all watch it together with the neighbors."

On hearing that, Lisa's eyes bulged out like frog's eyes over her taped mouth. Carmela watched her expression switch from one of rage to one of defeat as she realized that, yes, her mother really did intend to let her piss and shit herself in the chair, and film it too. And show it to others?

Mary grinned broadly at Lisa. "Okay, darling, just nod at everyone once you feel some pee-pee coming. We don't want to miss a drop of the fun."

Faced with that horrible, humiliating prospect—utterly unthinkable to a teenager—the rebellion ended. Not eating was one thing, making an infant-like mess of yourself with your family watching, and with your mother recording it for posterity, was totally another. That latter was simply not going to happen.

When questioned as to whether she was yet ready to quit her foolishness, Lisa nodded fiercely. Then she dutifully ate the portion of steak, fries, and salad placed before her, agreed to participate in all future family meals, and was promptly released.

Then she went upstairs to her room and concluded her tantrum by shredding her pillow with a pair of scissors. She considered running away from home in revenge, but instead decided to sit in front of her mirror and play princess, and plot her future revenge against the 'wicked old witch,' namely her mother.

(Even by the age of thirteen, Lisa had realized she was beautiful. She'd correctly interpreted the way her stepfather's eyes appraised her as she walked through the house. Should she? Could she? Would she? Maybe, just maybe. In her juvenile mind, it was simply a matter of 'when' not 'how' to make her play for him if she so chose to.)

So, no, Lisa wasn't Carmela's favorite person during their growing years. She pushed and shoved Carmela around a lot and eternally threatened to "beat the turds of stupidity out of your skinny ass."

Then, hooray! At age seventeen, grumpy elder sister went away to university somewhere (UMass Amherst to study Criminal Justice) and finally Carmela had the run of the house.

Being Kid One at home was fun. She was twelve and on the verge of YA womanhood and the world seemed to be her oyster. (Her mother did forget to give her her menses pep-talk, so when her menarche came she thought she was bleeding to death, but other than that everything was fine.) In time with the changes in her body, she was losing her interest in Barbie and switching it to the real-life Ken dolls at school, and wondering how she'd never noticed before she got bumps on her chest (and hair in strange places) how cute Joe and Ricky and Don and Mike and Matt and the other Joe and Gary all were.

It was a fun time for her.

And then Lisa came home for the summer holidays.

Carmela had no idea what to expect. She was worried that Lisa's return to the house meant a resumption of the old order of 'bossiness and total junior sister domination.'

But her fears proved groundless. Lisa was even more beautiful than before, as if going away to college had 'ripened' her into the sexual nymph she'd been destined to be. She seemed cooler too.

And most importantly, she was nicer to everyone. No more sulks or tantrums. (Lisa later admitted to Carmela—condescendingly of course—that she was an 'adult' now, and adults didn't behave like that, screaming at everything, or all the hot boys assumed you were still a spoilt brat and you didn't get asked out on dates.)

So peace and quiet reigned at home, and the summer passed happily enough. Lisa turned eighteen that July and they had a big birthday party for her. She went out on dates and got in on time and everyone, Carmela especially, was happy.

"Oh yes," she boasted to Tiffany 'Tiff' Hooper—the girl who lived next door to them—"I've got the best family in the world." (Tiff's parents were always at each other's throats. Her father was almost always drunk and disorderly [the police kept being called out to their house], and her older brother Tony had recently gotten his black girlfriend pregnant, and their mother was threatening to kick him out of their house if he didn't break up with 'that gold-digging slut.')

***

One hot August night that summer when Carmela couldn't sleep, she went downstairs for a glass of cold water.

Halfway down the stairs, she heard impassioned moaning coming from the living room. "Oh yes! Give it to me like that!"

Wow, it's mom and dad doing it! she thought, an innocent excitement growing in her budding breasts. Her next thought was, *Ha, ha! I'm gonna peek! I'm gonna watch!*

But then she remembered that her mother was away at the hospital on the night shift. So who were the couple making love in the living room?

Even more curious now, she padded downstairs, keeping very quiet, then peeped around the foot of the stairwell.

Ooh. It was Daddy and *Lisa* doing 'it' on the carpet. Lisa was on her back with her legs spread wide and their stepfather was inside her, and Lisa was moaning and gasping and clawing his back with her nails and biting on a finger in her mouth, while Daddy was thrusting away hard between her legs, and . . . Lisa sounded like she was having the time of her life . . . WOW!

It was the most exciting thing Carmela had ever seen. Without realizing she was doing so, she slipped her hands down inside the waistband of her pajamas and began rubbing herself like Tiff Hooper had confessed to her that she sometimes did when she felt 'strange,' usually after listening to her brother Tony and his girlfriend Shaniqua in bed through the walls (even though Tiff wasn't sure how they still did it with Shaniqua's belly so grossly big now.)

So Carmela masturbated to the sight of Lisa and their stepfather having sex on the living room rug, and shortly she exploded in the first orgasm of her life.

Then feeling suddenly ashamed of herself, she snuck away back upstairs to her room before they saw her. Her last view of the couple before she left the living room was of her stepfather ejaculating all over Lisa's breasts.

Her guilt soon passed though, to be replaced by a sense of female accomplishment, as if she'd just been initiated into the cult of womanhood. In fact, she was about going back downstairs to resume watching them when she heard Lisa coming up the stairs. Then she heard Lisa walk past her room and open and shut her bedroom door.

Carmela lay back in bed grinning at the ceiling. She was suddenly very satisfied in an way unfamiliar to a twelve-year-old, and also very tired. She was asleep before she realized it.

The next morning, everything was like nothing had happened. They all had breakfast together, then David left for his construction site and Lisa went out to see a matinee with her friends, and their mother went up to bed. Carmela was left alone with what she'd discovered: both that Lisa and David were having an affair, and also that she'd felt something special herself last night.

She decided not to tell her mother anything. By now she was already a nervous enough individual to dread the threefold drenching of rage certain to follow her revelation. And (and she later recognized this as her primary motivation for her silence), if she told her mother what she knew, it would stop, and she'd not have any more chances to observe them.

So it went on that summer. Each time Mary O'Connor worked the night shift at the hospital, David and Lisa worked overnight on the living room floor, once they thought Carmela had gone to bed.

Carmela meanwhile, perfected both her spying and masturbation skills. She told Tiff Hooper (now her best friend) what was going on at home. (Carmela's mother called the Hoopers 'suburban white trash' and didn't really approve of Carmela being friends with their daughter, but both girls attended Washington Irving Middle School, so it couldn't be helped.)

Tiff was a year older than Carmela. Having already kissed a boy at school, she considered herself an expert on relationships. She confirmed that, yes, Carmela had better not tell anyone what she'd seen or they'd be mad. Tiff knew adults were great at getting mad, like the time her father had punched out their picture window in a fit of rage at her mother and had had to be rushed to the ER as he'd gashed his arm badly and was bleeding to death.

Carmela agreed with Tiff. Each day she related Lisa and David's sexual shenanigan's to her. Even the 'more experienced' Tiff was surprised by some of the positions:

"You mean your dad put it in her *butt?* Oh my gosh . . . but won't that hurt?"

Carmela had wondered the same. "I don't know. I thought it would, but Lisa seemed to like it. She came. It made everywhere smell like poop though."

They both laughed.

But it had to end. And the end came unexpectedly and violently. A happy summer turning swiftly into a bloody autumn, with lives shed like leaves from trees.

Lisa had gone back to university. Back in school herself, Carmela was once again queen of the O'Connor household. If she didn't throw tantrums like Lisa once had, she still let her mother and stepfather know in no uncertain terms that she was a young woman now, and not one to be taken lightly.

Nowadays, Carmela experimented on her genitalia in private. The pleasure was the same, but oddly, she missed Lisa now, missed those exciting nights (and once, even on a Sunday afternoon when she'd returned home and peeked in the living room window after saying she was off to visit Tiff).

(In retrospect, Carmela was unsure if Lisa and David were really so careless about their affair, or simply too wrapped up in one another to notice her peeking at them, or if she was simply so expert and quiet that they never heard her. Another possibility *had* occurred to her— that they actually knew she was watching them, and that they either didn't care, or enjoyed having her as their voyeuristic audience. She preferred to think that she'd been expert in sneaking up on them.)

Her mother and stepfather had no problems that she could see. It was impossible to identify the crack in their relationship into which Lisa had slotted her young nubile body. David seemed as caring as ever for both Mary and herself, and if her mother seemed particularly anxious of late, it wasn't anything new. Carmela, who'd already begun nursing dreams of herself becoming a nurse, sometimes wondered how her mother didn't give patients the wrong injections at the hospital. She was just such a bundle of nerves sometimes, worried about everything and everyone and their dog's fleas. A far cry from the woman who'd terminated Lisa's hunger strike with one decisive, if zany, stroke.

(It was only as an adult that Carmela considered that her mother's odd way of stopping Lisa's protest might have been sociopathic and not loving.)

Sunday afternoon. Carmela had just gotten back from Tiff's house, where they'd been watching *Pretty Woman* on DVD to determine if Julia Roberts was actually pretty, or if maybe Michelle Bauer shouldn't have been cast in the lead role instead. Then there was their usual argument over who was hotter: Matt Damon, or Elvis, or Brad Pitt, or Harrison Ford in the early *Star Wars* films. (Definitely not Johnny Depp though. They both agreed on that.)

Carmela was just about opening her bedroom door when she heard the argument coming from her parent's bedroom.

She didn't need to eavesdrop; everything was loud and noisy:

"You sick bastard, David. How dare you fuck your own daughter!?"

"Mary, put the gun down. I'm telling you, it's all in your head, I didn't fuck her."

"You did, you son-of-a-bitch! I read the text message on your cellphone." Her voice pitched up mockingly. "'Oh, daddy dearest, I'm getting wet just thinking about your hard cock in my ass.'"

"Mary, it's not what you think—put the damn gun down, please!"

"You were *sodomizing* her, you sick animal? Your own kid?"

"Mary, you're crazy—there's no such text message in my phone. Look, here it is! See for yourself."

"Don't you dare call me crazy! I saw the text *before* you erased it, you asshole. How can you do this to me? To us?"

"Mary, put the gun down. Put the gun down. Please. Let's talk this over."

The words pounded in Carmela's young mind. *Gun? Mom's got a gun!?*

Horrified, confused, but clear-headed enough to know what to do in an emergency, Carmela pulled her cellphone from her pocket and dialed 911.

"Hello, this is 911. What is your emergency?"

"Hello, hello, my name's Carmela Cole! I'm twelve years old! I think my mom's gonna shoot my dad!"

"Where are you? What is your address?"

"117, Poplar Street—"

Bang!

"Mary, no! Stop, please!"

Bang! Bang! Bang!

Carmela dropped her phone and sprinted for the bedroom. She skidded to a halt in the bedroom doorway and gaped in horror.

David O'Connor lay in a pool of his own blood on the bedroom carpet. He was on his back with his purple dressing gown open, two bullet holes in his chest, and one in his neck from which blood was squirting in a thick red jet. His eyes were clenched shut in agony and he was coughing up blood, a red froth bubbling from his grimacing lips.

Oddly (and Carmela never forgot this—in later years it seemed to her clear proof that Mary O'Connor wasn't all there in the head), her mother was kneeling beside her prone, quivering husband, and holding his wrist. Carmela gasped when she understood what her mother was doing: she was taking David's pulse, her lips moving in a silent count.

Then Mary shook her head, looked up, frowned, and placed the muzzle of her large pistol directly over David's heart. "Go to hell, asshole."

"NO, MOM, DON'T!!!" Carmela screamed. "WHAT ARE YOU DOING!!?"

Bang! David's body jerked once then lay completely still. When Mary pulled the gun away, blood pumped from the fresh hole.

"Mom?"

Mary O'Connor got to her feet and turned to face her younger daughter. Her eyes were out of focus. (Carmela would never forget that either.) The lower half of her pale blue negligee was stained red with her husband's blood.

"He was raping Lisa," Mary told Carmela.

"Mom, Dad *wasn't* raping her!" Carmela blurted out. "She liked it!"

Mary's eyes widened in surprise. "You knew about it? Why didn't you tell me? We could have protected her."

"I . . . I . . . I . . ."

"You all ganged up against me? My own family?"

Carmela saw the sudden flush of rage in her mother's eyes. Then, that rage altered into another expression—one that Carmela didn't initially understand, something cold and 'unmotherly.' And then suddenly, she realized what it was. She was watching the disconnection of their familial relationship.

Her mother raised the gun and pointed it at her. "Goodbye, daughter."

Carmela turned to run, but she wasn't fast enough.

Bang!

The bullet hit her in the back, lifted her off her feet, and slammed her against the corridor wall.

She crashed to the floor then rolled forward, ending up on her right side. In this position, she could see into the bedroom, could see David's corpse. Agony racked her young body and she thought she was dying. She saw her mother walking towards her with the gun pointed down at her, and closed her eyes and pretended she was already dead.

It didn't work.

Bang!

This bullet hit her in the left shoulder. She felt her bones shatter and the pain seemed to force her body into the floor. Rendered speechless by her shock, Carmela could only stare up at her mother. She knew death was coming for her. She could feel the cold fingers of something ethereal tugging on her young soul, as if impatient to separate it from her body. And for once in her life, she realized she didn't feel nervous; she wasn't scared. Her time was up, that was all. She felt both feverish and cold, and the hurt from the bullets was spreading like a cloud through her body, but dulling itself at the same time.

Mary O'Connor bent down. Carmela felt her arm lifted, her wrist pressed and palpated. She realized that her mother was taking her pulse too. It meant little to her, was merely another part of her fade from reality.

Her mother let go of her wrist and peered into her eyes. "Goodbye, nasty little daughter. I'll see you soon."

Then she raised the gun again—the weapon looked impossibly HUGE to Carmela—turned its barrel into her own mouth, shoved it in deep and pulled the trigger.

Carmela watched the massive spray of brains out of her mother's head, then tracked her slow-motion fall. Mary collapsed with her head next to Carmela's, so that Carmela was forced to watch the blood squirt from the bullet's exit wound (some of it splashing her own face), and watch their blood seep and mingle in the dark matting of the corridor rug.

The police and paramedics found them like that: Carmela clinging on to life by a thread, and Mary and David both long dead.

***

Carmela lied to the police: she said she didn't know who her stepfather had been sleeping with. When she was out of the ICU and fit to be interviewed (which was a week later) she told them that her mother had accused her father of having an affair with a woman, but she had no idea who the woman was.

The detectives never doubted her. Seeing as no such woman existed, and the only witness to the shooting was Carmela herself (who was clearly too young to have any reason to lie about anything—how could she possibly be involved in the happenings?), and that, as Mary O'Connor had remarked to David before killing him, he had erased all the damning texts between himself and Lisa, the police were unable to track down David O'Connor's alleged mistress. After a while they stopped trying to.

Their final conclusion was that, in a fit of irrational jealousy, Mary O'Connor had lost her mind and shot first her husband and then her twelve-year-old daughter, before turning the gun on herself. The 'crazy' explanation for her actions was reinforced when her work colleagues told detectives how highly-strung she generally was.

Carmela had lied to protect Lisa. Lisa might have been at fault—though Carmela was still too young to understand how (Lisa and her stepfather had just been having fun, and their mother hadn't known) —but Carmela realized that with both their parents now dead, Lisa was the only person she had left in the world.

And she didn't want to lose her too.

On hearing about the shootings, Lisa was distraught, completely beside herself with grief. For days she sat from morning to night by Carmela's hospital bed with tears in her eyes.

Carmela never told her what she knew. And now, she realized that Lisa had never suspected she'd been spying on them. So there was really nothing to say except, "Why did mom do it? Oh, she shouldn't have done it."

Finally, Carmela was let out of hospital, and Lisa took her back home.

Almost immediately, there was a problem. The law demanded that someone be legally responsible for Carmela, who, just about to turn thirteen, was still a minor.

Carmela was horrified to hear that the social workers were planning to take her away and put her in either an orphanage or a foster home.

"Lisa, do something!" she wept, sobs wracking her body. "Don't let them take me away from you!"

Lisa (by that age already full of plans and schemes) did something. She bluntly refused to be separated from Carmela. "She's my sister and my responsibility," she protested doggedly, "no one else can have her." She hid Carmela over next door at the Hooper's, locked up their own house, and refused to let anyone inside, not even the police.

Finally, matters were resolved amicably. Lisa having turned eighteen in the summer, and as such legally an adult, the State of Massachusetts agreed to let her become Carmela's legal guardian, on the conditions that she 1) show a constant source of income, and 2) would agree to live at home and not at school.

Lisa had no source of income, but their dead parents had left them quite a lot of money—enough to live on comfortably for several years—which was an acceptable substitute. They also had their Poplar Street house—David O'Connor had built that himself.

Moving home from school was also easily accomplished. Lisa switched from UMass Amherst to UMass Boston to finish her Criminal Justice degree. Commuting to and from campus wasn't an issue—she had both their dead parents' cars at her disposal now.

And so it was that Lisa became both father and mother to Carmela.

At first the social workers called at the house twice a month to see how they were getting on. Once certain that Carmela was being adequately cared for and not being abused by Lisa, they reduced their frequency of visitation, then stopped them altogether.

***

On the surface, by all appearances, the sisters were happy. Lisa spared no expense of her time (or money, so far as they could afford it) in taking care of Carmela. She did her absolute best to singlehandedly raise her younger sister.

Carmela appreciated that. But the older she grew, once she began properly understanding the dynamics of male/female sexual relationships, and the dos and don'ts of the same, the harder it became for her to exonerate Lisa from guilt in their parents' violent deaths.

There was also the complicating factor (noticed and dismissed by Lisa due to her overfamiliarity with its source) that Carmela shared the late Mary O'Connor's temperament to a fault: her childhood inclination towards compulsive anxiety had blossomed along with her body, and now she worried whenever suitable occasion presented itself. Not just about general teenage concerns—boys, fashion, school grades, music and films, and how to be considered cool—but also about ethics, concepts, and . . . her memories.

Carmela knew Lisa was doing her utmost best to provide for her everything their parents would have. But still, in the dark hours, she would often lie awake in bed, imagining how different her life would have been if David and Mary O'Connor were still alive.

Oh, she was convinced, it would surely have been much, much better than living under Lisa's iron rule.

That was one thing that hadn't changed: Loving surrogate parent or not, Lisa Cole was still 'The Boss.' 'She Who Must Not Be Trifled With' as their stepfather had once jokingly dubbed her. You didn't talk back to her, or question her decisions. Or else . . .

(After being grounded for two weeks because of a screaming match they'd had over whether to buy vanilla or strawberry or chocolate ice cream, Carmela got the point.)

It seemed to Carmela that the more beautiful her older sister became—and by the time Lisa was twenty-two, she was an utterly gorgeous blonde bombshell and having to fend off male attention left, right, and center—the more ego-tripping she did, and mostly at Carmela's expense.

"Don't think about it too much," her best friend Tiff Hooper advised. "Soon, *you'll* be out of high school and off to college like me and you won't have to see her everyday anymore." Tiff, now a prettyish eighteen-year-old with a lot of lingering baby fat, had left home to study Economics at Western New England University in Springfield and was only ever home during school breaks and holidays.

She grinned at Carmela. "You'll never believe how great it was to escape the endless family drama. I've only been back for two days and already it feels like two years. Tony was home on shore leave yesterday. He was telling me how Shaniqua's pregnant with their third child now and my mom's *still* trying to break them up. And my dad? He got mad over losing a poker game and punched out a window again and ripped up his arm again. Can you imagine that?"

Carmela almost sobbed out her impatience. "Tiff, you're reading my mind. I can't wait to graduate high school like you and run away to nursing school and freedom."

"She loves you. You know that."

"Aw, she's just guilty over what happened."

"She doesn't know it was because of her, or even that you were watching them."

"Oh, Tiff, I *love* Lisa too—but she never gives ground on anything. Everything's either her way or I'm grounded. And she's only five-and-a-half years older than me."

Tiff nodded sagely. "In legal terms, that might as well be an eternity."

"And also . . . sometimes, I get so damn mad at her . . . normally when I'm thinking about how mom and dad died—oh, I really loved him!—and I can't get it out of my mind that it's all Lisa's fault because she's so damn selfish. And it just wells up inside me, and I can't help myself, and I feel like picking up a pair of scissors and stabbing her . . . then it dies down and I'm fine. But then Lisa pulls another of her control freak trips on me and it starts up again, and I find myself blaming her for everything bad that happened, and I want to kill her again . . . and then there's also Lisa's whole sex goddess scene going on that I need to deal with, 'cos see—"

"Ooh, sex is great!" Tiff interrupted her with a leer, her face aglow with lustful memory. Just make sure you aren't too drunk, and that the guy wears a rubber . . . or . . ." she giggled, "ensure that he comes on your bellybutton instead of inside you."

Carmela sighed with frustration. "Tiffany Hooper, can you get your head out of pornsville for five minutes and just listen to me?"

"Sorry, I just mean it—sex is utterly fantastic. You really have to try it soon. Alright, I'll stop preaching dick gospel to you, go on."

"Yes, yes, yes, I'm sure boys are better than fingers, and I do want to try one too, but I haven't yet, have I? And that's mainly Lisa's fault as well. And meanwhile, *she* keeps bringing all her boyfriends over to the house."

"Oh, I didn't know that. Did any of them molest you?"

"No, no, it's just them being here and knowing what she's up to and feeling guilty over how much fun she's having in her bedroom. She's so loud when she screws, you can hear her coming a mile off. And the slut changes boyfriends like catwalk models change outfits. And if *I* go out on a date—that's if she lets me—she gives me curfews and wants to know everything I've been up to, and who the boy is, and who his parents are . . . shit! Once she was going to forcefully inspect my panties for semen, till I bit her arm."

Tiff's eyes widened. "She just doesn't want you getting date-raped, or preggered. Look, girlfriend, I think Lisa is just trying to be a good parent, though I definitely understand your depression over how bossy she is. C'mon, let's just go to the mall for lunch and shop for underwear and watch the boys skateboard. That'll cheer you up."

"Yeah, I guess so."

That was how it was. A year later, Carmela left home for nursing school at the University of Massachusetts, Boston. Things instantly improved between the sisters. Besides, by then Lisa was working in law enforcement anyway, and even if Carmela had still been living under her supervision, wouldn't have had the time to order her about anymore.

But the resentment was still there.

And there were also unbidden, unwanted, and random reminders of past events that Carmela would much rather do without. Sometimes, for instance, when she saw Lisa's gun, her mind flashed back to the day when their mother had been pointing one at her. On most of those nights she had nightmares of being murdered.

For years, Carmela was haunted by memories of that moment when she'd seen the maternal affection vanish from Mary O'Connor's blue eyes, to be replaced by the clear intent to kill her—this child who was no longer her own.

***

With that image of maternal disinheritance burning in her mind, Carmela separated herself from her recollections. It was never wise to trudge down Memory Lane; too much pain lived there. And everything had happened so long ago—eleven years now—that blame and anger were both useless. Sometimes Carmela even doubted her own memories of the tragedy—she'd been so young. But her bullet scars were confirmation that everything *had* happened.

They'd crossed the intersection now and were halfway up Center Street.

As far as Carmela could tell from her feelings, she neither hated nor blamed Lisa anymore. Life had compensated her since the tragedy. As an adult, she realized that she'd not missed out on any teenage experiences (except maybe an unwanted pregnancy). She was a young successful woman, at the start of the satisfying nursing career she'd always dreamed of having.

Also, her ugly duckling fears hadn't played out. If she wasn't exactly a swan, she wasn't a barnyard chicken either. Men looked at her; even the middle-aged motel owner had earlier, when he'd thought she wasn't looking.

Except for her outbreaks of anxiety—and she had medication for that—she was content.

It was mainly when Lisa got them into a mess—like tonight's mess—through her bullheaded obstinacy and refusal to take advice (like about the need to wear gloves, for instance), that Carmela felt the return of her old anger. And then, her nervous condition made everything worse. And then she felt like hitting Lisa with something.

At the moment, her concerns were threatening to get the better of her. They could see the Fleming Oil gas station up ahead. There was no one there.

The closer they got to the gas station, the more Carmela felt the grip of her fears, like the night sky was falling on her. Even the air seemed thicker and harder to breathe.

"Shit, sis! Here we are in a strange town with two of our friends missing."

"Don't panic," Lisa said. "There has to be a logical explanation as to where they've gone."

They stood in the shadows a short distance from the gas station, staring at the deserted pumps.

"Maybe the pumps aren't working or something and they had to walk a bit farther," Lisa suggested after a while, though to Carmela's ears, she didn't sound convinced by her own explanation.

"Yeah, but how much farther? We're almost at the motel!"

"No we're not. Calm down. Let's reason this out."

Carmela shivered at the sudden thought that Tiff and Monique might be in danger. "I think we should turn on our phones," she suggested. "That way they can call us if they need our help. Yes, sis, I understand about the whole alibi thing and our signals bouncing off of phone towers, but this may be a life-or-death situation."

She was relieved when Lisa agreed with her without a fight. "Alright, if you insist. Turn yours on. If we use mine, Bobby might call me, and then . . . We'll destroy your phone in the morning, then you'll report it as being stolen yesterday."

Carmela nodded and turned on her phone. She immediately felt better. It had felt weird not to be able to contact anyone. Or have anyone contact her.

"Look, I'm gonna call Tiff," she said. "I'm getting so nervous now, I don't know what to do with myself."

She was prepared to insist on it, to fight to get her way. But again, Lisa just nodded.

"Yeah, yeah, do so," she said in a distracted voice that made Carmela look at her sharply.

Lisa wasn't even looking at her. Her gaze was fixed on the nearby gas station with its rows of deserted pumps like iron cacti in a concrete desert. She seemed deep in thought, her lips pressed tightly together, her brow crinkled up by her mental preoccupations.

Carmela also noticed that Lisa's right hand was fondling the gun in her pocket. *So she is worried too.*

She dialed Tiff's number. Of course, if Tiff's phone was still switched off, this was all a waste of time. She could only hope it wasn't.

The phone rang thrice then connected.

"Tiff? Where the hell are you two? We're at the damn filling station and you're not here and—"

"Well, hi there. I'm not Tiff." The voice was cheery and female. And no, it wasn't Tiff, nor Monique either.

"Huh?" Carmela jerked the phone away from her head and stared at it in shock. Yes, this was Tiff's number, she'd not dialed someone else by mistake. So what . . . ? About to return the phone to her ear, the full oddity of the situation dawned on her, and so she first tapped the onscreen 'speakerphone' icon so Lisa could listen in on the conversation as well. "Hey, who's this on the line?"

"Oh, my name's Nancy."

"*Nancy?* Who are you? Can I please speak to Tiff?" By now Lisa was looking at her in surprise.

"Not at the moment," the woman's voice replied with an amused chuckle. "She's preoccupied—"

Lisa snatched the phone away from Carmela. "Nancy, or whoever the fuck you are, what the hell are you doing with Tiff's phone? And where the hell are she and Monique? And why the hell can't they come to answer the phone?"

Carmela listened breathlessly to the giggled reply: "That's what I'm trying to explain, if you'll calm down and let me."

"We're listening."

The unknown woman laughed loudly. "Okay, the reason they can't come to the phone right now is because they're getting fucked by my brother Owlsy." She laughed even louder. "You need to see them go at it."

Lisa's mouth dropped open. "They're doing *what?*"

"Having sex. Apparently, Monique's an old flame of Owlsy's from way back and they met at the gas station and decided to drop over to our house for a quickie. And damn, can those two girls fuck. The fat one—Tiffany—is sucking Owlsy's balls like she hasn't had any in ages and—"

"Where's your house?"

"We're on Carver Street, two down from the motel, on the right." She giggled again. "You can't miss it. There's a green pickup truck with a load of baby pigs parked out in front of it."

"We're on our way."

"Are you sure you wanna bother? They'll be done soon, then Owlsy'll drop 'em both off by your van again."

"We're already at the Fleming Oil gas station at the Center Street junction. We'll be over there in ten minutes."

Another giggle. "Okay then, you're welcome to join in the party. Come and join in the fun. There's booze and some pot and . . . hey, you bringing any guys along? I need to get laid myself and I detest pussy."

Lisa's face squeezed up in anger, and she looked like she'd explode. But when she replied, her voice was calmness itself. "Nah, it's just us girls."

"Ah, too bad for my poor cooter then. I guess it's us and Mr. Rabbit again tonight." She giggled long and loud. "Okay, so I'll expect you two soon. I gotta get back into the bedroom and watch the show. Shit, that Tiffany can . . . Hey, now remember the directions—second house after the Sunflower and watch for the pig truck."

She hung up, leaving the two sisters gaping at each other in disbelief.

"Did you . . . ?" Lisa asked.

"I did . . ." Carmela replied.

"Do you . . . ?

"I've no idea what to think either."

"How can . . . ?"

"What were they . . . ?"

"Don't ask. Let's just get over there and knock some sense into their brains."

They set off up Broadway, growing angrier by the footstep. As their strides lengthened and became more rapid, Carmela was struck by the realization that this was one of the few times that she and Lisa had ever both been angry at the same time without it being directed at each other.

Beside her she could hear Lisa muttering angrily to herself. Carmela readied herself to stop Lisa from beating the shit out of Tiff and Monique.

They reached the Broadway–Carver Street intersection. Across the road lay the motel driveway.

"This is that slut Monique's fault," Lisa grumbled darkly. "I can't believe she'd try to turn a trick on a night like this. But once a hooker, always a hooker, I suppose, like selling their body is an infection in a prostitute's blood. Shit, what was I thinking to bring her along on this? I must've been crazy. She dragged Tiff off to ball a guy instead of buying gas? Shit!"

Carmela didn't reply. She didn't know what the hell was going on anymore. But as they angrily crossed the road into Carver Street, she had an intense sickening feeling in her gut of tonight being about to spiral completely out of control for them all in a really bad way.

CHAPTER 15

Peter

Hey—ain't this the vehicle Ida reported seeing?

Off-duty police detective Peter Claxton slowed, then parked his station wagon behind the black van. Flashlight and gun in hand, he got out to inspect it.

Right from the get-go, Peter had a bad feeling about this. The parked van—a black Mercedes Sprinter—looked abandoned. Shining his flashlight in through the windows confirmed this.

What the hell's goin' on here? Where's the driver gotten to?

The van was parked equidistant between driveways, leaving no suggestion that its missing occupants could have entered either of the houses that bordered it.

Peter pondered what to do. This just got stranger and stranger.

***

Peter Claxton had been having drinks with friends at Rudy's Truck Stop (out on Interstate 495) when he'd gotten a call from Ida Green.

"Peter, I can't find Josh!" she'd yelped in that horrible voice she had.

"Calm down, Ida. What're you . . . ? Hold on a minute while I step outside. The music's too loud to hear you clearly."

Peter excused himself from his table and stepped out into the night to finish the call. Out there, with the cool breeze blowing through his blonde hair, and peering in through the windows at Rudy's regulars twisting and turning to the country and western on the jukebox, he raised his phone to his ear again. "Alright, Ida, I'm listenin'. What'cha mean—you can't find Josh?"

There was the sound of heavy breathing over the line, then Ida said, "He's gone missing. We were supposed to meet up at the Liquid Solace bar once he'd closed shop for the night, but he didn't show. So I walked down the road—Willy Mandell is with me—to find him and when I got to the gas station, he wasn't there. His cellphone's here with all my missed calls on it, and the store door's unlocked, like he went to have a pee, but Josh ain't nowhere in sight. And we've been waitin' ages for him to get back, but he ain't showed up."

Peter frowned, his cop mind starting to tick into gear. He didn't like this. Josh Penham, even though a dubious sort of guy, was a conscientious dubious sort of guy. "Ida, how long've you and Willy been waiting for him?"

"Close to a hour now."

That *was* odd. Peter asked, "Did you notice anything strange when you arrived there?"

"No, not really." There was some talking in the background, then Ida said, "Yeah, there was a black van just leaving the gas station when we arrived."

"A black van?"

"Yeah, but Willy and I were too far off to see the people inside it." Then her voice broke. "Peter, I'm sure something bad's happened to Josh. What am I gonna do?"

"You and Willy wait for me at the gas station. I'll be right over. Might be that nothing's wrong, but I'll come have a look just the same."

"Peter, something *is* wrong!"

"Okay, I'm on my way."

Peter reentered the bar, paid his tab, said goodnight to his friends, and left.

***

Now, standing here by the parked van, Peter couldn't shake his unease. He didn't like Josh Penham, primarily because he was a troublemaker. The kind of rough uncouth fellow who became unmanageable after three or four drinks. Josh was a tall muscular man, and when drunk and unruly, he was a real handful to manage. They'd had him down to detox overnight in a cell at the station too many times to count. There was also his suspected marijuana business. But so far the Raynham PD hadn't been able to discover where Josh kept his stash.

In fact it was Josh's suspected dope dealing that had led to him meeting and dating Ida Green in the first place.

Peter still blamed himself for that. He'd busted Josh for smoking pot—Josh had a joint in his pocket—and brought him to the station to book him.

Ida had been there at the station at the time.

Ida was being booked too. In a fit of road rage ("Get outa my bloody fucking way, you stupid skanky piece-of-shit TV-star wannabe!"), she'd hurled a jar of peanut butter through the window of a car that had cut her off in the thick downtown midday traffic. The bottle had barely missed braining the woman driver who'd offended her, but she'd lost control of her car and driven off the road and crashed into a lamppost.

The horrified woman was taken off to hospital for treatment for minor cuts and bruises. Ida was hauled off to the police station.

There at the police station Ida met Josh, and they began flirting in handcuffs, and next thing, once released, they started dating.

Peter couldn't really be bothered by that. His main beef with their relationship was that for some reason, Ida now felt the need to labor him with all her woes over how Josh was treating (and not treating) her.

"He slapped me—but no, I don't want you to arrest him, he didn't mean it, he was just drunk." "He forgot my birthday again, the son-of-a-bitch." "I just can't stand Josh, Peter. How come you men are always such goddam insensitive disrespectful jerks? That prick was staring down that slut's cleavage while I was right beside him, and I could swear that Josh had a hard-on. I almost expected him to pull it out and start wanking in public, the disgusting, useless, no-good son-of-an-asshole. And I was right there! I was right there! And then . . ."

It wasn't all the time though, and Peter generally handled Ida's calls with good humor. For all her brazenness (and that horrible strident voice of hers), Ida Green was a good sort. She was divorced with two kids, and her old mother had Parkinson's disease and needed constant care. Peter had been over at their house and knew that Ida took really good care of her mom.

He sighed. If only she'd stop picking scumbags like Josh Penham to date. (Peter wasn't really judging Ida, mind; like her, he was divorced and understood how cracks could easily form in a once 'till death do us part' relationship. It was just that, reviewing her list of post-wedlock boyfriends, one couldn't help but conclude that Ida Green had defective mate selection genes. Indeed, Ida's talent for picking male scumbags out of the general populace was so good, she could have been employed as a criminal profiler, with a 100% success rate.)

And so it came to tonight, and now Josh Penham was apparently missing.

By the time Peter Claxton found the black Mercedes van, he'd been driving around town for over an hour, and had already passed this spot once before without seeing anything. (Unknown to him, the van had stopped here barely a minute after he'd driven by.) During that period, Ida had called him thrice, each time sounding louder and more distraught. Peter understood that: the woman was in love. But Peter was off duty and just wanted to get home, fall into bed, and get some well-earned shuteye. And the drinks he'd had at the bar weren't helping him stay awake either. (In fact, Peter doubted he'd pass a breathalyzer test if one was administered to him right now.) His limbs felt like redwood trees about to be felled—massive sticks glued to his body which he was expected to keep controlling.

So he'd been relieved to find the van. But not as relieved to find it deserted. Or maybe he was. The important thing (determined by shining his flashlight in through the side windows) was that Josh wasn't in the van. There was nothing in the vehicle except scattered Styrofoam packing and some empty cartons.

Peter began thinking this was all a wild goose chase. Sure, Ida was worried, but who on earth would want to kidnap Josh? Okay, maybe drug dealers he owed money. But if *they'd* abducted him, they'd do a professional job of it. At least Peter thought so. He didn't expect dope pushers to leave Josh's cellphone behind, or not bother to even lock up the shop either. And if it was them, why not just snatch him when he was at home?

Walking around the van one final time, Peter sighed, then yawned. Well, there wasn't anything else that could be done tonight. Josh was an adult, Ida had to wait twenty-four hours at least before officially reporting him as missing.

He checked his watch. It was one-twenty-two; definitely time for bed. *Sorry, Ida, but I've done the best I can tonight. I gotta be up early in the morning.*

Peter decided to drive back to the Red Eagle gas station to tell Ida in person. That way he could calm her nerves somewhat before heading on home himself.

It was then that he smelt the bad smell. A really horrible one. It smelt like something dead and rotten, but it also smelt like damp earth after a light rain. Peter hadn't ever smelt anything like it.

Having just completed a last circuit of the black cargo van, Peter was currently standing out in the road. The smell seemed to be coming from the van's other side, where a row of trees framed a lawn.

He groaned. *Aw, come on! No, you gotta be kiddin' me! That can't be Josh, can it? What's he done? Died and gone rotten in one hour?*

Wincing at the long night's work ahead of him if indeed Josh Penham did lie murdered on the lawn behind the van, Peter padded softly back around the front of the black vehicle, flashlight gripped in his left hand, service revolver in his right hand and poised to shoot.

The horrible rotting smell thickened around him as if he was walking into a cloud of it, or as if it was coming to meet him. Peter tightened his grip on his gun.

And then, just as he cleared the front of the van, he sensed a sudden blur of motion on his right, then felt a terrible sharp pain in his right wrist.

Peter stared down in shock. His right wrist was severed almost all the way through. Below the deep slash through his flesh and bones, his right hand hung limp and useless, his service revolver spilling from its nerveless fingers to clatter onto the sidewalk.

As blood spurted from the horrendous wound, horrible pain sped up his right arm, pain that threatened to paralyze him with its intensity.

Peter instinctively shoved his flashlight under his right armpit and grabbed his wounded forearm to stop the bleeding. At the same time he turned to see who had almost chopped his hand off. In his mind he had the image of a crack-head with a cleaver, maybe even the missing Josh Penham himself, all jacked up on PCP or some hallucinogen that had filled his head with delusions of being a ninja.

Peter was shocked to see Brainchew standing there by the van, illuminated by the flashlight beam and grinning at him. There was no mistaking that shape—that HUGE elongated head and muscular dwarf's body. He knew the monster first-hand; he'd helped bury it in the cemetery.

Now it was somehow both alive again and covered in blood, and its mouth—Peter had only seen it frozen and with its lips together— *Oh my good Lord, where'd it get so many teeth from!?*

He turned to run, but the monster grabbed him. Its smell cloaked them both now, thick and cloying, like he'd been dropped into a tub of rancid fat.

The flashlight fell from Peter's armpit and clattered to the ground.

He opened his mouth to scream for help, but Brainchew had already clamped a smelly hand over it. And now, worse still, it dug that hand in between his lips.

Peter tried fighting the intrusion of the razor-like claws digging between his lips and tearing both them and his tongue to shreds. With one useless hand, however, it was impossible; the monster proved too strong for him. Peter was in indescribable pain. The hurt from his torn right wrist paled to nothing in comparison to this fresh agony from his mouth.

The monster dragged him off his feet, away into the darkness bordering the van. In his desperation, Peter let go of his bleeding right arm and beat at Brainchew with his good hand. With vital blood spilling away over them, his right hand fingers twitched uselessly by his side, unable to respond to the impulses his desperate brain sent them. His wrist burnt like concentrated acid bubbled inside it.

Meanwhile, the creature kept forcing its three-fingered hand and claws deeper into Peter's mouth. Finally its claws punctured through his tongue and exited through the bottom of his face, exploding out behind his chin in a gush of blood. Peter screamed. With his tongue pinned down, however, his scream was a mere bleat that hardly qualified as noise.

Then, growling silently, Brainchew yanked its hand away from Peter's face. The action completely tore Peter's lower jaw off his head. As his skin and muscles shredded bloodily and his face separated in two, the claws impaling his tongue sliced it in half lengthwise, so that with his jaw ripped off his face, the speech muscle flapped uselessly amidst the red mess of gore that remained, unable to make more than quiet farting sounds amidst a froth of red bubbles.

Brainchew flung Peter's lower jaw across the nearby lawn.

Peter was almost out of his mind with pain and horror now. He suspected he was going to die here, and was suddenly very afraid to die, but had no idea of how to avert his horrible fate. This was crazy, just unbelievable; it almost seemed like he was merely having a nightmare, one he just couldn't awaken from.

And next, Peter discovered that the monster wasn't done with him yet. He had no idea what it was doing when it clamped its mouth around the raw gap where his mouth had been and began sucking on his face. (Its teeth were stuck in deep around the horrendous wound, in their turn ripping his skin up the more.)

Then he understood that it was drinking the blood from his wounds. It sucked away relentlessly, extracting liquid pain from his face. Horror had filled his mind so deep now that it had incapacitated him. Yes, he'd seen a lot of nasty things in his time as a policeman, but this . . . this . . . this was beyond comprehension.

Then Peter's phone began ringing. *Fuck! That must be Ida,* he thought.

***

Brainchew separated itself from the mouthless man. His blood had tasted sweet and refreshing. It grinned at the man. Blood was streaming down from below his nose, down his neck and onto his clothes. Brainchew's miniscule mind appreciated the disbelief and horror in the man's eyes, and how his body trembled with the pain from his mutilated face and arm.

(Music had suddenly started coming from the man's clothes. Brainchew listened to it, then forgot about it when it stopped.)

With no mouth, its victim no longer had a voice. Brainchew imagined however that he was begging for his life.

Though it was enjoying the man's pain, it had no desire to prolong his suffering further—it was in a hurry to feed on more people. (It had already wasted precious feeding time trying to free that 'other' it had found behind the 'glass wall' in its last victim's house, only to discover—when it finally smashed the wall—that the 'other' instantly vanished.)

With a grin of triumph, it spun the man around so he was pressed up against a tree trunk and next . . .

***

Peter Claxton was in too much agony to feel Brainchew clamp its teeth over the back of his head. He did, however, sense that his life was about to be snuffed out.

And then, with the sudden loud snap of the monster's teeth penetrating his skull, it was.

***

Brainchew chewed the dead man's brain with relish. It swallowed the tender salty flesh with regret, wishing there was more to eat in his head.

It should drink his urine too, but . . .

For the second time, music began emitting from somewhere in his clothes.

For a while Brainchew listened, finding the sounds pleasant (it had no idea what a cellphone was) and soothing. The music stopped, then, just as it was about leaving that grassy spot and going after the women who'd been in the black vehicle, the music started up again.

Brainchew listened some more, becoming now aware of a strange coincidence: it could smell traces of a particular woman on this man it had just killed, and a short distance from here . . . it smelt the same woman in person. She and someone else—a man—were in an isolated room. They were alone there. Interestingly, both of them smelt worried.

Best of all, these two people were nearby, much closer to it than the women from the van.

Grinning, and with officer Peter Claxton's blood dripping from its body and coloring its footprints red, Brainchew set off to pay the woman and her companion a visit.

After that it would seek out those who had woken it up and kill them too.

CHAPTER 16

Tiff & Monique / Nancy

"So you see, girls," Nancy Pine explained to her captives, "You two did Owlsy a favor by inviting yourselves over to our house. Otherwise, he was thinking of knocking you both out once he'd driven you back to your van"—she grinned, showing perfect teeth—"which, seeing as you had a taser as well as a gun on you, very well might have proved fatal for him." Her lips compressed into thin angry lines. "And that would've meant me losing both of my brothers in one night."

Hands on hips, she scowled at them. "Dammit, I just can't believe you two bitches murdered poor Josh like that. And for nothing?"

Behind her, Owlsy grinned and nodded. Tiff could sense his impatience. Owlsy held a large scalpel in hand. A scalpel still smeared with the blood of the woman piled in messy pieces in the buckets opposite them. (Kayoko, he'd said her name was. Who had she been? A Japanese tourist with the stereotypical camera, delighted to visit the USA for the first time?)

"Oh, we'll surely make you pay for that," Nancy continued.

Tiff wilted at her words, like she was a poor flower in the desert and Nancy's angry gaze the rays of the sun insisting she wouldn't grow. It wasn't the way that Nancy was glaring angrily at she and Monique that leeched her of hope and willpower, it was her knowledge that they'd gotten into this whole mess because of just *one* bad decision they'd made.

Just one mistake . . . ?

But considering that, she felt a sudden resurgence of hope. To err was human. Mistakes were the spice of life. She'd escaped the last time because Owlsy had made a mistake. *I can do it again. All Monique and I have to do is get through this first period of torture, then, when these two sickos have gone to bed, we'll find a way to bust out of here.*

So far though, these two seemed to have all their bases covered, and that really worried Tiff. Just five or so minutes ago, Tiff's cellphone had rung, meaning their captors had for some reason left it on after checking its battery charge. Tiff had hoped . . . no, she'd *prayed* . . . that Nancy would be dumb enough to answer the phone down here in the basement. Then she'd have screamed herself silly so Lisa and Carmela would know they were in danger; scream out the address of this place too before Nancy could disconnect the call. But no—Nancy had carried both she and Monique's cellphones upstairs with her, and had also shut the door behind her as she went.

For Tiff, watching that brown door close then had been almost like watching the last chapter of her life end.

She looked right, at Monique. The trans-woman was now also topless like herself, the upper half of her black catsuit dangling in strips around her waist, courtesy of a pair of Nancy's scissors. Monique's face was a mask of fearful tension. She was clearly scared shitless too—not the least because of Owlsy's scalpel.

We can make it, Tiff thought at her like she was telepathic, *we'll both make it.*

"Okay, so what we're going to do to you both is—"

"Let's just get to welcoming them home, Nancy," Owlsy interrupted her, and as he spoke, Tiff saw that the familiar look of insanity was back in his eyes again.

"Aw, okay," Nancy agreed, "I know you're impatient to romance your darling again." She glanced at him as he stepped past her towards Tiff. "So what you got in mind for your runaway princess?"

"A little breastfeeding," Owlsy said.

"No!" Tiff yelped as he raised the scalpel to her left breast and flicked her nipple with it. "Don't!"

Nancy licked her lips. "Yeah, breastfeeding it is then. Do it—cut the bitch!"

"Nooooo!" Tiff screamed. Then she gasped in soundless horror as a blade of white hot pain cut through her left breast.

Owlsy was slicing her nipple off.

She flailed her arms and legs, the cuffs peeling off her skin. Her eyes were riveted down on the sight of her flesh being mutilated, on the surgical blade deep inside her body, severing herself from herself, while blood bubbled from the parting. Owlsy had a wide smile on his face. His eyes too were fixed on his work.

And then, like morbid magic, the nipple and its aureole separated completely from the white hemisphere it had topped.

Owlsy held up his bloody prize in front of Tiff

Her voice returned, but it wasn't words that came out of her mouth, just a long horrified scream.

Her horror wasn't done yet.

"Yeah, breastfeeding." Owlsy popped Tiff's severed nipple into his mouth, chewed on it, and swallowed. He grinned at Tiff, who'd abruptly stopped screaming on seeing that follow-up act of his.

Tiff just stared at him, her mind unable to form thoughts other than the mental loop: *He ate it! He ate it! He ate it!*

"How's she taste, Owlsy?" asked Nancy with a grin.

"She's good," Owlsy replied her. He leaned in close to Tiff, then leered at his sister. "But you know what? I'm still damn hungry."

Nancy laughed back. "Thank God He gave each of us woman *two* breasts then, right?"

Tiff looked down at the bleeding hole in her chest where her left nipple had been and found her voice. "OH GOD NO! Please! Help me, somebody!"

But Owlsy already had a firm hold of her right nipple and was busy slicing that one off too.

Half insane with pain, and stricken voiceless again, Tiff glanced desperately sideways at Monique. But Monique had her own problems too.

Nancy had just discovered Monique's penis.

***

If anything, Monique's mental state was worse than Tiff's, because of her fearful anticipation of what would be done to *her*.

The moment Owlsy had sliced Tiff's left nipple off, Monique had pissed herself from fright, the urine departing her penis in a hot unnoticed stream that ran down the back of her legs to pool around her toes. Then, after cringing while watching the lunatic eat Tiff's nipple (all the while with that fixed loony smile on his face), she'd turned back to notice that Nancy was staring down at her feet. Which was when she realized that she'd wet herself.

(Nancy was wondering why the front of Monique's catsuit wasn't wet, why the urine had apparently made its trip to the floor down the *backs* of her legs . . .)

Next thing Monique knew, Nancy had fetched her scissors again from the table with the instruments, and, with a perplexed smile on her face, was cutting down through the crotch of the black catsuit.

Tiff was screaming again. Monique couldn't even look her way. She was filled with too much apprehension to think of anyone but herself.

Oh shit! She's gonna find my . . .

She'd expected to hear a gasp of surprise or of horror when Nancy saw her penis. Or at least a bigoted slur on her intergender status. But what she heard instead was:

"Wow, you ain't Jewish," Nancy said. Then she grinned up at Monique and smiled.

On seeing that smile, Monique felt the walls of hope collapse around her. On her left, she heard Tiff gasping in pain as she lost her other nipple down the lunatic's throat, but Tiff sounded far off, in another universe. Her entire world of agony paled into insignificance in comparison to this smile of Nancy's.

And Nancy herself looked oddly different now. Her face—its overlapping layers of muscle, skin, and emotions—was shifting like a sea surface. Monique had the clear, if absurd, impression of someone rebuilding Nancy from the inside out, giving her an extreme makeover from 'sane' to 'insane.'

After fondling Monique's penis and testicles for a few moments, Nancy grinned at her. "No, you ain't Jewish, girl. But your mohel, Ms. Pine here, sure can fix that for you."

Monique stared at her in incomprehension.

Nancy waved the scissors in her face. "I got a gift for you, smegma-bitch. It's called circumcision. Time for your belated bris."

And then Nancy began cutting Monique's foreskin off with the scissors, pulling the ring of skin away from the penis and cutting straight up to its point of attachment to the male organ.

"NOOO!!! STOP!!!" Monique screamed out of her horrible pain. She thrashed helplessly against her bonds but it was a waste of strength. Her whole world contracted down to just the agony in her genitals, where, now that she'd finished her initial first cut down through the foreskin, Nancy was cutting it off from around Monique's manhood in a bloody circle, with blood splashing her pink nightie.

Monique began pissing herself again.

Nancy looked up at her as the urine washed the blood off her fingers. Her eyes were bright as stars, and she giggled like she was in ecstasy. "Oh, so you're getting off on this too, eh? I frigging am."

Half of Monique's foreskin was now detached from her penis in a bleeding pink strip. Nancy grinned up at Monique, then dropped her scissors, and, after taking a firm grip on both penis and foreskin with separate hands, began tugging on both, attempting to tear the rest of the foreskin off Monique's body by sheer brute force.

The utter agony . . . Monique had never felt anything so painful in her life.

She passed out from the pain.

***

Tiff wondered how she'd not fainted herself. Glancing down first at the two bleeding circles on her breasts (and the red lines dribbling down from them to her crotch), and then at the smears of blood on Owlsy's smiling mouth, she knew it would have been a reprieve, even if only a temporary one. At the moment, her breasts felt like twin furnaces burnt in them.

Oh, God. Oh, God. Oh, God.

She managed to calm herself. *The one thing I mustn't do is freak out and lose it. Once I let my terror get the better of me, I'm done for . . . we're both done for.*

She glanced at Monique, who was out cold. While Owlsy watched with calm interest, Nancy was just as calmly ripping Monique's foreskin off.

With a sudden twist of flesh, Nancy was done. Both her hands were crimson with blood. Yet more blood dripped from Monique's mutilated manhood down into the pool of her urine.

Nancy shook the tiny strip of skin at her brother. "Hey, look what I got here—some man-bacon. You still hungry, Owlsy?"

"Yeah, sure, sis." And then Owlsy ate Monique's foreskin too. The maniac chewed it, swallowed it, and licked his bloody lips like it was delicious.

Tiff didn't wet herself, but she decided she was in Hell. At the moment, carrying Josh Penham off to the Pleasant Street Cemetery to execute her sweet vengeance on him with a baseball bat and a knife seemed as far off as a teenage dream.

Tiff stared at the psychotic pair. *There has to be a way to escape from here. There has to be a way to stall them both! There has to be!* Her thoughts were desperate, but she was in dire straits here.

"Hey, Owlsy darling," she called weakly. "So now I'm back home again, when do we have our first fuck?"

Nancy wiped her hands with her nightgown. A cautious look came into her eyes. "Now, Tiffany, you wouldn't be tryin' to tease my older brother, would you?"

"No, I recognize my mistakes now. I just wanna start loving him again."

Nancy smiled coldly. "We'll see. You're a strange girl, Tiffany. But if you're being straight with us, we might really let you fully into our family." She gazed fondly at her brother, who smiled back with a bovine expression on his face. "See, Owlsy's overdue for some real quality lovin', and from a woman who'll fuck him because she needs him inside her, not because she's terrified that he'll fuck her up if she doesn't." She leaned forward and peered intently into Tiff's face. "Do you understand the difference?"

Tiff nodded. She was thinking: *Oh, I understand the difference alright, you tiny psycho freak. Just give me one chance, and what I'll do to you two sickos will be unprintable.* She glanced behind Nancy, at the chopped-up body in the buckets. If she got out of here—*God please help me to!*—those damn farm pigs would have a whole lot more to eat.

She said, "Believe me, Nancy, you've proven your point—I've seen the frigging fluorescent illumination." She frowned at Owlsy as twin jolts of pain savaged her breasts. "But he shouldn't have eaten my nipples. What's he gonna suck on now when we fuck?" (Her words, with their suggestion of her getting intimate with this hulking lunatic brute who'd mutilated her and was even now digesting part of her flesh, utterly disgusted her and made her feel physically ill. But she was playing the game of survival here, and she needed an advantage, any advantage, no matter how little. She had to escape from this basement Hell before she too vanished like all the others before her.)

"It's too late now to cry over spilt breast milk," Nancy replied. It was then that Tiff realized that she and Nancy were of exactly the same body type: short and with a tendency to fatness. She wondered if maybe Owlsy particularly liked her because she reminded him of his sister. If that was so, it was something that might work in her favor. She might be able to turn him against Nancy. And then, oh God, how she was going to make them both pay. She'd first scalp Nancy, then skin her . . . slowly. And Owlsy? She wanted him bound like she was now and then she'd . . . she didn't know what she'd do to him yet, just that it would be utterly excruciating and it would last for *weeks*. She needed some quality time to mull on that.

Then, a lot calmer now, she remembered their cellphones. Both phones were still in the house. If she could just reach them, she could have the police over here in minutes. But Nancy might have locked them away somewhere.

Okay, first things first. The important thing now is to survive tonight. Hanging from her arms was starting to really hurt. In fact, she hurt everywhere. Even her vagina hurt from the suspicion that Owlsy might soon fuck it.

Owlsy was meanwhile busy throwing water in Monique's face to rouse her.

Monique sputtered awake. She awoke with a low moan of horror. Then she gaped down at her mutilated penis and let out a scared howl. She began weeping. "No . . . no . . . no . . ."

"Shut up, bitch," Nancy said. "I didn't castrate you."

"Now, now, don't you start putting ideas in my kid sister's head," Owlsy said.

"Okay, Owlsy," Nancy said, "What'cha wanna do to them now? Do we leave 'em for tonight and . . ." She bent and whispered something in his ear. Tiff strained her ears to catch what she was saying, but couldn't.

Owlsy's eyes, however, brightened with delight. "They are?"

Nancy placed a finger across his lips. "Shush." Then she grinned. "So you done with her for tonight or what?"

Say yes, you asshole! Tiff mentally screamed at him. *Say yes!*

But Owlsy instead, scratched his chin, then his tummy. "Nancy, it's odd, but I'se still feelin' hungry."

"What'cha wanna eat?"

Owlsy grinned and pointed at Monique. "I wanna breastfeed some more."

"Noooo!" Monique gasped. "No, stay away from me!"

"Shut up," Nancy chided her gently. "What'cha need nipples for anyway? You ain't ever gonna have babies to suckle."

"Please don't!" Monique gasped, as Owlsy, licking his lips and with his scalpel raised, stepped towards her.

Tiff had been thinking hard since Nancy had whispered into her brother's ear. *What is it that she doesn't want us knowing about? Could it be about Lisa and Carmela?* However, once she saw Owlsy heading for Monique, with the clear intent of cutting off her nipples too, she stopped her pondering. Her thoughts became anger at Owlsy. Her rage at him became hard, cutting words.

"Stop, you dickless bastard!" she screamed at Owlsy Pine. "Goddam let her alone, you impotent prick! Goddam asshole, limp-dicked cretin who can't get a girlfriend even for hire and has to resort to chopping up women in his basement to get a hard-on."

Owlsy froze at the beginning of Tiff's outburst. He turned and stared at her oddly. The scalpel fell from his hand.

Tiff stared at Nancy. Nancy looked horrified. Tiff ignored the warning look in Nancy's eyes, and the "Don't! Stop! Don't!" she repeatedly mouthed at her.

"Yeah," Tiff went on, heedless, "I'm sure you can't get it up at all, that's why you cut off women's nipples and eat them instead of sucking on them like real men do."

Owlsy's eyes turned cold. He turned from Tiff and walked back to the table with the surgical instruments.

"Yeah, go on, you pathetic loser!" Tiff screamed at his back. "That's all you know how to do, isn't it? Hey, I'm sure you didn't even screw me back then. You just pretended to. That's why you chloroformed me first each time, isn't it? So I wouldn't see you were using a dildo, you limp-dicked murderer? Hey look—I need a real man to fuck me. Not some asshole who's gay and scared to admit it."

Then she spat at him. She spat extra-hard, the ball of spit crossing the room to hit him on the back of his head.

She relaxed again. At least, she'd stopped him from mutilating Monique further.

She looked at Nancy. Nancy was shaking her head. *Screw you, bitch,* Tiff thought. She looked at Monique. Monique's expression was one of intense relief.

Tiff looked back at Owlsy. He was still facing away from her and doing something in his pants, like he was masturbating. *Oh god, how utterly pathetic.* She considered taunting him some more, then decided it would be unwise to anger him further. All she'd wanted was to stop him from hurting Monique. They both already hurt too much.

Now, if they'll just both leave us alone to plan our escape.

Owlsy turned around then.

Oh hell, so he isn't impotent, Tiff thought on seeing the hard erection poking from his undone pants. *He did fuck me back then.*

Then she gasped on seeing the HUGE carving knife he was brandishing at her.

And the look on his face . . . He was grinning, his lips stretched out to their limits and set in a too-wide smile over his bared teeth. His eyes were swollen and bloodshot and bulged from his head, like he'd just had an overdose of psycho-frog gene.

"You stupid twat," Nancy Pine told Tiff as Owlsy charged at her with the knife, his penis as stiff as if he planned on stabbing her with it too. "Now my brother's gonna cut your head off and screw your corpse, just to show you that he ain't impotent."

"Noooooo!" Monique yelled.

And then the next thing Tiff felt was the pain of the huge knife penetrating her belly. Too surprised by this sudden and unexpected turn of events to make a sound, she merely gaped down in horror. Owlsy had her body opened up and was pulling out her intestines and slashing at them, hacking her innards in pieces while her blood spattered his body. His throbbing erection glistened a bright red, coated with her blood.

She found her voice and began screaming. But that didn't last long. Barely a second had passed after she'd gotten her first loud cry out before Owlsy had his knife at her throat and was sawing through it. And then there was blood spilling everywhere from her neck, and Tiffany Hooper was dying, dying, dying; and it was the most horrible feeling ever, rocketing down to a black *nothing*, and she wanted to turn and gape her horror and fear of the afterlife at Monique, but Owlsy was fiercely severing the muscles in her neck so she couldn't even turn her head anymore.

In a final act of defiance, Tiff somehow managed to spit blood in Owlsy's grinning face, and then she died.

***

Monique gasped as Owlsy stepped away from Tiff's corpse and stepped towards her instead. Impossibly, his penis was still hard, and now dripped freely with Tiff's blood. In her terror, Monique almost imagined Owlsy's erection had a mouth that was lapping up the blood.

"Oh God, no!" she begged. "Please, man, it wasn't me. I didn't call you impotent. It was Tiff who did that and you've killed her. Let me live."

Owlsy, maniac grin seemingly stapled in place on his face, showed no sign of having heard her pleas. He stood looking her up and down, clearly sizing her up for something evil; maybe even the same sort of butchery he'd just performed on Tiff.

In desperation, Monique looked to Nancy for help. "Please! Make him stop!"

Nancy shrugged helplessly. "Sorry, darlin', but once someone's got him in this mood, he don't listen to no one."

And then Monique froze. Owlsy, his face still locked in that bug-eyed grimace, had grabbed a hold of her genitals, clamping both her penis and scrotum in one bloody gorilla-sized fist.

"NOOOOOOOO!" she screamed the next moment, when, in a savage burst of violence, he began slicing her genitals off. **"NOOOOOOOOOOOOOOOO!"**

The excruciating pain seemed to extend forever. It rocketed up and down from Monique's crotch, spreading out through her torso and further, to the tips of all four of her limbs, in torrents of absolute agony.

Owlsy was bent in front of her, focused on what he was doing. Then suddenly, he popped up again like a demonic jack-in-the-box, holding up a bloody mess that Monique recognized as once being attached to her.

Tears spurted from her eyes at the horrible sight. Yes, she'd wanted to be rid of her manhood, but not like this!!!

Then, while behind him his equally crazy younger sister bounced up and down and clapped her hands in glee, Owlsy forced Monique's teeth apart and shoved her castrated genitals into her mouth.

Despite the burning wound between her legs, Monique tried to spit her genitals out. She almost succeeded. But then Nancy ran forward and punched her in her wound, right in the middle of the blood running from her crotch. Monique gaped open her mouth to proclaim this fresh dose of agony, and Owlsy shoved the bloody penis and testicles back over her tongue and into her throat.

Suddenly Monique couldn't breathe. The genital obstruction was too thick to swallow and she couldn't get it back up into her mouth to spit out. And then Nancy duct-taped over her mouth anyway.

She was choking, with no oxygen, dying. And Owlsy and Nancy were laughing at her.

Then Owlsy turned to Nancy. "Get her untied, kiddo. I wanna fuck her ass while she's choking to death on her dick."

As Nancy hurried off to fetch the keys to the shackles, all Monique could do was hope to die quickly. And thankfully, death seemed to be coming fast for her.

Breathless, with her mind shutting down, she looked once at Tiff—dead, dead Tiff with her head hanging left on just her spinal cord; and with what seemed to be her belly's entire contents hanging out of it and splattered in heaps about her feet. And then she thought of herself, blood pouring from her crotch, her body in so much pain now that there were no words to describe her utter agony. *Shit—we both really took a wrong turn tonight!*

The thoughts somehow made it through the blackness filling her brain as it shut down. Monique thought she just might mercifully die before Owlsy entered her body. Because she could see that he was still as hard as a bone.

But then Nancy was back, and undoing Monique's arm and leg restraints, and dropping her on the bloody floor. And next, Monique suffered the final indignity of having Owlsy stuff his penis up her anus and start pumping away, ejaculating inside her just as her life ended.

The last words Monique Bangles ever heard were, "Shit, Nancy, this here is one slack ass. It's got less grip than a train tunnel."

***

While her older brother humped up and down on Monique's corpse, Nancy put his knife back on the tool table for him.

Shit! she thought, shooting a look of intense anger at Tiff's gutted corpse. *If only that fat slit had kept her mouth shut! Stupid blonde airhead!*

Nancy could care less about these two women's deaths. She was expecting their friends anyway. Owlsy could keep those two down here as replacements for his fun and games.

No, what was angering Nancy Pine was her sure-fire knowledge that Owlsy would now insist that she help him clean up the basement—chopping the bodies into bits that fit in the grinder in the shed out back, so they could mix them up with pig mash and bag them in sacks for the farm. Disposing of the evidence always took ages.

Nancy wouldn't have minded that even, except that she was really looking forward to today's outing with Ambrose. He'd said they drive out of town and . . .

***

Nancy Pine had been in love with Ambrose Duggan for as long as she'd known him. Which was all of the past four years, since he'd moved back to Raynham from West Virginia.

He'd been married then, so she'd kept her distance, just flashing him a wistful smile whenever he'd glanced her way. Back then, Ambrose had been living in this house along with his family, and their paths had rarely crossed, but when they did she'd made sure to catch his eye and smile. He'd grin back at her in that disarming way he had, and Nancy knew he thought she merely had a teen crush on him and would soon grow out of it.

But Nancy hadn't grown out of it. If anything, her feelings for him had deepened and grown more intense. Love at first sight, or maybe second or third, but it was there and it was a true heartfelt emotion.

She couldn't help it. She loved Ambrose with all of her heart.

(Even crazy women fell in love, and once they got what they wanted, they tended to be more devoted than sane, reasonable, 'normal' women. The most notable thing about insane women in love, however, was that they tended to stay that way, and woe betide anyone who got between them and the object of their affections. And even greater woe betide the object of their affections if he decided he wanted out of the relationship.

For crazy women, the old sayings "It ain't over until I say it is" and "If I can't have you, no one will," held painfully literal meanings.)

Nancy waited patiently for Ambrose. She had the unshakeable conviction that fate would cause their paths to merge, and that events would work out in her favor, so that at the end of the day she'd be Ambrose's woman.

When Brainchew had killed her love's family, Nancy had imagined her hour had come. But she'd not counted on Ambrose's losing it completely and going on a wild three-year drunk because of his loss.

The last thing Nancy wanted was a drunken husband. Dealing with Owlsy when he was in his cups was enough of a headache. Head-over-heels in love or not, she wasn't having another lush in the house.

(She wasn't so picky as to pass up a good thing though. If she didn't want him in *her* house, it didn't mean she couldn't go to *his*. One night during his drunken period, Nancy did just that—she crept over to the Sunflower and knocked on Ambrose's motel room door and fucked him. It had been akin to a wrestling match. Ambrose had been drunk as a skunk, and they'd rolled and grappled all over the bed and somehow had sex. He'd been deep inside her body and she'd loved it. Ooooh! And for some reason, he'd kept calling her Michelle, mistaking her for the cleaning lady. Drunk or not, the sex was nice and hot and dirty, and greatly satisfied, Nancy returned home and never told anyone.

The next time she saw Ambrose, he clearly didn't remember sleeping with her, and later, when Michelle came over to the grocery store where Nancy was working at the time, Nancy overheard her telling a friend how Ambrose's sister Dusty had railed at her for screwing him, and had warned her never to go in and clean his room again or she'd be fired.)

Nancy bided her time. She had the certainty that sooner or later, one way or another, by hook or by crook, Ambrose Duggan would be hers at the end of the day.

And, a week ago, it had finally happened. The man of her dreams— her middle-aged knight of the facial hair table—had finally looked her way and . . .

She still got all dizzy thinking of the first time he'd taken her to bed *sober* . . . how gentle and loving he'd been . . . how worried that he'd hurt her . . . how fantastic climaxing again with him after all this time had been . . .

It had been just one week, but it felt like they'd been together forever. It was utterly great. And now, Owlsy . . . ugh!

***

Nancy glared at her brother, who'd now gotten up off the dead transsexual redhead and was zipping up his pants.

"Look, Owlsy," she said. "I gotta date with Ambrose later today, and . . ."

He grinned. "And you ain't gonna be able to help me clean up, is that it?"

She nodded. "I've been telling you for a year—buy a goddam freezer for this place, then we won't have to worry about quick disposals of your girls' bodies."

He nodded back, then scratched his head. "Yeah, I guess you're right."

Then he prodded Monique's body with a foot as if to make sure she was really dead. He looked philosophical for a moment. "I never fucked a transsexual before. Her ass felt different somehow . . . sweeter, deeper, more experienced?" Then he looked inquiringly at Nancy. "When're their friends supposed to be gettin' here?"

"Shit!" Nancy yelped like she'd been pricked with a needle. "I plumb forgot! They should be arriving about now."

Owlsy in the lead, the siblings hurried up the basement stairs to clean themselves up, while hastily formulating a plan to trap the new arrivals.

In the wake of their departure, Tiff and Monique's corpses stared accusingly at the yellow walls.

CHAPTER 17

Lisa, mostly

"Well, this is it," Lisa said disgustedly. "Pigs, pickup truck, and all."

She and Carmela stood by Owlsy's green truck, staring at the old two-story house with the blue front door. Most of the piglets crated in the back of the truck were asleep, though every now and then one of them let out a gentle squeal like it was hungry.

"I dunno why, sis," Carmela said, "but I've got a bad feeling about this."

"Calm down," Lisa replied. "Turn off the worry tap. You get bad vibes about stuff like every two minutes. Just now, you thought the old guy in the motel lobby saw us."

"He did," Carmela insisted. "He looked up and—"

"Carmela," Lisa said patiently, "he couldn't have. He was bent hunchbacked over his laptop. I made sure he was occupied before we ran across the driveway." She peered intently at her sister, suddenly unsure whether to be exasperated or confused: Carmela sometimes behaved so much like their late mother that she might easily be her clone. "And even if he did happen to glance up as we crossed the drive, what would he have seen anyway? Not us—just two shadows that were likely a figment of his imagination."

"I wish I had your confidence."

"Me too. You're so wimpy I'm scared to let you out of my sight." Looking at Carmela then, Lisa was shocked: *Is she actually trembling?* She finally decided it was a trick of the light and returned her attention to the house.

"I don't care what you say," Carmela said, "I've got a bad feeling about us going in there."

"Give it a rest," Lisa snapped. But the harshness in her voice was forced, there only to prevent Carmela from freaking out. She agreed with her. Now that she'd calmed down, something about Tiff and Monique's no show at the filling station (and the weird invite they'd gotten over the phone to come over to this place) felt off to her too. Extremely off.

"All-right . . ." Carmela ventured, "if you're soooooo confident, why aren't you dragging me after you to go knock on the door?"

Lisa sagged against the green truck, then pulled Carmela out of sight into a crouch behind its tailgate.

"Alright, I admit it—I don't like this either. But I know Monique, this is the sort of nonsense crap she'd pull just to rile me up."

"Okay, that may be so. But what about Tiff? I *know* her; we both do. She's not the kind to do this kind of thing."

"Baby sister, your best friend—with our help of course—just murdered someone. She might need a hard anonymous fuck to get it out of her system." She raised her hands in a gesture of peace. "Don't get angry. I'm just saying."

"So what do we do?"

"We walk up to the front door and knock and enter, and . . ." Lisa pulled out her gun. "And if there's a problem . . . we solve it, like Vanilla Ice. Did you bring the other taser from the van?"

"Yeah, it's here." Carmela pulled it out of her jacket. "Please put the gun away; it's making me nervous."

Lisa sighed. "It's supposed to make you feel badass." But she tucked the pistol away again. "I don't really want to shoot anyone anyway. I mean, our alibi?"

"I think that's blown now, isn't it? Monique and Tiff?"

"Not necessarily. If this guy really is an old flame of hers . . ." Suddenly tiring of talking, Lisa straightened up. "Come on, let's go knock. They can't possibly know we're armed."

"Lisa, how about if I wait outside while you go in, then I can back you up if there's a problem?"

Lisa grimaced. Trust little sister to try to worm her way out of the situation. "Carmela, *I've* got the gun, and you can't shoot anyway." Then she laughed softly. "And besides, what the hell do you think they're gonna do to us? Kidnap us?"

She started toward the house. After a glance back to make sure Carmela was following, she climbed the porch steps and rang the buzzer with her left hand. Her right hand was in her pocket, fingers on the trigger of her pistol.

At the first sign of trouble, she was going to fire through her jacket. And heaven help whoever was standing in the way of the bullets.

CHAPTER 18

Willy & Ida

Willy Mandell peeked out of the doorway of the Red Eagle convenience store. A cool gust of night air blew in.

He looked around the gas station. The place was a glossy dead thing, one that demanded his cold aesthetic appraisal of its barren perfection. Its wide concrete floor shone dully under the lights. Its metal pumps seemed robots awaiting the command that would activate them. Its roof seemed the world's ceiling.

The only signs of life at this late hour were a blue scrap of paper caught up in a wind, and two cats meowing to each other as they walked along the wall on his right.

Across from Willy, the road was completely deserted. It was nearly thirty minutes since the last car had passed by.

It's like life on earth ended and forgot all about us, Willy thought to himself, his middle-aged face squeezing up as he did so. *Is this what it's always like this late at night? Like everyone else is dead, or on digital standby for eight hours?*

It was a sobering reflection. He looked outward at the sky. The moon was somewhere behind the store. The rest of the sky looked murky, like it was being stirred into an upset state.

"Any sign of them, Willy?" Ida enquired from behind him.

He turned to look at her. She was sitting behind the sales counter, moping. Ida Green was a tall thin woman, who on a good day would pass as very attractive. Now she just looked very miserable, her long pale face her personal Wailing Wall, her blue eyes wells of sadness framed by the Black Forest of her hair.

She wasn't crying yet, but Willy could tell she wasn't far from it. And then her mascara was going to run all the way down her face and drip onto her white tank top and . . .

Well, much better that than that she gets mad again and starts screamin', he thought grimly. He didn't want to endure that again.

When they'd first arrived here at the gas station (before Josh didn't come back), Ida had assumed Josh had hopped out back to bang some floozy. And, boy, had she let fly with her mouth: "God damn that no-good-for-nothing, shit-filled, slack stinking asshole with dick-sized hemorrhoids. How dare the shithead piss-riddled faggot cocksucker son-of-a-bitch slacker dunce stand me up for some herpes-riddled slut!?" And so on.

Willy had gotten an earful and then some. Ida cussed like a champ, like she had an 'insult thesaurus' wired to her tongue. And it wasn't just the words she used. Angry, her voice had that awful fingernails-on-blackboard tone everyone knew and dreaded. He wondered how Josh coped. But Josh didn't, did he? He just smacked Ida silent when she got too loud. That was how they kept winding up at the police station.

Looking at Ida now though, he thought he'd never seen anyone so worried. *Love sure is a crazy thing, ain't it? Here she is looking like she's gonna die if anything's happened to Josh, and the moment he turns up, she's gonna rip into him and rip him to shreds . . . and then they'll go make love.*

He smiled as reassuringly as he could. "There's no sign of him out there, Ida. No sign at all. But don't you worry, Josh is a big lad, he'll be fine."

Ida just sighed and went on looking morose and close-to-tears.

While leaning against the storefront wall, Willy checked out the time on the clock behind the sales counter. 01:37 a.m. Damn, he'd been comforting Ida for over two hours now. It felt like a lifetime ago when she'd leapt up angrily from their table at the Liquid Solace bar (where they'd both been drinking and waiting for her boyfriend to close up shop), and insisted she was going to look for Josh so he didn't stand her up and ruin her evening. (The Liquid Solace was up on Lincoln Street, five minutes walk from the Red Eagle gas station.)

And now, here we are. But where is he? Willy glumly looked around the store, peeking intently at the racked items like they knew where their seller had vanished too.

Ida said, "I'd feel much better if Peter would just answer my calls. His phone keeps going to voicemail."

Willy nodded. "Yeah, that's a bit odd." Then, seeing her alarmed look, he quickly added, "But it most likely just means there's nothing to tell you yet and he doesn't want you getting alarmed." To his relief, that calmed her again. But her words had started him thinking. *Yeah, where the hell is Peter Claxton? Fallen into the same wormhole that swallowed Josh? Don't tell me we've now got two missing people on our hands. And this late at night?*

"Peter shouldn't do that," Ida said after a bit. "He should call me. He knows how worried I am. He could at least tell me if he's found that black van or not."

Willy had no reply to that and so kept quiet. The inexplicable black van that they'd seen really bothered him too and he didn't want to express his unease to Ida. Instead of talking, he pushed the store door open again, and stared out at the night.

"Shit," Ida said suddenly. "I gotta call Traci and find out how mom is." (Traci was Ida's sixteen year old daughter.)

"Don't," Willy said without turning around. "They'll both likely be asleep by now and you'll just wake 'em up." That was one thing Willy really admired about Ida, how devoted she was to her old mother, who had that bad Parkinson's illness that once made someone snidely call her Mrs. Muhammad Ali. Old May Fenton walked like a robot, stuttered a lot, and had more tremors than an earthquake. Ida always told him that her ma's mind was still as clear as crystal, and it was just her muscles refusing to obey the commands her brain gave them, but watching Mrs. Fenton, Willy wasn't so sure; she seemed to have some dementia too. But maybe that was just normal senility mixing in with the Parkinson's.

"Yeah," Ida agreed after some thought. "But, Willy, what am I gonna do? I have to leave here soon. You know how mom always gets if I don't take her to church on Sundays, even though she thinks Reverend Ming is a commie spy. But . . . I'm not gonna be able to sleep if anything's happened to Josh."

Willy turned in the doorway at the sound of Ida getting up from her chair. He watched as she began pacing back and forth behind the counter, her heels doing a clackety-clack on the tiles.

He winced. She had a perturbed stare on her face that might at any moment morph into a fresh round of swearwords directed at his missing friend.

With a resigned shrug, he turned back to stare out at the shiny silver gas pumps and dull white pillars of the filling station; at the night world with its bug-noise silence and howls of mating cats and . . .

And that was when he smelt it.

It was a strange smell, and a horrible one. Like something had rotted underground, but up near the surface. Willy at first thought one of the toilet pipes had burst out in the restroom, but the smell was too specific for that. This wasn't any sewage leek. It stank more like rancid meat, but with a 'muddy' tinge to it.

Willy stepped out of the store and sniffed the air. *Shit, what a nasty, nasty stink. And it's getting thicker and more intense.*

And then he saw *it*.

Ida stopped her pacing, and asked, "Goddam it, Willy, did you just fart? What the damn fuck did you have for dinner? Are you trying to kill us in here?"

That was the exact moment when Willy saw the monster coming around the corner on his right.

There was no mistaking that he was seeing Brainchew, with its short pigmy body and monstrously elongated head, and its little red eyes like pools of fresh blood. Its gray skin was smeared all over with blood.

Willy turned to duck back inside the store and slam the door, but it was already there beside him.

They fought silently in the doorway. Willy pushing Brainchew's head back with both hands while it tried to close in on him. *Damn, the thing's teeth are so fucking BIG . . .*

Willy didn't yell for help; he knew it was pointless. There was no help coming from anywhere tonight. He also knew that Josh didn't keep a gun in the store, something to do with his criminal record not allowing him to own one. There were a few knives on the racks, but from what he'd heard of Brainchew, knives were next to useless against the creature.

Behind him, however, Ida was raving for all she was worth: "Shit, Willy, it's got you! Oh my God—the butt-ugly son-of-a-bitch has got you! It's got you, Willy! It's got you, man! Oh my God! Oh no, it's Brainchew! It's in the shop! Arrrrggh! Willy, do something!"

She was standing in front of the sales counter with her hands to her mouth and jabbering like a monkey intoxicated on bananas. Her freak-out was louder than if she was being raped. The noise was so strident and grating and distracting to Willy that he wished he spoke Brainchew's language, so he could tell it to first go eat her vocal cords before trying to kill him.

"Oh shit! WILLY! WILLY! WILLY!! Help! The stinky motherfucker's in here! Help help help, someone, please! Oh, my dear God, it's in here! OH NO, SHIT SHIT SHIT SHIT SHIT!!!!"

Then the monster raked Willy across his chest with its claws, cutting deep into his flesh so that his blood sprayed in jets on the open glass door. The pain made Willy let go of Brainchew's head.

And then, to his dismay, it had a hold of his own head, and it made a sudden violent twist of his head and he lost all sensation in his arms and legs.

The way Brainchew had yanked his head while breaking his neck, Willy now found he was staring behind himself, looking at Ida.

In the four seconds before he died, while Brainchew was fitting his head into its mouth, Willy watched Ida. She was trembling and pissing herself—the front of her jeans was soaked wet and the patch was spreading—and she was twitching like she had epilepsy. Willy hoped she wasn't shitting herself too. Her irritating jabbering had thankfully stopped now.

If she can just edge her way past the monster and run . . .

But then, just before Brainchew bit though Willy's skull and finished him off, Ida gave a final violent twitch, and her eyes rolled up in her skull and she fainted and collapsed to the floor.

Aw shucks! Willy thought. *Now she's a goner like me for sure.*

***

Brainchew ate the man's brain. It was delicious. One of the best so far tonight. (Like with Steve Birchfield's brain, this one also had a tinge of alcohol in it—though Brainchew had no idea what alcohol was—which enhanced the taste of the sweet soft head-meat it loved and craved.)

The fainted woman lay out cold a few yards in front of it. Easy meat. Once it was done with this man, it would eat her brain too. Too bad that in her fear she had urinated away all of her sweet waters. But this man still had all his urine in him; that would be enough compensation.

Brainchew drank a little of the man's blood, then stopped. Now that its initial hunger had been assuaged, it realized that something stank horribly in this place. The air reeked foully, the odor horrendous beyond belief.

The smell made the monster cringe.

It finally localized the stink to the unconscious woman on the floor.

Not gifted with great skills of recall, it took Brainchew several minutes—time spent nervously sucking on the hole it had made in the man's neck—to work out where it had smelt this utterly EVIL smell before.

And then, once its slow-witted mind had made the connection, it dropped the man it was draining of blood and backed out of the glass room.

NOOOOOOO! If it had had a voice, its scream would have echoed halfway across the town.

The unconscious woman had a disease! A brain disease—it smelled the illness on her like a poison. It now recalled once eating such a brain—millennia ago—and deep disgust flooded its foul soul. No, never again.

Without even bothering to drain the man's corpse of its urine, Brainchew turned and ran away. It ran as fast as it could, appalled to the very depths of its black heart by the obnoxious 'rotting' smell spilling from the woman's head.

When at last it was several streets away, it was utterly relieved to see the last of that terrible place.

***

And so it was that Ida Green survived the marauding monster, blissfully unaware that in ten years or so, just like her mother, she too was going to suffer from Parkinson's disease, and that that horrible affliction had just saved her life from Brainchew.

She was also three weeks pregnant for Josh Penham. Which she also had no idea about. That too, she'd discover in due course. Just a whole lot earlier.

CHAPTER 19

Lisa, mostly

Lisa rang the bell.

The blue front door opened immediately. Lisa found herself face-to-face with a short young woman in a frilly purple top and dark pants; her feet in brown slippers. Lisa's first impression of the woman was that she reminded her a lot of Tiff.

"Hi," Lisa said cautiously. "We called you from the gas station, and you said . . ."

"Yes, yes," the young woman said, nodding in an explosion of curly honey-brown hair, "I'm Nancy. I'm the one who called you." She stepped aside and held the door open. "Please come in. Tiff and Monique and Owlsy are in bed upstairs."

That statement brought back a part of Lisa's rage. "I-I-I don't understand how they could pull something like this."

Nancy giggled. "The way Monique whispered it to me, she loves Owlsy's 'ass-to-dick technique.'

Lisa peeked past Nancy into the living room. It seemed empty. She looked back. Carmela was dithering on the porch steps, looking left and right about her like she smelled danger in the night air.

Lisa grimaced and stepped into the house; she couldn't keep waiting for scaredy-cat. What she wanted to do right now was knock some sense into Monique and Tiff. Monique in particular.

The door swung to behind her as she heard Carmela's feet finally step up onto the porch.

"Neat place you got here," she said, looking around the living room.

Then she caught sight of a splash of blood on the green carpet. Her grip on the gun in her pocket tightened and she looked suspiciously at Nancy.

Several things now happened all at once: Behind Lisa, the front door clicked shut and Carmela, still outside, began buzzing to be let in; and Lisa also now heard deep breathing (as if someone had just stopped holding their breath), coming from behind (and slightly above) her.

Nancy—a shit-eating grin on her face—was standing in front of her, so that meant . . .

Lisa spun around to see who'd been hiding behind the open door, but she was knocked unconscious before she even completed the turn.

***

To Carmela's relief the front door finally opened again. Once the door had shut behind Lisa, Carmela's fear of entering this unknown house had inverted into a dread of being left outside it, all alone in the night. The sudden bump she'd heard from inside the house (or was it *outside?* Hadn't the sound come from behind her, near the truck?) almost made her jump out of her skin.

Carmela trembled with worries. *I still think this is a very bad idea. But if I don't go along, Lisa is going to be mad. Oh, God, why am I such a wimp at times? Oh, mom, I hate these jittery genes you left me! Okay, I gotta hold on to the taser, and if . . .*

Then she realized that the short young woman who'd been talking to Lisa was pointing a gun at her and waving her into the house.

Oh heck, Carmela thought as she meekly complied with the unspoken command, finding herself in a large living room with a huge, huge, huge ugly man, and Lisa lying unconscious on the floor, *I just knew this was a bad idea.*

***

Lisa woke up.

The throbbing in her brain was a maze she had to navigate back to consciousness, stepping between high walls of pain that threatened to at any moment short-circuit her back into senseless oblivion.

Once back to the land of the living, she got a fast update of her present situation. *Oh wow, did we just get suckered!*

She was propped up on a sofa in the living room. Carmela sat on her left, looking scared shitless, which was normal enough. Neither of them were tied up; there was clearly no need to restrain them. The short brunette who'd lured them over here with her lurid tale occupied an armchair on their right, legs crossed and a gun in her hand. And the person who'd knocked her out—a tall muscular man in dirty jeans—stood opposite them. Lisa's eyes rose up his body, from his bare feet to his denim pants, to the hands covering them with a shotgun, to his bare, hairy barrel of a chest to . . .

The first thing Lisa said on seeing Owlsy's face was, "Hey, you look just like that asshole Josh—" Then a horrified understanding hit her and she sagged back down on the sofa and smacked a hand against her forehead.

Oh no, Tiff didn't.

She swiveled to stare at Carmela. "Little sister, please tell me that your bestie didn't just execute the greatest fuck-up in human history."

Carmela, her lips pressed tightly together in her fright, could only nod repeatedly.

"Shit!" Lisa said, smacking her head hard again, scarcely noticing the pain the action triggered. "Shit! Shit! Shit!"

"You don't have to feel so bad about it," Owlsy said. "Happened all the time. Even the cops used to get us all mixed up."

Lisa nodded. This was a total nightmare. "Where're our two friends?" she asked, keeping any hint of nervousness out of her voice.

"They're downstairs," Nancy replied. She uncrossed her legs and stood up and stretched. "I wasn't lying about the sex part though. Owlsy here"—she flung her brother a loving glance—"literally fucked the poop out of Monique's ass."

Once again, Lisa was struck by how much this girl Nancy resembled Tiff. At least physically. There the similarity ended: Nancy had a confidence to her, a sureness to her actions which Tiff not only lacked, but had showed no signs of ever attaining. She also looked to be about twenty-three, Carmela's age.

While Nancy stretched herself, waving her gun like a flag over her petite plump form, Lisa scanned the room. If these two were the psychos who'd originally abducted Tiff, they were playing for keeps. There was no chance of talking sense into them; what was important now was keeping a clear head and working out a viable escape plan.

She instinctively felt her right jacket pocket for her gun. It wasn't there.

"You lookin' for this?"

She looked over at Owlsy. He was holding up her pistol. She watched him slip it back into the rear of his jeans waistband again. Shit!

"He's got your sister's taser too," Nancy added sweetly.

Hearing that, Lisa stole a quick glance at Carmela, willing her to keep calm. Carmela wasn't even looking her way, her gaze was fixed ahead on Owlsy. Her lips were trembling and she looked about to start crying.

Kid, don't you dare even fucking start that crap now, Lisa thought angrily. *You'd better hold it together. I really can't hold your hand at the moment.*

Then her anger faded and she felt silly over her mental raging. At the moment she had no choice but to hold Carmela's hand. That was what being family was all about.

"Now, you two pretty young ladies are most welcome to our family," Owlsy was saying.

Lisa looked at him. *Yes, he is mad. I can practically smell the waves of insanity blowing off him.* In the course of her job as a parole officer she'd met all types, including this man's type, the type that were so obviously not safe to let back into polite society that one questioned if the parole board members had been smoking reefer when they'd agreed to let them out. Agreed to 'unleash them on the world again' would be a better way of putting it. This man was a wolf, the kind that would kill and kill and kill until he got put down. Another really bad thing about him was that, like all successful serial killers/psychopaths, he had a deceptive appearance of normalcy. This house, for instance, wasn't a shit-den. It had no appearance of a ravenous beast's lair. And the man himself and his sister were both neat and properly groomed.

"You tell 'em, Owlsy," Nancy said, sitting back down and crossing her legs again.

"Welcome to our family," Owlsy repeated. "Now here's the rules we live by in this household. Firstly, we don't tolerate ungrateful bitches here. Second, we—"

"Second, we just jabber, jabber, jabber like Jabba the Hutt," Lisa interrupted in a tough voice. "Hey—news flash, amigo—we aren't staying. We ain't fallin' in love with you and getting married."

"Yes," Carmela said beside her, to her surprise. "We came here to collect our friends and leave. My sister's a law enforcement officer, and you're breaking the law by keeping us here against our will." Lisa was pleased; Carmela's voice was nervous but determined. *So you finally grew a pair?*

"Oh, is that so?" Owlsy replied in clear amusement. (Lisa hated the smile that had spread over his thick-lipped face at their protests. Such an ugly face it was. And, wow!—she began to forgive Tiff her mistake in fingering the wrong man—the resemblance between this guy and the one they'd killed was uncanny). He laughed and scratched his sideburns. "Goddam, a policewoman? Well, ain't you a legal catch then."

"Cops or not, you're staying," Nancy said.

"Fuck you," Carmela spat at her. "Release us at once!"

"No. We're keeping you. Downstairs, where it's nice and warm, with your friends and the rats and bugs."

"Hey, you're breaking the law; you can't get away with this," Lisa said. She glared at Owlsy. "Let us go, you sick fuck!"

On her angry demand, a scary and visible change came over his face. His eyes suddenly went 'flat,' like all the humanity had drained out of their pale depths; both sisters had the same impression of staring at shiny cold gray marbles implanted in dough. In addition, Owlsy's nose began twitching and his lips puckered out with rapid gusts of breath.

He strode forward and grabbed Lisa by her hair and jerked her up to her feet. Ouch! Lisa could practically feel her hair coming out at the roots.

"Who you talking to, bitch? Me?" He had his face close to hers, and was slobbering and . . . she felt a sudden charge of excitement at the primal nature of their close contact, and a desire to shed blood herself. *I could headbutt him now and kick him in the balls and . . .*

But Nancy had that gun trained on her and didn't look like she'd mind firing it.

"Easy now, Owlsy," Nancy cautioned. "Take a deep breath to calm down. If you fuck the bitch up now, how you gonna fuck her later, if she don't look so good anymore?"

Lisa felt him release her hair. She plopped back down on the seat. Owlsy stepped back from her. His facial expression normalized again as he went.

Carmela grabbed her and leaned in close, so close that Lisa could smell her shampoo. Cherry blossom and ginseng.

So strange, she thought, *so strange how Carmela and I are becoming closer than ever tonight. Like another's death is the tie that binds our hearts. Exactly like when our parents died. But, even at the cost of someone's else's passing, it's nice to feel loved.*

Her pleasure sobered on reviewing their situation. *Right now, we need to find a chink in these two psychos' mental armor and get the hell out of here. And rescue Tiff and Monique too. Thank heavens Carmela isn't cracking under the pressure!* Then she winced. *Oh, shit, I can't get over the fact that we killed an innocent man! How could we, after all the time I spent planning this?* It was damning knowledge she didn't wish to deal with.

Owlsy had meanwhile strolled off to the living room window and was peering out over the porch.

"Something's agitating the damn porkers," he told his sister.

"You see anything out there?" Nancy asked without taking either her eyes or gun off their captives.

"Nah, but I sure can smell it. Aw, makes me wanna puke. Like one of 'em's been dead for a week."

Lisa listened. She became aware of noises from outside, along with a strangely horrible smell. The smell was just like Owlsy had described it: something rotting. The young pigs, most of whom had previously been asleep, now sounded like they were all wide awake again. They were squealing like they were frightened for their lives.

"Maybe just some damn bobcat," Owlsy said, looking back from the window at Nancy. "I'll go have a look. You keep an eye on those two."

"Alright, but be careful. You don't wanna have to get another rabies shot like last time with Mortimer's dog."

Owlsy nodded. He pulled on a pair of boots sitting by the door, then waved to Lisa and Carmela. "Keep what's in your panties nice and warm for me, girls. I'll be right back."

The door clicked shut behind him.

Lisa heard the clump of his feet descending the porch steps, then his voice: "What the hell's wrong with you damn hogs tonight? C'mon, get your stinky li'l asses back asleep, ya li'l bastards, before I fry y'all as bacon. Shit! It stinks worse than the farm out here!"

Lisa regarded Nancy through hooded eyes. Nancy smiled back at her.

I need to take out this bitch and fast, Lisa thought desperately. *This opportunity—us with her alone—might not present itself again. What? They're planning to keep all four of us in their basement, odalisques in a psycho sheik's harem? Hell no, that ain't ever happening—I need to kick her ass fast before her brother comes back inside. Hmmm, but what do I do about the gun? I need a distraction. The easiest thing will be to tell her I need to pee, and then . . .*

She looked sideways at Carmela, who was still pressed up against her. Carmela looked calm enough, her expression placid. Lisa knew that was deceptive. Inside, her sister must be boiling with anxiety.

"So what's it like down in your basement?" she asked Nancy. "Do Tiff and Monique like it down there?"

Nancy kept her smile, and her grip on the gun never faltered (which began to worry Lisa). "Oh yeah, they really do. You'll like it too, once Owlsy gets to—"

She was interrupted by Owlsy's loud gasps from outside: "What the hell? You? What the goddam hell are *you* doing here, you evil son-of-a-bitch? Hey, friggin' let go of me!"

This outburst was followed by a weird silence that Lisa found ominous. In that surreal moment even the piglets were more quiet than a corpse. Then the pig racket was back redoubled; and cutting through their energetic squealing (and the horrible stink that now threatened to make her puke), Lisa made out the sounds of a violent scuffle.

Then they all clearly heard Owlsy yelling: "Hey, hey, get the hell offa my back, you smelly asshole! Nancy, help—the fucker's got me!"

Nancy had been keeping her eyes determinedly fixed on the captives. On this cry for help of Owlsy's, however, she instinctively cast her gaze right to look at the porch window.

That was all the window of opportunity Lisa needed. She flung herself so fast at Nancy that Carmela, who'd been leaning snugly against her, toppled over and fell flat on the sofa.

Before Nancy could turn back towards them again, Lisa had disarmed her.

Gun now in her possession, she dragged Nancy to her feet and pushed her towards the porch window.

She dug the gun into Nancy's back to encourage her. "Alright, get over there and don't try any tricks. I haven't shot anyone in ages and I'm impatient to do so again. C'mon, move it—I want to see what's going on out there."

Without a murmur of protest, Nancy hurried over to the window. Lisa sensed that for the moment, Nancy was more concerned about whatever was happening to her brother out in their yard than about herself being disarmed.

Outside, the unseen struggle grew even louder amidst the pig clamor. Lisa imagined the entire neighborhood waking up and someone directing the police over here. *Dammit, we don't need this nonsense! We're in enough of a mess already!*

All Lisa's thoughts froze in her brain the moment they reached the window and peered out. *What the hell is THAT?*

Owlsy and 'something' were grappling in front of his pickup truck. The porch light let her see the 'something' quite clearly. It was short and very muscular and was up on Owlsy's back, and (while he staggered around and pushed up against it with both hands) was clearly trying to fit its mouth over his head.

As far as Lisa could tell from her vantage point, the monster's head was almost as long as its body. Its eyes were sunken deep in its face and it appeared to be noseless. Its bloody lips formed a demonic halo around the brown fringe of Owlsy's hair, its mouth a yawning pit filled with hooks.

Owlsy wasn't yelling anymore because the monster now had a hand clamped over his mouth. Its claws had ripped open his left cheek and were buried out of sight in his face. Blood rushed bright red down his neck and into the thick hair on his bare chest.

Lisa had no idea what the thing was.

"What in God's name is that?" Carmela asked nervously, announcing her arrival beside them.

"Shit, shit, shit!" Nancy gasped in horror. "That's Brainchew! Oh, Jesus, help us!"

Brainchew? It suddenly made sense to Lisa as to why the monster was up on Owlsy's back and trying to fit its mouth around his head. *Brainchew?*

Of Owlsy's shotgun, there was no sign. The two had likely battled around the truck with the man trying to get back up onto the porch again before the monster killed him. Of the fact that it was deadly, Lisa had no doubt—it was soaked in blood, and from the shape and size of its dentition, it clearly didn't subsist on vegetables.

Brainchew?

Nancy, formerly the picture of feminine self-confidence, was now whimpering like a baby. That might have had something to do with the gun Lisa had stuck in her back, but Lisa doubted it.

Brainchew?

Outside the deadly contest was still on. Owlsy kept shifting his head just fast enough to stop the monster riding his back from getting its mouth into position. Lisa could only speculate on what would happen once 'Brainchew' succeeded in its objective.

Owlsy was climbing the porch steps. He was staring in through the window at them and silently gesturing for help, his eyes frantic and pleading. The monster had its legs locked around the front of his body. He had no chance whatever of shaking it off. His naked chest and belly both ran with bright red streams. In addition to the blood still gushing from his ripped-open face, blood also poured from holes in Owlsy's belly where the creature's claws had dug deep into his abdominal wall and shredded his muscles.

Nancy began squirming desperately against Lisa. "We've gotta help him!" she moaned. "It's gonna kill him. We've gotta do something!"

"Shut up," Lisa warned her. "You open that door and I'll push you outside for it to get too."

Nancy went limp and began mumbling incomprehensibly. Lisa heard Carmela breathing superfast like she was going to faint.

And then, just as Owlsy stepped up onto the porch, he slipped on a splatter of his own blood and lost his balance. And as he struggled to right himself again, the monster—Brainchew—finally got its mouth in the right position over his head.

Lisa cringed as the horrid maw yawned wide. *My god—all those teeth!*

Then she heard a sharp snap like someone breaking a bone, and the monster's teeth vanished completely inside Owlsy's head. And then the pair of them fell backwards off the porch and rolled down the steps and down towards the pickup truck.

Nancy began weeping loudly.

"Be quiet!" Lisa warned her harshly. Her mind still reeled from what she'd just seen. She cast one last gaze outside the window. Still wrapped around Owlsy's body where they lay on the ground, the monster was chewing something while looking towards the house. Owlsy was clearly dead. His eyes stared wide in his torn-to-shreds face.

Holding her by the scruff of her neck, Lisa dragged Nancy away from the window. She pushed her towards a chair, and forced her down into it. Nancy sat there, tears streaming down her face, seemingly incapable of even the least resistance now.

Lisa turned to Carmela, who'd trailed them over. "Go back and shut the drapes, and then lock and bolt the door."

Carmela nodded and hurried to do so. While she pulled the curtains together, Lisa poked Nancy in the head with the muzzle of her gun. (It was actually *Monique's* gun; *hers* had been the one that Owlsy had stuck in his waistband, and which was now lost somewhere outside along with his shotgun.) "Hey, cut out the goddam weeping act before I start slapping you. Hey, bitch, I mean you!"

Nancy looked tearfully up at her. "My brothers . . . my brothers . . ."

"Yeah, yeah," Lisa said. "We both saw what the hell happened. And it couldn't have happened to a nicer man now, could it?"

Nancy's teary face contorted in rage. "How dare you?"

Lisa smirked. "Now that's more like it; bring out the tough bitch in you. And hey—don't you look at me like that. Were you expecting sympathy? That we'd shed tears over some rapist jerk who just got his just deserts? His dying merely saves us the bother of offing him ourselves, you piece of trash."

Nancy still looked enraged, but resumed weeping. "My brothers . . . my brothers."

Lisa felt Carmela tapping her on the shoulder. She looked up. "What, kid?"

"Three things: First, we need to find out about the other entrances to this house that that thing can get in through. Second, we need to go get Tiff and Monique . . . and rethink our plan for tonight. And third, we need to figure out what to do about that thing outside."

Lisa nodded. "Yeah, you're right. And there's a fourth too—what the hell *is* that thing? But first things first . . ." She peered hard and cold at the weeping brunette seated facing her. "Hey, you heard my sister. Are there any other entrances through which that thing can get in?"

Nancy wiped her eyes dry, then shook her head. "No, the back door and kitchen door are both locked."

"Good, that buys us some time then." Lisa ran fingers through her pale hair.

"So now we go fetch Tiff and Monique," Carmela said. "She said they're downstairs in the basement."

(On her statement, Nancy looked up, a strange dread filling her dark eyes. Neither sister, however, both being preoccupied with other things, noticed how curious that glance had been.)

"Tiff and Monique," Carmela repeated pointedly, when Lisa didn't seem in a hurry to head off to look for them.

"Hold on," Lisa said. "If they aren't dead yet, a five-minute wait won't kill them." She peered coldly at Nancy again. "Now, that thing outside there . . . you called it 'Brainchew.' Start talking—what the hell is it? And why did it attack your brother?"

She repressed a shudder. The image of the monster they'd glimpsed through the window was vivid in her mind—the massive abnormal head, the bloodstained gray skin, the flesh-rending claws— and she needed an explanation fast before she began visibly trembling like Carmela was doing.

When Nancy didn't talk fast enough, she slapped her hard. Once, twice.

"Hey, snap out of your damn funk and start talking, before I push you out the front door for that thing to get. I mean it, I ain't playing with you."

The slaps seemed to bring Nancy back to the present.

"It's called Brainchew," she mumbled.

"We already know *that*. Tell us *the rest*." Lisa pulled up a chair to face Nancy, then sat with her gun pointed at her. "Out with it."

"They're gone," Carmela called from the window.

"What?" Lisa didn't look at her in case Nancy had reserves of courage left.

"Both the monster and Owlsy's body. They're both gone."

Lisa winced at the 'loud and clear' anxiety in Carmela's voice. *Just what we don't need.*

Nancy began sniffling again. Lisa slapped her again. "Hey, bitch, I'm still waiting for your explanation. Or do I need to shoot you first? And . . ." this time she did fling a quick glance sideways, "Carmela, for God's sake, stop pooping yourself with fear beside the goddam window and come listen to this."

***

"Brainchew," Nancy explained, "is a monster that feed on human brains. That's both the long and short of it. Brainchew is kinda like

Raynham's very own urban legend; like New York's 'alligators in the sewers' sort of thing. Only in this case, the damn thing is as real as moonlight. And if you encounter it, you're very likely gonna wind up dead."

"Yeah," Carmela agreed. "We just saw that."

"Okay, how do we kill it?" Lisa asked.

"You can't kill it."

A cold shiver ran through Lisa. She shook it off. "Don't give us that hogwash. Everything can be killed."

"Not this thing. Not Brainchew. Guns won't stop it, nor will fire or explosives. Believe me, the cops have tried everything."

Lisa was relieved that Nancy had stopped sniveling over her asshole brother's death. She was tired of having to slap her. *Did she honestly expect us to give a shit?*

"You're serious that there's no way to kill that thing?" Carmela asked. "No way at all?"

"Yeah, you're lying," Lisa said, a thought occurring to her. "Because, if you're telling the truth, how come the population of Raynham isn't zero by now? Why hasn't this Brainchew monster eaten everyone's brains already?"

"There's a knife that can stop it," Nancy admitted. "It freezes Brainchew solid, but it won't be dead for real; that's what I meant. Given the right conditions, it'll wake up again, and just as hungry as before."

"Don't worry about *afterwards*," Lisa retorted. "We intend to be gone from here long before the 'right conditions' return."

"Who's got the knife?" Carmela asked in a desperate voice. "Tell us—who has it?"

"My boyfriend Ambrose," Nancy revealed.

"Where is he?"

"He runs the Sunflower Motel, two houses away from here."

"The tall, bearded, middle-aged guy?"

Nancy nodded.

Lisa raised an eyebrow at Carmela. A plan had begun forming in her mind. She turned back to Nancy. "Alright, girl, now take us down to our friends." This time she didn't miss the look of horror that immediately came over Nancy's face. "*What?* You've done something bad to them?"

"We . . . we . . ." Nancy cringed, the look of horror remaining on her face.

Lisa had no idea what to make of their former captor's strange behavior.

Carmela had seen it too, and had reached her own conclusion. Unsure of where she was heading, she turned and charged off down the adjoining hallway, howling, "Tiff!? Tiff!? Are you okay!?"

Lisa leaned towards Nancy, who shrank back from her. "Get up, you. Let's go find out exactly what you and your brother were up to before we arrived. And it had better not be what I'm thinking."

She dragged Nancy away by her hair across the living room.

CHAPTER 20

Ambrose

In the lobby of the Sunflower Motel, Ambrose looked up from his laptop. Had he just smelt what he thought he had?

No, that was impossible.

He rubbed his temples, then his eyes. *Hey, for a moment there, I thought I smelt Brainchew.*

He sniffed the air, but it smelt clean again; there was no rotting meat reek to alarm him.

Still, Ambrose couldn't relax after that. The motel's books were in order, except that he'd discovered he'd overbilled a Detroit couple who'd stayed here last week by $200. He'd need to call them in the morning and refund the money. That was all.

He got up and stretched, then walked out from behind the reception desk and over to the front door. He unlocked it, rolled up the metal shutter beyond, and stepped outside. He walked down the lobby steps onto the front lot and looked around.

All at once he felt silly. There was nothing out here except the night—the black sky, the cold breeze tickling his mustache and beard, and the subliminal hum that assured one that though the human world was asleep at the moment, the insect world was wide awake and going about its business.

Ambrose walked towards the driveway. Then he stopped on hearing a sudden cascade of sounds coming from his right. He turned that way and listened hard. That had to Owlsy's pigs, the fresh load he'd not yet dropped off at McKinney's farm.

The wind shifted slightly and traces of smell from that direction came his way. Damn, it sure did stink like Brainchew a bit; but it was most likely just the damn pigs shitting up the rear of Owlsy's pickup truck. *How similar they smell. And, damn, do the little beasts sound agitated tonight. As if . . .*

He snuffed the thought out. One had to think logically about stuff like this. If (by the wildest stretch of the imagination possible) Brainchew *had* somehow crawled out of its grave again and found its way up here, surely it would come looking for *him*, and not pass him by and head over to Nancy's house instead.

We're old enemies, Brainchew and I, he thought. *Sure, the damn thing is dumber that a sackful of horseshit, but at least it knows it hates me. And vice-versa, I hate the stupid demon prick worse than I hate pedophiles.* He looked far across the motel parking lot, down the length of the front block, squinting to see beyond the silver Honda Accord belonging to the four young women. There was nothing over there, just night-draped trees.

Besides, he thought, turning to return to the lobby, *if Brainchew somehow got lost and ran over to Nancy's place instead of coming here, she can just call me on the phone and I'll . . .*

He froze in sudden shock. Inside the motel lobby, his phone was ringing. *Paranoid* blasting loud and clear as FM Radio.

Aw heck, no! In a panic, Ambrose dashed over to the steps and up into the reception building.

He grabbed up his phone and heaved a sigh of relief. No, Nancy wasn't in any danger. It was just Crystal calling him again.

"Hi, darling," came her voice over the line once he accepted the call, "how you doing?"

"Crystal, ain't you supposed to be getting double-teamed?"

She giggled. "Oh, I got the rest of the night off. See, I was right about Cody and Jimmy secretly being in love with each other. Once they were both inside my ass at the same time, rubbing their dicks against one another's, they got around to kissing each other and now . . . now they're busy performing sixty-nine on each other and making plans to get married." She giggled again. "They're giving me a huge bonus for helping them come out of the closet."

Ambrose sighed. "That's nice, Crystal, really wonderful."

She sighed back, a desolate and miserable sound. "You know, Ambrose, I've been thinking about what we were discussing earlier. Maybe you're right, maybe I really should stop selling my gash for cash and come sit down in Raynham and help you run the motel. I think I'm getting too damn old for this damn prostitute's game."

"Yeah?" Ambrose asked cautiously, having heard the notes of despair in her voice. "What's giving you that sudden change of heart? I thought you loved hustling." Inwardly, he was wincing in almost physical pain. *Oh no, Crystal, you can't quit now; you gotta keep selling yourself! You quitting prostitution will spell the end of my fledgling romance with Nancy Pine. And next thing, you're gonna suggest that me and you get married and live happily ever after.* At that moment it was a terrifying and very real possibility to Ambrose: having a wife that half the men in town had slept with.

Crystal said, "Oh, baby, watching these two guys having sex out there in the bedroom like I'm not even here, I just feel obsolete. It's like I've been devalued by the US Pussy Treasury, or the Vagina Stock Exchange, or something. Oh, I dunno, Ambrose, I just feel so shitty. Maybe by morning I'll feel better."

He sighed with relief. His best friend just had the hooker blues that afflicted her every once in a while. When those came, Crystal felt her life wasn't worth living anymore. That lasted until the next guy flashed a wad of cash in her face and asked for some ass.

"Yeah, baby," he said soothingly. "I feel that way too sometimes. Most time it's just stress and exhaustion. I'm sure you'll feel better after some sleep."

"You really think so, Ambrose?"

"I'm positive about it. There ain't nothing like a good night's rest to restore a call girl's proper perspective of the value of selling her body to advance the male sexual cause."

"Huh? Yeah, you're right. And you know what?"

"What?"

"Suddenly, I don't feel so obsolete anymore. Right now I'm gonna go back out into that bedroom and lick each of those guys' assholes while they're fellating one another. I'll teach those cocksuckers how to ream each other's butts—earn my bonus. Hey, how's that for prostitute positivity?"

Ambrose was speechless. It now occurred to him that maybe she'd been doing some coke or speed too; her words had that hyped-up, jagged rhythm to them. *Well at least she ain't gonna come home and split me and Nancy up anymore.*

Then Crystal asked, "Hey, Ambrose, you seen Brainchew yet? Has your favorite enemy been over to the motel to say 'hi' tonight?"

The question jolted Ambrose like an electric shock. "*What?* What?"

"Ha ha, baby! Just joking! Thanks for always being there to listen to me."

And she hung up.

Ambrose sat back down behind the reception desk, staring across the lobby and out into the night. *What the hell was that all about? Can't tonight just be normal for even a few minutes?*

Then, a sudden inexplicable chill coming over him, he stopped staring outside the lobby, and instead gazed down into the shelves in the rear of the desk, at the stone knife resting beside his shotgun.

Oh, dear God, I ain't gonna have to use this tonight, am I?

Across the room the clock read 01:40.

215

CHAPTER 21

Mostly Carmela

Once they were down in the basement, Carmela lost it.

For a long disbelieving moment, she stared in shock at Tiff's gutted and almost decapitated body dangling from the yellow wall. Tiff's eyes were open, looking fixedly at nothing. She seemed to have a gaping toothless mouth in the middle of her neck, one which had vomited red paint all over her breasts and shoulders. Her bloody innards hung in tattered loops out of her belly, draped down over Monique's gagged and equally bloody corpse, which lay by her feet. (Monique's buttocks were smeared with feces, like she'd defecated violently while dying.)

Carmela's moment of absolute disbelief ended. She turned to Lisa then pointed at Nancy. "Shoot her," she said in a tight, almost hysterical voice, "Put her out of her misery before I rip her to shreds."

"The noise," Lisa replied. Her eyes were cold, and she was clearly distressed too by all she was seeing. Still, she didn't look as upset as Carmela would have liked. Those nerves of steel again.

"Lisa, we're down in her goddam psycho basement. No one'll hear. Shoot the bitch."

"No." Lisa was gripping Nancy by her curls. Nancy had a permanent wince fixed on her face from the tugging on her hair. She had a pleading look in her eyes that neither sister bothered with.

Carmela looked around, her eyes falling on the table with the surgical implements.

"Don't," Lisa said, correctly reading the intent in her teary eyes. "We need her to call her boyfriend, so we can get out of here without that monster emptying our heads too like it did her brother's."

Mention of the monster got through to Carmela. What 'Brainchew' had done—what they'd all watched it do—was almost more horrible than the sight of these two corpses down here. Oh, no, that wasn't being done to *her*. Nothing was eating *her* brain like that.

She froze at another horrible sight—a diced human corpse in several buckets. Shit. What the unholy hell was this crap? The set of a torture-porn flick? *SAW 8* versus *Hostel 14* versus *The Texas Chainsaw Massacre*? How many people had these two psychopaths butchered down here? Back when Tiff had told her what this basement was like, she'd thought she understood. Now, seeing Tiff hung on the wall like fresh meat, her head almost fully severed from her body, she realized she hadn't understood a thing. Nothing at all. Seeing Monique lying dead there on the floor, a floor so smeared with her blood that it looked almost like her red hair had melted into it, was unnerving.

Indeed, Carmela was certain she'd have turned and fled screaming from this room of horrors if she wasn't so angry. And if she didn't have an obvious target to vent her anger on:

Nancy.

But Lisa, her lips compressed with disgust at the human carnage everywhere, was insisting that they mustn't kill the fat little bitch. *And Lisa is of course Decider-In-Chief of Cole family opinion. She Who Must Not Be Trifled With. I must do what she says. It's always been that way and will likely never change. Lisa is always right. And of course, I agree with Lisa: we need this psycho Nancy cunt alive. But . . .*

She glanced once more at Tiff's corpse, then frowned at her sister.

"Okay, so maybe I won't kill her," she told Lisa in a voice so steely that she hardly recognized it as her own. "But I'm gonna hurt her badly whether you like it or not."

"Be my guest," Lisa said, shoving the cringing Nancy at her. "You've got five minutes to beat all the shit out of her that you want. And you . . ." she reached forward and tugged Nancy's curls again, "if you dare resist whatever she does to you, I'll put a bullet in each of your buttocks. Don't doubt that I will, not after seeing this little torture dungeon you two have been running down here."

She smiled at Carmela. "Go on, little sis. The bitch is all yours."

Carmela wasn't sure what possessed her then. It felt like she was filled by the spirits of both Tiff and Monique, both angry as goddam fuck with Nancy and impatient and desperate to get even with her.

She charged forward and slammed into Nancy like a battering ram, aware only of a red rage filling the space behind her eyes, a rage focused on the small brunette in front of her who'd robbed her of her best friend.

Tiff, Tiff, Tiff. Little harmless Tiffany Hooper who never hurt a soul in her damned life and you went and cut her open like she was a sheep been prepared for a barbeque? Oh God.

Carmela didn't even realize she was crying while she took out her rage on Nancy Pine (whom she too had already noticed looked distressingly similar to Tiff, just somehow sexier). Carmela just knew that she was throwing HARD punches and kicking and slamming Nancy left and right, flinging the other woman across the basement like she was in the grip of a human tornado.

Nancy, seeing as Lisa was covering her with the gun, could do nothing but take the beating. And Carmela had truckloads of animosity to let loose on her victim. Oh, Carmela let loose a virtual universe of girl-on-girl violence on her.

Finally, Carmela felt Lisa pulling her off Nancy. "Alright, time's up, that's enough."

"Let go of me, you bitch—I'm not done yet."

"Oh yes you are. If you do any more you'll kill her."

Slowly the red rage departed from Carmela's mind; the corresponding crimson haze faded from her eyes. She stood up.

"Wow," Lisa said admiringly. "That was some beating. I didn't know you had it in you."

Carmela didn't reply. Lisa's smugness in the face of all this death and horror was beginning to irritate her.

Instead, she looked down at Nancy, who lay all disheveled on the floor.

Nancy was bleeding from both mouth and nose, and her hair looked like a rat's nest. Her top was torn into rags. Her eyes were open and staring and she was gasping for breath. There was blood on her pants from Carmela dragging her over Monique's corpse to ram her head against the far wall. She sat up, gasping in pain as she got her torso upright. She looked up at her tormentor, one hand grabbing her head as if to prevent it toppling off her shoulders. In addition to a look of agony, there was fury in her eyes.

"Fuck you, bitch," she spat at Carmela, in the process spitting out two of her front teeth, "is that all you got?"

As her response, Carmela let fly with a final kick to the ribs that curled Nancy up and left her gasping for pain on her back again. She felt satisfied; on that last kick she'd heard something crack. Hopefully it was one of the bitch's ribs, if she hadn't already broken them all.

"What now?" she asked Lisa.

Lisa met her gaze coolly. She pointed down at Nancy. "We get her upstairs and rethink the plan."

Carmela couldn't believe her ears. "Rethink the plan? The *plan?* Lisa, the goddam plan is already fucked up its ass by both John Holmes and Ron Jeremy doing a DP on it."

"And here I was thinking I was the only one who watched vintage porn," Lisa replied sweetly. "Yes, our original plan might have hemorrhoids, but that doesn't mean we give up sodomizing life's butthole. We can't. You wanna spend the rest of your life in jail for murdering Josh Penham?"

Carmela didn't reply.

Lisa nodded. "No, I didn't think so. So give me a hand with getting this little piece of shit upstairs to where the air doesn't reek of blood and our brains will work better."

Carmela reached down and viciously jerked Nancy up by her hair. "You heard the boss—get a fucking move on."

***

"Listen, Nancy, we'll make a deal with you," Lisa said once the three of them were again seated upstairs in the living room. (Outside, the smell of monster had dispersed. For the moment at least, they appeared safe.)

"A deal?" Carmela and Nancy asked simultaneously.

"Yes, a frigging deal."

"What is it?" Carmela and Nancy both enquired, again speaking at the same time.

"Will you two just let me finish talking?"

Both nodded.

Lisa cleared her throat and brushed her blonde hair out of her eyes. Carmela felt a moment's envy over how beautiful her older sister was, but felt even more intensely jealous over how unruffled she still seemed after this night's procession of ever-increasing horrors.

Fuck! Saying Lisa has nerves of steel is an understatement. And me? Oh, I have nerves of well-boiled spaghetti; long limp terrified strings of them linking my brain to my muscles.

The adrenalin surge of rage that Carmela had experienced on finding Tiff dead had now passed, and she felt empty, her emotional space a deep hole with walls of copiously dripping anxiety. Tiff, her best friend and confidante for eleven years was dead, and at the moment the magnitude of that loss seemed impossible for Carmela to quantify.

And now, despite everything, we're having to worry about going to jail after all. Oh, I was so against this whole plan to begin with!

Lisa, meanwhile, was addressing them both:

"Here's the deal, Nancy. You'll call your boyfriend Ambrose over here to come kill Brainchew, and after that we'll go our separate ways. We'll forget about you and the contents of your basement, and you'll forget that you ever met us, or that we ever mentioned Josh Penham's death to you." She leaned close to the woman. "What do you say?"

Nancy wiped blood from her face. "I don't know," she said cautiously. "How do I know you won't kill me once Ambrose subdues Brainchew?"

"Use your goddam brains. We're all criminals and murderers here. You know about Josh, we know about you and your brother's killing spree. There's no benefits to either side if we don't work together. We all keep our mouths shut and none of us goes to jail."

"Okay," Nancy agreed slowly.

"I don't like this," Carmela said. She hated the fact that they were dealing with Nancy at all—this evil murderess! But then, the damning import of Lisa's words hit her. They were murderesses too—Josh Penham had never laid a finger on Tiff, and look what they'd done to him. *Okay, it was Tiff who slit his throat, but I drugged him after we abducted him, and Lisa thought up the plan to abduct him in the first place . . . and beautiful Monique? Oh, Monique's crime was just having too much urine on hand, I guess.*

"What're we gonna do about Tiff and Monique's bodies?" she asked.

"She'll get rid of them," Lisa said, gesturing at Nancy with her pistol. "Won't you?"

"I'll get rid of them," Nancy agreed, a cold smile settling over her battered face. (Carmela felt somewhat embarrassed on seeing the woman now had two black eyes, and her nose too looked crooked and swollen.) "Mr. McKinney's hogs won't mind a little more high-protein mash. I'll explain it as bags of feed that Josh forgot to deliver." She leaned forward and spat out blood on the green carpet. "But you need to figure out an explanation as to why both girls went missing. One that won't lead back here."

"Don't worry about that; I got that covered," Lisa said.

Nancy's expression now turned quizzical. "Okay, now that I'm disposing of bodies, where did you leave Josh's, so I can lose it too?"

Despite her hatred of the woman, Carmela was impressed by Nancy's nerve. "You're not worried?"

Nancy grinned, revealing her three missing teeth, then winced and gingerly felt her nose. "Shit, I think you broke it." Then she seemed to forget the pain. "Look, it's still the middle of the night now, there's next to no danger. Once Ambrose takes care of Brainchew, I'll drive off to get the body. There'll be loads of cops over here of course 'cos of Owlsy, but I'll sneak it into the house somehow, and . . ." She looked expectantly at them. "So where is it?"

"We left it in the Pleasant Street Cemetery. Hey—what's wrong? Nancy? Nancy? Why d'you look so shocked?"

Nancy had gone the color of whitewash. "Aw shit," she said finally. "That's what woke Brainchew up again."

Carmela and Lisa paled also. *"Us?"*

Nancy seemed to get over her shock. "Yeah. Where exactly did you leave the body?"

"In a deep corner of the graveyard. On the left, under a group of trees."

"Was it bleeding?"

"A whole damn lot."

Nancy shrugged. "That's all it takes; blood wakes Brainchew up. You're fortunate. If you hadn't gotten out of there, it would have killed all four of you." She sniffed the air. "Yeah, it's still around somewhere. It won't go away until it's eaten our brains too."

Carmela found it odd how they were all talking like old friends now. She desperately wanted to continue hating Nancy for taking Tiff away from her, but it was impossible. Now that they were partners in crime, the pot had no business despising the kettle. And now (along with Lisa), she remembered clearly those strange vibrations that had rumbled the 'Brian Chu' grave.

"Well, we'd better get your boyfriend over here," Lisa said. "And the faster the better. Okay, when he arrives, Carmela and I are gonna hide upstairs. Our alibi for tonight is that we're asleep in the motel, so . . ."

"You can sneak back across behind the next house afterward. It's empty, no one'll see you. But you need to leave before the police arrive, and . . . shit! Shit! Shit!"

While speaking, Nancy had been getting her phone out of her pants pocket.

"What's the matter?" Lisa asked.

Nancy held the cellphone up for her inspection. Carmela winced on seeing its completely shattered screen, realizing it had gotten smashed when she'd been beating the crap out of Nancy. "Oops—no way to call Ambrose now."

Lisa and Nancy turned to look at Carmela.

Carmela thought she had to defend herself against the unvoiced accusations. "Look, I didn't know it was in her pock . . . Hey, both of you stop staring at me like I . . ." Then she stared pointedly back at Nancy, and reached into her pocket for her own phone. "I don't see what the fuss is—just call him on my line." She looked to Lisa for confirmation. "That's fine, isn't it, since she'll be getting rid of Josh's body too?"

Lisa nodded. "Yeah, it is."

Then Carmela realized that Nancy wasn't taking the phone from her. "What is it now? Surely even if he doesn't recognize the number calling, you can still text him?"

"It's not that."

"Then what the fuck is it!? I can smell that damn monster outside!" This was true: a wayward draft of air had just blown Brainchew's stink into the living room. The smell reminded Carmela of the monster's horrible appearance (all those teeth!) and she instantly felt like wetting herself. Also, Owlsy's piglets had abruptly begun squealing again.

"I don't know Ambrose's number off-hand," Nancy admitted finally.

Lisa and Carmela both stared at her. "What?" they said together.

"Some girlfriend you are," Lisa blurted out disgustedly.

"What sort of girlfriend are you?" Carmela was forced to ask.

Nancy looked very offended by the statement/question. "Hey, stop judging me. We've only been dating for a week."

"Even so . . ." Lisa said. (Lisa knew Bobby Finch's phone numbers—office phone, cellphone, apartment phone—better than she knew her own social security number.) "To a proper girlfriend, a man's numbers are of the highest priority."

"Yes," Carmela agreed. "Who you gonna call otherwise? Ghostbusters?"

"Besides, there was no need to memorize it anyway," Nancy continued in an aggrieved voice. "It was stored in my phone and he lives fifty yards away." She gestured in the direction of the motel. "All I need to do to see him is *walk over there.*"

Lisa got up and paced towards the front door, then turned back and stared at the other two. "Yes," she said, "that's what were gonna do then: walk over there."

"What!?" Nancy and Carmela both yelped. Carmela now decided that there was something fundamentally wrong with tonight, a misalignment of the stars that was breeding coincidental speech.

Leaning against the front door, Lisa shrugged. "We either head for the motel, or wait for Brainchew to break in here. In which case, seeing as you've said bullets won't stop it, we three are all as good as dead with emptied heads. So, which is it, girls—we walk or we wait?"

"We walk," Nancy said immediately.

Lisa's gaze swept to Carmela. Carmela always hated the pressure of Lisa's eyes on her. It was simply more domination; more bossing about.

"We walk," she agreed finally, accepting that they were all caught between a rock and a hard place.

Wow, Carmela thought, *what a fantastically sticky mess we've gotten ourselves into tonight!* In a way, she was almost amused. But then, not for the first (or as she suspected, the last) time in her life, she put her faith in Lisa to see them safely through. Brainchew might be unkillable, but Lisa was indestructible.

Like the other two, Carmela now began mentally preparing herself for the trip across to the motel, while Brainchew's obscene reek percolated in and out of the Pines' living room amidst the racket of alarmed piglets. She suspected that their chances of making it across to the motel alive or dying trying were an even 50/50.

CHAPTER 22

The Monster

Brainchew was confused. Concealed amidst the roadside trees near the Pine house driveway, its feet surrounded by fresh piglet carcasses, and with the exquisite taste of the big man's head still fresh in its mind, it pondered its next move:

Should it attack Ambrose in the 'Sunflower?' (From long association with the place, Brainchew knew the motel's name.) Or should it instead try to enter this nearby house with the three scared women (oh, how it relished their terror!), which even now had three already dead brains underground?

Hunger versus hatred. Lust versus ego gratification. The contest for dominance raged between its desires. It needed to feed, but its want for revenge on Ambrose poisoned its gluttonous craving, turning the food bitter in its mouth.

Oh, how Brainchew *hated* Ambrose!

But it feared him too, was terrified of him, this puny human whom it could kill with a single swipe of its claws.

Brainchew bent and plucked a squealing piglet from the crate it had carried off from the green vehicle. It raised the terrified animal's head to its mouth and bit deeply. It sucked out the bloody, juicy brain. Then, almost instantly, it spat the piglet's brain out again. It raved in disgust at the pig-brain's corrupted flavor. Its hatred was too great; these little porcine appetizers tasted as bland as salted sand to its palate.

It flung the brainless piglet over to its right, where the shredded corpse of the man it had killed (and drank both his blood and urine) lay draped across a stretch of tree-shaded grass. The dead piglet hit the big man and almost rolled into the hole in his head.

Brainchew looked once more towards the house with the scared women. They were no match at all for it. It would return for them; all it needed to do here was find a way into the house.

But for now, it was going to settle its score with Ambrose once and for all.

Yes. *KILL AMBROSE! KILL AMBROSE!! KILL AMBROSE!!!* its miniscule mind raved in its grotesque head.

Taking cautious steps, it started towards the motel. It was cowardly in its fear. It didn't dare take on its nemesis face-to-face again. It would stalk him with animal cunning; with the self-preservative instinct of the desperate hunted beast. It would make a noise, and then, when he came out to investigate, it would ambush him—it would tear out his throat with its claws and it would watch in pleasure while, in rising horror, he stared his death in the face. And then, when his terror of dying was at its highest, only then would it place its mouth around his head and clamp its teeth down tight on his skull, then bite through the puny resistance of the bone and sink its teeth into his brain. Ah, it would savor the taste of Ambrose's brain for ages, letting the man's blood seep out of the soft meat cushion and pool in its mouth, and it would chew delicately on its enemy's center of thought, and then . . .

It had stepped out of the cover of trees into the moonlight. It gazed up at the moon, bathing in the celestial body's crystalline radiance.

. . . And then, once Ambrose was dead and no longer able to stop its rampaging, it would kill kill kill kill KILL KILL KILL KILL KILL **KILL KILL KILL KILL KILL!!!**

Infernal joy thrilling in its evil heart, Brainchew walked forward into the line of trees that bordered the Sunflower Motel.

CHAPTER 23

Carmela, with Lisa & Nancy

"Okay, remember," Lisa admonished as they prepared to exit Nancy's house through the back door. "Stay close to me. We're not going to run, because we might run right into it. We'll all just walk very fast. Understood?"

The other two young women nodded.

"Too bad we lost Owlsy's shotgun," Nancy said.

"We'll be okay," Lisa said reassuringly, indicating her own gun. "Even if this doesn't stop it, the shots will buy us enough time to make it across to the motel. And also, Brainchew stinks like the Devil's farts. It can't get near us without us smelling it far off."

"Yeah, but it's as fast as a fart too," Nancy pointed out.

"Shit, that's true. We need to all keep as alert as possible then."

Carmela didn't say anything. Now that they were about going into action with Lisa's latest plan (didn't Lisa ever run out of plans? And each one more dangerous than the last?), she was doing her best to remain brave. She was certain that if that Brainchew monster came charging at her, she would freeze in her tracks and piss herself and lose her mind and simply play the role of the classic, perfect victim— she couldn't get the monster's huge head and seemingly even HUGER mouth, and impossibly HUGEST teeth out of her mind. Try hard as she could to flush this mental garbage, she kept seeing the images, like her memory was a video stuck in a loop.

Carmela and Nancy had armed themselves with two large knives that Nancy had fetched from the basement. Carmela had refused to return down there. One more sight of Tiff's corpse and she'd freak out completely.

"Alright," Lisa said. "Let's do this."

Nancy unlatched the back door and they stepped outside. Afterwards, Nancy made certain to lock the door behind them. "If we miss it on our way over there," she said, "I don't want to come home later and find it inside waiting to welcome me."

The night air embraced them. The rear yard was more shadowy than its front counterpart, mostly due to a large tree in its middle, to the left of which stood a white shed which Carmela suspected contained the Pine sibling's 'body grinder.'

Considering the shed's gory function helped increase Carmela's worries. She felt surrounded by insanity—it appeared to be everywhere she turned. She quickly looked away from the shed and followed the others (Lisa already leading the way) off to the right of the house.

A few steps later they were all out in the moonlight.

As they hurried across the yard, Carmela looked right, down the Pine's driveway. There was blood smeared along the side of the pickup truck. She shuddered and made sure she kept close to the others.

Penetrating the tree line separating the yards formed a brief interlude in their transit. Then they were in the shadows of the next building, a small cottage with unmown knee-high grass.

"Stop, I can smell it!" Nancy whispered all of a sudden.

The other two froze. All three women huddled close. They stood back-to-back like Lisa had instructed, knives and gun held out as protection.

"Yeah, I can smell it too," Lisa acknowledged after sniffing the air. "It smells like it's over towards the motel though."

"The wind keeps shifting," Nancy said, "that's the problem."

"Let's move closer to the house," Lisa said. "That way, we'll only need to watch on one side."

They pressed themselves against the cottage wall, with Carmela in between Lisa (who was once again in front) and Nancy. Staring wide-eyed into the darkness and across at the border of trees separating them from their destination, they made their way forward with slow, painfully quiet steps.

As they neared the far side of the cottage, Brainchew's smell began thickening around them.

"I think it's heading back this way," Nancy said.

"It could be anywhere," Carmela said in a quaking voice, feeling her mind about to melt from fear. "The smell is getting stronger and stronger!"

"Calm down," Lisa whispered gently to her. "Don't get into a panic, it might just be the wind changing direction again. If we can't make it across now, we'll break a window and hide in this house until the smell's gone again."

"The smell's dying down," Nancy said.

Then they all heard it—the loud 'krak' of a foot snapping a fallen branch. Even Lisa leapt back at the noise, which had come from in front of them.

"It's here," Nancy gasped.

"Shit."

During their progress along the wall, they'd gotten shuffled up again. Nancy was now in front and Lisa in the middle, while Carmela brought up the rear.

Lisa prodded Nancy with a finger and whispered, "Try and peek around the side of the house. See if it's there. If it's not we'll chance a dash across the yard."

"Okay," Nancy whispered back, while Carmela again marveled at how, in the interests of survival, the three of them previously at loggerheads were now working together as a single cohesive unit.

Nancy inched forward towards the end of the wall. The smell of monster was everywhere now, impossible to pin-point, settling all around them as if the night winds were conspiring to deliver Brainchew's horrible scent here from all the other places it had previously visited tonight. The smell filled their nostrils and choked them, and it threatened to drive Carmela mad with terror.

And then, suddenly, Carmela became conscious of an unseen pair of eyes watching her. This creepy sensation crept up on her in stages: At first she didn't even understand what was making her feel queasy, she just had an uncomfortable prickly feeling, like a bug was walking down the back of her neck. Next, the spot between her shoulder blades began feeling awkwardly warm.

Then, in a horrified flash, she understood. She imagined the observer's eyes, those blood-red sunken eyes, and its teeth, those horrible teeth like black hooks set in pink flesh, and the knife-sharp claws on its three-fingered hands.

Without alerting the others (Nancy, knife held high as if to stab someone, was now peeking around the side of the house, and Lisa was watching her), Carmela looked behind her. Oh yes, it was there. She saw its red eyes and gaping maw—was it grinning at her?—in the shadows. And in its intense EVIL gaze she read its clear intent to feast on her brains, to scoop them out of her head like they were jello. She wasn't going to escape from here with her head intact. No, she wasn't . . .

And then the monster was rushing at her, and Carmela was suddenly twelve-years-old again and watching her mother pointing a gun at her to kill her, and she knew she was about to lose her life for something that was actually Lisa's fault.

But, oh no, Carmela wasn't going to be hurt again, not for Lisa's sake. This time, Lisa was paying for her own sins.

Without thinking, Carmela stepped forward, and with the handle of her knife, clubbed Lisa as hard as she could in the back of the head. A violent blow that almost knocked Lisa unconscious. And then, while Lisa reeled stunned, Carmela stepped around her and pushed her straight into the onrushing monster's path.

When Lisa wasn't moving fast enough away from her and towards Brainchew, Carmela stuck a foot in her belly and kicked her towards the monster, which only seemed the more terrible the nearer it got.

She had the barest of impressions of her sister's shock at what was happening to her; and then Brainchew had Lisa and was hauling her away from Carmela into the night; and Lisa vanished around the far corner of the house.

***

Carmela was expecting to hear a gunshot, but no sound came round the corner except a LOUD wet 'Krak!' like someone was shattering the shell of a monster walnut.

I'm safe now, Carmela thought, her terror subsiding somewhat. She looked behind her. Nancy was staring at her in shock, her mouth wide open.

"Come on, let's run!" Nancy grabbed Carmela's arm and pulled her towards the tree border. And then they were both running in a crazy panic, like foxes with their tails on fire. Carmela looked back once, but the monster wasn't coming after them.

"Whatever did you do that for?" Nancy gasped as they burst through the trees and dashed across the motel's parking lot for the reception building. "You sacrificed your own sister!"

"I don't know why," Carmela answered, now weeping as she ran. "I really don't know." And now that that moment of inexpressible terror was past, she really didn't know why she'd done it anymore.

***

Brainchew had been surprised when the three women had left their house to come after it. It had turned back again in the hope of feeding on them, and its hope had been realized. (It had in fact been scared of confronting Ambrose, and thus glad of the excuse to delay their combat which the female trio's emergence had provided it with.)

This woman with the yellow hair had a sweet, sweet brain, and her horror and terror as she'd died had made her head-meat even tastier.

The only thing that puzzled Brainchew was that the yellow-haired woman had kept on sadly muttering, "Why, Carmela, why? Why, baby sis, why?" right up to the moment when it bit into her head.

But the monster had no understanding of human languages and as such found the words meaningless.

CHAPTER 24

Ambrose

The lobby door swung open and two scared women ran in. Both were clutching large knives.

One of the scared women was the pretty guest who reminded Ambrose of his late wife. The other one . . .

It was a long moment before Ambrose recognized Nancy Pine.

Yes, that lovely plush petite body and those honey-toned curls were unmistakable. But she had two black eyes, was missing several teeth, and her nose looked squashed. In addition to which, her top was all ripped up and bloody.

"Ambrose . . ." she gasped breathlessly, "baby."

What the . . . ?

He dashed around the desk and took her in his arms. "What happened to you? What the hell happened to you?"

"I got the shit kicked out of me."

He looked at the young woman with the black hair—Carmela; yeah, that was her name. She was weeping copiously. For a moment his mind replayed the sequence of their entry into the lobby: had she been chasing his darling?

He gaped at Carmela in horror. "You? *You* did this to her? You beat her black and blue like this?"

"Not her," Nancy moaned against him, "it was her elder sister, the crazy bitch."

Ambrose's face clouded with anger. "Where the hell is she? She and I are gonna have a long talk about this."

Nancy stepped back out of his embrace. "She's dead, baby. Brainchew got her." She nodded at the blank expression that came over his face. "Brainchew's back, Ambrose. It killed Owlsy too, then it killed her sister Lisa and we ran over here."

231

The blank expression remained on Ambrose's face. *Brainchew?* At first Nancy's words didn't really register with him; they seemed an extension of Crystal's earlier jokes on the phone. *Brainchew just killed again?* After the night's premonition of horrors to come, this—someone's death—was almost expected, yet was still completely unexpected. *Nah, that son-of-a-bitch can't have woken up again.*

And the weird way he was finding this out—the odd couple bringing the information—wasn't helping him believe it quickly either. These two young women's presence *together* didn't add up.

He looked hard at Carmela. "I thought you girls went off to sleep," he said slowly. "How'd you meet up with Nancy and . . . ?"

"I-I-I . . . we-we-we . . ." she stuttered through her tears. Ambrose could see that she was on the verge of a nervous collapse. No doubt something had scared her real bad. But Brainchew? Frigging Brainchew?

"Ambrose, we ain't got time for that!" Nancy snapped at him. "Okay, listen, baby. Her sister came out to get some air and she heard me walkin' through the trees, and we—"

"Nancy, what were *you* doing outside at this hour?"

"I got lonely in bed and was coming to see you. And Lisa heard me and startled me amidst the trees and we got into a fight. Then Carmela came out to look for Lisa and cleared up our misunderstanding. And then we all began discussing the empty Matthews house next door . . . and that's when Brainchew . . ." She paused speaking to look pleadingly at him. "C'mon, baby, do something. You gotta do something about Brainchew before it murders everyone in town!"

Do something, Ambrose mused, finally accepting that Nancy *was* telling the truth, and that he suddenly had a major crisis on his hands. There was only one thing to do, wasn't there? He had to kill the monster.

Still, he didn't immediately rush off looking for it. Like Nancy had said, Lisa Cole was certain to already be dead. Brainchew never wasted time with feeding. It ate quickly, and ate and ate and ate.

But even so, Ambrose knew he had to hurry. If the monster got away, it'd be the devil's business trying to find it again before it killed someone else. A lot of other someone else's. And once it found a lair and hid itself . . . *Owlsy and that young woman are dead already? Shit!*

He hurried behind the reception desk and got out the stone knife. Its weight felt comforting in his hand. He placed it on top of the desk, then got out his shotgun and set that down on the desk too.

"Alright," he said, "you two ladies wait here."

"Baby, where the hell else did you imagine we planned on going?" Nancy asked.

"If you see Brainchew, fire the shotgun. That'll alert me that you're in danger."

"But . . . don't you need it?" Carmela asked nervously. She'd dried her eyes now and seemed less near the hysterical cliff edge.

He shook his head at her, then picked up the knife. "I only need *this*, and to find the damn demon." He slipped his cellphone into his pocket; he'd need to call the police afterwards. "Did you see where it dragged your sister off to?"

"It took her behind that empty house," Carmela said. "On Nancy's side of it."

"I hope it's still there." Grabbing a flashlight, Ambrose ran out from behind the desk and crossed the lobby to the front door.

"Hey, wait!" Nancy yelped just as he was stepping outside.

He paused in the doorway and turned to look at her. His heart instantly went out to her; she looked like the victim of an abusive relationship. "What is it, sweetheart?" he asked gently.

She tapped her head. "You ain't wearing any headgear, Ambrose."

"Oh." Thank heavens she'd remembered. Women were great at remembering stuff like that. He ran back past both women, and into the hallway beyond the lobby. There he found a motorbike helmet and strapped it on. Then he hurried back outside without stopping and entered the night. He set off running across the front lot towards the trees at its far end.

Now, Brainchew, you stinky demon son-of-Hell, where the hell are you?

CHAPTER 25

Nancy & Carmela

Once Ambrose had vanished from sight, Nancy turned to Carmela. "I really hope he finds—" Then she gasped in horror. "Hey stop! What are you doing?"

Carmela had Ambrose's shotgun. She was holding it vertically, with the shotgun's muzzle placed under her chin and her thumb on the trigger. The slightest application of pressure would blow her head off.

"What's it look like?" she replied. "I'm about to kill myself." Her voice sounded as flat and lifeless as if she was already dead. "I can't live with myself after what I just did to Lisa."

Nancy had expected anything but this. She raised her hands in a placatory gesture. "Hold on. Don't do it, don't you dare do it. Just listen to me for a minute."

Carmela, her right thumb firm on the shotgun's trigger, its muzzle wedged tightly under her face, nodded. "Okay, I'm listening. You got your minute. But I can't see you saying anything to make me change my mind about this."

***

Carmela felt a weight of immense darkness covering her. The very air around her called to her to end her miserable existence. Now, the full horror of what she'd done to Lisa settled on her.

In her head, a voice (it sounded distressingly like Tiff's) accused her. She defended herself as best she could:

"She loved you and raised you from a tween, you piece of shit! How could you?"

"She was too bossy—thought she knew everything about everything—that's why! She kept running my goddam life for me, even now that I'm an adult."

"Bossy? Just listen to yourself. You killed her just because she was bossy?"

"Shut up! Shut up! You don't know anything about this! Lisa is responsible for everything going wrong! She robbed me of our parents' love!"

The voice had no reply to this, likely because it knew she was right. Just like she'd been outside a few minutes ago, Carmela was suddenly twelve again, this time being rushed out to an ambulance by appalled paramedics. As she slipped in and out of consciousness, a morbid mantra drummed in her head. The logic was simple enough: *Two hours ago I had two loving parents. Now I have none, and it's all Lisa's fault.*

It almost seemed that blaming Lisa back then had kept Carmela alive, so she could see her and blame her in person. *But I never did, did I? I never said a word to her—never let on what I knew about her and Daddy. I kept the pain and anger and bitter reproach deep inside my heart, a rotten seed determined to grow and bear fruit no matter what. And now it has borne fruit. But, God—did I have to?*

Almost unconsciously, the pressure of her thumb on the shotgun trigger increased. But not enough to make that fatal click. The weapon's tip felt cold as ice on her chin. She felt herself totter on the edge of the void, about to discover the secrets religion only hinted at. Soon she'd know for sure if God and Jesus and the Devil really existed, or if the afterlife was just hogwash.

She almost killed herself then out of sheer curiosity, but . . .

No, hold on, girl. Nancy has something she wants to say first, right? A pre-epitaph. Well, I'm fucking listening. But it won't make the slightest difference. I'm garbage and I feel like garbage and I don't deserve to live.

In retrospect, she saw now that darkness had always been a part of her heart, her endless anxiety the end-product of its seepage into her soul.

And then, the most damning piece of the puzzle fit in Carmela's overwrought emotions, that bit of incontrovertible evidence that convinced her mental jury to award her the death sentence:

I'm exactly like mom. She killed, I killed. She started, I finished. Stepfather and stepdaughter, Dad and Lisa. Both fucked each other, and both are now dead by our hands. Though it took eleven years to accomplish, still I'm an instrument of mother's vengeance. But, oh no, mom, I don't wanna be like you. It's bad enough that you've given me crappy genes to start with, I don't wanna spend my life acting like you. I didn't want to kill Lisa. I loved Lisa with all of my heart. You POSSESSED me, mother. YOU MADE ME DO IT! I'm not like you. I'm not you! I WON'T BE YOU!!

She almost killed herself then too. Oh, she'd never be a replay of her mother's life, too scared to live and love and have a happy family because she felt inadequate and responsible for a heap of genetically hinted-at crimes, and all due to a nebulous strand of guilt transmitted down her hereditary pipeline. Who'd been the first woman in their lineage to feel this way? Who would be the last? *I can be the last. It can end with me. All I need to do is force down this trigger and blow my head off. And then I won't pass my crappy DNA down to any more daughters, making miserable incomplete women too scared to piss with the lights off.*

But Nancy was talking to her. Carmela wasn't really listening, but Nancy just kept on speaking. And little by little, her words made a breech in Carmela's emotional wall of deadness, and built a bridge over her emotional void:

***

"Don't do it, Carmela. Please, don't do it."

"And why shouldn't I? Tell me, Nancy, what have I got left to live for? My fucking life is completely empty now. I've no family, no friends—"

"I'll be your friend."

"And worst of all, I'm losing my mind! I'm going psycho like my mom did."

"So what's new? Oh, you'll get used to being mad, take it from me. After a while being crazy doesn't hurt as much anymore. You'll even think of marriage and kids, like I'm doing now. I got Ambrose and I love him madly and he loves me too. And you're prettier than me; tall and slim like most men prefer. You'll easily find a guy of your own. Now, please, lower the damn shotgun."

"Okay, so let's say I don't kill myself. I'll get caught by the police anyway. They're gonna connect Lisa's death to Josh's death and then . . ."

"Trust me, I got that covered. We'll move Josh's body."

"How? When? There's no time, no time. I'm fucked, fucked, fucked, fucked, fucked, fucked."

"Carmela, the last place the cops are gonna go tonight is the Pleasant Street Cemetery. They *know* Brainchew won't be there. Tonight, they'll just collect all the bodies and launch a proper investigation in the morning."

"There's still our broke-down van. The detectives will find that for sure."

"Forget it. What's important is that we remove Josh from the cemetery before the police find *him*. No body equals no crime." Nancy paused, waving a finger in the air to make her point. "Once Ambrose has the cops over here, we'll find some pretext to slip away for half an hour and do the graveyard cleanup."

"Nancy, that's not all—the van was *stolen*."

"Wow, you sure do worry a lot, don't ya? Listen, do you have a criminal record?"

"No? What's that go to do with this?"

"It means your fingerprints aren't on file. Forget the van then; there's no way its theft can be traced to you."

"You're right I guess."

"Sure I am. See? So relax, that's all settled then. Now, lower the shotgun away from your head."

"Nancy, why are you helping me now that Lisa's dead? I mean, you even lied to your boyfriend that it wasn't me that beat you up?"

Nancy stroked Carmela's cheek. "'Cos I like you, that's why. No, not in a lezzie way; I mean, I don't wanna sleep with you. But you're honest, and like me, you're half mad. But you've got a conscience too. Besides, now that Owlsy's dead, I think it's about time I left the serial killing lifestyle behind. And I could do with a good, reliable friend. Someone like you."

As an illustration of her point, she touched her broken nose and winced. "I know you only attacked me because Owlsy killed your friend. You've got a good heart, Carmela."

"A good heart? I just killed my older sister, pushed her to her death at that monster's hands. I'll never forgive myself for that."

"Don't worry 'bout it, no one's perfect. And remember, you were scared shitless at the time. You did it to save yourself . . . to save both of us. So that now we can be besties."

"I traded my life for hers. That's unforgiveable."

"Maybe. Now just stay calm and stick to the plan."

"The plan? The plan? *The plan?* You're starting to sound like Lisa."

"Ha ha ha. Just don't push me in front of a car then."

"Don't you ever, *ever* talk to me about fucking *plans*. That's all I've been hearing for over a decade—plans to do this and that and everything else."

"Alright, I won't. And now you need to trust me, huh? Just trust me. I'll get us through this and then we'll be best friends forever, united by our bloody secrets." She smiled at Carmela. "Deal?"

It took a nervous few seconds, but Carmela finally smiled back, "Okay, deal."

"Hugs then. But put that goddam shotgun down first."

"Okay, okay, okay—I'm lowering the gun. But I'm warning you— don't you dare mention any goddam plans to me, or I'll blow you away instead."

"Yeah, sure. Whew! Now just hug me, will you?"

***

They hugged, then separated and held each other at arm's length.

"So how d'you feel now?" Nancy asked. "Better?"

"Yes, much better," Carmela admitted.

"Good. All you need to do now is pretend to be sane around sane people. Don't worry about that—I'll teach you. I've had years of practice."

"Nancy, I don't know for how long this 'normal' feeling is going to last. Five minutes ago, my life had absolutely no meaning to me. What am I gonna do if I suddenly start feeling that way again?"

"Oh, don't worry, sis, we'll get you through that."

Sis? Did she just call me her sister? That shook Carmela. Nancy wore a Madonna smile on her battered face, and a look in her eyes that said, 'we're all crazy in here, mama.' Carmela was appalled to realize that she and Nancy were now essentially the same.

"We need each other," Nancy told her. "I ain't got any family left anymore—both of my brothers are dead." She looked inquisitively at Carmela. "How 'bout you? You got any more siblings stashed away somewhere? Any parents?"

Carmela shook her head.

Nancy grinned. "So we'll be each other's family then. We'll be each other's *blood* sisters."

Then she sobered a little. She looked worriedly at Carmela. "Hey, I really hope Ambrose doesn't get killed taking on Brainchew."

"Don't worry, he'll be fine."

"He'd better be. If anything happens to him, I'll be the one putting the shotgun to my face."

CHAPTER 26

Ambrose

Ambrose found Lisa's corpse lying by the front porch of the empty house.

He winced when the flashlight beam revealed the damage to her body. In addition to the gaping hole in her head, Brainchew had also ripped open her belly to reach her bladder. That of course, after first drinking her blood—Lisa's neck was slashed open and her blood was splashed far and wide over the porch.

Ambrose took a long look at the mutilated corpse. He winced at the waste. *Damn, this Lisa sure was one beautiful young woman.* Then he remembered his girlfriend's battered face. *But she must've been crazy too. Why the hell else would she beat Nancy up so bad, like she utterly hated her?*

He switched off his flashlight and stood in the darkness with his back to the building's front wall. No way did he want Brainchew sneaking up on him from behind.

Now where's the damn demon hiding?

He was out of breath from his mad charge over here and waited a few minutes to let his breathing normalize again.

It was time to think.

He could smell Brainchew. At the moment, the creature's stink was the air he was breathing, like he was drowning in quicksand mixed with rotten burger patty. But that meant it could be just about anywhere around here. And he knew from experience that given a choice, Brainchew would try to ambush him, to sneak up on him from behind.

He tapped his helmet. *You tried that once before, asshole, and it didn't work.*

Ambrose tried not to ponder on how the monster could have possibly gotten out of its place of confinement. It was too mindboggling. *Yeah, yeah, it might wake up, but breaking free of that thick metal coffin? That's just unbelieve—*

His phone rang. Black Sabbath thrashing out *Paranoid* at full volume again. He winced at the noise. *Damn, dude, you really need to change this thing to Stairway to Heaven. Even Ace of Spades would be quieter, God rest Lemmy Kilmister's soul.*

Keeping a firm grip on the stone knife, he jammed the flashlight into his pocket, then pulled out the phone to silence it. He winced when he saw it was Crystal calling him again.

The sensible thing to do now would be to ignore her. The thing was, when drunk or upset (or both), Crystal didn't mind calling back ten or fifteen times till she got through to him. And Ambrose didn't want to turn off the phone in case Nancy called from the lobby. True, he could put it on vibrate, but then Crystal would keep vibrating his pocket, which would still be distracting.

Totally against his better judgment, Ambrose accepted the call.

"Oh, Ambrose darling, are you alright?" Crystal gushed immediately. "I had this absolutely horrible premonition about you, and I just had to call and find out if you're okay."

"Yeah, I'm fine, baby. Look, I really, really, really, really, really can't talk at the moment."

"What's the matter, darling? Brainchew?"

He wondered how she knew. "Yeah."

"Oh, I sure hope you kill it again, darling."

"Me too, Crystal."

He was about hanging up when she said. "Ambrose, don't hang up yet."

"Yeah, what's the matter?"

"Okay, now I know you don't have much time for me at the moment, but I really have to talk to you about this. I don't want to wait till morning, 'cos then I might forget. So, Ambrose . . ."

"I'm listening, but please hurry it up. Make it real snappy. I can smell Brainchew everywhere around me at the moment."

"Okay, okay. See, I've been wondering about this for quite a few years: do you guys prefer oral sex, anal, or just plain everyday pussy fucking?"

Ambrose grimaced. *Aw shucks, she's stoned again.* He considered hanging up, but then she'd just ring back and they'd start over from the beginning. Better to just soldier this one through.

"Or do men enjoy wanking more than sex? But don't answer that now, darling. You can think about it and ask some of your friends too, and give me a reply when I'm back in Raynham. I'm thinking of writing my memoirs about my sexual escapades, and I think this is an important topic to address. I'm gonna call my autobiography 'My Fucking Life.'"

"Yeah." Most definitely she was stoned out of her mind.

She was silent for a moment, then said, "I just had a quick peek out into the bedroom. Cody and Jimmy are at it again—sucking each other off, I mean. Damn, they each must've come a full condom's-worth of jism tonight. I guess that's true love for you, ain't it, Ambrose? Swallowing each others semen?"

"Yeah, I guess," Ambrose replied, then added quickly, "But only if you're gay."

"And that's really why I called you now, Ambrose. I really had to let you know that I love you with all my heart, and I don't want anything bad to ever happen to you, 'cos if it did, I'd kill myself. I really would. I'd slit my wrists, or wrap my car around a tree, or jump off a bridge or OD, or I'd . . ."

Ambrose stood there, stone knife held pointed in front of him, listening. *Yeah, yeah, she'd hate anything to happen to me. And yet, with a brain-eating monster on the rampage that I have to subdue, she's calling me in the middle of the night to chat about straight sex and gay sex and . . . love, and I'm certain her whorish thought processes will shortly rotate full circle and she's gonna begin telling me how much she loves sex and being paid for it . . . and then she's gonna start singing Donna Summer again. Crystal, for fuck's sake, goddam shut the fuck up!*

But he didn't say it and she went on talking. She seemed unable to stop her mouth chattering. And for his own part, he seemed unable to hang up on her. There was an earnestness about her speech—not the words themselves, but their heartfelt honesty—that compelled him to listen to her regardless.

Or maybe, just maybe, her voice was steadying his nerves?

". . . Throw myself under a train if you were to die and leave me. Shit, man, if you ever die, I'll drink a whole bottle of bleach and chase it down with antifreeze and rat poison . . ."

He heard a sound then, off towards the west side of the house. Keeping the phone pressed to his ear, he set off towards it. There was no way he could hold the flashlight while at the same time both

holding the phone to his ear and the stone knife in his free hand, so
he left it stuck in his pocket and turned off, trusting in the phone's
faint glow to illuminate objects in his way.

"So," Crystal was saying, "I really mean it, Ambrose darling. You're
my bestest friend ever, and make sure you murder that stupid prick
Brainchew, and then . . ."

If you don't get me killed first, honey. The noise had grown louder as he
neared the side of the house, and now it separated into a mess of
pitiful squeals.

On turning the corner, Ambrose found himself looking down at a
crate of young piglets. The little pigs sounded terrified, but in a
subdued way, like they'd squealed themselves into exhaustion. In the
light of the moon he made out a dark splash on the crate, some of
which liquid had dripped down onto the pigs.

"You know, Ambrose, it's really weird how nobody is as friendly
as they should be nowadays. Not like you are to me. And it's all over
the place now too. Jimmy was earlier telling us how his mom's older
sister got shot in the leg by a cranky neighbor, and all because of an
argument over . . . Ambrose can you hear me?"

"Hold on, Crystal." Finding the box of piglets had Ambrose really
bothered. He knew the pigs must have come from Owlsy's pickup
truck. And if Owlsy was dead like Nancy said, then *he* wasn't the one
who'd moved the pigs over here. That had to be . . .

The monster's thick stink enveloped him again just as he heard it
coming around the side of the building behind him.

"Hey, Ambrose—are you still there? I need you to listen to this,
darling. It's important!"

Ambrose spun around to face Brainchew.

It was leaping at him as he turned, and, simply as a reflex while
ducking out of its way, he flung his phone at it.

The phone vanished into Brainchew's mouth, its screen flashing
blue, white, and green as it went. The monster swallowed the
unfamiliar meal whole, belched, and backed off from Ambrose.

What was weird about this now was that Ambrose could still hear
Crystal's voice coming through Brainchew's body, as if the creature's
flesh was an amplifier.

". . . So you see, Ambrose darling," she was saying, "that's why I
think we working girls really ought to stick together. If Heidi and

Maria hadn't had that falling out, Heidi would have been there that night, and that maniac Carlos wouldn't have . . ."

Ambrose got out his flashlight and shone it on Brainchew. It was crouched opposite him, ready to leap and rend him with its claws. Ambrose knew how sharp those claws were—he bore the scars from an earlier encounter with the monster. The blood smeared all over its gray body (the most recent coatings from the beautiful corpse on the porch) made him want to puke.

"Hey, Ambrose, are you there? I mean, I was so upset when I heard Maria was dead that I charged all my customers triple for the next two weeks so I could put a huge bouquet of orchids on her grave. That's good payback, right?" Her voice boomed out of Brainchew's body.

Ambrose now also realized that Brainchew had left the crate of piglets here to distract him, and then stalked around the house to ambush him from behind. Such a previously unencountered display of rudimentary cunning and intelligence worried him—it made the creature even more dangerous.

Considering the monster's rows of teeth, he also wondered if it wouldn't have been wiser to face it drunk. He shook his queasiness off—this was no time to turn wino again. Besides, even if he wanted to, there was no time now to get drunk anyway.

I gotta stop it now. If it gets away from me tonight, there's no telling the kinda havoc it'll wreak on the townsfolk.

Knife in right hand, flashlight in left, Ambrose prepared to battle his archenemy. "Okay, you stinky bastard, let's dance."

Now that they were face-to-face again, Ambrose could almost feel Brainchew's intense hatred of him. But there was something else. Something unexpected and very odd was going on:

Brainchew didn't seem interested in attacking him anymore. Ambrose suddenly understood the problem. The monster was completely distracted and perplexed by the loud noises coming out of its body:

" . . . And so, Ambrose, that's why I'm gonna wave my fuck flag high no matter what!" Crystal was yelling now. "I'm gonna fuck and fuck and fuck and fuck and fuck until women everywhere beg me to orgasm and stop!"

Brainchew reached up with both hands and grabbed its head by the sides. Then it began lurching left and right like it had a headache.

Crystal, meanwhile, had launched into a LOUD rendition of Donna Summer's *She Works Hard for the Money*. "I fuck hard for my money, fuck hard for my money. I get screwed thrice daily, so you better treat me right! Yeah, you better treat me right!"

Ambrose was amazed. Crystal's voice was projecting through Brainchew's body with pristine clarity, the sort of clarity audio engineers would happily sell their souls to achieve in recording studios. The crackle over the line came through clearly too, giving her voice an eerie ambience.

"Hell yeah, Cody and Jimmy, you better treat me right! Yes, you better fuck me right, and pay me lots tonight . . . !"

Brainchew was still gripping its head as if the sound was giving it a migraine. Shining his light on it, Ambrose saw it was totally confused.

Indeed, Brainchew was so clearly utterly perplexed and miserable now that Ambrose almost felt sorry for it. It also looked like its head was going to burst from the noise. Ambrose was *almost* tempted to wait and see if it did.

Almost. He quickly stepped forward and stabbed it with the stone knife.

Ambrose was uncertain which gave him more relief, Brainchew once again reverting back to a stone statue and toppling over lifeless, or the sudden silence which announced the fact that he needed to buy himself a new cellphone.

But losing the phone was worth it not to have to keep listening to Crystal. Best friend or not, a man's tolerance had its limits.

Ambrose shone his flashlight on the petrified monster now lying motionless on the grass. Then, once he'd convinced himself that it was properly frozen and wouldn't be going anywhere, he strode off towards the motel to call the police.

Then, struck by a worry, he walked back and picked up the crate of piglets and carried them away with him. He didn't want any brains—any kind of brains—near enough to Brainchew to tempt it to rouse itself again.

Sure, Ambrose had never heard of lightning striking four times in the same place before, but if he'd learnt anything tonight, it was that it was dumb to tempt fate.

CHAPTER 27

Ambrose, Nancy, and Carmela

The moment Ambrose walked through the lobby door, Nancy launched herself straight into his arms.

"Oh, darling, darling, I was so worried," she sobbed into his chest. Then she pulled back a little and stared inquisitively at him. "Is it dead? Is Brainchew dead?"

"As dead as it can get," he replied.

"Oh, thank the heavens. Yes!" She hugged him close again.

Ambrose held her tight; he would slot her right into his heart if he could. It felt great to be back and still alive. It felt great to hold Nancy close again, while realizing that he'd survived yet another encounter with Brainchew. "Nancy, honey," he said, "you wouldn't believe in a thousand years what happened out there just now."

"What happened?" Carmela asked.

Ambrose looked over Nancy's head at her. Carmela seemed composed now; well, as composed as could be expected if your sister just died. He frowned, uncertain of how much to say. Then he decided to just say what had happened. He'd have to tell the police anyway. "A friend of mine named Crystal called me on the phone while I was tracking Brain—"

Nancy stiffened against him. "Crystal? *Crystal?* What is wrong with that woman?" Nancy pulled away from him. She looked utterly enraged, which, combined with the mess that had been made of her face, meant she looked utterly ugly.

Nancy raged, "Is she trying to get you killed or what!?"

"Now, honey, take it easy. It's nothing like that. C'mon, you know she's my best friend."

"And I'm your girlfriend. What is that slut doing calling you at . . ." she looked over at the lobby clock, "ten-past-two in the morning? Or is she expecting you to fly condoms down to Texas for her?"

"Hey, watch your mouth. I won't have you talking about Crystal like that, okay?"

"Ambrose, I'll goddam say whatever the hell I damn the fuck want about her. O.K., just suppose she'd gotten you killed tonight; what was I supposed to do then, huh?" Then she suddenly looked about to cry.

Ambrose decided not to bother explaining anymore how he'd defeated Brainchew. He found it scary: Nancy looked angry enough to actually *kill* Crystal. To literally murder her. He winced at the distortion and damage to her features. *Damn, I need to get her to both a doctor and a dentist fast.*

"Alright, now calm down, baby, you're reading this all the wrong way. It ain't at all what you're thinking. She was just feeling miserable; she gets that way sometimes."

"So tell the whore to change jobs then."

"C'mon, Nancy, don't be like this. Don't call her a whore."

"So what should I call her then? A hooker? A sex worker? A lady of the night? She ain't Canadian else I'd call her 'la fille de joie.'"

"Just . . . don't call . . . Aw shucks, Nancy, look what you've gone and done now with all your green-eyed-monster-truckin'. You've made me forget I gotta call the cops."

"Hell no, baby, you ain't calling anyone till we settle this Crystal prostitute business!"

***

From her chair across the room, Carmela stared morosely into the shadows in the passageway that led off the lobby. Nancy and Ambrose's argument blew past her like the wind. Every now and then though, she'd look Nancy's way, waiting for the agreed signal for them to leave this place.

Carmela felt much more composed now, though claws of guilt still raked her soul. *What I did back there was just . . .*

She'd snapped. Quite literally too. She'd never been that terrified before in her life. No, not even when her mother had had that gun pointed at her. And now she had to live with the consequences of her actions.

She looked over at the shotgun on the reception desk. Six or seven steps would put the weapon in her hands again. If she wanted, she could end everything before Nancy or Ambrose could stop her.

But did she want to? No, she didn't want that anymore. At least not at the moment. Of course, the time might come when her feelings of guilt and self-reproach would become too much for her to bear, and then she might put another gun to her head, somewhere else, but it wasn't going to be either here or tonight. Nancy's words had made a definite impact on her psyche. At the moment suicide didn't seem worth it.

Maybe Nancy was right, maybe she'd get through this okay. She doubted it, but . . .

Then she grinned. Nancy looked comical, the way she was gesticulating furiously at Ambrose, blocking him off from picking up the lobby phone.

"Nancy, for God Almighty's sake, get out of the damn way. I need to call the police."

"Liar, you just want to call Crystal again."

"Nancy, that ain't true. You know that."

Nancy stepped back. Ambrose picked up the phone and dialed.

"Hello, Tom? . . . Yeah, it's Ambrose. Dude, I just stopped Brainchew again; you guys might wanna come pick up the pieces. . . . What? Ida Green just called you too that it was at Josh's store and killed Willy Mandell? Shit, man!"

Carmela didn't pay attention to the rest of the conversation. Nancy was winking at her.

"Let's go," she mouthed.

Carmela leapt up and hurried over to her side. Nancy waved at Ambrose. "We'll be right back. We each need to take a crap after being frightened so bad."

And then Carmela was hurrying out of the lobby after Nancy. And next, both of them were running across the front parking lot towards the far tree border.

"Hey, wait!" Carmela gasped as they reached her car. "Let's just take this one." She felt through her pockets and came up with the key to Room 9, dashed inside the motel room, and was soon outside again with the car keys in hand.

Nancy took them from her. "Okay, but hold on tight. We're gonna be breaking the speed limits tonight."

***

Ambrose was at first puzzled when he saw the silver Honda Accord drive past the lobby with Nancy at the wheel. But when the vehicle turned right once out of the driveway, he relaxed.

Nancy and Carmela were clearly headed for Nancy's house. And, women being what they were, they were apparently too scared to walk back the way they'd come. It didn't matter if the rampaging monster had been slain or not, the memory remained and was equally as daunting.

He felt sad for both young women, particularly Nancy. He'd liked Owlsy Pine, as fine a fellow as they came, he was.

He returned his attention to the phone. "Yeah, Tom, Brainchew's on ice. It ain't waking up for the next hundred years or two . . . . at least I damn sure hope so. . . . What? You can't get Peter Claxton on the phone? . . . Just wake up the Chief then. Tina ain't gonna be happy though. . . . Yeah, buddy, I know how you guys gotta keep everything under wraps 'cos of the town's reputation, but you're gonna have to find everyone Brainchew killed before daylight then. You got a long messy night ahead of you . . ."

***

Nancy drove the Honda to the Pleasant Street Cemetery along a carefully thought out route, one that shunned Raynham's main roads in favor of smaller ones more likely to be deserted at this time of night. She kept the car lights off while crossing the Orchard Street intersection that led to the police station.

The graveyard was silent, and looked undisturbed.

"Great," she told Carmela.

Carmela was at first too scared to get out of the car.

"Look, you have to come too," Nancy insisted. "I ain't gonna be able to move him alone. Remember how big Josh is?"

Carmela got out and accompanied her to the grave. Nancy had a penlight which she shone on the tomb.

"Dang!" she exclaimed on seeing the shattered concrete slabs and Josh's brainless body beside it. "Alright, let's get him outa here."

Wheezing from his dead weight, they carried Josh Penham out from beneath the trees, with his clothes piled on top of him. Nancy realized that Carmela was largely on autopilot at this point, but the job had to be done.

(In Carmela, Nancy recognized not so much a kindred soul, as the sister she'd always wanted to have. And she was going to protect that tonight. Two brothers for one sister? Hopefully, the sibling exchange would prove worth it. *Josh never knew he was related to me anyway.*)

They got Josh into the trunk of Carmela's car and left the cemetery. Nancy drove carefully now, back the same way they'd come. She left the headlights off for almost the entire trip.

Carmela, possibly traumatized by having to move Josh's corpse, wasn't saying anything. Nancy let her be. The hard part was done. All that remained to do now was driving home, parking around the back of the house, and carrying Josh in through the back door and down to the basement. Then they'd clean up the car and the house. Nancy knew there was no reason the police would enter the house except to comfort her or take her statement, and the blood on the rug could easily be explained away: a large amount of it was hers. Besides, from what Ambrose had told her about Brainchew, the police were bound to be too preoccupied with hushing up the deaths anyway to look for any additional criminal stink. They'd most likely just assume Brainchew had killed Josh too and dragged his body off somewhere and hidden it.

Nancy felt sorry for Josh's girlfriend Ida. The two of them had really loved each other, and now Ida would never know what had happened to him. It was real sad, but couldn't be helped.

And Owlsy too. Nancy had no idea where Brainchew had left his corpse. The police would have to find it for her.

As touching Owlsy's dying, she felt deeply, deeply saddened. The pain of losing him hadn't even begun yet, she knew. Even if Owlsy did tend to drink too much at times and couldn't keep a steady girlfriend alive, he'd otherwise been such a wonderful brother to her.

She wiped away tears.

She turned the car back onto Carver Street, entering it via the same way as she'd departed for the cemetery, by the farther end from the Sunflower Motel.

Great, there was no sign yet of the police. Or if they were around, they were still talking with her darling Ambrose at the motel.

Then, on thinking of Ambrose, Nancy remembered Crystal Parr again, and just like that, her face clouded over with anger as the 'CRAZY' clicked back into place in her brain. *Ambrose is mine, mine, mine. No one else is gonna have him.*

As far as Nancy could see, there was only threat standing in her way where Ambrose was concerned: *That greedy slut Crystal.*

Nancy grimaced. She didn't get it. *I'm competing for Ambrose's love with a hooker? Crystal can have almost any man in the country, but instead she wants mine?* The anger simmered in her bosom, building to a crescendo of madness so intense that for a moment Nancy lost sight of the road, and was driving the silver Honda along the freeways of lunacy in her head. Then the insane flicker ended, and she stabilized again between the high walls of her intense love for Ambrose and of her equally monumental hatred of his best friend.

A messed-up girl like me tries to go on the straight-and-narrow, Nancy thought darkly, *but there's always some bitch somewhere who contrives to pull me out of line again. Crystal, you . . . you . . . you . . .*

Nancy was suddenly so enraged with Crystal Parr that she actually shat herself on the car seat while pulling into her driveway. Just like that, a hot turd popped out of her ass. Thankfully, it was only a little one; Carmela was unlikely to smell it.

Oh, was Nancy so going to teach Crystal a lesson once she got back from Texas or wherever the hell it was down south that she was currently selling her body.

Oh yeah, it looked like she and Owlsy's bloody basement was going to have one final female visitor before she shut it down for good.

Feeling immensely pleased and warmed by that thought, Nancy took her right hand off the steering wheel and reached over and patted Carmela's arm. (They were just rolling past the side of the porch with the fallen-out stone slab that had enabled Tiff to identify the house.)

Nancy parked the car in the back yard, beside the shed that housed the meat grinder. Then she turned and smiled at Carmela.

"Well, we made it, sis. See, I told you not to worry, that everything was gonna be okay."

She felt tingles of delight when Carmela smiled back at her. Carmela's smile was beautiful to see. It was an expression of genuine heartfelt pleasure, filled with love and friendship and the promise of a truthful and honest relationship between them.

Nancy smiled back at Carmela. Oh, yes, she thought happily, everything *was* gonna be alright now. She had her new sister, and she had her darling Ambrose, and she, Nancy Pine, was on top of the world.

The End

ABOUT THE AUTHOR

Wol-vriey is Nigerian, and quite tall.

He currently resides in a state of uneasy stalemate with his threatening-to-thin-beyond-redemption hair, and believes there actually are things that go bump in the night.

Wol-vriey recycles the ridiculous into reasonable reality for the reader.

His WEIRRRD philosophy?

WEIRRRD = Warp/Write Everything into Realistic Ridiculous Readable Distorted Dream Dimension Descriptions.

Wol-vriey blogs at:

http://oddityfarm.wordpress.com

WOL-VRIEY
BIZARRO AND TRANSGRESSIVE FICTION

BOSTON POSH (BUD MALONE #1)

In 2028 AD, the USA is a nation ravaged by hungry dragons and dinosaurs. In Boston, Massachusetts, private eye Bud Malone is hired to rescue a kidnapped heiress. But nothing is as it seems.

Malone works to unravel a tangled web involving Boston Chinatown, a 200-year-old woman with a 9-year-old body, white robots, a human-liver-eating psychopath, a golem, a porcelain dragon, and a snake goddess with a crush on him. There's also a woman obsessed with chicken sex. Then Malone meets Posh Lane, a gorgeous call girl who's desperate to quit her pimp.

Romantic sparks ignite between Posh and Malone, but Posh's past suddenly catches up with her in a BIG way. To save Posh, Malone agrees to run a quest for Earth's new rulers, the Forks. But, Malone has no idea that agreeing to the Fork's odd request will send him on the weirdest trip he's ever been on in his life.

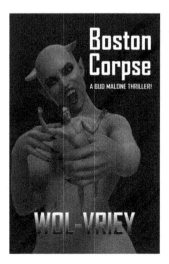

BOSTON CORPSE (BUD MALONE #2)

MAGIC CAN BE MURDER! - Drag queen Lucy Tang is back in Boston, and is hell-bent on settling her vindetta against casino owner Sookie Ling. And suddenly, Bud Malone, PI, has the case of his life to resolve.

When Boston's robot police force are baffled by a mind transfer case, they come to Malone for help. The one person who can likely help Malone out here is the witch Soledad Bathory. But Soledad seems to know a lot more than she's telling him. It's a case not made easier when Malone meets Soledad's beautiful cousin, Josephine 'Slave' Bailey. Slave has her own plans for Malone, most of which involve teaching him BDSM and making him her new Master.

Oh, and Rick Rogers owes Sookie Ling a whole lot of money, a gambling debt that's going to be literally Hell to pay!

BOSTON CORPSE - Not your average detective novel!

Burning Bulb
PUBLISHING

WOL-VRIEY
BIZARRO AND TRANSGRESSIVE FICTION

BOSTON LUST (BUD MALONE #3)

"Bless it, Father, for she has sinned."

Seven murdered gay women, all their bodies completely drained of blood. All also with large parts of their bodies dissolved away like acid has been pumped into their veins.

Bud Malone has to find the female vampire preying on Boston's lesbian population.

Then Malone meets the beautiful Trudi Carmen and the case gets even more tangled. Trudi needs Malone's help in recovering a ring that's gone missing. But how in the world is one little black ring related to either the dead women or their killer?

Resolving this case will lead Malone deep into Lucy Tang's legacy—The Abstracta. And then to the city of Genesis.

Boston Lust—Just when you thought Bean Town was safe to visit again.

HELL DANCER

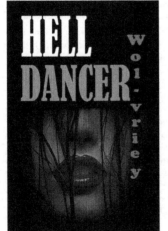

Six people find themselves trapped in Detention, a nightmare realm where the demonic Schoolmaster is hell-bent on reforming them . . . until they die.

Porn superstar Venus Deluxe came to Springfield, MA to party, and next found her life hanging by a thread. One wrong answer will mean her death.

Suspended BPD detective Tanya Rockford was trying to stop one kind of violence, but found a terrifying another. With her and her companion's lives hanging in the balance, it's going to take all of her courage and resourcefulness to escape this hell she's stumbled into.

Porn stud Chad Cannon has made a career from his ten-inch penis. Here in Detention, however, it's his brains that matter. He'll soon be hoping all the pot he's smoked over the years hasn't completely messed up his memory.

The three students, Sherri, Jordan, and Mike? They were all just in the wrong place at the right time. Will anyone survive Detention? The evil Schoolmaster doesn't plan on letting that happen . . .

Burning Bulb
PUBLISHING

WOL-VRIEY
BIZARRO AND TRANSGRESSIVE FICTION

VAGINA MUNDI

Rachel Risk is a professional thief with super-strong hair that can stretch like tentacles to manipulate objects. Ashley Status has both a digitally augmented brain, and 'muscle-purses' in her arms and legs in which she stores inflatable objects—cars, guns, rocket launchers, etc.

When Raye is framed as the fall girl in a jewel robbery, the pair flee Chicago's vengeful robot gangsters and take refuge in the Hotel Bizarre, where the gorgeous 'vagina singer,' Femina, is performing for a week.

But the Hotel Bizarre is even stranger than its name suggests, and very soon Raye and Ash are involved in an deadly adventure, a struggle for survival the likes of which they'd never imagined possible—with loads of deviant sex, drugs, music, and violence at every turn. And just what is the old woman in the skin desert really doing with all those cats glued to her walls?

VAGINA MUNDI—a Bizarro Hymn in praise of WOMAN!

VEGAN VAMPIRE VAGINAS

The biggest bank heist in US history. And Tom Palmer can't remember pulling it off. And no, this isn't your standard case of amnesia. After a one-night-stand gone horribly wrong, Boston salesman Tom Palmer wakes up with a vagina implanted in his left hand. Then his day gets worse.

Tom is transported across space-time to a nightmare version of Boston, one where the Bizarro virus has transformed half the population into cannibals. Worst of all, Tom discovers that in this new Boston, he's the infamous gangster Pussypalm, wanted for robbing the Federal Reserve Bank of Boston a year ago. He also learns that the vagina in his hand is prophetic, i.e. it talks . . . after sex.

With 130 people left dead during his bank heist and six billion dollars missing, Tom knows he's living on borrowed time. It is in his best interests not to remember anything. Because once he does . . .

Burning Bulb
PUBLISHING

WOL-VRIEY
BIZARRO AND TRANSGRESSIVE FICTION

Dr. Orgasm

Courtney Taylor is young, intelligent, beautiful, and successful. She also has a boyfriend who loves her deeply. The problem is, no matter what Courtney does, she can't climax during sex.

When Florence Rigid's communist forces destroy the city of Metaphor, Courtney and her friends Teresa, Highball, Miki, and Heather are cast into the midst of a quest to find the only person able to save the land of Innuendo—Dr. Carol Orgasm, wanted by the communists for developing the O-Pill, a wonder drug that grants women sexual ecstasy on demand.

The communists will do anything to get their hands on the O-Pill and prevent its reaching the millions of Innuendo's women. But Courtney desperately wants that pill too. And so it's now a race between Courtney and the communists to find Dr. Orgasm first.

And Courtney has no choice but to win this race. She must win it: For her own orgasm . . . and for the freedom of female sexuality everywhere.

PUSSY TRANSMISSION

Pussy Transmission were the most decadent Pop Art ensemble of the 90's. Led by the beautiful painter Isis Lynch, the trio revolutionized the art world. Then suddenly, without explanation, Pussy Transmission vanished into historical obscurity. Now, twenty years later, three women come to Lynch Place. Lily and Nina are journalists desperate to interview Isis Lynch. Raven, on the other hand, wants to find her boyfriend, who's gone missing inside Isis's house. Raven's worried—she's heard that Pussy Transmission broke up because Isis began dabbling in black magic . . . with devastating results. All three women will shortly wish they'd never left home. Particularly once the rats in Lynch Place start warning them that they're going to die . . . and Raven meets Betty Butcher, the bouncy supernatural psycho who's intent on chopping her into bits. Pussy Transmission, Baby! Just because . . .

Burning Bulb
PUBLISHING

WOL-VRIEY
BIZARRO AND TRANSGRESSIVE FICTION

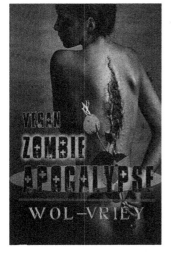

VEGAN ZOMBIE APOCALYPSE

In the post-apocalypse worlderness, zombies rule the earth. They're allergic to meat, and brains literally make them explode. Zombies now eat blood potatoes, parasitic tubers grown in the flesh of humancows corralled in maximum security farms. Two fugitives meet in the ancient ruins of Texas. The first is Soil 15-f, a womancow who's escaped her farm a week before she's due to be killed and her blood potato crop harvested. The second fugitive is Able Kane, former head necros food technician, now sentenced to death for heresy. But Soil is no ordinary humancow.

Unknown to herself, she's the vegan zombie agricultural revolution, and the zombies desperately want her back. And the necros equally desperately want Able Kane dead. He's fled with a forbidden discovery which will reshape the world for the worse if used. And Able is just hardheaded/misguided enough to use it.

MELANIE NEMESIS CATCHPOLE

In Springfield, Massachusetts, Melanie Catchpole is hired to fetch back a magic teddy bear worth millions of dollars from a warehouse across town. Problem is, the warehouse is down in Springfield's O-Zone-that totally weird sector of the city where Bizarro fell to Earth. The 'O' is a fairytale land, a place where dreams and nightmares literally live and breathe.

Worse still, the gingers—mutant cannibals—prowl the O. The gingers have already eaten everyone else Melanie's employers sent to get back the magic teddy bear.

Accompanied by the handsome but ruthless Doug Fisher (who she finds sexy but doesn't dare entrust her heart to), Melanie enters the O-Zone. Melanie and Doug are instantly caught up in an adventure they'd never have believed credible even if written as fiction . . . and Melanie's used to experiencing the very weird as the norm.

And now, additionally, there's a mystery to unravel: What does the dark, freezing-cold being called The Fixer want with Mary, the barkeep's daughter?

Burning Bulb
PUBLISHING

WOL-VRIEY
BIZARRO AND TRANSGRESSIVE FICTION

BIG TROUBLE IN LITTLE ASS

From Bizarro master storyteller Wol-vriey comes a truly weird western tale that will leave you awe-struck and on the edge of your seat...

In the town named Little Ass, tight-assed prostitute Rosa over-hears a gunslinger's plans to assassinate rancher Edison Bennett. Once the badass Bennett learns of the plot, he ensures there'll be hell to pay for any attempt on his life!

Yes, it's going to take all of gunslinger Jude's shooting prowess, his eclectic collection of strange firearms, a trusty horse that requires an owners' manual, and the help of the lovely and invigorating Nell (who's EXTREMELY odd when the going gets weird), to survive the Bizarro hell that Edison Bennett unleashes in order to hold onto the land that he'd stolen from Madam Zizi.

BIZARRO 101 (A BASIC PRIMER)

Welcome to the strange place:

A collection of 37 flash fiction stories designed to introduce one to the Bizarro/New Weird Genre.

Weird, dreamy, nightmarish, absurd, sad, surreal, humorous . . . this collection of tales is all this and more.

***

"This primer is the very essence of any and all styles and types of Bizarro writing. Wol-vriey collects, distills, and bottles up these 37 tiny stories for your sensory enjoyment. This is an absolute must-read for anyone new to the genre, because it demonstrates the scope of what Bizarro is, and what it can be."
—Teresa Pollack, Bizarro commentator and blogger

Burning Bulb
PUBLISHING

WOL-VRIEY
BIZARRO AND TRANSGRESSIVE FICTION

GIRLS ARE NOT SMILING

Welcome To The Road Trip From Hell

Pagan is demon-possessed.

Lori is suicidal.

Britt is just terminally pissed off.

Meet three young Boston women on the run from the law, each with problems that will fuse into more than the sum of their individual parts, becoming a holocaust of sex and violence and terror, a literal rain of blood and horror and gore and evil.

And if that wasn't already bad enough, Pagan's pet demon is slowly transforming her into something both unspeakable and unholy. Truly, these girls aren't smiling.

BRAINCHEW

It was supposed to be a simple jewel heist, but it went badly wrong. Chuck got shot and died.

Lance hid his friend's corpse in the Pleasant Street Cemetery. But that was a big mistake—there was something undead, something extremely hungry . . . something eXXXtremely horrible, buried in the Pleasant Street Cemetery.

And Lance had just woken it up.

They called the monster Brainchew because it ate brains. Human brains. And it preferred those brains fresh from the heads . . . of the living.

And now it was awake again, Brainchew planned on feeding big-time tonight. Oh hell yes, it did.

Burning Bulb
PUBLISHING

OTHER GREAT TITLES FROM

Burning Bulb

PUBLISHING

WWW.BURNINGBULBPUBLISHING.COM

BELLY TIMBER

From the writers of Darkened Hills, Detour to Armageddon and Night of the Living Dead comes a novel unlike any other...

In the 1800's, ordinary people learned the secret of the Kala and undertook extraordinary measures to rid the earth of this evil. This is their story.

For John McCormick, life on the Indiana frontier held nothing but promise. His settlement along the White River would soon become the crossroads of America. Friends and family from back in Ohio and other points east were all making plans to see what all the fuss was about in the newly-formed city of Indianapolis. Yes, things were good. John had his general store and his friend George Pogue had his blacksmith business. Claims were being staked and relations with the native Indians were amicable. The town was growing and nothing could be better... or so he thought.

In Ohio, an evil was brewing. The Lecky Family, a group of ruthless Mongolian nomads, had made their way to America and were practicing their cannibalistic religion of Kala with reckless abandon. No one was safe, not even John McCormick's family.

Burning Bulb
PUBLISHING

ANTHOLOGIES
BIZARRO AND TRANSGRESSIVE FICTION

THE BIG BOOK OF BIZARRO

The Big Book of Bizarro brings together the peculiar prose of an international cast of the most grotesquely-gonzo, genre-grinding modern writers who ever put pen to paper (or mouse to pad), including:

NIGHT OF THE LIVING DEAD horror writers John Russo & George Kosana; HUSTLER MAGAZINE erotica contributors Eva Hore, Andrée Lachapelle, & J. Troy Seate and established Bizarro genre authors D. Harlan Wilson, William Pauley III, Wol-vriey, Laird Long, Richard Godwin and so many more!

From Alien abductions to Zombie sex, The Big Book of Bizarro contains OVER FIFTY STORIES of the most outrélandish transgressive fiction that you'll ever lay your capricious and curious hands upon!

WESTWARD HOES

Nine outlaw writers rode into town from obscurity to pen nine tantalizing tales of horror and fantasy, and leaving once they branded their own personal marks on the weird western genre and became living legends of the American Frontier experience.

Like drunken Indian scouts, the writers fervidly tracked down and captured the Western genre, tore off its fashionable veneer and ravished its exposed essence.

So belly up to the bar with your favorite soiled dove and enjoy perusing these thrilling tales of Old West debauchery, danger and desire; compiled by the publisher of The Big Book of Bizarro and featuring the bizarro novella *Big Trouble in Little Ass* by Wol-vriey.

Burning Bulb
PUBLISHING

ANTHOLOGIES
BIZARRO AND TRANSGRESSIVE FICTION

THE BIG BOOK OF BIZARRO SPECIAL KINDLE EDITIONS

OTHER AWESOME COLLECTIONS

Burning Bulb
PUBLISHING

GARY LEE VINCENT'S
DARKENED
THE WEST VIRGINIA VAMPIRE SERIES

DARKENED HILLS

When evil descends on a small West Virginia town, who will survive?

Jonathan did not start out his life to become a rambler, it justworked out that way. William was a troubled youth with something to hide. Both were from Melas, a small town tucked away in the West Virginia hills... a town where disappearances are happening more and more frequently.

After the suicide of a wanted serial killer, the townsfolk thought the nightmare was over. But when a centuries-old vampire is discovered they find out the hard way it's just getting started. Dark secrets can only stay hidden for so long and when the devil comes to collect, there will be hell to pay. Can Jonathan and William find a way to stop the vampire before it's too late? Find out in *Darkened Hills!*

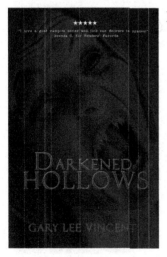

DARKENED HOLLOWS

In the heart-stopping sequel to the award-winning *Darkened Hills*, Jonathan and William must return to West Virginia to face possible criminal charges stemming from their last visit to the damned town of Melas, where both had narrowly escaped the clutches of a vampire seethe.

And as livestock start mysteriously getting murdered with all of their blood drained, worried farmers are searching for answers - leaving the local Sheriff and his deputy racing against time to learn the cause before a more violent crime is committed.

Burning Bulb
PUBLISHING

WWW.*DARKENEDHILLS*.COM

GARY LEE VINCENT'S
DARKENED
THE WEST VIRGINIA VAMPIRE SERIES

DARKENED WATERS

When the world goes to hell, the chosen must arise!

As Talman Cane orchestrates a flood of epic proportions in this third installment of the *Darkened* series the towns of Melas and Tarklin are caught completely off guard by the deluge. Hell-bent on finishing what they started, the evil brothers return to the lunatic asylum to take care of the witnesses and add to the ever-growing army of the undead.

Aided by Lucifer himself and the insane vampire demon Legion, the stage is set to channel all of the forces of hell to come forth. In an all-out race to survive, Jonathan, William, and Amanda soon discover they are up against impossible odds as Lucifer opens the Gateway to Hell, ushering in the zombie apocalypse and the End Times.

Find out who will survive this cosmic battle of the ages in *Darkened Waters*!

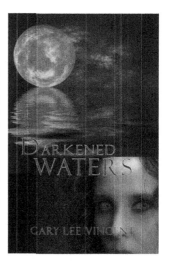

DARKENED SOULS

Melas and the Madison House are about to be rebuilt.
True evil is about to be reborne!

Young ex-priest and vampire-killer William is drawn back to the West Virginian town that almost killed him, where his vampire arch-enemy Victor Rothenstein still stalks the earth.

The town of Melas lies destroyed after the battle of the End of Days. But why is wealthy Jackie Nixon so eager to rebuild it using the bone dust of murdered souls?

Terrible evil has visited before, but the Gateway to Hell is about to be reopened in a horrific climax. And this time – it's personal.

WWW.DARKENEDHILLS.COM

Burning Bulb
PUBLISHING

GARY LEE VINCENT'S
DARKENED
THE WEST VIRGINIA VAMPIRE SERIES

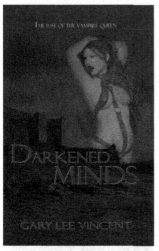

DARKENED MINDS

Jackie Nixon intends to become Vampire Queen, but at what blood-drenched cost?

In this continuation to the explosive infernal saga begun in Darkened Souls, newly-turned vampire Jackie Nixon is taking no prisoners. Accompanied by her daughter, Kate, and by the captive vampire lord Victor Rothenstein, Jackie Nixon explores the Darkness. There, she intends to rouse the slumbering vampire race, bound under an ancient curse, and with their help, rule the human world.

But there's a deadly threat to Jackie's plans. Not just William who is trying to stop her, but her own royal ambitions. If Jackie performs the ritual to wake the sleeping vampires the wrong way, she could instead free the Red Beast of Hell, an unspeakable evil that even the undead fear.

DARKENED DESTINIES

With over 45 people missing after Jackie Nixon's party, the mysteries surrounding Melas and the Madison House keep getting darker.

Now, with legions of vampires at her command, can anything or anyone stop her from gaining complete control over all mankind?

The final battle has begun! As the Vampire Queen ascends her throne and sets to unleash the full forces of darkness, the fate of all things good hangs in the balance.

Burning Bulb
PUBLISHING

WWW. DARKENEDHILLS.COM

DAVID J. FAIRHEAD

"David Fairhead writes compelling stories that offer very human characters and very inhuman monsters. There is no subtlety in Fairhead's imagination - he is simply dying to scare the hell out of you." - Nelson W Pyles author of DEMONS, DOLLS AND MILKSHAKES

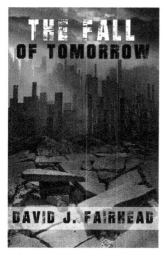

THE FALL

Hopelessness... How do you protect your loved ones when Hell itself opens its insidious mouth?

Horror... Nightmarish Creatures invade your world and there is nowhere to hide.

Blood... How long can you hold out before they come for you?

Pain... Where do you run to avoid being eaten alive by monsters with a voracious appetite for your flesh?

Screams... While you selfishly run for your own life.

Questions... Who is to blame? Where did they come from? How many people survived...and how does the human race find the means to fight back?

THE FALL OF TOMORROW is man's last tale of desperation told by those that are striving to salvage some hope against a ravenous bastion of evil beasts bent on ruling our world.

DWELLING IN THE DARK

From David J. Fairhead, author of the FALL OF TOMORROW, comes DWELLING IN THE DARK- A soulful anthology of creeping terror to keep you up in the small hours with horror set in the past, present and future. Overlapping bits of puzzle fitting each other, before and after The Fall of Tomorrow.

A place where three children facing a monstrous foe can only pray that their bloody summer would just come to an end. Go back to the 1960's- THE COMMUNE where overindulging hippies use a mage's diary to control the end of the world, only to see first-hand that their drug induced visions have horrific ramifications. Where a young boy's visit to a haunted house becomes a lesson in RESIDUAL morality. The story, DEEPER- plunges two brothers into a sinkhole only to find they were being hunted by an insidious creature from its depths. Visit the old west as hero Dekker Collins battles evil gunslingers in DEMONEYE.

And so much more...!

Burning Bulb
PUBLISHING

WWW. FAIRLY DARK PRODUCTIONS.COM

WEST VIRGINIA-THEMED HUMORROROTICA
BY RICH BOTTLES JR.

HELLHOLE WEST VIRGINIA

From the heights of Mothman's perch high atop the Silver Bridge in Point Pleasant to the depths of Hellhole Cavern in Pendleton County, evil lurks within the shadows as the sun sets upon the haunted hills and hollows of West Virginia.

Bizarro author Rich Bottles Jr. blows the coffin lid off horror genre clichés with this tour de force cast of Eco-friendly vampires, beach-yearning zombies and sex-starved she-devils.

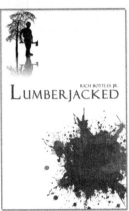

LUMBERJACKED

If you are easily offended or do not possess a truly depraved sense of humor, this story may not be the light summer reading fare you desire. As for the four feisty female freshmen stranded on top of West Virginia's third highest mountain, they have no choice but to experience the sick, twisted debauchery and perverted mayhem described deep inside the tight unbroken bindings of this horrific missive.

Lumberjacked takes the reader to a nightmarish world where character development and aesthetic integrity are prematurely cut short by the swinging axes of maniacal lumberjacks, who are hell bent on death and destruction in the remote forests of Appalachia. And at the climax, when paranoia crosses over to the paranormal, Lumberjacked makes Deliverance look like a family raft trip down the Lower Gauley.

THE MANACLED

What happens when twin brothers lease out the former West Virginia State Penitentiary with the false purpose of filming a documentary on supernatural phenomena, but their true intention is to make a pornographic movie?

Chaos ensues as the disturbed spirits of murdered convicts, along with the reanimated dead from the neighboring Indian Burial Mound, take their vengeance on the unwary and undressed trespassers.

Zombies, ghosts, mobsters and porn collide in this bizarre tale from horror author Rich Bottles Jr.

Burning Bulb
PUBLISHING

WEST VIRGINIA-THEMED HUMORROROTICA

BY RICH BOTTLES JR.

BY

A collection of short stories from Rich Bottles Jr. Be forewarned that the graphic sex and violence described in this book of bizarre short stories may provoke psychological or emotional triggers for some unstable or weak-minded readers, including, but not limited to, the following extreme content: Rape, Torture, Murder, Mayhem, Kidnapping, Cannibalism, Necrophilia, Poisoning, Prostitution, Pornography, Nazis, War Crimes, Ethnic Cleansing, Terrorism, Incarceration, Bondage & Discipline, Sadomasochism, Corporal Punishment, Foot Fetishism, Masturbation, Alcoholism, Drug Abuse, Eating Disorders, Domestic Violence, Mental Illness, Suicide, Drowning, Religious Intolerance, The Occult, Adult Language, Homosexuality, Sodomy, Unwanted Pregnancy, Amputees, Adultery, Incest, Shoplifting, Bukkake, Penis Envy, Cigarette Smoking, and Heavy Metal Music.

THE VAMPIRE WHO SAVES CHRISTMAS

Cantankerous demon Krampus is out to ruin Christmas for everyone, but Mrs. Claus and Jolly Ole Saint Nicholas will do everything in their power to stop his diabolical plan, even if it means becoming vampires to fight the evil villain! Join Alfie the Elf, Rudolpho the Reindeer Trainer, and all the other merry residents of Christmasland in this hilarious yuletide adventure that is sure to become a joyous holiday classic!

THE TAILSMAN

He's hot on the trail, looking for some tail! Follow the adventures of Sly Franko in this ornery comic book set in the *Westward Hoes* universe by Gary Lee Vincent, Rich Bottles Jr., and Stuart Brown.

Burning Bulb
PUBLISHING

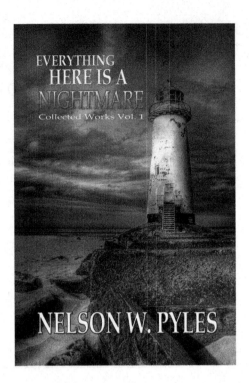

EVERYTHING HERE IS A NIGHTMARE
Collected Works Vol 1.

"Pyles makes it look easy. His characters come instantly alive with the cocksure verve and swagger of rock stars."
- Daniel Knauf, creator of HBO's "Carnivale,"
Executive Producer/Writer, ABC's "The Blacklist."

The critically acclaimed author of Demons, Dolls and Milkshakes returns with fifteen tales of horror and suspense with Everything Here is a Nightmare.

From zombies in the old west, to a young boy tempted by the Devil. From vampires with romantic longing, to an abandoned lighthouse haunted by vengeful spirits. From a serial killer getting unholy justice, to a haunted English race car, Nelson W Pyles invites you to explore a landscape of fear, suspense and horror.

Take his hand and hold on tight. Remember that whatever you find here, whatever you see, no matter what you might think it could be... know this: Everything Here is a Nightmare.

Burning Bulb
PUBLISHING

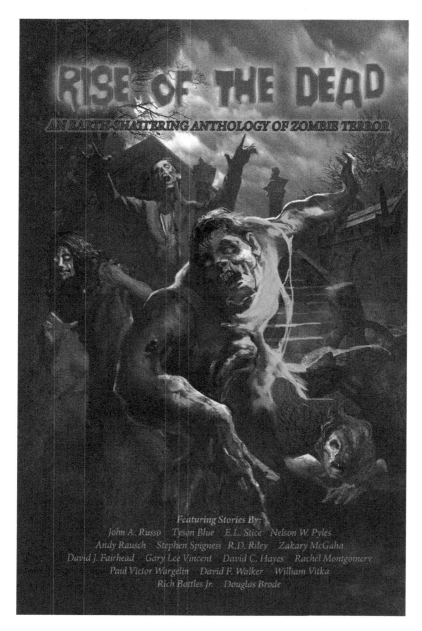

Featuring Stories By:

John A. Russo   Tyson Blue   E.L. Stice   Nelson W. Pyles
Andy Rausch   Stephen Spignesi   R.D. Riley   Zakary McGaha
David J. Fairhead   Gary Lee Vincent   David C. Hayes   Rachel Montgomery
Paul Victor Wargelin   David F. Walker   William Vitka
Rich Bottles Jr.   Douglas Brode

RISE OF THE DEAD - a collection of seventeen tales of unspeakable
zombie terror. Featuring a foreword and short story by John A. Russo!

www.TheJohnRusso.com

Burning Bulb
PUBLISHING

NIGHT OF THE LIVING DEAD

Why does Night of the Living Dead hit with such chilling impact?

Is it because everyday people in a commonplace house are suddenly the victims of a monstrous invasion? Or is it because the ghouls who surround the house with grasping claws were once ordinary people, too?

Decide for yourself as you read, and the horror grips you.

All the cannibalism, suspense and frenzy of the smash-hit move are here in the novel.

www.TheJohnRusso.com

THE BOOBY HATCH

With NIGHT OF THE LIVING DEAD, John Russo helped blaze a path in the horror genre that has never been equalled. In this hillarious erotic novel, he blazes a path through the wild, zany Sex Revolution of the 1970s.

Sweet, innocent Cherry Jankowski works for Joyful Novelties, where she tests sex toys ranging from the ridiculous to the sublime. But she can't find love or peace of mind and her efforts are hampered by a Peeping Tom, an exhibitionist, a cross-dressing boyfriend, a quack psychiatrist, and even her own product-testing partner, Marcello Fettucini, who can't get it up anymore and is scared of losing his job!

www.TheJohnRusso.com

Burning Bulb
PUBLISHING

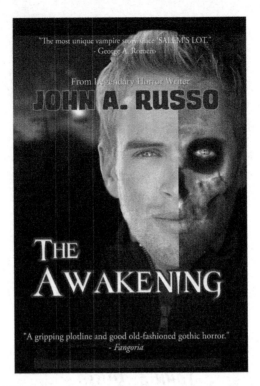

THE AWAKENING

For two hundred years, he has rested. Now he rises. Now he will be satisfied. Nothing can stop him. No one can resist him.

Benjamin Latham is young and handsome, his eighteenth-century mind wakened to a bizarre twentieth-century world. And there is the need deep within . . . an animal need, frightening, murderous, unholy . . . a vital need that must be fed.

And with his need comes a power over men and women to do his bidding, to quiet his dark craving . . .

Until the murders begin. And the inquiries. All suggesting the same hideous truth.

Now Benjamin must find a sanctuary: a lover, a partner, a friend. Someone who can share his darkness. Someone he can lead to . . . The Awakening.

www.TheJohnRusso.com

Burning Bulb
PUBLISHING

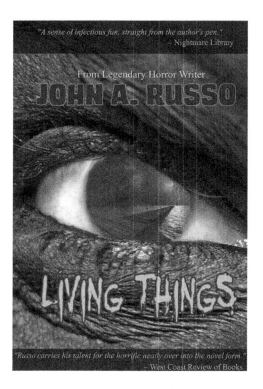

"A sense of infectious fun, straight from the author's pen."
– Nightmare Library

From Legendary Horror Writer
JOHN A. RUSSO

LIVING THINGS

"Russo carries his talent for the horrific neatly over into the novel form."
– West Coast Review of Books

LIVING THINGS

Beneath the shimmering Miami sun sprawls one of the Mafia's biggest empires, a glittering worldof lavish beachfront mansions, neon-painted nightclubs, beautiful women, expensive cars—and absolute control over the state's billion-dollar drug trade. But, one by one, its ganglords and henchmen are falling prey to a new rival. His powers are fueled by monstrous ancient rituals; his hellish undead legions slaughter mobsters and innocent citizens alike, his unholylust for power is virtually unstoppable.

Now a burned-out ex-detective and a brilliant anthropologist must enter a gruesome, nightmare world to fight this master of malevolence and illusion. Their time is short, their weapons few, and they face an ultimate, terrifying choice - annihilation or the loss of their souls to the eternal torment of those who never die. . .

www.TheJohnRusso.com

Burning Bulb
PUBLISHING

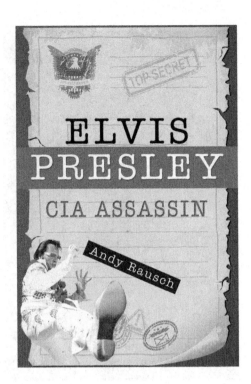

ELVIS PRESLEY, CIA ASSASSIN BY ANDY RAUSCH

"I can guarantee you. Read this book and you'll never look at Elvis the same way again!"
~ Douglas Brode, author of ELVIS CINEMA AND POPULAR CULTURE

SOON TO BE A MAJOR MOTION PICTURE

In 1970, singer Elvis Presley secretly met with President Richard Nixon. This new comedic novel imagines that Presley became a Central Intelligence Agency operative, eventually moving up through the ranks to become a skilled assassin.

Presented in an oral history fashion, the book tells us about Presley's secret transformation by the people who knew him best.

Did he fake his death in 1977? Was Presley involved with the Watergate scandal? The Iran hostage crisis? Communicating with aliens?

Read this book to find out the answers to these and many more questions.

Burning Bulb
PUBLISHING

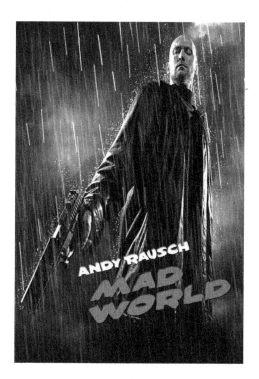

MAD WORLD BY ANDY RAUSCH

"*Mad World* is dark, twisted, no-holds-barred fun."
—Jason Starr, author of *Bust*, *Slide*, and *The Max*

EVERYONE'S PLAYING AN ANGLE IN THE CITY OF ANGELS

Mad World tells the stories of a black hitman who doubles as a university professor, a Catholic priest who longs to be a gangster, a would-be author from Kansas, a gay phone sex operator who claims he's straight, a group of rich twentysomethings playing a deadly game of life and death, a vicious Mafia boss, and a sleazy Hollywood movie director. As each of their stories intersect, the body count piles up and the action comes nonstop in this tense, white-knuckle thriller by first-time author Andy Rausch.

"A wild ride. If you like it gangster, *Mad World* delivers."
—Daniel Birch, author of *Get Some*

Burning Bulb
PUBLISHING

THE HAGS OF BLACK COUNTY

by Michelle Bowser

Ruled by a committee of Hags, and fueled by toothless rivalries, Black County lurks just far enough out of the way to be completely unnoticed by the rest of civilization. Its inhabitants have been mentally warped for generations and the land itself seems to have the power to drive anyone unlucky enough to visit into ridiculous hillbilly madness. When a construction Company needs to bury a pipeline through its ludicrous hills and valleys, a twisted charm goes to work and every aspect of already bizarre Black County life takes a gory turn for the hysterical. Take a preposterous trip along with its citizens, both native and new, through escapades such as the Hag parade, the grand opening of Madame Skunk's House of Ill Repute, the demolition derby riot and the rabid, zombie clown apocalypse.

THE ABANDONED SOUL

by Daniel Sellers

After spending most of his 20s in a drug and alcohol fueled daze, a young man finally hits rock bottom. Having used up his friends and their good graces, he ends up squatting in an abandoned house. Forcibly sobering he begins to realize that he is not alone in this abandoned house. Left with one last friend and a mountain of regrets, he must decide if this presence is a guilty conscience, or a malicious hunter.

WE WISH YOU A HAPPY KILLDAY

by Jason Heroux

"We Wish You a Happy Killday" is the story of an international b eloved holiday called "Killday" where one day a year everyone over the age of fifteen is permitted to register for a license allowing them to kill one other person. But this year Chad Ovenstock doesn't feel like killing anyone. His friends and family urge him to participate in the festivities, but he can't seem to get into the holiday spirit. On the day before Killday Chad comes in contact with Ambrose, an old friend who suffered a nervous breakdown and is now part of The One Ant Army, a mysterious cult dedicated to making the future disappear. When the holiday finally arrives Chad refuses to participate and tries to survive on his own, surrounded by constant gunfire, countless corpses, and the nagging suspicion that Ambrose may have secretly brainwashed him into becoming a member of The One Ant Army cult.

Burning Bulb
PUBLISHING

Made in the USA
Middletown, DE
26 November 2022

16049908R00159